OUTLAWS

OUTLAWS

Javier Cercas

Translated from the Spanish by Anne McLean

BLOOMSBURY

LONDON · NEW DELHI · NEW YORK · SYDNEY

First published in Great Britain 2014

Originally published in Spain 2012 by Random House Mondadori, S.A., as *Las leyes de la frontera*

Copyright © Javier Cercas 2012
English translation © Anne McLean 2014

This work has been published with a subsidy from the Directorate General of Books,
Archives and Libraries of the Spanish Ministry of Culture

Bloomsbury Publishing Plc
50 Bedford Square
London
WC1B 3DP

www.bloomsbury.com

Bloomsbury is a trademark of Bloomsbury Publishing Plc

Bloomsbury Publishing, London, New Delhi, New York and Sydney

A CIP catalogue record for this book is available from the British Library

Hardback ISBN 978 1 4088 5045 9
Trade paperback ISBN 978 1 4088 4422 9

10 9 8 7 6 5 4 3 2 1

Typeset by Hewer Text UK Ltd, Edinburgh
Printed and bound in Great Britain by CPI Group (UK) Ltd, Croydon CR0 4YY

For Raül Cercas and Mercè Mas.
For the gang, for forty-odd years of friendship.

We get so used to disguising ourselves to others that, in the end, we become disguised to ourselves.

François de la Rochefoucauld

Contents

Part I

Over There

I

'Shall we begin?'

'Yes, but first let me ask one more question. The last one.'

'Go ahead.'

'Why have you agreed to write this book?'

'Didn't I tell you already? For the money. I'm a writer, that's how I make my living.'

'Yes, I know, but is that the only reason you agreed?'

'Well, it's not every day you get an opportunity to write about a character like El Zarco, if that's what you mean.'

'You mean you were interested in Zarco before you were asked to write about him?'

'Of course, isn't everybody?'

'Yeah. Anyway, the story I'm going to tell you isn't Zarco's story but the story of my relationship with Zarco; with Zarco and with . . .'

'Yes, I know, we've talked about that too. Can we begin?'

'We can.'

'Tell me when you met Zarco.'

'At the beginning of the summer of 1978. It was a strange time. Or that's how I remember it. Franco had died three years earlier, but the country was still governed by Franco's laws and still smelled exactly the same as it did under Franco: like shit. I was sixteen years old back then, and so was Zarco. We lived very near each other, and very far away from each other.'

3

'What do you mean?'

'Do you know the city?'

'Roughly.'

'That's almost better: the city today has very little in common with what it was back then. In its way, Gerona at that time was still a post-war city, a dark, ecclesiastical dump, encircled by the countryside and covered in fog all winter; I'm not saying that today's Gerona is better – in some ways it's worse – I'm only saying it's different. At that time, for example, the city was surrounded by outlying neighbourhoods where the *charnegos* lived. The word's fallen out of fashion, but in those days it was used to refer to immigrants from other parts of Spain who'd come to Catalonia, incomers, people who generally didn't have a cent to their name and who'd come here to try to get by . . . Though you already know all this. What you might not know is, as I was saying, at the end of the seventies the city was ringed by *charnego* neighbourhoods: Salt, Pont Major, Germans Sàbat, Vilarroja. That's where the dregs accumulated.'

'That's where Zarco lived?'

'No: Zarco lived with the dregs of the dregs, in the prefabs, *los albergues provisionales*, temporary housing on the city's north-east border, set up in the fifties for the influx of workers and still in use somehow. And I lived barely two hundred metres away: the difference is that he lived over the border, across from where the River Ter and La Devesa Park marked the divide. I lived on Caterina Albert Street, in the neighbourhood now called La Devesa but back then it was nothing or almost nothing, a bunch of gardens and vacant lots where the city petered out; there, ten years earlier, at the end of the sixties, they'd put up a couple of isolated tower blocks where my parents had rented a flat. In a way it was also an incomer neighbourhood, but the people who lived there weren't as poor as most *charnegos* usually were: most of the families were those of middle-class civil servants, like mine – my father had a low-level position working for the council – families who weren't originally from the city but who didn't consider themselves *charnegos* and in any case didn't want anything to do with real *charnegos* or at least with the poor ones, the ones in Salt, Pont Major, Germans Sàbat and Vilarroja. Or, of course, with the people who still lived in the prefabs. In fact, I'm sure that the majority of the people who lived on Caterina Albert (not to mention the people from the city) never set foot anywhere near the prefabs. Some perhaps didn't even know they existed, or pretended not to know. I did know. I didn't really know quite what they were and I'd never been there, but I knew they were there or that it was said they were there, like a legend that nobody had confirmed or denied: actually, I think that for us, the neighbourhood kids, the very name of *los albergues* added a touch of prestige by evoking an image of refuge in inhospitable times, like an inn or a hostel in a tale of epic adventure. And all this is why I told you that back then I lived very near and very far away from Zarco: because there was a border separating us.'

'And how did you cross it? I mean, how did a middle-class kid make friends with a kid like Zarco?'

'Because at sixteen all borders are porous, or at least they were then. And also by chance. But before I tell you that story I should tell you another one.'

'Go ahead.'

'I've never told anybody this; well, nobody except my analyst. But unless I do you won't understand how and why I met Zarco.'

'Don't worry: if you don't want it to go in the book, I won't use it; if I do use it and you don't like how it sounds, I'll cut it. That was the deal, and I'm not going to break it.'

'OK. You know what? People always say that childhood is cruel, but I think adolescence is much crueller. In my case it was.

I had a group of friends on Caterina Albert: my best friend was Matías Giral, but there was also Canales, Ruiz, Intxausti, the Boix brothers, Herrero and one or two others. We were all more or less the same age, had all known each other since we were eight or nine, lived our lives in the street and went to the school run by the Marist Brothers, which was the closest one; and of course we were all *charnegos*, except for the Boix brothers, who were from Sabadell and spoke Catalan among themselves. In short: I didn't have any brothers, just one sister, and I don't think I'm exaggerating if I say that in practice those friends filled the vacant role of brothers in my childhood.

'But in adolescence they stopped doing so. The change began almost a year before I met Zarco, when a new kid came to the school. His name was Narciso Batista and he was repeating his second year of high school. His father was chairman of the council and my father's boss; we knew each other from having crossed paths a couple of times. So, also because our surnames meant we sat at the same desk (in the class list Cañas followed Batista), I was his first friend at the school; thanks to me he made friends with Matías, and thanks to Matías and me he made friends with the rest of my friends. He also turned into the leader of the group, a group that up till then had never had a leader (or I hadn't been aware that it did) and perhaps needed one, because the essential feeling of adolescence is fear and fear needs leaders with which to fight it. Batista was a couple of years older than us, physically strong and knew how to make himself heard; besides, he had everything any teenage *charnego* might desire: to start with, a solid, rich, Catalan family (although he considered himself very Spanish and despised everything Catalan, not to mention *catalanista*, especially if it came from Barcelona); also, a large apartment in the new part of the city, a tennis-club membership, a summer house in S'Agaró and a winter one in La Molina, a 75cc

Lobito to get around on and his own place on La Rutlla Street, a tumbledown old garage to spend the evenings listening to rock and roll, smoking and drinking beer.

'Up to here, everything's normal; from here on in, nothing was. I mean in just a few months Batista's attitude towards me changed, his sympathy turned into antipathy, his antipathy into hatred and his hatred into violence. Why? I don't know. I've often thought I was simply the scapegoat Batista invented to ward off the group's essential fear. But I really don't know; the only thing I know is that in a very short time I went from being his friend to being his victim.

'The word victim is melodramatic, but I prefer the risk of melodrama to that of lying. Batista began taunting me: although his mother tongue was Catalan, he laughed at me for speaking Catalan, not because I spoke it badly, but because he despised those who spoke Catalan without being Catalan; he laughed at my appearance and called me Dumbo, because he said I had ears as big as the Disney elephant's; he also laughed at my awkwardness with girls, at my studious-looking glasses, my studious-looking grades. These taunts became increasingly ferocious, and I couldn't stop them, and my friends, who just laughed at first, ended up joining in. Soon words were not enough. Batista got a taste for half-joking and half-seriously punching me in the shoulders or ribs and giving me an occasional slap; perplexed, I answered with laughter, playing at returning the blows, trying to take the gravity out of the violence and turn it into a joke. That was at the start. Later, when it was no longer possible to disguise the brutality as fun, my laughter turned into tears and the desire for escape. Batista, I insist, was not alone: he was the big bully, the origin and catalyst of the violence, but the rest of my friends (with the occasional exception of Matías, who sometimes tried to put the brakes on Batista) at times turned into a pack of hounds. For years I wanted to forget that time, until not long ago I forced myself to remember it and realized I still had some of those scenes stuck in my head like a knife in the guts. Once Batista threw me into a freezing stream that runs through, or used to run through, La Devesa Park. Another time, one afternoon when we were at his place on La Rutlla, my friends stripped me and locked me in the darkness of the loft, and for hours all I could do was hold back my tears and listen through the wall to their laughter, their shouts, their conversations and the music they put on. Another time – a Saturday I'd told my parents I was sleeping over at Batista's parents' place in S'Agaró – they left me again at the place on La Rutlla, and I had to spend almost twenty-four hours there – from Saturday afternoon to midday on Sunday – alone and in the dark, with nothing to eat or drink. Another time, towards the end of term, when I was no longer doing anything but avoiding Batista, I got so scared I thought he was trying to kill me, because he and Canales, Herrero, the Boix brothers and another one or two trapped me in the washrooms off the patio at school and, for what must have been a few seconds but felt like a very, very long time, held my face inside a toilet they'd all just pissed in, while I listened to my friends' laughter behind me. Shall I go on?'

'Not if you don't want to. But if it makes you feel better, go ahead.'

'No, talking about it doesn't make me feel any better; not any more. I'm surprised to be telling you, though, which feels different. The Batista thing has become like so many things from that time: it's not like I lived through them but more like I dreamt them. Although you'll be wondering what all this has to do with Zarco.'

'No: I was wondering why you didn't report the bullying.'

'Who was I supposed to report it to? My teachers? I had a good reputation at school, but I didn't have any proof of what was going on, and reporting it would have turned me into a liar or a snitch (or both), and that was the best way to make everything worse. Or my parents? My father and mother were good people; they loved me and I loved them, but over those months our relationship had deteriorated so much that I wouldn't have dared tell them. Besides, how would I have told them? And what would I have told them? On top of everything else, as I already said, my father was subordinate to Batista's father at work, so if I told him what was going on, aside from turning into a liar and a snitch, I would have put my father in an impossible situation. In spite of that, more than once I was tempted to tell him, more than once I was on the brink of telling him, but in the end I always shied away. And if I wasn't going to report it to them, who was I going to tell?

'The thing is that going to school every day turned into an ordeal for me. For months I cried myself to sleep. I was scared. I felt enraged and embittered and humiliated and most of all guilty, because the worst thing about humiliation is that it makes the one who suffers it feel guilty. I felt trapped. I wanted to die. And don't think what you're thinking: all that shit didn't teach me a thing. Knowing absolute evil – that's what Batista was to me – earlier than most, doesn't make you better than others; it makes you worse. And it's absolutely no use whatsoever.'

'It was useful to you in that it led you to meet Zarco.'

'That's true, but that was its only use. That happened not long after term finished, when I'd gone for a while without seeing my friends. With the classrooms closed there were more possibilities of hiding from them, although the truth is, in a city as small as Gerona, there weren't really that many either and it wasn't easy to drop out of circulation, which is what I needed to do so my friends would forget about me. I had to avoid bumping into them in the neighbourhood, avoid the places we used to hang out, avoid going near Batista's place on La Rutlla, even avoid or evade visits or phone calls from Matías, who kept inviting me to come out with them, probably to ease his guilty conscience and hide the actual harassment they were subjecting me to behind his apparent generosity. Anyway: my plan that summer was to go outside as little as possible until August when we'd go away on holiday, and to spend those weeks staying in reading and watching TV. That was the idea. But the reality is that, no matter how dejected or cowardly, a sixteen-year-old kid is incapable of spending all day at home, or at least I was incapable of it. So I soon started venturing out into the street, and one afternoon I went into the Vilaró games arcade.

'That was where I saw Zarco for the first time. The Vilaró arcade was on Bonastruc de Porta Street, still in La Devesa neighbourhood, across from the railway overpass. It was one of those amusement arcades for teenagers that proliferated in the seventies and eighties. What I remember of that one is a big warehouse with bare walls and a six-lane Scalextric track; I also remember several table-football games, a few Space Invaders consoles and six or seven pinball machines lined up against one of the side walls; at the back there was a drinks machine and the washrooms, and at the entrance was the glass-walled booth where Señor Tomàs sat, a stooped, balding, round-bellied old man who was only distracted from his crossword-puzzle books by the odd practical problem (a jammed machine, a clogged toilet) or, in the case of an altercation, to throw out the troublemakers or re-establish order with his shrill voice. I used to go there with my friends, but more or less since Batista showed up I'd stopped going; my friends had too and, maybe for that reason, it seemed like a safe place, like the hole where a shell had just landed during a bombardment.

'The afternoon I met Zarco I'd arrived at the arcade not long after Señor Tomàs opened up and started playing my favourite pinball machine – Rocky Balboa. A good machine: five balls, an extra ball for not many points and at the end bonus points that let you make the next level easily. For a while I was the only one play-ing in the empty place, but soon a group of kids came in and headed over to the Scalextric track. A little while later a couple more showed up. A guy and a girl, who looked older than sixteen but younger than nineteen, and my first impression when I saw them was that they seemed like they might be related somehow, but mostly that they were a couple of tough *charnegos*, from the outskirts, maybe even *quinquis* or delinquents. Señor Tomàs sensed the threat as soon as they walked past his window. Hey, you two, he called after them, opening the door to his booth. Where're you going? They both stopped short. What's up, chief?, asked the guy, raising his hands as if offering to be searched; he wasn't smiling, but gave the impression that the situation amused him. He said: We just want to have a game. Can we? Señor Tomàs looked them both up and down with suspicion, and when he finished his examination said something that I didn't quite catch; then realized what it was: I don't want any trouble. Anyone who gives me trouble is out. Is that clear? Absolutely, said the guy, gesturing in a conciliatory way and lowering his hands. Don't worry about us, boss. Señor Tomàs seemed to be half satisfied with the reply, returned to his booth and must have gone back to his crossword puzzle while the pair walked into the arcade.'

'It was them.'

'Yes: the guy was Zarco; the girl was Tere.'

'Tere was Zarco's girlfriend?'

'Good question: if I'd known the answer in time I would have saved myself a lot of trouble; I'll come to that later. The thing is that, like Señor Tomàs, as soon as I saw Zarco and Tere walk in I immediately felt wary, felt that from this moment on anything might happen in the arcade, and my first instinct was to abandon Rocky Balboa and split.

'I stayed. I tried to forget the pair, act like they weren't there, and carry on playing. I didn't manage it, and a moment later felt a slap on my shoulder that made me stagger. What's up, Gafitas?, asked Zarco, taking my place at the controls of the machine. He looked me in my bespectacled eyes with his very blue ones, spoke with a husky voice, had a centre parting in his hair and wore a tight denim jacket over a tight beige T-shirt. He repeated, defiantly, What's up? I was scared. Holding up my hands I said: I just finished. I turned to leave, but at that moment Tere stepped in my way and my face was a handspan from hers. My first impression was surprise; my second, of being completely dazzled. Like Zarco, Tere was very thin, dark, not very tall, with that springy outdoors air *quinquis* used to have back then. She had straight dark hair and cruel green eyes, and a beauty spot beside her nose. Her whole body radiated the composure of a young woman who was very sure of herself, except for one tic: her left leg moved up and down like a piston. She was wearing jeans and a white T-shirt and her handbag strap crossed her chest. Going already?, she asked, smiling with her full, strawberry-red lips. I couldn't answer because Zarco grabbed my arm and forced me to turn back around. You stay right there, Gafitas, he ordered, and started playing pinball on the Rocky Balboa machine.

'He wasn't very good at it, so the game was soon over. Shit, he said, punching the machine. He looked at me furiously, but before he could say anything Tere laughed, pushed him aside and put a coin in the slot. Grumbling, Zarco leaned on the table right next to me watching Tere play. Both of them commented on the game without paying any attention to me, although every once in a while, between one ball and the next, Tere would glance over at me out of the corner of her eye. People kept coming in and out of the arcade; Señor Tomàs came out of his booth more often than usual. Gradually I began to calm down, but was still a bit jittery and didn't dare leave. Tere didn't take long to finish her game either. When she did she stepped back from the machine and pointed at it. Your turn, she said. I didn't open my mouth, didn't move. What's the matter, Gafitas?, Zarco asked. You don't want to play any more? I kept quiet. He added: Cat got your tongue? No, I answered. So?, he insisted. I've run out of money, I said. Zarco looked at me curiously. You're out of cash?, he asked. I nodded. Really?, he asked again. I nodded again. How much did you have? I told him the truth. Fuck, Tere, Zarco laughed. That wouldn't be enough for me and you to wipe our asses with. Tere didn't laugh; she stared at me. Zarco shoved me aside again and said: Well, if you ain't got cash, you're fucked.

'He put some more coins in the machine and started a new game. As he played he started talking to me; or rather: he started interrogating me. He asked me how old I was and I told him. He asked me where I lived and I told him. He asked me if I went to school and I said yes and told him which school I went to. Then he asked me if I spoke Catalan; the question seemed strange to me, but I answered yes again. After that he asked me if I came to the arcade often and if I knew Señor Tomàs and what time the place opened and what time it closed and other similar questions, which I don't remember specifically, but I do remember answering them or answering as far as I could. I also remember that his last question was whether I needed money, and I didn't know how to answer that. Zarco answered for me: If you do, tell me. Come to La Font and tell me. We'll talk business. Zarco swore at a ball that got past him and punched the machine again; then he asked me: Do you or don't you, Gafitas? I didn't answer; before I could a tall blond guy in a Fred Perry polo shirt who'd just walked into the arcade came over. The guy said hi to Zarco, whispered with him for a moment and then the two of them went outside. Tere stood there looking at me. I noticed her eyes again, her mouth, the mole beside her nose, and I remember thinking she was the most gorgeous girl I'd ever seen. Will you come?, she asked. Where?, I asked. To La Font, she answered. I asked what La Font was and Tere told me it was a bar in the district and I understood that the district was the red-light district. Tere asked me again if I'd go to La Font; although I was sure I wasn't going to, I said: I don't know. But then quickly added: I probably will. Tere smiled and stroked the beauty spot beside her nose with one finger; then she pointed at Rocky Balboa and, before following Zarco and the guy in the Fred Perry shirt, said: You've got three balls left.

'That was our first meeting and that's how it went. Left on my own I breathed a sigh of relief and, I don't know whether for pleasure or because I thought Zarco and Tere might still be hanging around outside the arcade and I didn't want to risk running into them again, I started playing the balls left in the machine. I'd just begun when Señor Tomàs came over. Do you know who those kids were, son?, he asked, pointing at the door. He was obviously referring to Zarco and Tere; I said no. What were you talking about?, he asked. I explained. Señor Tomàs clicked his tongue and made me repeat the explanation. He seemed anxious, and after a moment he went away mumbling something. The next day I arrived at the arcade in the late afternoon. When I passed the booth on my way in, Señor Tomàs rapped on the glass with his knuckles and asked me to wait; when he came out he put a hand on my shoulder. Hey, son, he began. Would you be interested in a job? The question took me by surprise. What job?, I asked. I need a helper, he said. He gestured vaguely around the whole place before making his offer: You help me close up every night and in exchange I'll give you ten free plays a day.

'I didn't even need to give it a second thought. I accepted, and from then on my afternoons began to follow a single pattern. I arrived at the Vilaró arcade as soon as it opened, sometimes a little later, played my ten free games on whichever machine I felt like playing (almost always the Rocky Balboa) and, around eight-thirty or nine in the evening, I'd help Señor Tomàs close up: while he opened the machines and took out the coins, counted the day's takings and filled in a sort of inventory, I made sure there was no one left in the main part of the building or in the wash-rooms, and then between the two of us we pulled the metal shutters down over the door; when we finished, Señor Tomàs got onto his Mobylette with the money and I walked home. That was all. Do I mean by this that I soon forgot about Zarco and Tere? Not at all. At first I was afraid they'd show up at the arcade again, but after a few days I was surprised to find myself wishing they would, or at least that Tere would. It never crossed my mind, however, to accept Zarco's invitation, to go into the red-light district one afternoon and turn up at La Font: at sixteen years of age I had an approximate but sufficient idea of what the district was, and I didn't like the idea of going there, or maybe I was just scared. In any case, I soon convinced myself that I'd met Zarco and Tere because some unlikely coincidence had made them stray outside their territory; I also convinced myself that, as well as unlikely, the coincidence was unrepeatable, and that I would not see them again.

'The same day I arrived at this conclusion I had a terrible scare. I was on my way home after having helped Señor Tomàs close the arcade when I saw a group of kids walking towards me on Joaquim Vayreda. There were four of them, coming from Caterina Albert, on the same side of the street as me and, in spite of the fact that they were still quite a way off and it was getting dark, I recognized them immediately: it was Batista, Matías and two of the Boix brothers, Joan and Dani. I wanted to just keep walking along, but before I could take another two or three steps I felt my legs buck-ling and I started to sweat. Trying not to give in to panic, I began to cross the street; before I reached the other side I saw that Batista was doing the same. Then I couldn't help it: instinctively I took off running, reached the kerb and turned right down an alley that led into La Devesa; just as I got to the park Batista jumped me; he brought me down and, kneeling on my back and twisting my arm behind me, immobilized me on the ground. Where're you going, asshole?, he asked. He was panting like a dog; I was panting too, face down in the dirt of La Devesa. I'd lost my glasses. Looking around desperately for them, I asked Batista to let me up, but instead he asked me the same question again. Home, I said. Through here?, Batista asked, digging his knee into my back and twisting my arm till I screamed. You're a fucking liar.

'At that moment I heard Matías and the Boix brothers catch up. From the ground, in the leaden light shining from a streetlamp, I saw a blurry confusion of jean-clad legs and feet in sneakers or sandals. Nearby I caught sight of my glasses: they didn't look broken. I begged them to pick them up and someone who wasn't Batista picked them up but didn't give them to me. Then Matías and the Boix brothers asked what was going on. Nothing, said Batista. This fucking *catalanufo*, he's always lying. I didn't lie, I managed to say in my defence. I just said I was going home. See?, said Batista, twisting my arm harder. Another lie! I screamed again. Let him go, Matías said. He hasn't done anything to us. I felt Batista turn to look at him without letting go of me. He hasn't done anything?, he asked. Are you a dickhead or what? If he hasn't done anything why does he take off running as soon as he sees us, eh? And why has he been hiding? And why does he keep lying? He paused and added: Well, Dumbo, tell the truth for a change: where were you coming from? I didn't say anything; as well as my back and arm, my face was hurting too, pressed against the ground. See?, said Batista. He keeps quiet. And a guy keeps quiet when he has something to hide. Just like a guy who runs away. Yes or no? Let me go, please, I whined. Batista laughed. As well as a liar you're a dickhead, he said. You think we don't know where you've been hiding? You think we're idiots? Eh? What do you think? Batista seemed to be waiting for an answer; suddenly he twisted my arm even harder and asked: What did you say? I hadn't said anything and I said I hadn't said anything. Yes you did, said Batista. I heard you call me a son of a bitch. I said: That's not true. Batista brought his face up to my face as he twisted my arm nearly out of its socket; I thought he was going to break it. Feeling his breath on my face I screamed. Batista paid no attention to my screams. Are you calling me a liar?, he asked again. Matías intervened again, tried to ask Batista to leave me alone; Batista cut him off: told him to shut up and called him an idiot. Straight away he asked me again if I was calling him a liar. I said no. Unexpectedly, this answer seemed to pacify him, and after a second or two I felt the pressure ease up on my arm. Then, without another word, Batista let me go and stood up.

'As quickly as possible I did the same, brushing the dirt off my cheek with the palm of my hand. Matías handed me my glasses, but before I could take them Batista grabbed them. I stood looking at him. He was smiling; in the darkness of the park, under the plane trees, his features appeared vaguely feline. You want them?, he said, holding out my glasses. As I reached out my hand towards them, he pulled them away. Then he held them out again. If you want them, lick my shoes, he said. I stared back at him for several seconds, and then looked at Matías and the Boix brothers, who were watching me in expectation. Then I knelt down in front of Batista, licked his shoes – they tasted of leather and dust – stood up again and stared back at him. His eyes seemed to sparkle for an instant before he let out a snort that sounded like laughter or a laugh that sounded like a snort. You're a coward, he finally said, throwing my glasses on the ground. You disgust me.

'I spent the night tossing and turning in bed while trying not to feel completely ashamed of the incident with Batista and trying to find some relief for my humiliation. I didn't manage either one, and after that I decided not to return to the Vilaró arcade. I feared that Batista had been telling the truth and knew where I was hiding and would come looking for me. What might have happened if he had found me?, you'll be wondering. Nothing, you'll say to yourself, and I suppose you'd probably be right; but fear is not rational, and I was afraid. Whatever the case, soon loneliness and boredom overcame my fear, and two or three days later I went back to the arcade. When he saw me Señor Tomàs asked what had happened and I told him I'd been sick; I asked him if our deal still held. Of course, kid, he answered.

'That afternoon something happened that changed my life. I'd spent quite a while playing the Rocky Balboa machine when I was startled by a group of people bursting into the place. At first I thought, in panic, that it was Batista and my friends; with relief, almost with joy, I soon saw that it was Zarco and Tere. This time they weren't alone: they were accompanied by two guys; this time Señor Tomàs didn't stop them on their way in: he just watched them from the door of his booth, his hands on his hips and his crossword-puzzle book in one of them. After a moment, the relief and joy faded and the worry returned, especially when the four recent arrivals made straight for me. What's up, Gafitas?, asked Zarco. Not planning to come to La Font? I stepped back from the machine and ceded the controls to him; he stopped short; pointing at me with a smile he turned to the two guys: See? This is my Gafitas: I don't even have to say anything before he does what I want him to. While Zarco took over the game I'd started, Tere said hi. She said she'd been waiting for me at La Font and asked why I hadn't gone there. The other two guys watched me with interest. Later I found out they were called Gordo and Tío: Gordo, or Fatso, because he was so skinny he always seemed to be in profile; Tío, because that's what everyone called him. Gordo wore tight bellbottoms and had wavy, shoulder-length hair that looked like it was kept in place with hairspray; Tío was shorter than him and, even though he was the oldest of all of them, had a sort of childlike air about him, his mouth always half-open, his jaw a little loose. I answered Tere's question with excuses, but nobody paid any attention to my reply: Zarco was concentrating on the Rocky Balboa machine and Gordo and Tío were playing the pinball machine next to it; as for Tere, she too soon seemed to lose interest in me. But I stayed beside her anyway while her friends played, not daring or not wanting to walk away, listening to the comments the four of them made, watching Señor Tomàs go in and out of his booth and watching the regulars glance over at us out of the corners of their eyes.

'Zarco had finished his turn and given his place to Tere when the guy in the Fred Perry shirt came back into the arcade. Zarco exchanged a few words with him and Gordo and Tío stopped playing and the four of them went outside together. Tere went on playing pinball. Now, instead of looking at the table all the time, I looked at her every once in a while, furtively, and at a certain moment she caught me; as a cover-up I asked who the Fred Perry guy was. A dealer, she answered. Then she asked me if I smoked. I said yes. Hash, Tere clarified; I knew what hash was (just as I knew what a dealer was), but I'd never tried it and didn't say anything. Tere guessed the truth. Do you want to try it?, she asked. I shrugged. If you want to try some come to La Font, Tere said. In a pause between one ball and the next, she looked at me and asked: Are you going to come or not? I had no intention of going, but I didn't want to tell her. I looked at the image of Rocky Balboa looming over the pinball table; I'd seen it a thousand times: Rocky, muscular and triumphant, wearing nothing but a pair of shorts with the American flag printed on them, raising his arms to

19

the clamouring stadium while a defeated boxer lies in the ring at his feet. I looked at this image and remembered myself licking Batista's shoes and felt the shame of my humiliation all over again. As if fearing that the silence could reveal what I was feeling, I hurried to answer Tere's question with another question: Do you go every day? I meant to La Font; Tere understood. More or less, she answered, and launched the next ball; when that one got swallowed by the machine too she asked again: Why? Are you going to come? I don't know, I said, adding: Probably not. Why not?, Tere insisted. I shrugged again, and she kept playing.

'I kept looking at her. I pretended to look at the pinball table, but I was looking at her. Tere noticed. The proof was that she hadn't even finished playing that ball when she said: Not bad-looking, am I, Gafitas? I blushed; I immediately regretted having blushed. The arcade was very noisy, but I had the impression that in the centre of the uproar was an absolute silence, which only I could hear. I pretended I hadn't really heard her question. Tere didn't repeat it; she finished playing the ball unhurriedly and, leaving the game half-finished, took me by the hand and said: C'mon.

'Have I already told you that some of the things that happened that summer feel like things I've dreamt rather than things I've experienced? What happened next was one of those. Tere dragged me to the back of the arcade, dodging the people that were beginning to fill the place, and without letting go of my hand we went into the women's washroom. It was exactly the same as the men's — there was a long hallway with a big mirror on the wall, opposite the line of stalls — and at that moment it was almost empty: just a couple of girls in high heels and mini-skirts applying mascara in front of the mirror. When Tere and I came in, the girls looked at us, but didn't say anything. Tere opened the door of the first stall and invited me in. Where are we going?, I asked. In here, she answered. Disconcerted, I looked at the two girls, who were still looking at us. What? Tere hissed at them. Take a picture; it'll last longer.

'Startled, the girls turned back to the mirror. Tere pushed me into the stall, stepped in behind me, closed the door and bolted it. The stall was a minuscule space where only a toilet and tank fit; the floor was cement and the walls wood and they didn't reach all the way to the floor. I leaned back against one of them; Tere pushed her handbag around to her back and gave me an order: Drop your trousers. What?, I asked. Tere's reply was to kiss me on the mouth: a long, dense, wet kiss, with her tongue twirling around mine. It was the first time in my life that a woman had kissed me. Drop your trousers, she repeated. Like a sleepwalker I unbuckled my belt and undid my zipper. Pants too, said Tere. I obeyed. When I finished, Tere took me in her hand. And now pay attention, Gafitas, she said. Then she crouched down, put it in her mouth and started to suck. It was all over very quickly, because, although I tried not to, I came almost immediately. Tere stood up and kissed me on the lips; now her mouth tasted of semen. Did you like that?, she asked, still holding my exhausted dick in her hand. I managed to mumble something. Then Tere smiled fleetingly but perfectly, let go of me and, before walking out of the stall, said: Tomorrow I'll be expecting you at La Font.

'I don't know how long I stayed there with my pants round my ankles, trying to recover from the shock, or how long it took me to get dressed again. But when I came out of the stall the washroom was empty. And when I came out of the washroom, Tere was not in the arcade; Zarco wasn't there either, Gordo and Tío had come back in. I went to the door, leaned outside and looked up and down the street, but I didn't see anybody. Señor Tomàs appeared beside me. Where did you get to?, he asked. I looked at him: he had his hands in his pockets, and he hadn't noticed that the

21

pressure of his gut had popped two buttons of his shirt; a clump of curly, grey hair poked through the opening. Before I could answer he asked another question: Hey, kid, are you all right? You don't look so good. I told him I was fine but that I'd just thrown up in the washroom, though I felt better now, and that maybe I wasn't entirely recovered. Well, you take care, kid, Señor Tomàs warned me. You don't want a relapse. Then he asked me what I'd been talking about with Zarco and Tere and the others and I told him that time we hadn't talked about anything. Señor Tomàs clicked his tongue. I don't trust those *quinquis* one bit, he said. Then he said: Don't take your eyes off them if they come back, OK? I said OK and, looking at the double row of cars parked under the train overpass, for a moment I thought I'd never see Tere again and asked: Do you think they'll be back? I don't know, answered Señor Tomàs; and as we walked back to his booth added: With those people you never know.

'The next day I went to La Font.'

2

'Yes: I'm a police officer. Why did I join the police? I don't know. I'm sure my father being a Civil Guard had something to do with it, though. And besides, I imagine at the time I was as idealistic and fond of novelty as any other kid my age; you know what I mean: in the movies the cop was the good guy who saved the good people from the bad guys, and that's what I wanted to be.

'The fact is that at the age of sixteen I prepared for the exam to become an inspector of the General Police Corps, the secret police. I was a terrible student, but for nine months I studied like crazy and at the end of that time I sat the exam and passed it and even got a good grade. How do you like that? To do my practical training I had to move from Cáceres to Madrid; I took a room in a house on Jacometrezo from which I came and went daily to the Police Academy, at number five Miguel Ángel Street. At that time I began to realize what this job actually entailed. And you know what? I wasn't disappointed; well, some things did disappoint me – you know, the obligatory routines, stupid colleagues, oceans of red tape, things like that – but on the other hand I made a discovery that should have surprised me a lot and didn't surprise me at all, and it was that being a police officer was exactly like I'd always thought it was going to be. I already told you I was an idealist, and such a stubborn idealist that for a long time I believed my job was the best job in the world; now that I've spent almost forty years doing it I know it's the worst, apart from all the rest of them.

'What were we talking about? Oh, yes. My practical training. I found Madrid a bit intimidating, in part because I'd always lived in a small city and in part because it was a difficult time and the veterans of the force with whom I patrolled the city and I were always coming across altercations in the streets: one day it was an illegal demonstration, the next it would be a terrorist attack, and then another day a bank robbery. Or whatever. The thing is I knew almost immediately that level of commotion was too much for me and that neither Madrid nor any other big city was right for me at the time.

'That is one of the reasons behind the decision I took when I finished my practical training: requesting a position here, in Gerona. I both did and didn't want to go back to Cáceres. I liked the city, but I didn't like the idea of going back to live there again one bit, and much less with my parents. And then I thought Gerona could be a good solution to that wanting and not wanting, because it wasn't Cáceres but it was very similar – both were tranquil, historic provincial capitals, with a large old quarter and all that – and I thought that would make me not feel such a stranger in Gerona; I must have also thought I could get a head start there before going home or choosing a better posting, doing easier and less demanding work than I would have had to do in a big city. Besides (this might seem stupid to you but it was very important), I don't know why but I was very curious about the Catalan people, especially the people of Gerona. I'm lying, I do know: I was curious because during my practical training I read *Gerona*, the novel by Galdós. Do you know it? It's a portrait of the city during the siege by Napoleon's troops. When I read it, forty years ago, I loved it; it was damn good: the total tragedy of war, the greatness of a whole city up in arms and defended by an iron-willed people, the heroism of General Álvarez de Castro, a character of mythic stature who refused to surrender the ruined and starving city to the French, and whom Galdós portrayed as the greatest patriot of his age. In 1974 I was only nineteen years old and things like that made an impression on me, so I thought Gerona would be the ideal place to start.

'I requested Gerona and they sent me here.

'I remember the day I arrived as if it were yesterday. I'd come on the train with five other new recruits and we went straight from the station to the Hotel Condal, where they had reserved rooms for us. It must have been seven or seven-thirty in the evening and, since it was February, night had already fallen and everything was dark. That was my first impression of Gerona: the sensation of darkness; the second was the sensation of damp; the third was the sensation of dirtiness; the fourth (and most intense) was the sensation of loneliness: a complete and absolute loneliness, such as I hadn't even felt in my first days in Madrid, alone in my room in the boarding house on Jacometrezo. When we got to the hotel we unpacked, had a quick wash and went out to find some dinner. One of the other recruits was from Barcelona and knew the city, so we followed him. Looking for a restaurant we walked up Jaume I, crossed the Marquès de Camps and Sant Agustí Plazas, past the statue of Álvarez de Castro and the city's defenders, which I didn't see or didn't notice that night; then we crossed the Onyar and in the dark could just barely make out its filthy water and the sadness of the façades overlooking the river, covered in clothes hung out to dry; then we wandered through the old city and walked the Rambla from bottom to top and crossed the Plaza de Cataluña and, when we were about to give up and say to hell with it all and go to bed on empty stomachs after that depressing stroll and that exhausting trip, we came across a place that was open very close to the hotel. It was the Rhin Bar. There, after haggling with the owner, who was closing and didn't want to serve us, we drank a glass of milk. So I managed to go to bed that night not completely starving, and as I did so I thought I'd made a mistake and that as soon as I could I'd request a transfer and leave that godforsaken city.

'I never did: I didn't request a transfer or return to Cáceres or ever leave this city. Now it's my city. My wife's from here, my children are from here, my father and mother are buried here, and I love it and hate it more or less the way a person loves and hates what matters most to him. Although, on reflection, it's not true: the truth is that I love this city a lot more than I hate it; how do you think I've put up with it for so long? Sometimes I even feel proud of it, because I've done as much as the next guy to make it what it is today; and believe me: it's a lot better than it was when I got here . . . Back then, as I've already told you, it was a horrible city, but still, I soon got used to it. I lived with my five friends in a rented flat on Montseny Street, in the Santa Eugènia neighbourhood, and I worked at the station on Jaume I, near Sant Agustí Plaza. Gerona has always been as calm as a mill-pond, but it was even more so back then, when Franco hadn't yet died, so as I'd expected, my work was much easier and less dangerous than what I'd done during my practical training. I was under the command of the deputy superintendent in charge of the Criminal Investigation Squad (Deputy Superintendent Martínez) and a veteran inspector in charge of one of the two groups the squad was divided into (Police Inspector Vives). Martínez was a good person and a good cop, but I soon discovered that Vives, who could be a lot of fun, deep down was a brainless thug. Why should I lie to you: there were lots of cops like that then. But luckily none of the guys with whom I had to share the flat and the squad, because I was living with them all hours of the day: we spent our mornings at the station, had lunch at Can Lloret, Can Barnet or El Ánfora, in the afternoons we walked our beats, at night we slept under the same roof and on our days off we tried to amuse ourselves together, something that in the Gerona of those days was almost more difficult than doing a good job. It's true that the resources the Squad had at its disposal were very sparse (we only had, for example, two undercover cars, which everyone recognized anyway because they were always parked in front of the station), but we didn't really need that much more either, because there was very little crime in the city and it was all concentrated in the red-light district, and that made it pretty easy to keep it under surveillance: all the crooks congregated in the district, all the jobs were cooked up in the district, and in the district, sooner or later, everyone knew everything about everyone. So all we needed to do was pass through the red-light district every evening and every night to control most of what went on in the city without too much difficulty.'

'And that's where you met El Zarco?'

'Exactly: that's where I met him.'

3

'As I told you before: at the age of sixteen I'd heard of the red-light district, although the only thing I knew about it was that it was not a highly recommended place and was on the other side of the river, in the old part of the city. In spite of my ignorance, the first time I went to La Font I didn't get lost.

'That afternoon I took the Sant Agustí bridge across the Onyar, and once I was in the old quarter I turned left on Ballesteries Street, continued up Calderas and, as I left the Church of Sant Fèlix behind on my right and turned into La Barca Street, realized I'd arrived in the district. I realized that from the stench of garbage and piss rising up like a thick waft from the paving stones heated by the siesta-hour sunshine; also from the people at the corner of Portal de la Barca, taking advantage of the stingy shade those decrepit buildings cast: an old man with sucked-in cheeks, a couple of sinister-looking adults, three or four *quinquis* in their twenties, all smoking and holding glasses of wine or bottles of beer. I passed them without looking at them and once I'd crossed Portal de la Barca I saw the Sargento bar; next door to it was La Font. I stopped at the door and looked through the glass. It was a small place, long and narrow, with a bar on the left and a space that ran along in front of it towards the back where it opened out into a little room. The place was almost empty: there were a few tables in the little back room, but I didn't see anybody

28

sitting at any of them; a couple of customers were chatting by the bar; behind the bar a woman was rinsing out glasses in the sink; above the woman, stuck on the wall, a sign read: "Smoking joints strictly forbidden". I didn't dare go in and kept going along La Barca to the corner of Bellaire, the border of the district. I hung around there for a good long while, between the railway overpass and Sant Pere Church, wondering whether I should go home or try again, until at some point I gathered my courage, returned to La Font and went in.

'There were quite a few more people in the bar now, although not Tere or Zarco. A bit intimidated, I planted myself at the end of the bar, near the door, and the landlady – a grim-faced redhead in a stain-covered apron – soon came over and asked me what I wanted; I asked for Zarco and she said he hadn't arrived yet; then I asked if she knew when he was going to get there and she told me she didn't; then she stood there looking at me. What's wrong?, she finally said. Aren't you going to order anything? I asked for a Coca-Cola, paid for it and began to wait.

'It wasn't long before Tere and Zarco showed up. As soon as they came through the door of La Font they saw me; as soon as they saw me, Tere's face lit up. Zarco patted me on the back. Fuck, Gafitas! he said. About time, eh? They took me to the back of the place and we sat at a table where two young guys were sitting: one, freckled and with almond-shaped eyes, they called Chino; the other chain-smoked constantly and was very small and very nervous, had a face full of pimples and they called him Colilla, or cigarette butt. Zarco made me sit between him and Tere, and while he was ordering beers from the landlady, Lina appeared, a blonde in a miniskirt and fuchsia-coloured sneakers who, I later found out, was Gordo's girlfriend. No one introduced me to anyone and no one said anything to me: Tere was talking to Lina, Colilla and Chino talked to Zarco; Gordo and Tío didn't even give any sign

29

of recognizing me when they showed up after a while. I felt totally out of place, but never for a minute did I consider leaving.

'A little while later a slightly older guy came over to sit with us. He was wearing cowboy boots, very tight flared jeans and his shirt unbuttoned; a gold chain shone on his chest. The guy sat astride a chair, beside Zarco, leaned his forearms on the chairback and pointed at me: And this posh kid? Everybody shut up; I suddenly noticed eight pairs of eyes staring at me. Zarco broke the silence. Fuck, Guille! he admonished. He's the guy from Vilaró: I told you he'd show up eventually. Guille made a face like he didn't know what Zarco was talking about. Zarco was about to go on when the landlady appeared with more beers and with a kid they called Drácula. When the landlady left (and Drácula stayed: they called him that because one of his eye teeth stuck out over his lip), Zarco continued: Go on, Gafitas, tell Guille what you told me the other day. Although I guessed what he meant, I asked him what he meant. What you told me about the arcade, he said. I told him; flattered by my momentary prominence, maybe trying to score points in front of the group (or just in front of Tere), I added that now I was helping Señor Tomàs close the place. Zarco asked me a couple of questions, among them how much money Señor Tomàs collected each day. I don't know, I said, honestly. More or less, Zarco insisted. I said a figure that was too high, and Zarco looked at Guille and I looked at Tere and at that moment I guessed I shouldn't have said what I'd just said.

'I soon forgot my hunch, and spent the rest of the afternoon with them. After my starring moment on account of the arcade and Señor Tomàs, I barely opened my mouth again; all I did was try to go unnoticed and listen while they drank beer at La Font and went out to smoke joints sitting on the rail of the bridge over Galligants, in the Sant Pere Plaza. That was how I found out three things: the first is that Zarco and Tere lived in the prefabs (as I later learned, the rest of them lived in Pont Major, Vilarroja and Germans Sàbat, but all of them or almost all of them had lived in the prefabs and most of them knew each other from there); the second is that, apart from Zarco, who was from Barcelona and had only been living in Gerona for a few months, they were all from Gerona or had been living here for years; and the third is that Zarco, Guille, Gordo and Drácula had all spent time in reform school (as I later learned, between the previous summer and the winter of that very year Zarco had been in Barcelona's Modelo Prison, even though he hadn't yet turned sixteen and was still a minor). As for the rest of it, until that day I had never tried hashish, so towards evening, after the feeling of well-being and uncontrollable laughter that a couple of tokes provoked had passed, I started to feel bad and, while we were on our way back to La Font from Sant Pere Plaza, I slipped away from the group and walked down Bellaire Street away from the district.

'Walking through La Devesa did me good. When I arrived at the arcade it was still open, and as I walked past Señor Tomàs' booth I waved to him, but didn't stop to talk. I went directly to the washrooms; I looked at myself in the mirror: I was pale and my eyes were red. I still felt like I was floating in a thick fog; to clear my head I urinated, took off my glasses, washed my face and hands. Then, as I looked back at myself in the mirror again, I remembered Zarco and Guille's conversation about Señor Tomàs and the arcade. On my way out of the washroom I bumped straight into the old man; as if he'd caught me doing something wrong, I was startled. What's wrong?, asked Señor Tomàs. Have you been sick again? I said no. Well, you still look ill, son, said Señor Tomàs. You should go to the doctor. We'd started to walk towards his booth. The arcade was still full of people, but Señor Tomàs announced: We'll close in ten minutes. At that moment I thought

I should tell him what I'd told Zarco and Guille and the rest of them at La Font, and what I was starting to suspect about them; only then did I realize that maybe he had suspected it much earlier than me, since the first afternoon Zarco and Tere showed up at the arcade, and that this was precisely why he'd offered to make me his helper. Even so, I didn't dare confess my suspicions – after all, doing so would have also meant confessing that I'd been with Zarco and the others and in a sense had turned into their accomplice, or at least that I'd said too much – and ten minutes later I helped him close up.

'That same night I had my first fight with my father. I mean the first more or less serious fight, of course, because we'd already had quite a few unimportant fights; not many, really: up till then I'd behaved like a good boy, and the one who had fights in my house was my sister, who was the eldest (and who, therefore, because I was a good kid and never confronted my parents, accused me of being a coward, a hypocrite, faint-hearted and accommodating). But over the last little while things had begun to change and the run-ins between my parents and me – mostly between my father and me – had become habitual; I suppose it was logical: after all I was a teenager; I suppose as well that, since nothing is as satisfactory as being able to blame someone else for all our woes, part of me blamed my parents for my troubles, or at least all the trouble Batista was giving me, as if I'd arrived at the conclusion that the inevitable result of my meek *charnego* upbringing was the horror in which Batista had me imprisoned, or as if this horror were part of the natural logic of things and Batista was just doing to me what, without my knowing or anyone having told me, his father had always done to my father.

'I don't know. The thing is that for months a wordless grudge against my parents had been growing in my guts, a silent fury that surfaced then, the first day I drank a few beers and smoked joints with Zarco's gang. I have a sort of hazy memory of what happened that night, maybe because during that summer there were various similar episodes and in my memory they all tend to blend into a single one: one of those interchangeable quarrels between fathers and sons in which everyone says brutal things and everyone's right. What I do remember is that when I got home it was after nine and my parents and my sister were having dinner. You're home late, said my father. I mumbled an apology and sat down at the table; my mother served my dinner and sat down again. They were eating with the television news on, though the volume was so low that it barely interfered with conversation. I began to eat without lifting my eyes from my plate, except to look at the television screen every once in a while. My sister was absorbing my parents' attention: she'd just finished high school at the Vicens Vives Institute and, while preparing to start university the following year, she had a summer job in a pharmaceutical lab. When my sister stopped talking (or maybe just paused), my father turned to me and asked how I was; avoiding his gaze, I said I was fine. Then he asked me where I'd been and I said outside. Oh oh oh, my sister intervened, as if she couldn't stand not being the centre of attention for every second of the meal. But look at the eyes on you! What've you been smoking? A hush fell over the dining room, disturbed only by the sound of the television, where there was news of an attack by ETA. Shut up, you idiot, I said before I could stop myself. There's no need to insult anybody, said my mother. Besides, your sister's right, she added, putting her hand on my forehead. Your eyes are red. Are you feeling all right? Pulling my forehead away I said yes and kept eating.

'Out of the corner of my eye I saw my sister observing me with her eyebrows arched mockingly; before she or my mother could add anything, my father asked: Who were you with? I didn't answer. He insisted: Have you been drinking? Have you been smoking? I thought: What's it to you? But I didn't say it, and I suddenly felt a great serenity, a great self-confidence, just as if all the confusion of the beers and the joints had cleared in one second and had left only a lucid form of rapture. What is this?, I asked without getting upset. An interrogation? My father's expression hardened. Is something going on with you?, he asked. Let it go, Andrés, my mother chimed in, trying again to restore the peace. Keep quiet, please, my father cut her off. Now I was staring back at him; my father insisted. I asked you what's going on. Nothing, I answered. Then why don't you answer me?, he asked. Because I don't have anything to say, I replied. My father kept quiet and turned towards my mother, who half-closed her eyes and begged him in silence to let it go; my sister was watching the scene with barely disguised satisfaction. Look, Ignacio, said my father. I don't know what's going on with you lately, but I don't like you behaving the way you've been behaving: if you're going to keep living in this house . . . And I don't like to be lectured, I inter-rupted; then I continued, fired-up: When did you start drinking? When did you start smoking? At the age of fourteen? Fifteen? I'm sixteen, so leave me alone. My father didn't interrupt me; but, when I finished speaking, he left his cutlery on his plate and said without raising his voice: The next time you speak to me like that, I'll knock your teeth out. It felt like a blow to the chest and throat, I looked at my almost empty plate and then at the TV: on the screen, the Minister of the Interior – a man with square-framed glasses and a severe countenance – was condemning the terrorist attack on behalf of the government. As I stood up from the table I murmured: Fuck right off.

'My father's shouts chased me to my room. My sister was the first to come to offer her understanding and advice; naturally, I ignored her. I ignored my mother too, although she seemed truly worried. Lying on my bed, trying in vain to read, I felt too proud of myself, and wondered why I wasn't capable of confronting Batista as serenely as I confronted my father; before falling asleep I promised myself, full of resolve, that the next day I'd go to La Font and speak to Zarco to ask him not to bother Señor Tomàs, and then I'd speak to Tere to ask her if she was going out with Zarco: if the answer was no, I promised myself, I'd ask her to go out with me.

'The next day I went to La Font without stopping in at the arcade. At the same table as the day before were Gordo, Lina, Drácula and Chino, who didn't seem surprised when I joined them. Zarco and Tere arrived a little while later. Yesterday you left without saying goodbye, said Tere, sitting down beside me. I didn't think you'd come back. I apologized with the truth – or half the truth: I told her I'd gone to close up the arcade – and remembered the double promise I'd made myself the night before. Feeling incapable of speaking to Zarco, but not to Tere, after a while I told Tere I wanted to speak to her. What about?, she asked. Two things, I answered. Tere waited for me to begin. I nodded towards Zarco and the rest and said: Not here.

'We went outside. Tere leaned on the wall beside the door to La Font, folded her arms and asked me what I wanted to talk about. I immediately knew I wasn't brave enough to ask her if she was Zarco's girlfriend. I decided to talk to her about the arcade and, after pressing up against the wall to let a drinks truck past that barely fit in La Barca Street, I asked her: Are you guys going to do something to Señor Tomàs? Who's Señor Tomàs?, asked Tere. The old man who runs the Vilaró arcade, I answered. Are you going to rob him? Tere looked surprised, she laughed and unfolded her arms. Where did you get that idea?, she wanted to know. Yesterday Zarco asked me about the arcade, I answered. And the first day we met as well. So I thought that . . . Second thing, Tere

35

interrupted me. What?, I asked. Second thing, she repeated. You told me you wanted to talk about two things, didn't you? The first is fucking stupid; what's the second? She stared at me with all the cruelty her eyes were capable of and her lips curved into a half-ironic half-contemptuous sneer; I wondered where the girl from the arcade washroom had gone and why she'd made me go to La Font, was glad I hadn't asked her if she was going out with Zarco, and felt completely ridiculous. There is no second thing, I said. Tere shrugged and went back inside the bar.

'We spent the rest of the afternoon as we had the previous afternoon, back and forth from La Font to the Galligants bridge, smoking and drinking. On one of these comings and goings Zarco grabbed my arm at the intersection of La Barca and Bellaire. Hey, Gafitas, he said, forcing me to stop. Tere told me you're a bit pissed off. I watched Tere and the rest disappear down La Barca towards La Font. It was Friday and, although it hadn't started to get dark yet, groups of drinkers were already beginning to arrive in the district. Zarco went on: Is it true you thought we were going to rip off the place in Vilaró? There was no sense in denying it, so I didn't deny it. And where did you get that idea?, he asked. I told him. He listened to me attentively, but I hadn't finished talking when he let go of my arm and put his hand on my shoulder. Anyway, what if it is true?, he asked. You told me you didn't have money, right? Well that's how you get money: you tell us how things work, we do the job and then you get your share of the take. He paused before concluding: There's no risk. It's a great deal. What more do you want? He stared at me waiting for my reply. Nothing, I answered. So why are you pissed off?, he insisted. I didn't know how to explain it to him. I explained: Well, I'm not really like you guys. Zarco smiled: a hard smile, showing off-white teeth. And what do you mean by that?, he asked. Before answering I reflected. It means I don't want a share, I said, and added quickly: I don't want to make a deal. I don't want anything to happen to the old man and it to be my fault. I don't want you to rob him. Now Zarco's expression turned uncertain and his eyes narrowed so much that they were reduced to two slits, just a touch of blue showing through. What's the deal?, he finally asked. The old man's a mate of yours? More or less, I answered. Really?, he insisted, opening his eyes wide. I nodded. Zarco took a few seconds to process my reply; then he took his hand off my shoulder and looked somewhat resigned and somewhat understanding. OK, he said in another tone of voice. If he's your mate that changes things. Does that mean you guys aren't going to do anything to the old man?, I asked. Of course, Zarco answered, sticking his hands in his pockets. Friendship's sacred, Gafitas. Don't you think so?

'I said I did. We were in the shade, but the air was still hot and beyond the sidewalk the sun was still beating down on the cobblestones. Behind Zarco, the Gerona bar was heaving. People kept arriving in the district. So there's no job, Zarco decided. Mates are mates. I'll tell Guille and the rest. They'll understand. And if they don't understand, fuck them: I'm the leader of this pack. Thanks, I said. Don't thank me, said Zarco. You do owe me one, though. He took his right hand out of his pocket and pointed the long, dirty nail of his index finger at me while moving it up and down and adding: I scratch your back, you scratch mine. That said we went back to La Font. A while later, when I was going to leave the district without any further mention of the subject, Zarco grabbed me by the wrist and pointed at me again while Tere watched us. Don't forget you owe me one, Gafitas, he said. And he repeated: I scratch your back, you scratch mine.

'That night I made the decision not to return to La Font. I'd had enough: my two incursions into the district had entailed an enormous risk and had been about to lead to a calamity for Señor

37

Tomàs; but most of all they'd been enough to convince me that Tere wasn't the girl for me and that what happened between us in the washrooms at the arcade could never happen again. Although I'm not so sure of the last bit; I mean I'm not so sure that I was sure of that. Whatever the case, my impression was that I had nothing to show for my walk on the wild side, except the certainty that, on the other side of the river, there was a world that bore no relation to the one that I knew.

'I spent the weekend between my house and the Vilaró arcade, reading and watching TV and playing the free games I'd accumulated on account of the help I gave Señor Tomàs, help I knew Señor Tomàs no longer needed, or rather that I hoped he didn't need. On Monday I continued my new routine. In the afternoon I was at the arcade and at dusk I helped Señor Tomàs close up and said goodbye to him. Then, on my way home, just after I'd passed one of the columns that supported the railway overpass, somebody made a sound behind me. A cold shiver ran down my spine. I turned around; it wasn't Batista: it was Tere. She was leaning against the overpass column smoking a cigarette. Hiya, Gafitas, she said. In two strides she was in front of me; she was wearing her usual sneakers and jeans, but it seemed like her handbag strap across her white T-shirt accentuated her chest more than ever. How are you?, she asked. Fine, I said. She nodded and rubbed the mole beside her nose and asked: Aren't you coming back to La Font? Of course I'm coming back, I lied. Tere looked at me inquisitively. I explained: It's just that this weekend I was tied up. At the arcade?, she asked. I said yes. Tere nodded again and took a drag of her cigarette; as she blew out the smoke she gestured behind her: How's the old man? I understood that she meant Señor Tomàs and I said he was fine. That's good, said Tere. I didn't know you were friends. Zarco told me. She paused and then added: Does he know he owes you one? She meant Señor Tomàs

38

again, but this time I didn't say anything. Well he does, said Tere. You better believe he owes you one. You should have seen the stink Guille made. He wanted to do the arcade job whether anybody else wanted to or not. Luckily Zarco stopped him. If not for him, the old man would have had a rough time. Thanks to him and to you, of course. At that moment a train started to pass over our heads; the noise was deafening, and we kept quiet for a few seconds. When the sound of the train began to fade into the distance, Tere took a last drag of her cigarette; then she threw the butt on the ground, stepped on it and asked: What were we talking about? You lied to me, I improvised. What?, asked Tere. You lied, I insisted. You told me you guys weren't planning on hitting the arcade and you were planning it. Tere looked like she was thinking it over; then she made a gesture of indifference; then her expression brightened. Oh, yeah, she said. Now I remember what we were talking about: about how the old man owes you one. She paused. And that you owe Zarco one, she said. Remember? She pointed at me with her index finger the same way Zarco had pointed when we said goodbye at La Font on Friday and said: He scratched your back now you scratch his.

'We looked at each other for a moment. Tere leaned on the hood of a car parked next to us and explained that Guille had been talking for some time about a housing development in Lloret, that it was the perfect place to rob because it was really isolated and the owners were rich people, and it was the perfect moment too because June wasn't over yet and lots of houses were still empty, waiting for their owners to come and stay for July and August. Finally she said that Zarco was going to do a job there and needed me to help him. Then she changed the singular for the plural: You'll help us, right? I had no intention of helping them and, to gain time, for a moment I thought of asking her why Zarco didn't ask me himself, why he sent her to ask me; instead of beating about the bush I said: I'm sorry. I can't. Tere opened her arms and looked at me with astonishment that struck me as genuine. Why?, she asked. The only thing that occurred to me was to answer the same way I'd answered Zarco. Because I'm not like you guys, I said. I've never done that. You've never done what?, she asked. Stolen anything, I answered. Nobody's asking you to steal, she said. We're the ones who're going to do the stealing. What you have to do is something else. And it's dead easy, so easy that it's almost nothing. So why doesn't somebody else do it then?, I asked. Because we need someone like you, she answered. Someone who speaks Catalan and looks like a good kid. Come on, Gafitas, for fuck's sake: are you going to leave us high and dry after what Zarco did for you? Pay us what you owe and we'll be even. She fell quiet. The streetlamps of Bonastruc de Porta had been on for a while and they tinged Tere's dark hair, her green eyes, her red, full lips with their golden light. What do you say?, she asked. I looked behind her at the closed blinds of the Vilaró arcade and thought that, if I said no, I'd never see Tere again; I felt my legs go weak as I said: What do I have to do?

'I don't remember exactly what Tere's reply was; only that she assured me that the next day Zarco would explain what I had to do and that she said goodbye with two sentences. Be on time. Tomorrow at La Font at three. I spent a horrible night wondering whether to go or not, deciding not to go and then a minute later deciding to go. In the end I went, and before three in the afternoon I was already at La Font. A little while later Zarco arrived and Tere, wearing a pair of shorts that revealed her long, tanned legs; Guille was the last to show up. Zarco wasn't surprised by my presence there, didn't explain what it was we were going to do, and I didn't ask him either; I was too worried. As we left the district, Zarco, Tere and Guille started checking out the cars parked along the streets and, when we came up to a Seat 124 parked in a solitary alley that led out onto Pedret Avenue, Tere took a small sawblade with a hook on one end out of her bag and handed it to Zarco while Guille took off running up to the next sidestreet; then Tere ran to the one behind us. I stayed with Zarco and saw him stick the sawblade into the slot between the Seat 124's door and window and, after feeling around for a couple of seconds with the blade, I heard a click and the door opened. Zarco sat in the driver's seat, yanked the steering wheel around, reached underneath it and brought out a handful of wires, connected one wire to another, touched another wire to them and the engine immediately started. The whole operation lasted a minute, maybe less than a minute. A little while later we were on our way out of the other side of the city riding in the 124.

'We arrived in Lloret around four. We drove in on a wide street that led to the centre, flanked by souvenir shops, cheap restaurants, closed discotheques and groups of tourists in flip-flops and swimsuits, and when we came to the sea we turned left and followed a promenade dotted with patio bars that ran parallel to the beach. Finally we turned left again, drove away from the sea for a moment and then came back towards it up a winding road that clung to the cliffs, until we saw a sign that said: La Montgoda. It's here, said Guille, and Zarco parked the car on a slope, at the entrance to the housing development; then he turned around to face the back seat and started to explain what I had to do while Tere took a comb, an eyebrow pencil and lipstick out of her bag. I don't know if I understood Zarco's whole explanation, but when he asked me if I'd understood I answered yes; then he said: OK, now forget everything I told you and just do what you see Tere doing. I said yes again, and at that moment Guille caught my eye in the rear-view mirror. Gafitas is shitting himself, he scoffed. All the bastard can say is yes. Zarco told him to shut up while I turned and looked helplessly at Tere and Tere winked at me while carrying on combing her hair. Zarco added: And you, Gafitas, don't let it get to you: do what I told you and everything'll be fine. OK? I was about to say yes again, but I just nodded my head.

'Once she'd finished getting ready, Tere put her comb, eyeliner and lipstick back in her bag and said: Let's go. When we got out of the car she took me by the hand and we started walking up the badly paved slope. The housing development seemed deserted; the only noise we could hear was the sound of the sea. When we saw the first house appear among the pine trees, Tere instructed me. Let me do the talking, she said. Nobody's going to say anything to you, but, if someone speaks in Catalan, you talk. If not, keep quiet. Do what I do. Most of all, whatever happens, stay with me. And one more thing: is what Guille said true? My heart was beating through my ribs like a caged bird; I'd started to sweat, and Tere's hand was slipping in my soaking wet hand; I managed to say: Yes. Tere laughed; I laughed too, and that simultaneous laughter filled me with courage.

'We got to the first house, walked through the garden and Tere rang the doorbell. The door opened and a woman who looked like she'd just got out of bed questioned us in silence, with her eyes half-closed against the strong sun; Tere answered the questioning look with a question: she asked if Pablo was home. Unexpectedly friendly, the woman answered that no one called Pablo lived in that house, and Tere apologized. We left the garden and walked down the street. How's it going?, asked Tere. How's what going?, I asked. How's everything going?, she clarified. I don't know, I said, truthfully. Does that mean you're not nervous any more?, she asked. More or less, I answered. Then stop squeezing my hand, would you, she said. You're going to break it. I let go of her hand and dried mine on my trousers, but she was soon holding it again. We didn't call at the house next door or the next one, but at the one after that we tried again. This door opened too, this time an old man in a T-shirt with whom Tere exchanged a series of questions and answers similar to the exchange she'd had with the first woman, only longer; in fact, at one point it seemed to me that the old man, who couldn't take his eyes off Tere's legs, was undressing her in his mind and that, instead of trying to cut short the dialogue, he was trying to lengthen it.

'The third house we tried was the one. Nobody answered when we rang the bell and, as soon as we made sure the villa was empty, that the villa next door was empty and that on the other side of the villa next door there was nothing but a brick wall behind which was a vacant lot full of shrubs, we walked back to the entrance of the development, where Zarco and Guille were waiting for us in the 124. Go up to the end of the street, Tere said to Zarco, who started up the car as soon as we got in. It's the last house on the right. As we drove into the development in slow motion, Tere answered questions from Zarco and Guille and, after a Citroën with a woman and two children in it passed us on its way out, we arrived at the brick wall at the end, and parked in front of the door with the car facing back the way we came.

'That's where the real danger began. As Zarco and Guille walked into the garden and around the house – a two-storey house with a flat roof, a big willow tree shading the entrance – Tere put her bag behind her back, leaned against the hood of the 124, pulled me towards her, wrapped her arms around my neck and wedged her bare knee in between my legs. Now we're going to do like they do in the movies, Gafitas, she told me. If nobody comes along, we stay here nice and quiet until Zarco and Guille call us. But, if someone decides to come by here, I'm going to snog you to within an inch of your life. So you can start praying that someone comes by. This last bit she said with half a smile; I was so scared I just nodded. Anyway, nobody came past, and I don't know how long the two of us were leaning against the car, joined in that fake embrace, but shortly after seeing Zarco and Guille disappear beneath the branches of the willow, towards the back of the garden, I was startled to hear in the absolute silence of siesta time a vague crunch of breaking wood coming from the house and then an unmistakable crash of broken glass. Tere tried to calm me down by pressing her knee into my crotch and talking. I don't know what she talked about; all I know is that at a certain point I started to get a massive hard-on, which I tried to hide but couldn't, and that, when she noticed my erection, a happy smile revealed her teeth. Fuck, Gafitas, she said. What a time to get horny!

'Tere had barely finished that sentence when the door of the house opened and Zarco and Guille came out carrying bags. They put them in the trunk of the car, asked me to stay there, keeping an eye out, and went back inside the house, this time with Tere. After a while they came out with a couple more bags, a Telefunken television, a Philips radio-cassette player and a turntable. When everything was loaded into the trunk, we got into the car and drove unhurriedly out of La Montgoda.

'That was my baptism by fire. Of the return trip to Gerona I remember only that I felt not the slightest relief because the danger had passed; on the contrary: instead I swapped the fright for euphoria, the wild rush of the robbery with adrenaline coming out my ears. And I also remember that when we got to Gerona we went directly to sell what we'd stolen. Or did we sell it the next day? No, I think it was the same day. But I'm not sure. Anyway. That week I still went back to the arcade a few times to help Señor Tomàs (and sometimes, on my way past, to play a few games of pinball before going to La Font); but, when I started going out at night without telling anybody, treating my family with no consideration, further embittering my relationship with my father and multiplying our fights, I stopped going to the arcade entirely, and one afternoon, on my way to La Font, I went in and told Señor

Tomàs that I was going on holiday and probably wouldn't be back for a long time. Don't worry, son, Señor Tomàs said. I'll find someone to help me close up. If you like, I said. But you won't need to. Nobody's going to bother you. Señor Tomàs looked at me intrigued. And how do you know that?, he asked. Privately proud of myself, I said: I just do. From then on I started to go to La Font almost every afternoon.'

'But you didn't have to: you'd paid Zarco back the favour in La Montgoda and you were even.'

'Yeah, but there was Tere.'

'You mean you joined Zarco's gang for Tere?'

'I mean that, if it hadn't been for Tere, I most likely wouldn't have done it: although I'd arrived at the conclusion that she wasn't the girl for me, I wanted to think that, while we were near to each other, what had happened in the Vilaró arcade washrooms could always happen again; and I think I was willing to run any risk in order to keep open some possibility of that happening again. That said, you're a writer and must know that, even if we find it very comforting to find an explanation for what we do, the truth is that most of what we do doesn't have a single explanation, supposing that it even has any.'

'You told me before that robbing the house was a rush. Does that mean you enjoyed it?'

'It means what it means. What do you want me to say? That I loved it? That the day I stole stuff in La Montgoda I discovered that there was no way back, that Zarco's game was a very serious game, where everything was at stake, that I could no longer be satisfied playing the Rocky Balboa pinball machine, where I had nothing at stake? You want me to say that playing that game I felt I was getting even with my parents? Or you want me to tell you that I was getting revenge for all my humiliations and the guilt that had been accumulating over the last year and that, as Batista

45

represented absolute evil for me, this game that liberated me from Batista represented absolute good? If you want I'll say it; maybe I've already said it. And it may be true. But do me a favour: don't ask me for explanations; ask me for facts.'

'Agreed. Let's get back to the facts. The robbery in La Montgoda was the first in a series of robberies you participated in with Zarco. You told me before that when you got to Gerona that day you went to sell what you'd stolen. Where did you sell it? Who did you sell it to? Because I can't imagine it would have been easy.'

'Selling it was easy; what wasn't easy was getting good money for it. There was only one fence in Gerona, or at least only one serious fence, so since he had practically no competition, he did whatever he wanted. He was the General. They called him that because he bragged about having been an officer in the Spanish Foreign Legion; also because he wore long bushy sideburns like a comic-strip general. I only met him three or four times. He lived in an Andalusian-style house in the middle of an open field in Torre Alfonso XII and he was a peculiar guy, although maybe the peculiar thing was him and his wife as a couple. I clearly remember the afternoon we went to sell him the loot from La Montgoda, which was the first time I saw him. As I told you before, it might have been the same afternoon as the robbery, but it might have been another, because we often stashed what we stole and took a few days to sell it. As a precaution. The thing is that day we – Zarco, Tere, Guille and I, the same ones who'd gone to La Montgoda – went that day, parked the car in front of the General's house and Zarco went to the door and soon came back and announced that the General was busy although his wife said he'd soon be finished and we could go in shortly. They want to fuck with the guys who are with the General, Zarco said. Guille and Tere laughed; I didn't get the joke, but didn't think anything of it either. Between the four of us we carried all the stuff into the house guarded by the General's wife, a skinny, scraggy woman, with vague eyes, messy hair and a grey housecoat. When we went out to the yard we saw the General and a couple of men at one side in front of a large cardboard box with a radio-cassette player sticking out of it. The men looked angry when they saw us and immediately turned their backs. The General seemed to be trying to placate them; he greeted us with a slight nod. We left our load in the middle of the yard (at the other side there was a jumble of bed frames, bicycles, scrapped motorbikes, furniture and appliances), and waited for the General to finish what he was doing. He soon did, and the two men left in a hurry without even looking at us, accompanied by the General and his wife.

'We were left alone in the yard, and Zarco amused himself by looking through the big cardboard box with the radio-cassette sticking out of it while Guille, Tere and I smoked and talked. A while later the General came back without his wife. He seemed cheerful and relaxed, but before he could say a word Zarco pointed to the gate. Who were those guys?, he asked. The ones who just left?, asked the General. Yeah, answered Zarco. Why do you want to know?, asked the General. Zarco shrugged. No reason, he said. Just wondering what that pair of dickheads were called. The answer didn't seem to annoy the General. He looked at Zarco with interest and then turned for a second towards his wife, who'd come back out to the yard while they were talking and was standing a few metres away, with her head leaning on one shoulder and hands in the pockets of her housecoat, apparently oblivious to the conversation. The General asked: What's up, Zarquito? Did you come here to piss me off? Zarco smiled modestly, as if the General was trying to flatter him. Not at all, he said. Then would you mind telling me what you're talking about?, said the General. Zarco pointed to the cardboard box he'd just looked through. How much did you pay for what's in there?, he asked. What's it to you?, replied the General. Zarco didn't say anything. After a silence the General said: Fourteen thousand pesetas. Satisfied? Zarco continued smiling with his eyes, but pursed his lips sceptically. It's worth a lot more, he said. And how do you know?, asked the General. Because I know, answered Zarco. Anyone other than those two dickheads knows it; what a pair: as soon as they saw us they shat themselves and could only think of how fast they could get out of here. He paused and added: What a bastard you can be. Zarco said this calmly looking at the General, with no malice in his tone of voice. As I told you, it was the first time I went to that house and I didn't know what Zarco's relationship was with the man he was talking to or how to take that verbal sparring, but I was reassured by the fact that neither Tere nor Guille seemed anxious or surprised. The fence didn't either, just scratched a sideburn thoughtfully and sighed. Look, kid, he said afterwards. Everyone does business the way they like, or the way they can. Besides, as I've told you many times: in this world things are worth what people pay for them, and in this house things are worth what I say they're worth. Not one peseta more. And anyone who doesn't like it shouldn't come here. Is that clear? Zarco rushed to answer, still a bit mocking but conciliatory now: Crystal. Then, turning to the merchandise that we'd left in the middle of the yard, he asked: And according to you how much is this worth?

'The General looked at Zarco with distrust, but soon followed him, just as Tere, Guille and I did; then his wife followed. For quite a long time the General was examining the stuff, crouched down, with his wife standing beside him: he'd pick something up, describe it, list its defects (many, according to him) and virtues (according to him, few) and then he'd move on to the next. As I watched the scene I understood that the General was listing and describing more for his wife than for himself, and for a moment I thought his wife had trouble with her eyesight or that she was actually blind. When they finished the inventory and valuation, the General and his wife moved a few steps away, exchanged a few inaudible words and soon the man returned, crouched down again beside the Telefunken television set, passed his hand over the screen as if he wanted to get the dust off it, pressed the on-off button a couple of times to no effect and asked: How much do you want? Double, answered Zarco without a thought. Double what?, asked the General. Double what you paid those dupes, answered Zarco. This time it was the General who smiled. Then he placed his hands on his knees, stood up with a groan and looked his wife in the eye; his wife didn't look at him; she was staring beyond the fences of the yard, as if something in the sky had caught her attention. The General looked at the empty sky and then looked back at Zarco. I'll give you sixteen thousand, he said. Zarco pretended to think it over for a moment before turning to me. Hey, Gafitas, he said. You've been to school: is sixteen thousand double fourteen thousand? I shook my head slightly and Zarco turned back to the General and copied my gesture. You're crazy, said the General without the smile leaving his face. I'm making you a good offer. It doesn't seem that good to me, said Zarco. Nobody's going to pay what you're asking, insisted the General. We'll see about that, replied Zarco. He immediately signalled to Guille and the two of them picked up the television while I carried the record player and Tere the speakers, but we hadn't even started walking when we saw that the General's wife was waiting for us at the door to the house, as if she wanted to say goodbye or rather as if she wanted to prevent us from leaving. Twenty thousand, the General said then. Carrying the television, Zarco looked at him, looked at his wife, looked at me and asked: Is twenty thousand double fourteen thousand? Before I could answer, the General said: Twenty-three thousand. It's my final offer. Then Zarco gestured to Guille that they should put the television down and, once they'd done so,

49

went over to the General, held out his hand and said: Twenty-five thousand and there's no more to be said.

'Nothing more was said: the General reluctantly accepted the deal and paid us the twenty-five thousand pesetas in thousand-peso notes.'

'Zarco twisted his arm.'

'That's what it seemed like, that's what I thought that day, but I don't believe it: what we'd stolen was surely worth a lot more than that; otherwise the General wouldn't have paid what he paid. He was smart, and his wife was even smarter. They always seemed to give ground, but they never actually did, or at least they never lost out; when I think about it, the very opposite happened to Zarco, and not only with the General and his wife: although he sometimes seemed to win, he always ended up losing. Of course it took me a long time to understand that. The first time I saw him, at the Vilaró arcade, Zarco seemed to me like one of those unpredictable, violent, tough guys who inspire fear because they feel no fear, exactly the opposite of what I was or how I felt then: I felt like a born loser, so he could only be a born winner, a guy who was going to conquer the world; that's what I think Zarco was to me, and maybe not just for that summer. As I said, it took me a long time to figure out that he was actually a born loser, and when I did figure it out it was too late and the world had already conquered him . . . Anyway. I just remembered a story. It doesn't have to do directly with Zarco, but indirectly it does. Or at least I feel it has to do with him.'

'Go ahead.'

'Tere told the story, I don't remember when or where. In any case it was one of many I heard about the prefabs, something they talked a lot about in Zarco's gang, as if they were all really proud of having lived there or as if having lived there was the only thing that really united them. It had happened some eight years earlier, before Zarco lived in the prefabs but when the rest of them did, and so, some more and some less, they all remembered it or had heard it told. The story had started the day a man caught his wife in bed with the next-door neighbour; according to Tere's version, the man was a good man, but the neighbour was an awful brute who'd been making his life impossible for years. And so, when the good man saw that his wife was cheating on him, and who she was cheating with, he freaked out and ended up setting fire to the place next door. The problem was that this happened in the wooden prefabs (housing that, as Tere pointed out, no longer existed), and the flames spread very quickly and the fire ended up devouring thirty-two homes. It was a dramatic story, which had apparently caused the worst disaster in the whole history of the prefabs, but Tere told it as if it were a comical story or we'd all smoked so much hash and drunk so many beers and popped so many pills that we listened to it as if it were a comical story, laughing till tears were streaming down our faces, interrupting her constantly. Anyway, what I remember most clearly isn't the story itself but what happened after Tere finished telling it. I asked how it had ended for the two protagonists. That's the best part of the story, interrupted Guille, who never let an opportunity for sarcasm pass him by. In the end the bastard got off and the cheated-on husband owned up. Poor sucker got at least a couple of years in the can. We all laughed again, even harder. It's what always happens, man, Gordo philosophized, suddenly serious, patting his lacquered shoulder-length hair. The good guys lose and the bad guys win. Don't be a wanker, Gordo, Zarco leapt in. That's what happens when the good guys are dickheads and the bad guys are smart. Oh man, Tío then burst in, with an innocence that for a moment I interpreted as a form of irony. Don't fucking tell me that now you want to be a good guy? Zarco seemed doubtful, seemed to think over his reply or to realize all of a sudden that we were all waiting for his reply and had stopped laughing. Of course, don't you?, he finally said. But I'd rather be a bad guy than a dickhead. A wave of laughter met Zarco's reply. And that's where we left it.'

'Are you telling me that, as well as a born winner, during that summer you saw Zarco as a good guy turned by circumstances into an arsonist?'

'No. I've just told you a small story that forms part of a larger story; take it however you like, but not before I finish telling the whole story. Remember: facts, not explanations; ask me to tell you things, not interpret them.'

'OK. Tell me then. You said that the General gave you twenty-five thousand pesetas for what you'd stolen in La Montgoda. That was quite a lot of money back then. What did you do with it?'

'We spent it immediately. That's what we always did. Money burned holes in our pockets: one afternoon we'd have twenty-five, thirty, forty thousand pesetas, and the next morning we'd have nothing left. That was normal for us. Of course we all spent the money and not just the ones who'd participated in the theft.'

'When you say all you mean the whole gang?'

'Yeah.'

'That was the norm? Everything they stole got divvied up in equal portions?'

'More or less. Sometimes we shared out what we earned and other times it went into a sort of kitty. But the money was every-body's and we spent it between all of us.'

'What did you spend it on?'

'Drink, food and smokes. And drugs, naturally.'

'What drugs did you use?'

'Hash. Pills too: uppers, downers, stuff like that. Sometimes mescaline. But not cocaine.'

'Did any of you use heroin?'

'No. Heroin came in later, same with coke. I don't remember anyone doing heroin back then in the district.'

'Not even Zarco?'

'Not even Zarco.'

'Are you sure?'

'Totally. The thing about him being addicted to heroin from the age of thirteen or fourteen is a lie. A legend like so many that circulate about him.'

'Tell me how you got hold of the drugs.'

'It wasn't as easy as you might think. During the spring Zarco and the rest of them had been supplied by a couple of dealers who were regulars at La Font, but a little while before I joined the gang the police had made two or three raids and cleaned the dealers out of the district, so, when I showed up, they were in jail or had scarpered. That explains why Zarco and Tere were at the Vilaró arcade when we met; as Tere told me, the guy in the Fred Perry shirt was a dealer: he'd told them to meet him there. And it also explains why we had to go outside the district all summer to sort ourselves out. Luckily the Fred Perry dealer didn't arrange to meet Zarco at the arcade again (he must have sensibly realized it was not a suitable place for his business dealings); they met in bars in the old quarter: in the Pub Groc, in L'Enderroc, in Freaks. Later, towards the middle of July or the beginning of August, the Fred Perry dealer disappeared and we started frequenting the Flor, a bar with big windows that overlooked Mayor Street in Salt; we had several dealers there from the middle of July or the beginning of August until the middle of September: some guy called Dani, a Rodri, a Gómez, maybe another one or two.'

'Did they never suggest becoming dealers? It would have solved the supply problem.'

'But it would have created much worse problems. No. It was never suggested. Not as far as I know.'

'Everybody took everything?'

'Yeah. Some were greedier than others, but in general, yeah: we all took everything. Maybe the girls were more sensible, including Tere, but not the rest of them.'

'You took everything too?'

'Of course. I wouldn't have fitted into the gang if I hadn't. Supposing I eventually did fit in, that is.'

'Didn't you?'

'I tried to. Sometimes I think I managed it, but other times I think not; depends on what you understand by fitting in, I suppose. It's true that, as I've told you, after a certain point I went to La Font almost every day, hung out with them and did more or less whatever they were doing. But it's also true that I never felt entirely like just one more member of the gang: I was and wasn't, I did and didn't, I was inside and out, like a witness or onlooker who participated in everything but most of all watched everyone participate. That's how I think I felt deep down, and I think that's how they felt about me; the proof is that, aside from Zarco and Tere (and only on exceptional occasions), I barely spoke to anyone on my own, and I wasn't close to any of them. For all of them I was what I obviously was: a meteorite, a disorientated kid, a posh brat lost among them, the top dog's protégé, their leader's whim, someone who didn't have much to do with them, although they accepted him and could fraternize with him once in a while.

'But, to get back to the facts, yes, I took everything. At first I had a hard time keeping up with the rest of them, and I had a few bad days, but I soon got used to it.'

'What other things did you have to do to fit in?'

'Lots. But, please, don't misinterpret: I didn't take drugs to be accepted; I took them because I liked it. Let's say I started off doing it out of some sort of obligation, or curiosity, and ended up doing it for pleasure, or habit.'

'Like what happened with the robberies, no?'

'In a certain sense. With other things.'

'For example?'

'For example with hookers.'

'You went to hookers.'

'Of course. In the district there was a brothel every couple of steps and we were sixteen, seventeen years old, walking around with a permanent overdose of testosterone, we had money; how could we not go to hookers? Actually, I think we spent most of our money on hookers. Although, to be perfectly honest, it was much harder for me to get used to the hookers than the drugs; I got much more hooked on drugs than hookers. I did like some hookers, but the truth is, especially at first, most of them gave me the creeps. I can tell you about my first visit to a brothel; I remember that night very clearly because something strange happened.'

'I'm listening.'

'It was at La Vedette, a brothel that was where most of the red-light district brothels were, on Pou Rodó, parallel to La Barca. It was the most expensive place in the neighbourhood, and also the best, though it was still a filthy, dark cave; imagine what the rest were like. It was run by a madam who was also called Vedette, a woman in her fifties with a reputation for ruling her business with unceremonious authority. That day the place was only half full, there wouldn't have been more than ten or twelve men leaning on the bar or against the walls, drinking or breathing in the atmosphere saturated with smoke, cheap perfume and the smell of sweat, sex and alcohol. The girls swarmed around them, wearing very tight clothes and with faces caked in make-up, and a full-volume rumba shut down the conversations. It must have been right after the robbery in La Montgoda, or at least right after one of the first jobs I was involved in, among other reasons because after a job was when we could afford the luxury of going to La Vedette. The thing is that a few minutes after we got there all my friends had paired off and disappeared, and I suddenly found myself alone at the bar, after several girls had given up on me when they understood I didn't have the slightest intention of bedding them. At that moment Vedette strolled calmly over from the other side of the room. Hello, handsome, she said. Don't you like any of my girls? Vedette had bleached blonde hair, big breasts, big bones and hard features, and her powerful proximity was more intimidating than that of her charges, but for that very reason I found it easy to lie. Of course I like them, I answered. Vedette spilled her cleavage over the bar and asked: Well then? I smiled and put my empty beer glass to my lips and averted my gaze as I searched for a reply. Don't tell me it's your first time?, she asked. Before I could tell her another lie, the woman let out a terrifying cackle; terrifying until I realized that nobody in the place had heard it. Little angel, she said, exhaling her mentholated breath in my face. If I wasn't retired I'd deflower you myself. She let me go and added: But if you want I'll introduce you to the girl you need. She pointed to a place in the shadows. It's her over there, she continued. Do you want me to call her? Go on, don't be silly, you'll see how much you like it. I didn't see who Vedette was pointing at, but it didn't matter: the mere idea of shutting myself up in a dark room with one of those big painted women was so revolting that it killed the slightest twinge of desire. Vedette must have sensed this (or maybe I shook my head), because she sighed, defeated, and asked, pointing at my beer: Do you want another?

'I still hadn't finished drinking my second beer when Zarco and the rest started to come downstairs. They all asked me the same thing and I answered them all the same way and they all insisted I choose a girl and go upstairs with her; none of them suspected what Vedette had guessed, or at least no one voiced the suspicion out loud, and finally their insistence and my fear the secret would come to light overcame my disgust and I went over to Vedette and told her to introduce me to her candidate. Her name was Trini and she turned out to be a little brunette with short hair and swaying hips who pulled my arm around her waist and, while Zarco and the rest of the guys gestured euphorically at the other end of the bar, led me upstairs to one of the bedrooms. There she stepped down out of her high heels, stripped me and helped me strip her. Then she took me into the bathroom and washed and washed me and pushed me down on the bed and started sucking me off. It was the second time in my life something like this had happened to me, although the truth is it seemed like two different things and not the same thing done by two different women. After a while Trini managed to get it up, but as soon as she tried to get me inside her it shrank again. She tried to reassure me, saying it was normal for the first time, and then she went back to work on me with her mouth. I was very flustered, afraid of a total fiasco, and I concentrated until I came up with the solution: imagining that we weren't in one of La Vedette's rooms but in the washrooms of the Vilaró arcade and that those were Tere's fingers and lips down there and not Trini's, I got an erection and came right away.

'That was when the strange thing I mentioned before happened. I was starting to get dressed when a red light came on beside the door and Trini said: Shit. What's going on?, I asked. Nothing, said Trini. But we can't leave. She pointed to the light and added: Cops are downstairs. I felt my legs weaken and a wave of heat enveloped me. In the bar? I asked. Yes, Trini answered. Don't worry, they won't come up; but until they leave we can't go down. So it would be better for you to take it easy. I tried to take it easy. I finished getting dressed while Trini told me that, each time a pair of cops on their round came into the bar, Vedette or her husband pressed a button behind the bar and a red light turned on in all the bedrooms; then, when the police left, they pressed the button again and the lights went out. Trini insisted that I shouldn't worry and just had to have patience, because, although naturally the police knew just what was going on (knew that there were girls and their clients in the rooms upstairs, knew that Vedette and her husband alerted them when they walked in), they always went away without bothering anyone after talking to Vedette for a while.

'She was right: that's what happened. Trini and I sat on the bed for a while, dressed, side by side without even touching, telling each other lies, until after a while the red light went out and we went downstairs. That was my first visit to a brothel. And that was how we spent the money.'

'Did the girls in the gang know about it?'

'What? That we spent the money on hookers?'

'Yes.'

'I don't know. I never asked myself that question.'

'Ask yourself now.'

'I don't know if they knew. I don't think so. Obviously, we went to the brothels without telling them, and I don't remember anyone ever saying anything about it in front of them. I suppose in theory they didn't know, although it's hard to believe that in practice they didn't suspect. As I said that's where most of the money went.'

'Well, I guess it mustn't have been too difficult to hide it from the girls; after all there were only two of them, and one was Zarco's girl and the other was Gordo's.'

'That there were only two is true: there were lots of girls who came in and out or circled around the gang, but only Tere and Lina belonged to it. The other part, however, is not true, or not entirely, or I didn't have the impression that it was, or I only did for a time: Lina was Gordo's girlfriend, yes, but as for Tere being Zarco's girl . . . Well, as I said before if I'd known the truth in time everything would have been different; or if I'd seen from the beginning that she and Zarco behaved like Gordo and Lina did, which was more or less like most couples behaved back then: in that case I wouldn't have got my hopes up or gone to La Font or done everything possible to fit in with the gang. It's probable. But the fact is that Zarco and Tere did not behave like a couple, and unlike Lina, who gave the impression of being in the gang as Gordo's girlfriend, Tere gave the impression of being in the gang like any of the rest of us. So how was I not going to get my hopes up and think I might have a chance? How was I going to forget what had happened with Tere in the arcade washrooms? It's true that after that Tere acted like nothing had happened, but the fact is that it had happened and I didn't get any signal that it could never happen again (or if I did I hadn't been able to decipher it). Because it's also true that in the early days I thought Tere was Zarco's girl-friend, but it soon struck me that, even if she were, she and Zarco did their own thing when they felt like it.'

'When did you start to think that?'

'Pretty soon, like I said. I remember, for example, one of the first nights I went with them to Rufus, a discotheque in Pont Major, on the way out of the city on the highway to La Bisbal. That's where Gerona's *charnegos* and *quinquis* used to hang out and, as I later discovered, where the gang ended up every night, or almost every night. It was the first discotheque I'd been to, though if you asked me to describe it now I wouldn't be able to: I always arrived high, and the only thing I remember is a foyer where the bouncers and the ticket office were, a big dance floor with strobe lights and disco balls, a bar on the right and some sofas in the darkest section, where the couples hid.

'There, as I was telling you, we ended up almost every night that summer. We'd get there about midnight or twelve-thirty and leave when they closed, about three or four in the morning. I spent those two or three hours drinking beer, smoking joints in the washrooms and watching Tere dance from a corner of the bar. At first I never danced: I would have liked to, but I was embarrassed; besides, in general the guys in the gang never danced, I don't know whether for the same reasons I didn't or because they considered themselves tough guys and thought tough guys don't dance. I say in general because, when they played slow songs – things by Umberto Tozzi or José Luis Perales or people like that – Gordo would run down to the dance floor as fast as he could to dance with Lina and, when they played rumbas by Peret or Los Amaya, or songs by Las Grecas, sometimes Tío, Chino and Drácula would dance to them. The girls, however, danced much more, especially Tere, who never stopped from the moment she arrived until we left the place. I, as I said, concentrated on her for hours, watching her as I couldn't anywhere else, without anyone bothering me or suspecting me (or that's what I thought). I never got tired of watching her: not only because she was the most attractive girl in the disco or because more than dance she seemed to float over the floor; also because of something else I discovered with time: lots of people – Lina, for example – danced non-stop, but they danced the same way to almost all the songs, while Tere danced differently to every song, as if she adapted to the music the way a glove does to a hand or as if her movements came out of each song as naturally as heat comes off a fire.

'Sorry: I've strayed off on a tangent. I was telling you about one of the first times I went to Rufus. The truth is I don't remember very clearly what happened that night in the discotheque, but I do remember at two-thirty or three in the morning, when I'd been in there for a while, I felt a hot foam bubbling up in my stomach, went outside and threw up in the parking lot beside the river. After that I felt better and wanted to go back inside, but when I reached the door realized I was incapable of making my way through that mass of humanity enveloped in smoke, music and intermittent lights, and told myself the party was over.

'I'd gone to Rufus with Zarco and Tere, but decided to go home on my own. I'd been walking for quite a while back towards the city when, very close to the Pedret bridge, a Seat 124 Sport braked beside me. At the wheel was a guy who looked like John Travolta in *Saturday Night Fever*, which was not strange because that summer the nights were full of guys trying to look like John Travolta in *Saturday Night Fever*; at his side was Tere, which was not strange either because that night I'd seen her dance with tons of guys, among them the John Travolta lookalike. Where did you get to, Gafitas?, asked Tere, rolling down the window. I couldn't think up an excuse to improvise, so I had to resign myself to the truth. I wasn't feeling well, I said, and leant on the roof of the 124 and down to the window. I puked, but I feel better now. It was true: the night air had begun to clear my wooziness. I gestured towards the nearly dark highway. I'm going home, I announced. Tere opened the car door as she said: We'll give you a lift. Thanks, I answered. But I'd rather walk. Tere insisted: Get in. That's when Travolta intervened: Let him do what he wants and let's get out of here, he said. You shut up, dickhead, Tere cut him off, getting out of the car and pushing her seat forward so I could get in the back. She repeated: Get in.

'I got in. Tere got back into the front seat and, before Travolta pulled out back onto the highway, she grabbed his earlobe, tugged it hard and said as if she were talking to me at first and then to him at the end: He's a dickhead but he looks good enough to eat. And tonight I'm going to screw him. Aren't I, tough guy? Travolta swatted her away, mumbled something and pulled out. Five minutes later, after crossing the bridge over the Onyar and driving all the way up the Paseo de La Devesa, we stopped at Caterina Albert. Tere got out of the car and let me out. Thanks, I said, once

I was outside. No problem, said Tere. Are you all right? Yeah, I answered. Then why do you have that pissed-off look on your face?, she asked. I don't know what look I've got on my face, I answered. I'm tired, but I'm not pissed off. You sure?, she asked. Tere put the palms of her hands on my cheeks. You're not pissed off because I'm going to screw this dickhead tonight?, she insisted, pointing with her head inside the car. No, I said. She smiled and, without another word, kissed me softly on the lips, scrutinized me for a couple of seconds, then said: Next time me and you'll have a shag, OK? I didn't say anything and Tere got back in the 124 and the 124 turned around and drove away.

'That's how the night ended. And that's why I was saying that from that moment on my way of looking at things changed: because that's when I realized that whatever the relationship tying Tere and Zarco to each other, Tere did what she liked with whomever she liked.'

'And Zarco did too?'

'Yeah. And it didn't seem to bother him that Tere did, either.'

'And you?'

'What about me?'

'Did it bother you that Tere slept with other guys?'

'Of course. I liked Tere a lot, I'd joined Zarco's gang for her, I would have liked her to sleep with me; I don't mean that she'd only sleep with me: I mean that she'd at least sleep with me. But what could I do? Things were the way they were, and I didn't have any choice but to wait for my chance, assuming I'd get one. Besides, I didn't have anything better to do.'

'Did you idealize Tere?'

'If falling in love with someone doesn't consist of idealizing them, you tell me what it does consist of.'

'And Zarco? Did you idealize him too?'

'I don't know; maybe. Now I detest those who did – actually, that's one of the reasons I agreed to talk to you: to put a stop to the falsehoods and tell the truth about him – but maybe the first one to idealize him was me. It could be. In a certain way it would be logical. Look, at the beginning of that summer I was just a baby-faced, frightened kid who practically from one day to the next had seen his best friends turn into his worst enemies and realized his family wasn't capable of protecting him and that all the things he'd learned up till then had been useless and mistaken, so, after the worry and fear of the first days, why wouldn't I prefer to stay with Zarco and his gang? Why wouldn't I not be pleased with someone who in those circumstances offered me respect, adventure, money, fun and pleasure? How could I help but idealize him a little? And by the way, do you know what I called Zarco's gang?'

'What?'

'The outlaws of Liang Shan Po. Have you ever heard that name?'

'No.'

'No, of course not; you're too young. But I bet you anything the majority of people my age remember it. It was made famous by the first Japanese television series to be shown in Europe. *The Water Margin*, and here in Spain it was called *La Frontera Azul*, the blue border. It was so spectacularly successful that two or three weeks after it started there was barely a teenager in the country who didn't watch it. It must have gone on air in April or May of that year, because, when I met Zarco and Tere, I was already addicted to it.

'It was a sort of Oriental version of Robin Hood. I remember the opening sequence really well: over a background tune I could still hum, the images revealed a rag-tag army of men on foot and horseback carrying weapons and standards, while the narrator's voice-over recited a couple of identical phrases every week: "The ancient sages said: Do not despise the snake for having no horns, for who is to say it will not become a dragon? So may one just man become an army." The storyline was simple. It was set in the Middle Ages, when China was governed by I don't know which dynasty and the empire had fallen into the hands of Kao Chiu, the emperor's favourite, a corrupt and cruel man who had converted a prosperous land into a desert with no future. Only one group of upstanding men, led by former imperial guard Lin Chung, rose up against the oppression; among them was one woman: Hu San-Niang, Lin Chung's most faithful deputy. The members of the group were condemned by the oppressor's laws to a life in exile on the banks of the Liang Shan Po, a river near the capital that was also the blue border or water margin of the title, a real border but especially a symbolic border: the border between good and evil, between justice and injustice. Anyway, all the episodes of the series followed a similar outline: because of the humiliations inflicted by Kao Chiu, one or several honourable citizens found themselves obliged to cross to the other side of the Liang Shan Po to join Lin Chung and Hu San-Niang and the other honourable outlaws. That was the story repeated without too many variations in each episode.'

'And you somehow began to identify with it.'

'Drop the somehow: what are stories for if not to identify with? And especially: what good are they to a teenager? That's why I'm sure that in a way, in my instinct, in my fantasy, in my feelings, in the depths of my heart, during that summer my city was China, Batista was Kao Chiu, Zarco was Lin Chung, Tere was Hu San-Niang, the Ter and the Onyar were the Liang Shan Po and everyone who lived on the far side of the Ter and the Onyar were the Water Margin outlaws, but above them all were those who lived in the prefabs. As for me, I was an upstanding citizen who had rebelled against tyranny and was anxious not to go on being just a snake (or just one man) and aspired to be a dragon (or an army) and, every time I crossed the Ter or the Onyar to go and meet Zarco and Tere, it was as if I were crossing the water margin, the border between good and evil and between justice and injustice. Something that, if you stop and think, has some truth to it, doesn't it?'

4

'Have you ever heard of Liang Shan Po?'

'Of what?'

'Liang Shan Po.'

'No. What's that?'

'It doesn't matter. Tell me about the first time you saw El Zarco.'

'It was the spring of 1978. I remember because I'd just turned twenty-three, had spent four uninterrupted years living in Gerona (uninterrupted or with no interruption other than the months I spent in Madrid doing my military service, at the headquarters of the Intelligence Service and the State Security Office), had just moved out of the apartment on Montseny Street I shared with other inspectors and had just married my wife, Ángeles, a nurse at the Muñoz clinic I met while recuperating from an appendectomy. Back then Gerona was still a damp, dark, lonely and filthy city, but there was nowhere damper, darker, lonelier or more filthy than the red-light district.

'I should know, since I practically lived there for years. Like I said, all or almost all the city's delinquents got together in the district, so all we had to do was keep an eye on that part of town to make sure nobody went too wild. Why should I lie: it wasn't hard work. The district was just a handful of blocks of ancient buildings that formed a spiderweb of narrow, stinking, gloomy streets: Bellaire, Barca, Portal de la Barca, Pou Rodó, Mosques and Pujada del Rei Martí; those five or six streets squeezed between churches and convents were once the city's entrance; prostitution had always thrived there and still did. In fact, at the end of the seventies the district enjoyed its final glory days, before drugs and apathy took over in the eighties and nineties and the council took advantage of its decline to clean it up, throw people out and turn it into what it is today: the most elegant part of the city, a place where there's now nothing but trendy restaurants, chic stores, loft apartments for the rich and so on and so forth. How do you like that?

'But in my day, like I say, it wasn't like that. Back then it was a neighbourhood where families who'd been there for generations lived cheek by jowl with the penniless, with immigrants, gypsies and *quinquis*; there were the hookers as well, in my day more than two hundred of them. We had them all on file. We knew who they were and where they worked, we kept an inventory of hirings and firings, made sure there were no minors or criminals among them, every once in a while we checked to make sure none of them were being forced to work as prostitutes. There was no lack of places for them to work, believe me: we counted fifteen just on Portal de la Barca and Pou Rodó Streets, which were the centre of the district and where most of the joints were. I knew them all, actually for years there was hardly a week when I didn't go in one or another of them; I can still recite the names from memory: there was La Cuadra, Las Vegas and Capri on Portal de la Barca; the rest were on Pou Rodó: Ester's, Nuri's, Mari's, the Copacabana, La Vedette, Trébol, Málaga, Río, Chit, Los Faroles and Lina's. Almost all the girls who worked in those places were Spanish, had children and didn't want any trouble. We had a good relationship with them and their madams; we had an unsigned pact advantageous to both sides: we wouldn't bother them and in exchange they would keep us informed. This pact also meant that we should all respect certain formalities; for example: although we knew that the majority of the bars in the red-light district had prostitution going on, we pretended they were normal bars, and everybody had to play along, so, when we entered one of them, normal activity was paralyzed, the girls and their clients stopped going up to the rooms and the madam let the ones who were already upstairs know that we'd arrived and everybody had to stay put and keep quiet until we left. It's true that the pact wasn't always honoured: sometimes because the girls or their bosses kept information from us, something they naturally did whenever they could get away with it; other times because we abused our power, which was enormous. In my early days of patrolling the district I was on the beat with Vives, my section boss. I already told you that Vives was a brainless thug and I soon saw that he would drink and screw on the house every night in the district, but sometimes he'd go crazy and make a big scene and sow panic among the girls. I was still an idealist who thought the police were the good guys and we saved good people from the bad guys, so I didn't like what Vives was doing and once or twice I reproached him. How do you like that? He didn't pay me a blind bit of notice, of course: he'd tell me to fuck off and mind my own business, and I didn't have the guts to report him to Deputy Superintendent Martínez; the only thing I dared do was ask him to assign me a new partner, something he did without asking why, probably because the deputy superintendent knew Vives better than I did and, although he didn't want to get rid of a guy like that, or couldn't, his opinion of him was even lower than mine.

But I insist: in general we cops and the girls tended to respect the pact, which allowed us to keep crime under control with relative ease in the district and also in the city, like I said, because sooner or later all criminals passed through the district and because everything that went on in the district ended up reaching the ears of the girls. Mind you, I'm talking about the spring of '78; after that all this changed. What I think is that two things made it change: drugs and juvenile delinquency. Two things we knew nothing about back then.'

'Two things that everybody associates with Zarco.'

'Sure. How can they not associate them with him when he ended up becoming this country's official drug addict and *quinqui*? Who was going to tell us that then, eh? Though, why should I lie, I've always thought that we at least should have been able to tell a bit more.'

'What do you mean?'

'I'll tell you about the first time I saw him. You'll say there was nothing special about it, or almost nothing, except that it was the first; but for me there was. It happened on the way out of La Font, one of the few normal bars in the district, along with the Gerona and El Sargento; normal is just a figure of speech: what I mean is that they weren't hooker joints but basic dives where *quinquis* got together, so, for us, anyone going in or coming out of one of them was suspicious, as was anybody wandering around the district, actually. We knew most of them, but not Zarco: so that afternoon, as soon as we saw him, we stopped him, asked for his ID, searched him and so forth. I was with Hidalgo, who was my partner on the beat then. Zarco wasn't alone either; he was with two or three other kids, all around about the same age as him, all just as unknown to us. We asked them for their documentation as well and frisked them. Of course you could see from a long way off that Zarco was the ringleader, but maybe we would have let him go straight away if we hadn't found a lump of hash in his pocket when we searched him. Hidalgo examined it, showed it to him and asked him where he'd got it. Zarco answered that he'd found it in the street. Then Hidalgo got mad: he grabbed him by the arm, pinned him up against the wall, leaned his face right up to Zarco's and asked him if he thought

69

he looked like an imbecile. Zarco seemed surprised but didn't react, didn't resist, didn't look away; finally he said no. Without letting go of him, Hidalgo asked what they were doing there, and Zarco said nothing, just going for a walk. In an undefiant voice he added: Is that against the law? He said that and smiled at us, first at Hidalgo and then at me, and that's when I saw he had very blue eyes; that smile disarmed me: I instantly noticed the tension level drop and Hidalgo and Zarco and the guys with Zarco noticed it too. Then Hidalgo let go of Zarco, but before we went on with our rounds he threatened him. You watch out, kid, he said, although he didn't sound convincing any more. You don't want me to have to give you a smack next time I see you round here.

'That was it. In other words, like I said, it was hardly anything, practically nothing. But I've thought many times since that maybe that little nothing or whatever it was should have put us on the alert about Zarco.'

'What do you mean?'

'Well from that first encounter I could have guessed that Zarco wasn't just another teenager in the district, one of many clever kids without much to lose who tried to act hard with us because deep down they were soft, one of so many little tough guys from the outskirts running as fast as they could to nowhere or one of so many teenage *quinquis* unable to escape their *quinqui* fate . . . What do I know. He was, of course, but that's not all he was; he also had something else that was immediately visible: that serenity, that coldness. And also that sort of joy or lightness or self-confidence, as if everything he was doing was a pastime and nothing could cause him problems.'

'Are you sure that was what you thought back then? We're all very good at predicting the past: are you sure this isn't a retrospective thought, something you say in the light of what later became of Zarco?'

'Of course it's a retrospective thought, of course I didn't think that back then, but that is precisely the problem: that I could have thought of it, that I should have thought of it. Or at least guessed. If I had, everything would have been easier. For me and for everyone.'

'Your partner, Hidalgo, threatened him: could you have carried out the threat, could you have kept him from coming back to the district and forming his gang there?'

'How were we going to prevent him? He hadn't done anything wrong, or at least we couldn't prove that he had: were we going to arrest him for drinking beer in La Font, for smoking joints, for taking pills, for doing what all the *quinquis* in the district were doing? We couldn't; and if we could have we wouldn't have wanted to: in Gerona a guy like Zarco could only go to the district, and that suited us, because in the district we could control him better than anywhere else. Anyway. The result was that Zarco and his gang became another part of the landscape of the district that spring. It's true that they were a special part, and that this should also have put us on our guard. Because in the district there were a lot of *quinquis* like them, more or less the same age as them, but they all got together with older guys, who were the ones in charge, who pointed out objectives and took advantage of them; whereas Zarco and his gang did everything their own way and didn't take orders from anybody. And this, later, when things got serious, made them much more uncontrollable.'

'When did that happen?'

'Pretty early: as soon as the gang took shape.'

'And when did the gang finish taking shape?'

'I'd say around the beginning of the summer.'

'More or less when Gafitas joined?'

'You know who Gafitas was?'

'Of course.'

'Who told you?'

'What do you mean who told me? Everybody knows: Zarco's ex-wife has been telling anyone who'd listen for years that Cañas was part of her ex-husband's gang. Cañas himself told me that they called him Gafitas. He agreed to talk to me too; actually he's my principal source, if it weren't for him I wouldn't have been commissioned to write this book.'

'I didn't know you were talking to him as well.'

'You didn't ask.'

'Who else are you talking to?'

'No one yet. Shall we go on?'

'Sure.'

'You were saying that the gang settled into shape more or less when Gafitas joined.'

'I think so. More or less. But you'd be better off asking Cañas.'

5

'Inspector Cuenca says that Zarco's gang settled into shape when you joined.'

'Is that what he says?'

'Yes. I think what he means is that you were like the leavening that makes the dough rise into bread.'

'Yeah. It could be, but I don't think so. In any case, if it was like that, I didn't do anything to raise it; and even if I had: remember that I was the lowest guy on the totem pole, who'd just arrived, who was a complete nobody and who was living in a sort of permanent beatified state of shock, to give it a name. On the other hand, what is certain is that Zarco had looked out for himself in his own way for ever, and since arriving in Gerona he'd been gathering around him a group made up mostly of old friends of Tere's, who she'd grown up with in the prefabs and at Germans Sàbat school. So, when I arrived, the group was already formed and had been doing jobs for months.

'No, I don't think I made anything take shape. What is true is that my arrival coincided with the first of the two qualitative leaps the gang made; it wasn't me who provoked them, but the summer, which changed everything by filling the coast up with tourists and turning it into an irresistible lure. This increased the gang's activity, maybe turning it into a real criminal gang and in any case and for practical reasons caused it to divide into two groups, which outside the district acted with relative independence: on one side there was Zarco, Tere, Gordo and me, and on the other Guille, Tío, Colilla, Chino and Drácula. Those two groups came into being more or less spontaneously, without anyone suggesting it and without regulation by any explicit hierarchy; it wasn't necessary: we all took it for granted that Guille was in charge of the second group and Zarco was in charge directly of the first and indirectly of the second. Of course neither the composition of the gang nor that of the two groups was fixed: sometimes people from the second group worked with the first and other times the first group worked with the second; and sometimes people who didn't belong to the gang or who in theory didn't belong to the gang acted with the gang, like Latas and Jou and other regulars from La Font or Rufus, not to mention Lina, who belonged to the gang but almost never worked with either of the two groups, I don't know whether because she didn't want to or because Gordo wouldn't let her. I insist that Tere was a case apart: to all intents and purposes she was the same as everyone else; well, to all intents and purposes except for one, because sometimes she didn't show up at La Font and didn't always come along on jobs with us and then we had to find someone to take her place. One night I asked Tere about these disappearances, but she smiled, winked at me and didn't answer. Another night I asked Gordo while smoking a joint with him in the toilet of Rufus, and Gordo answered me with a confusing explanation about Tere's family from which I only caught clearly that her father was dead or missing, that she lived with her mother and older sister in the prefabs, as well as two nieces, and that she had another sister who'd left home more than a year ago but had just returned, pregnant with her first child.

'One person who never or almost never missed those daily meetings in La Font was me. Shortly before getting into Zarco's gang I began to live by an invariable routine: I'd get up about noon, have breakfast, read or loaf around until lunchtime and, when my parents went to have their siesta and my sister went back to work at the pharmaceutical lab, I left and didn't come back till the early hours of the morning. Around three or three-thirty in the afternoon I'd get to La Font and, while waiting for my friends, I'd talk to the landlady or her customers. I sort of made friends with some of them, especially with Córdoba, a small, scraggy man with a felt hat, always dressed in black and always with a tooth-pick between his lips, who often bought me beers while we talked about red-light-district things; but I also made friends with an old Communist prostitute called Eulalia, who never raised her large glasses of anisette without toasting the health of La Pasionaria and the hoped-for death of the traitor Carrillo; or with a salesman of pipes, peanuts and candies called Herminio, who would show up at La Font mostly on the weekends and talk about bullfighting and recite poetry in an impossible Catalan and predict the end of the world and the invasion of the planet by extraterrestrials, before visiting all the brothels, offering his wares in a wicker basket; or with a couple of lingerie and trinket salesmen whose names I never knew or have forgotten, two twin brothers who'd arrive after eating lunch in a downtown restaurant, fat, congested and sweaty, with a couple of cheap cigars in their mouths and a couple of patched suitcases in their hands, and leave at dinner time bragging at the top of their voices of having sold their best pieces.

'My friends would start to show up about four or four-thirty, and from that moment on we'd spend the afternoon talking, going out to smoke joints on Galligants Bridge and drinking beer among the lush collection of hookers, Gypsies, hawkers, hustlers, *quin-quis*, lost causes and crooks who tended to congregate in La Font, until around midnight, after eating a snack somewhere, we went to Rufus to end the day. This happened especially at the beginning, during the first two or three weeks, when there were whole evenings when we practically never left the district. Then we began to escape as a rule to the coast or inland, and La Font became just a meeting place. But by then we were already a fully fledged criminal gang, or just about, and everything had changed.'

'Before you tell me, let me ask you a question I've been wondering about for a while now.'

'Go ahead.'

'Didn't you see your friends from Caterina Albert Street again?'

'That summer? Once or twice, hardly at all, and only just in passing. As I said I would leave the house at three or three-thirty in the afternoon and not return until the early hours, so it was unlikely I'd run into them; besides, we didn't go to the same places. Anyway, the one I didn't bump into again was Batista. Why do you ask?'

'I was wondering if you hadn't wanted to take revenge on them, if it hadn't at least occurred to you. You could have tried to get Zarco and company to teach Batista a lesson, for example.'

'I might have thought about it at some point, but I doubt it: I never had enough confidence with them to dare to ask them something like that. For one thing because I would have had to tell them what Batista and the rest had done to me, and I didn't want to do that. Don't you understand? I felt ashamed and guilty about what had happened, I wanted to erase it. I suppose that's also why I'd gone with Zarco and Tere: to begin a new life, as they say, because I wanted to be someone else, reinvent myself, change my skin, stop being a snake and turn into a dragon, like the heroes of Liang Shan Po. That was what I wanted and, although of course I would have enjoyed getting revenge, given the circumstances it was impossible, at least for the moment. Besides, remember that I had the impression that my old friends and Zarco's gang lived in different worlds, just like my parents

76

and I, just like my old self and the new me; like I said before: Zarco and I lived very close to each other and very far away, separated by an abyss.'

'The water margin.'

'Yes, that border, Liang Shan Po: call it whatever you want.'

'One more thing. Inspector Cuenca told me that at the time the police had absolute control of the red-light district.'

'It's true. Absolute or almost absolute. Later, in the eighties and nineties, everything changed: they abandoned the neighbourhood to its fate, washed their hands of it, and the neighbourhood deteriorated and ended up going to hell. Or not, depending on your point of view. In any case the district disappeared. But in my day they controlled everything: there were always a couple of secret police there, they inspected the bars and the brothels, kept an eye on the hookers, stopped people in the street at all hours, asked for your papers, searched you, asked you what you were doing, where you were going.'

'Did they ever stop you?'

'Lots of times.'

'And didn't it matter? I mean: weren't you scared? Didn't you think the police might tell your parents? Didn't you think you might get arrested and locked up?'

'Of course I thought all that, of course I was scared. Anybody would be. But that was just the first few times. Not later. After a while, getting stopped by the cops became part of the routine. Bear in mind that what my parents thought or might no longer think mattered less and less to me. And, as far as getting caught, well, I was sixteen years old and knew that at my age I wasn't going to end up in juvenile court or a reformatory, but directly in jail, but it seems to me that for any kid that age prison, until he gets locked up there or actually sees the writing on the wall, is more or less like death: something that happens to other people.'

'You're right, only you weren't just any old kid: you didn't stop committing crimes from the time you met Zarco, or helping to commit them; in other words you didn't stop giving them reasons to put you in jail.'

'True, but that's the secret: the more crimes you commit without anything happening to you, the less fear you have of everything and the more convinced you are that they'll never catch you and that prison is not for you. It's as if you're anaesthetized, or armour-plated. You feel good; or to put it a better way, you feel fucking great: apart from sex and drugs, at sixteen I didn't know anything better than that.'

'Tell me about the crimes you guys committed.'

'At first, more or less up to the month of August, we mostly snatched handbags, robbed houses and stole cars. Stealing cars was so easy that we'd steal them at the drop of a hat, sometimes more than one a day, not always because we needed one but simply because we liked the car and wanted to take a ride in it, or to see who could steal one faster. The fastest were Zarco and Tío, who could get a car open in less than a minute and that's why they were always in different groups. I learned to open cars straight away, and to start them and drive them. There's no secret to driving cars, much less to hot-wiring them: first you snap the steering lock with a sharp turn of the wheel, then you identify the power wire, the contact wire and the starter wire and finally you put the three of them together. Getting the cars open, however, was another story; there were several systems: the simplest was to kick in the little window beside the driver's window, reach in and open the door with your hand; for the more sophisticated method you needed a sawblade with a hook at one end and enough skill to get the blade through the crack between the window and the door and the hook around the lock so you could pull it up. This is the system we tended to use, because it was quicker and more discreet (I watched with my own eyes as Zarco resorted to it on various occasions in places full of people, in plain view of everyone and without anyone noticing what he was doing); but the most common system was to open the car door by picking the lock with one of those keys for opening a tin of sardines or tuna. Anyway, everyone in the gang – some more, some less – knew how to do all these things, and Zarco better than anybody, because he'd been stealing cars since he was six or seven years old. But just because it was very easy to do and we did it every day doesn't mean that every once in a while we didn't get a good scare and sometimes, I at least, was very scared while doing it.'

'In spite of the anaesthesia and armour-plating?'

'In spite of the anaesthesia and armour-plating. Habit teaches you how to handle part of the fear; but you can never learn how to handle fear as a whole: it almost always handles you.

'I remember for example one time in La Bisbal, an afternoon in the middle of July. Zarco, Gordo, Drácula and I were in a Renault 5, and as we drove through town we decided to stop for a beer. We parked in a street backing off the main highway, drank a beer while we played table football in a bar called El Teatret and when we went back to the car we saw a Citroën Tiburón parked next to it. Do you remember that beauty? Now it's an old relic, although back then you didn't see too many of them either. Anyway. There was no one in sight, so we didn't even have to exchange a single word before deciding we'd take it. Drácula ran to one corner of the street and I went to the other while Zarco and Gordo stayed by the Tiburón and got down to work. Since the street was not long, I got to my corner straight away, and as soon as I leaned around it saw two cops coming towards me on motorbikes; I should say: I didn't see them coming but bearing down on me. I doubt the cops suspected what we were up to, but I turned around and ran towards my friends shouting that the cops were coming. All three took off as fast as they could: Drácula immediately vanished and behind him Zarco and Gordo vanished too. Hearing the noise of the motorbikes getting closer and closer, I ran past the Tiburón, turned the corner my friends had just turned, saw that I'd lost them and, as I turned the next corner, found myself running alone under a colonnade, beside the main road, through a commotion of pedestrians getting out of my way and people sitting on the patios of bars. That was when panic overcame me and I knew for certain two complementary things at once: the first was that the two cops had got off their motorbikes and given up chasing my friends and were now only chasing me; the second is that they were going to trap me because I wasn't going to have time to get to the next corner. And that was when I made an irrational decision, an absurd decision dictated by panic that in hindsight seems dictated by someone who has learned to handle panic: in the middle of the crowd coming out of the shops and bars, drawn by the disturbance, I stopped dead, took off my jean jacket, threw it on the ground, turned around and, pretending to limp and with my heart pounding in my throat, started to walk towards the two cops, who flashed past and vanished behind me around a corner while I quickened my pace and vanished around the opposite corner.'

'You were saved by a miracle.'

'Literally.'

'Now I understand why you said that was a very serious game, in which you risked everything.'

'Did I say that?'

'Yes.'

'Well it's true. And it was also an unending game; or rather, the end could only be catastrophic: the risk anaesthetized you, armour-plated you, but to keep playing you had to keep taking risks, you had to do something for which neither the anaesthetic nor the armour-plating could protect you, so you constantly had to run greater risks. I don't know if this was conscious, maybe not, or not entirely, but that's how it was. The fact is that as well as stealing cars, and robbing the occasional house, at first we mainly snatched handbags (tanks, we called them), probably because it seemed as simple and low risk as stealing cars. The proof is that sometimes we'd do it when we didn't even need money, like stealing cars, almost as a sport or a bit of entertainment; the best proof is that I dared to do it very soon.'

'How did you do it?'

'The way we all did: grabbing them. I've since read that a famous juvenile delinquent of the time said that Zarco invented the grab and all he did was borrow it from Zarco or from Zarco's film character; maybe you read that too in some cutting in my file . . . It might be true, I'm not saying it's not, although I tend to believe that this kind of thing says more about Zarco's legend than reality: after all, there's almost nothing connected to the juvenile violence of the time that hasn't been attributed directly or indirectly to him. Because when it comes down to it grabbing a handbag is such an elemental thing that nobody really needed to invent it. All you had to do was steal a car and choose a suitable victim and location: the ideal victim was an older woman with a wealthy appearance if possible and the ideal location was an out-of-the-way sidestreet, solitary if possible; once chosen, the driver approached the victim from behind and drove slowly beside her and at this moment I, who would be sitting in the front passenger seat, had two options: one – the simplest and best – consisted of sticking my body out the window and grabbing the handbag away from the victim in one yank; the other – more complicated, that we'd only use when there was no other choice – consisted of jumping out of the moving car, running to the victim, snatching the bag and, once it was in my hands, running and jumping back in the car. The only precaution I took in both cases consisted of taking off my glasses so the victim couldn't recognize me by them. Like I said it was a very simple thing, and comparatively low risk; of course low earning too, because there normally wasn't a lot of money in the stolen handbags. Anyhow, at first that was the kind of robbery in which I most frequently played the part of protagonist, although not the only one: now I remember, for example, one afternoon when I stole the day's takings from a refreshment stand on the beach in Tossa while Tere distracted the manager by flirting with him. But that wasn't very usual. The usual was that I played the part of bait or front, or I just kept a lookout while the rest worked, or did both successively. That's what I'd done the first time I robbed with them, the afternoon in La Montgoda, and that's what I kept doing throughout the month of July, up until Guille's death and Chino, Tío and Drácula's arrest changed things.'

'It's odd. The way you tell the story, anyone might think that it wasn't you who joined up with Zarco's gang but Zarco who recruited you.'

'It doesn't strike me as a mistaken deduction. Although probably the two things happened at once; in other words: that I needed what Zarco had and that Zarco needed what I had.'

'I understand what you might have needed from Zarco, but what could Zarco have needed from you? That you acted as bait or a front, as you put it?'

'Sure. That was useful for a gang like that; besides, remember what Tere told me to convince me to come with them on the robbery in La Montgoda: they needed someone like me, someone who looked like a student at the Marists' school with a face like he'd never broken a plate, someone who spoke Catalan . . . I think that's what Zarco thought of me, at least at first. Do you remember the character of Gafitas in the first part of that film *Wild Boys*? Obviously, that's based on me, was inspired by me, and the Zarco of the film recruits him for his fictional gang for the same reason I believe the real Zarco recruited me for his gang in reality: so I could act as bait or as a front. Anyway, I'm not saying that Zarco went to the Vilaró arcade looking for me on purpose or anything like that; what I think happened is that our paths crossed by chance at the arcade and that, when he realized I could be useful to him, he did everything he could to keep me. Probably including inventing an attack on the arcade.'

'What do you mean?'

'Well, most likely Zarco never had any intention of robbing the Vilaró arcade. Neither Zarco nor Guille, or anybody else either. It's possible. The truth is it wasn't the kind of job they were doing then, without guns or anything, so it's possible that Zarco invented it to scare me so I would ask him not to do it and he would do me a false favour and I would feel obliged to owe him one.'

'Are you sure of that?'

'No, not sure, although once Zarco told me that was what happened.'

'What other things do you think Zarco might have done to recruit you?'

'Are you thinking of something in particular?'

'The same as you.'

'What am I thinking of?'

'Tere. Do you think Zarco could have convinced her to do what she did?'

'You mean what happened in the washrooms of the Vilaró arcade?'

'Yeah.'

'I don't know. There were times when I thought that and other times when I thought not; now I don't know what to think. Besides, I don't think this has anything to do with your book, so we better change the subject.'

83

'Sorry. You're right. Let's talk about something else. You mentioned Guille's death and Chino, Tío and Drácula's arrest. What happened? How did Guille die? How did the other three get arrested? How did it affect the gang?'

'I'm sorry. I didn't mean to be rude. Of course what happened in the arcade has to do with your book, at least in my case, every-thing to do with Tere has to do with Zarco and vice versa; so if you don't understand my relationship with Tere you won't under-stand my relationship with Zarco, which is what this is about. Did I tell you I joined Zarco's gang for Tere?'

'Yes, but you also said that she probably wasn't the only reason.'

'I'm not saying she was the only reason; I do say she was deci-sive. How would I have dared to get into that gang of *quinquis* and do what I did if it wasn't the only way to get close to Tere? She was what I most needed of what Zarco's gang had. Love made me brave. I'd fallen in love before, but not like I fell in love with Tere. At first it even passed through my head that Tere could be my girlfriend, the first girl I'd go out with; after my first few days in the gang I ruled that out, of course, and not because it was impossible in theory – after all, whether or not she was Zarco's girl, Tere slept with whoever she wanted and even flirted with me once in a while or I had the impression that she was flirt-ing with me – but because she seemed too much for me: too independent, too good-looking, too much of a tease, too grown-up, too dangerous; in reality, I don't know what I aspired to with her: I probably just hoped that what happened in the washrooms of the Vilaró arcade would happen again, and that she'd sleep with me every once in a while.'

'Yeah, you told me that too.'

'The thing is Tere turned into an obsession. I'd been mastur-bating since I was thirteen or fourteen, but that summer I must have broken the world wanking record; and up till then I'd masturbated over photos from *The Book of Woman*, illustrations in comics, movie actresses, heroines of novels and girls in nude magazines or garage mechanics' calendars, from then on Tere was the absolute protagonist of my imaginary harem. So much so that I often felt that Tere wasn't one character but two: the real character I met every afternoon at La Font and the fictional character with whom I went to bed morning, noon and night in my fantasies. If I'm honest, I sometimes had my doubts about which one of the two had shared the washrooms of the Vilaró arcade with me.

'Until one night in late July it seemed like the real person and the fictional character finally merged into one, and that meant that everything was going to change between us. It's one of the nights of that summer that I remember best, maybe because over the years since I've gone over and over what happened. If you like I'll tell you.'

'Please do.'

'It's a bit of a long story; we'll have to leave Guille's death and Chino, Tío and Drácula's arrest for another time.'

'Not to worry.'

'All right. As I was saying, it was one of the last nights in July, not long after the scare over the Tiburón in La Bisbal and not long before Guille's death and the arrest of the others. It was a Friday or Saturday night, in Montgó, a beach in L'Escala. We'd been in the district till dusk, and then Tere, Zarco, Gordo, Lina and I stole a Volkswagen and drove off towards the coast.

'As far as I recall we didn't have any plan and we weren't going to any particular place, but when we got to Calella de Palafrugell we felt hungry and thirsty and decided to stop. It was a pitch-black night. We parked on a patch of ground at the edge of the village, took a second round of uppers, went down to the beach, looked unsuccessfully for a table on one of the patios and finally went into a bar, maybe Ca la Raquel. There we ordered beers and sandwiches at the bar and Zarco started talking about his family, something I'd never heard him do before. He talked about his Uncle Joaquín, one of his mother's brothers with whom, as he later told in his memoir, he'd spent two years of his childhood travelling here and there in a DKW, helping him earn a living through robberies and shady deals; he also talked, with admiration, of his three older brothers, who were in their twenties back then and in prison. He might have talked about something else, though I don't remember now. The thing is that at some point I went to the washroom and, when I came back, two girls had joined the group. One, the one who was beside Zarco, was called Elena and she was petite, dark-haired and pretty, like a doll; the second was called Piti and she was taller and had reddish hair and pale freckly skin. I grabbed my beer and started listening to Zarco, who was telling Elena that we lived in Palamós and were students, although, he added in the same unconcerned tone, we spent the summer doing jobs; the lie didn't surprise me, because it was inoffensive, but the truth did, because it was indiscreet, and, since Zarco didn't usually commit indiscretions, I thought he'd taken such a fancy to that doll that he was willing to do anything to seduce her. Jobs?, asked Elena. We nick cars, break into houses, all sorts, Zarco explained. Elena looked at me, looked back at Zarco and laughed; I tried to laugh, but I couldn't. That's a lie, said Elena. And how do you know?, asked Zarco without laughing. Simple, answered Elena. Because people who do jobs like that never say they do. Shit, said Zarco, pretending to be frustrated, and added, pretending to be guileless: Tell me something else: Do people who have dosh go around saying they do? Elena seemed to consider the question, amused. If they have a little, they do, but if they have a lot, then no, she said at last. Then we can't say we do, said Zarco, looking at me with feigned annoyance. Why do you want to say you've got dosh?, Elena asked, prolonging the flirtation. To impress us? Of course not, said Zarco. Just to buy you another round. Elena laughed again. We accept, she said. Zarco immediately ordered another round of beers and, while we were drinking them, Elena told us that she and her friend lived in Alicante, that they'd been travelling around Catalonia for two weeks, that they were staying in a cheap hotel in L'Escala and that they'd hitchhiked that afternoon from L'Escala to Calella. When she finished talking, the girl leaned over to Zarco and whispered something in his ear. Zarco nodded. Sure, he said. He paid and we left.

We wandered the streets a bit looking for a quiet place to roll some joints, until we got to a plaza in front of the village church. We sat there for quite a while smoking and talking around a bench and, when we started to think about moving on, Elena mentioned a discotheque where they'd gone dancing a couple of times; Piti said the disco was called Marocco and it was near L'Escala, and Zarco suggested we go check it out. Have you guys got a car?, Piti asked. Of course, answered Zarco. Great, said Elena. We only have one car, Gordo pointed out. And there's seven of us. That doesn't matter, said Elena. We'll all fit. Don't pay any fucking attention to Gordo, Zarco interrupted. He's always joking around: no respect for anyone. And he added: we actually came in two cars. Before anyone could deny it, Zarco asked Elena and Piti if they both knew the way to the Marocco; they said they did and then Zarco jumped off the back of the bench where he was sitting, landed on the flagstones and said: Cool. Gordo, I'll take Elena, Tere and Gafitas in the Volkswagen; you bring Lina and Piti in your dad's car. What car?, asked Lina. But Zarco had already started walking out of the plaza and we all followed him and nobody paid any attention to Lina, not even Gordo, who just fixed his lacquered hair a little with a resigned look on his face, draped his arm over his girlfriend's shoulder while telling her to shut up and cursing Zarco's mother.

'So that's how we ended up that night in Montgó, which was the cove where the Marocco was hidden. From Calella it couldn't have taken us more than half an hour to get there, and that was in spite of Elena getting us lost and, after crossing L'Escala, spending a while driving in circles around a housing development. But eventually we saw a sign advertising the place, went down a dirt road and managed to park in a clearing in a pine forest crammed full of cars and illuminated by the lights of the discotheque, shining in the distance, way down by the beach.

'Marocco turned out to be a disco for foreign tourists and hippy stragglers, but the music playing inside was no different from what they played at Rufus, probably because that summer all the discos played more or less the same music or because it seemed more or less the same to me: rock and pop hits alternating with disco songs (and once in a while a rumba, quite frequently at Rufus). Before going inside the discotheque we'd smoked one last joint, and Zarco, Tere and I popped our third upper; as soon as we went in I lost sight of Zarco and Elena, not Tere, who went straight onto the dance floor. I stood at the bar and watched her while I drank a beer, at times with the smug sensation (which sometimes struck me at Rufus as well) that she was dancing for me or at least that she knew I was watching her, always with the feeling that the movements of her body adapted to the music like a glove to a hand. After a while Gordo, Lina and Piti arrived, said hi and ordered drinks. Gordo and Lina went to sit on a sofa or got lost on the dance floor, and Piti asked me where Elena was; I answered that I didn't know though I thought she was with Zarco. Then Piti asked me if we'd been there long and I said yes and then she told me, as if I didn't know or as if apologizing, that it had taken them longer than expected to get there; I interrupted her to say that we'd got lost too, but Piti answered that they hadn't taken so long because they got lost but because Gordo had forgotten where he'd parked the car, and she and Lina had had to wait for him until he found it and came back to pick them up. I clicked my tongue and said, shaking my head back and forth: Not again. The same thing every time. He always forgets where he parks his car?, she asked. No, I answered. Only when he drives his dad's car. Really?, she asked. Really, I answered; I added: He should go see a psychoanalyst. We looked at each other and then burst out laughing. Then we carried on talking, until Tere interrupted us. Piti asked her where Elena was. Tere said she didn't know and then the two of them started talking. I didn't hear what they were talking about, but a short time later Piti left the bar as fast as she could. What happened to her?, I asked. Nothing, answered Tere. It looked like she was crying, I insisted. You're seeing things, Gafitas, Tere teased. Then she asked: So, are you dancing or what?

'I was gobsmacked: Tere had never asked me to dance, and I'd never even considered the possibility that I might dance with her, in part (I think I already told you) out of embarrassment, and in part because I didn't know how to dance. But that night I discovered that to dance, or at least to dance to the music they played at the discos, you didn't have to know how to dance, you just needed to want to move around a bit. It was Tere who revealed this to me. But it was when we finished dancing that what I wanted to tell you about happened. When the music stopped and they turned on the lights in the discotheque, Tere and I realized that our friends had disappeared. We spent a while looking for them, first inside the place and then on the way out, on a patio full of night owls prowling around a closed refreshment stand, not yet ready to consider the night over. We didn't find any of them, and I told Tere that they'd probably all left and we'd better go too. Tere didn't answer. We walked to the parking lot, swept at this hour by the lights of departing cars. We didn't know what car Gordo had nicked in Calella, but our Volkswagen was still parked between two pine

89

trees. At least Zarco hasn't gone, said Tere when she saw it. How do you know?, I replied, thinking she was probably right. He might have stolen another car. I had absolutely no desire to see Zarco, I wanted to go on spending the night alone with Tere, so I concluded: It's almost five; come on, let's go. Tere stood still and took a while to answer. What's your hurry, Gafitas?, she finally said. Then she took me by the arm and pulled me around and forced me to walk back to the Marocco as she said, Come on. Let's see if we can find them.

'We walked past the patio of the discotheque, almost empty now, towards the darkness and started walking along the beach. In the sky a bright full moon was shining and, as my eyes adjusted to the darkness and as we approached the water, it revealed a cove bordered by two hills and strewn with lumps on the sand like shadowy shells. They're here, on the beach, whispered Tere when we got to the water's edge, sitting down on the sand; she added: We'll smoke a reefer. How do you know?, I asked. What a question, she said. Because I'm going to roll one. How do you know they're here?, I clarified. Tere licked the paper of a cigarette, peeled it, emptied the tobacco into the rolling paper she had spread out in her hand and answered: Because I do. She finished rolling the joint, lit it, took five or six tokes and passed it to me.

'I sat down next to her and smoked listening to the sound of the waves breaking against the shore and watching the moonlight bouncing off the surface of the sea and diffusing a silver brilliance over the whole cove. Tere didn't say anything and neither did I, as if we were both exhausted or lost in thought or hypnotized by the spectacle of the beach at night. After a while Tere stubbed out the joint and buried it in the sand; she stood up and said: I'm going for a swim. Before I could say anything she stripped off and walked into the sea that looked like an enormous and silent black sheet. She swam away from the shore and, at some point, stopped and started calling me with muffled little shouts that echoed around the whole cove. I took off my clothes and ran into the water.

'It was almost warm. I swam out to sea a bit, away from Tere and, when I stopped, I turned around and realized I was in the middle of an immense darkness and that the few little dots of light on the beach were very far away and Tere had disappeared. I swam back towards shore, with strong strokes, but when I stood up I still couldn't see Tere. With the water up to my waist I looked for her without finding her, and during a moment of panic I imagined she'd left and taken my clothes with her, but then I saw her silhouette emerging from the water to my left, twenty or thirty metres away. I walked out of the water too, feeling that the swim had dissipated the inebriation of the alcohol and hash and calmed the tachycardia of the uppers, and, when I got to Tere, she had already covered up with her T-shirt and was barefoot and sitting on her jeans. Standing up, I put my underwear and jeans on as fast as I could, and still hadn't finished buttoning my shirt when Tere asked: Hey, Gafitas, me and you haven't had a shag yet, have we? I got my buttons all mixed up. No, I managed to say. I don't think so. Tere stood up, took my hands away from my shirt and started unbuttoning the ones I'd got mixed up; I thought she was unbuttoning them to button them up properly, but while she was still unbuttoning them she kissed me, and while she was kissing me I guessed that she was naked from the waist down. Again she asked: Well it's about time we did, don't you think?

'You can imagine the rest. And, as I told you before, as a result of what happened that night I believed everything was going to change between Tere and me and from then on Tere would stop being an imaginary character in my imaginary harem to become only a real character, or that the real character and the imaginary one would meld together into a single one; and I also thought that, although from then on she might not become my girlfriend, at least we'd sleep together every once in a while. It wasn't like that. Maybe the fact that this episode happened very close to the time of Guille's death and Chino, Tío and Drácula's arrest might have contributed to it not turning out like that, but the truth is it wasn't like that. And everything got complicated. But that, if you don't mind, I'll tell you next time. Now I'm running late: I have to get going.'

'Of course. But I wouldn't like to stop without you telling me what happened to your friends that night.'

'Ah, nothing important. The next day I found out at La Font. Gordo and Lina left the Marocco early, they took Piti back to the hotel in L'Escala and went home. Zarco slept with Elena in some hotel in L'Escala, and in the morning went back to Gerona too, just like Tere and I did. We never heard any more from Piti and Elena.'

'So it wasn't true that night that Zarco and Elena were on the beach, as Tere had said.'

'No.'

'Do you think Tere knew or suspected and lied to you because she wanted to seduce you?'

'It's possible.'

'I'll put the question another way: did you never think that Tere had slept with you that night out of spite, to get even with Zarco, because he'd left with Elena?'

'Yeah. But I didn't think that then. I thought it later. And only briefly.'

'And later? I mean: and now?'

'Now what?'

'Now what do you think about that?'

'That it's not true.'

6

'Tell me about Gafitas.'

'What do you want me to tell you? A policeman's life is full of strange stories, but the story of Gafitas is among the strangest that's happened to me since I started this job. At first perhaps you might not think so: after all it's not that rare to see a case of a middle-class kid or upper middle-class or even an upper-class kid get involved with a gang of *quinquis* and suchlike. At least it wasn't so rare back then; in fact, a while later I knew of a similar case, although that was in the tough years when kids were going astray on drugs, while in Gafitas's day drugs were only just starting to arrive and it's harder to find an explanation for what happened. I at least don't have one, and this is something I've never talked to Cañas about since; I've talked to Cañas about other things, but never this: for us it's as if it never happened. How do you like that? But anyway, if he's telling you the story of his relationship with Zarco, I imagine you'll already have an explanation of why he ended up in his gang.'

'Cañas says it was by chance.'

'That's not an explanation: everything happens by chance.'

'What I mean is that Cañas says he met Zarco by chance; the reasons he joined his gang are something else. According to him, the main reason is that he fell in love with Zarco's girl.'

'You mean Tere?'

'Who else?'

'Zarco had a lot of girls; and Tere a lot of guys.'

'He means Tere. Does that surprise you?'

'No: I think it's interesting. What other explanations has Cañas given you?'

'He's told me that Zarco went looking for him. Or that he didn't just join Zarco, rather Zarco also recruited him: according to Cañas, Zarco needed someone like him, someone who spoke Catalan and looked like a nice boy and could act as a decoy for their jobs.'

'That sounds a bit unlikely to me. I mean, I'm not saying that a good decoy couldn't have come in handy for Zarco, but I don't think it would have mattered to him enough to go out and look for one, among other reasons because he used to do things bare-faced, without any screen.'

'Not that he was looking: he just found one.'

'Well, then maybe so. In any case it's true that Gafitas wasn't like the rest of the gang; that was clear as day: although he soon started dressing like them, and combing his hair and walking and talking like them, he never looked like one of them; he always looked like what he was.'

'And what was he? A middle-class teenager taking a walk on the wild side?'

'More or less.'

'Do you mean that he never took what he was doing with Zarco seriously?'

'No: of course he took it seriously; if not he never would have gone as far as he went. What I mean is that he always thought, as serious as it was, that it was just temporary, that he'd stop and return to the fold and then it would be as if nothing had ever happened. That's my impression. Maybe I'm wrong, but I don't think so. In any case, ask Cañas. Or don't waste your time: I'm sure Cañas will say I'm wrong. Up to you.'

'From what you say, you guys didn't see Gafitas the same way you saw the rest of them.'

'We saw him for what he was, as I said, just that he wasn't like the rest. And if you mean did we treat him differently from the rest, the answer is no . . . Although maybe I should qualify this. The truth is at first, when he showed up in the district with Zarco and the rest, we thought it would just be a fleeting thing, one of those strange things the district sometimes turned up; the surprise was that he lasted and after a short time he was just one more of them. As for the end, well, judging by what happened in the end maybe you're right: maybe we did always see him in a different light. But we'll talk about the end later, right?'

'Yeah. Let's go back to the beginning. The other day you told me that the gang settled into shape when Gafitas arrived on the scene.'

'That's what I believe. Of course before Gafitas showed up there was already a gang more or less in existence: they stole cars and broke into holiday villas, snatched purses and stuff; but when Gafitas showed up things changed. Not because Gafitas wanted them to, of course, just because; these things happen all the time: something is added by chance to a mechanism and it unintentionally changes the way it works. That's what might have happened when Gafitas joined Zarco's gang. Or when Zarco recruited him, as Cañas says.'

'Was it at that moment when you guys detected that there was a gang of delinquents operating in the city?'

'No, it was earlier. I remember very well because for me the case began then. One morning Deputy Superintendent Martínez called all sixteen inspectors of the Squad into his office. That wasn't too out of the ordinary; what was out of the ordinary is that the provincial superintendent was present at the meeting: that meant it was a serious matter. During the meeting the superintendent said very little, but Martínez explained that for some time they'd been receiving recurrent reports of robberies in the city and the towns and housing developments of the province; at that time the systems of suspect detection were very rudimentary, we didn't have a computerized registry of fingerprints like they do nowadays and everything had to be done by hand, imagine what that was like. In any case the repetition of the robbery methods, Martínez told us, led them to believe that we were dealing with a more or less organized gang: the handbags were always snatched the same way, the cars always hot-wired the same way and the houses always broken into through doors or windows when they were empty; furthermore, witnesses spoke of kids doing the robberies. Here things got complicated because, as I think I told you already, there was no such thing as a teenage gang back then, or they didn't exist the way they later did, or at least we didn't know about them, so Martínez's conjectures did not indicate a gang of teenagers but an adult gang who used kids to help them. This meant it wasn't going to occur to anybody at first that Zarco's gang had anything to do with those robberies, first because we didn't even think of them as a criminal gang exactly, and second because, as far as we knew, they weren't associated with any adults. Be that as it may, Martínez asked the whole brigade to be alert and assigned Vives to take charge of the case; our group had several things on our hands already, and Vives decided to divide us in two and asked me to devote myself exclusively to this case with the help of Hidalgo and Mejía.

'That's how I began to pursue Zarco without yet knowing I was pursuing him. Apart from bureaucratic tasks, my job up till then consisted mostly of interrogating victims and suspects, gathering evidence and spending the afternoons and evenings doing the rounds of the bars of the district, identifying, frisking and questioning anyone and everyone, keeping my eyes and ears wide open; from that moment on my job would still be the same, except that now my main objective was to arrest the gang we'd just been alerted to. Just at that time Gafitas showed up in the district, but I'd been trying to complete my mission for a relatively short time and hadn't yet associated the gang I was looking for with Zarco's gang.'

'When did you associate them?'

'Some time later. Actually, during the first weeks I was so disoriented that I only managed to establish that the robberies were the work of one gang and not a bunch of different gangs or isolated individuals, which is what I thought more than once at the beginning; I also came to think that the gang had no connection to the city or to the red-light district, that it had its centre of operations outside – in Barcelona, perhaps, or maybe in some housing development or town on the coast – and that they only came into the city on jobs and then left. It was a preposterous idea, but ignorance produces preposterous ideas, don't you think? I had a few at least, until one day I began to suspect that Zarco and his guys could be connected to the robberies.'

'How did you reach that conclusion?'

'Thanks to Vedette.'

'You mean the madam?'

'Do you know her?'

'I've heard about her.'

'Of course, lots of people have heard about her, she was a legend in the district. The truth is she was a remarkable woman, and one who stood out in that scene. When I met her she was already getting on, but she still had her faux-grande-dame bearing, she still behaved with the arrogance of a woman who was once very beautiful and still ran her business with an iron fist. She was the proprietor of two clubs, La Vedette and the Eden; the best known was La Vedette, which also had a reputation for being the best hooker bar in the district, as in times gone by the Salón Rosa or the Racó used to have. It was a small L-shaped place, without a single table but with lots of stools lined up against the walls, opposite a bar that began just to the left of the entrance then turned left again and continued to the back, where two doors opened, one to the kitchen and the other to a stairway leading to the rooms upstairs; the walls were wood-lined and had no windows, several columns came out of the bar and reached up to the ceiling mouldings, a reddish light made objects and faces look unreal, the music of Los Chunguitos, Los Chichos and people like that was playing at all hours. Back then it was often full, especially on Saturdays and Sundays, just when we tended not to go to the district so we wouldn't ruin the bar owners' businesses by scaring away their abundant weekend clientele.

'The day I'm talking about must have been a Monday or a Tuesday because there weren't many people in the bar and Mondays and Tuesdays were slow days in the district. When we went in Hidalgo and I always carried on straight to the back, where we could get a good view of the whole place, and we stayed there while Vedette or her husband pressed the button that turned the red light on in the rooms and the girls moved away looking at us from the other end of the bar with the usual mixture of suspicion and indifference. We talked for a while with Vedette, and then I left her with Hidalgo and went to talk to three girls who were alone at the bar. The first two didn't tell me anything out of the ordinary, but, after a few minutes of conversation, the third told me or led me to understand – or maybe it slipped out – that Zarco and his gang had spent a fortune in the place the previous Saturday night. I spoke to the first two girls again, who confirmed the story a bit reluctantly, and one of them added, probably to make up for her previous silence, that one of the kids had mentioned that he or someone from the gang or the whole gang had been in Lloret that afternoon. I went back to the bar and told the owner what her girls had told me; a little grimace gave her away: because it was in her interest, Vedette had always behaved very well towards us, but she was an astute woman and knew that information was power and liked to be the one who handled it and doled it out; in any case she immediately realized that she neither could nor should refute what her charges had said, so she had no choice but to confirm it, although she tried to play down Saturday's orgy, assuring us that Zarco and the rest had spent much less money than the girls had claimed and denied having heard anything to do with Lloret.

'The first thing I did when I got to the station the next morning was to ask whether there'd been any robberies in the city or province that we hadn't heard about. Nobody knew anything, but Hidalgo, Mejía and I started making inquiries and soon found out that the Civil Guard in Lloret had received a complaint the previous day of a break-in at a bungalow in a housing development called La Montgoda. That's how we connected one thing to the other. And that's how I got my first suspicion that the gang we were looking for was Zarco's gang. How do you like that?'

7

'It was at the beginning of August, not long after I slept with Tere on the Montgó beach, outside the Marocco, and it was like cresting a hill not least because from that moment on the gang was reduced almost by half. I'm talking about Guille's death and the arrests of Chino, Tío and Drácula.

'It happened at the same time as my parents went away on holiday. Until then I'd always gone with them, but I spent the month of July announcing to my mother that I was going to stay in Gerona with my sister and she and my father finally accepted it. My parents' departure simplified things, because it allowed me to stop leading a double life – that of a *quinqui* with Zarco's gang, that of a conventional teenager with my family – and to enjoy much more liberty than I'd ever enjoyed before. I don't think my parents left without me calmly, but I don't think they had much choice either, because at sixteen it was impossible to force me to go with them and on top of that they must have been more than fed up with the arguments, complaints, rude remarks and hostile silences, and maybe they thought it would do me good to spend a month apart from them. What my parents did try to do was keep me under control through my sister, although she wasn't much help to them: as soon as I understood that they'd put her in charge of keeping an eye on me and keeping them informed, I threatened her, told her I knew a lot about her and that, if she told our parents anything I was up to, I'd do the same; of course, I was bluffing, I had no idea what kind of life my sister was leading and had not the slightest interest in finding out, but she didn't know that and she did know I was serious, that I'd changed in that brief month and a half of summer and was no longer the fragile adolescent or faint-hearted little brother I used to be, and on account of that she had begun to fear my reactions, if not respect me. So she had no choice but to shut up and accept the blackmail.

'I'm sure I don't need to clarify that my parents' departure affected me, not the gang; what affected the gang was, as I was saying, Guille's death and Chino, Tío and Drácula's arrest. The episode was pretty confusing, and I wasn't involved, so what I'm going to tell you is not what happened but what I reconstructed after it happened. That afternoon Guille's group didn't even come into La Font; I knew they were up to something but I didn't know exactly what, which was quite normal anyway, because normally only Zarco and Guille knew what we were all up to and the rest of us knew nothing or only knew about stuff once it had already happened. This ignorance wasn't premeditated, a security measure or anything like that; it was just a symptom of our absolute subordination to Zarco and Guille, proof that, in the hierarchy of the group, those of us who weren't Zarco and Guille were no more than extras. The thing is that Guille and his group had planned a robbery in a village near Figueras that afternoon and the robbery went wrong because, as we began to learn that night and as was related in the newspapers the next day, while Guille and Drácula were inside the house the owner and two of his sons showed up firing hunting rifles and scared them away. Everything would have ended at that if some neighbours, alerted by the gunshots, hadn't called the police and if not for the coincidence that there was a milk cart, which is what we called the white Seat 131s of the police fleet, nearby; these two things meant that, when our guys pulled out onto the main road fleeing the failed robbery, they practically crashed into the cop car and a full-speed chase ensued that ended a few kilometres further on, when Tío took the curve of the Bàscara bridge too fast and lost control of the Seat 124 they were in, and the car flipped over several times before going over the railings and falling into the river. Guille got stabbed in the sternum with the gear stick and died instantly; Tío, Chino and Drácula survived, although Tío broke his spinal column in several places and was left a quadriplegic.

'The days following the accident were very strange. None of us went to Guille's funeral or visited the injured guys in hospital or showed any concern for them or their families (only some time later Tere did); actually, everything went on as if that catastrophe hadn't happened, except for the fact that for three days we were sort of dormant, we even stopped stealing cars, and people in the district and at Rufus bombarded us with questions and the secret police interrogated us several times. But between ourselves, as far as I remember, we barely mentioned the accident, or we only mentioned it in a neutral and dispassionate way as if it had nothing to do with us. I don't have any explanation for that either. Perhaps it was all a pose, or we were like punch-drunk boxers, or in reality the accident and its consequences overwhelmed us, and that's why we talked so little about it. You could say that, but I'm not sure it's true.

'What is true is that the incident changed everything. I remember very well how the change began. One afternoon, after about four or five days of total paralysis, Zarco, Gordo and Colilla went into a villa at La Fosca beach, between Calella and Palamós, while I stood guard by the door, and they came out of there with an armour-plated safe they could barely carry between the three of them; and we put it in the trunk and tried to open it in an empty field, but we quickly realized we wouldn't be able to without help and took it to the General's house. The expression on the General's face changed when we told him what we had in the car and he told us to leave the safe in the yard and then asked us to wait there. We waited there, accompanied or guarded by the General's wife, who came in and out of the yard in silence, with her grey hair and grey housecoat and vague eyes. The General came straight back. With him came two men carrying two toolboxes. After examining the safe, the men took out some safety goggles, gloves and a pair of blowtorches and got to work. An hour later they'd destroyed the lock and opened the safe.

'The General saw the two men out. As he did so we looked through the safe: inside were stacks of files full of documents and a gold ring with a precious stone set in it. When he came back out of the house, the General found his wife examining the gemstone against the light. When she saw him, the woman rubbed the stone against her housecoat, as if she'd sullied it and wanted to shine it up again, and then she handed it to Gordo, who in turn handed it to Zarco, who in turn handed it to the General. How much do you want for this? the General asked Zarco, after studying the ring and gem carefully. Nothing, said Zarco. The General looked at him with distrust. I don't want cash, Zarco clarified. I want hardware. The General's expression went from distrust to incredulity; I looked at Gordo and Colilla and realized they were as perplexed as the General or, for that matter, as I was: Zarco hadn't said a word to them about weapons either. The General looked sceptical, scratched his sideburns and said: What happened to Guille has upset you, son. Zarco smiled and shrugged, although he didn't say anything; his silence was his way of insisting, or that's how the General took it, and he added: I don't have weapons: you should know that. Yeah, I know, said Zarco. But you can get some if you want. The General asked: What do you want them for? What's it to you?, Zarco replied softly; and just as softly asked:

Do you want it or not? If yes, fine; if not, fine too: I'll find someone who does. Before the General could reply something nobody expected happened: his wife intervened in the discussion. Get them for him, she said. We all looked at her; standing between us and the General, the woman had her hands hanging down at her sides and, with her blind-woman's eyes, she seemed not to be looking at anyone or to be looking at us all at once. It was the first time I'd heard her speak and her voice sounded cold and piercing, like the tyrannical voice of a spoiled child. After a moment of silence she repeated: Get them for him. Have you gone crazy too?, the General asked then. What if they turn us in? Can't you see they're just little kids and that . . . ? They're not kids, his wife cut him off. They're men. As much as you are. Or more. They won't turn us in. Give them guns. Indecisive or furious, the General put the gem in his shirt pocket, walked over to his wife, grabbed her by the arm and dragged her to the back of the yard; there they stayed for a while, whispering (the General was gesturing, as well), and then both of them went inside the house and a short time later the General came out alone. What do you need?, he asked briskly. Not much, replied Zarco. A pistol and a couple of sawn-off shotguns. That's a lot, said the General. That's a lot less than the stone's worth, Zarco replied. The General only thought for a second. All right, he said. Come by tomorrow afternoon and they'll be here. Before we could consider the deal done he looked at each of the four of us one by one and said: One last thing. It's a message from my wife. She's asked me to tell you just once and I'm only going to say it once: anyone who lets it out is dead.

'The next day the General presented us with a long-barrelled 9mm Star pistol, two homemade sawn-off shotguns, a couple of magazines and a couple of boxes of ammunition. That same afternoon we spent several hours shooting at empty tin cans in a forest in Aiguaviva, and two days later we held up a grocer's shop in

Sant Feliu de Guíxols at gunpoint. The takings were scant, but the job was safe and comfortable, because the shopkeeper was so startled that he offered no resistance and didn't even report the robbery to the police. I don't know if our first armed robbery made us think that they'd all be very easy; if it did, the illusion didn't last long at all.

'Two days later we tried to rob a gas station on the way to Barcelona, near Sils. The plan was simple. It consisted of Zarco and Tere going into the station and pointing their guns at the guy behind the counter while Gordo and I waited outside, with the engine running, ready to drive out at full speed as soon as they came out with the money; the car, incidentally, was a Seat 124, which was the car we started to use systematically for our hold-ups because it was fast and powerful and easy to handle, and didn't attract attention.

'The plan was simple, but it went wrong. As soon as we stopped at the gas station, Zarco and Tere got out and started filling up the tank; meanwhile, Gordo and I stayed in the car, watching as two men waited to pay at the cash register inside the glass-walled station shop, and, when the second man finished paying and left, Gordo gave a signal to Zarco who gave a signal to Tere and they both pulled stockings over their heads at the same time, got out the guns – Zarco the Star and Tere a sawn-off shotgun – and walked into the glass-walled shop aiming them at the proprietor. I saw it all from inside the car, holding my breath beside Gordo, clutching the other shotgun and keeping one eye on the entrance to the gas station and the other on the glass-walled shop: through the huge windows I saw how the owner of the station raised his arms, how then, slowly, he lowered them and how, when he'd lowered them already, he made a strange quick movement. Then there was the thunder of a gunshot followed by a muffled swearword from Gordo, I looked at Gordo and then I looked back at the shop, but now I couldn't see anything or I only saw shattered glass. A couple of seconds later Zarco and Tere rushed into the car and Gordo pulled away and skidded out through the entrance to take the highway in the direction of Blanes, while in the back seat Zarco explained, swearing his head off, that the money wasn't where they'd expected it to be or where it should have been and that the owner of the gas station had tried to grab the pistol and in the struggle, while Tere shouted threats at the man, the gun had gone off and the shot shattered the window. Now we were speeding as fast as possible down the main highway, Zarco and Tere seemed calm in the back seat (or maybe it's just that I was so nervous in the front seat) and, as we got further away from the gas station, Gordo began to ease off a bit on the accelerator, until after a little while, when we were almost going normal speed and the four of us were beginning to feel that the fright had passed, he said, looking in the rear-view mirror: We're being followed.

'It was true. We all turned around and the first thing we saw was one of the secret police's Seat 1430s about a hundred and fifty metres behind us, and at that moment the driver and the officer beside him realized we'd recognized them and put the flashing light on the roof of the car and turned on the siren. What do we do?, asked Gordo. Speed up, said Zarco. Although on that stretch the highway was narrow and curved, Gordo floored it and in the blink of an eye we'd overtaken a pick-up truck and a couple of cars, but the police car easily replicated Gordo's manoeuvre and was back on our tail. It was then that the real chase began. Gordo drove the 124 as fast as its engine would go, the cars in front of us and oncoming traffic started to get out of our way, the police car got close enough to bang into our bumper and twice pulled up next to us and sideswiped us trying to push us into the ditch. Before they could try for a third time, Gordo took the next exit, which turned out to be a dirt track full of potholes that we started jolting along into a little pine forest with the police not very far behind, and at some moment the first shot was fired, and then the second and the third, and before I knew it we were in the middle of a full-scale shootout, with bullets coming through the back windscreen and whistling between us and going out through the front windscreen while Zarco and Tere leaned out the side windows and began to shoot back at our pursuers and Gordo tried to dodge the shots by zigzagging through the pines and driving off the track and back onto it and I cringed in the passenger seat, petrified with fear, incapable of using my sawn-off shotgun, silently imploring that we might get out of that trap, something that actually happened right at the moment it appeared they were going to catch us, when the track ended all of a sudden and we went down an embankment with great difficulty and landed on a sort of semi-paved forest floor while the secret police's 1430 tried to get there faster than us from behind and halfway down the embankment flipped over spectacularly to the euphoric delight of Zarco and Tere, and also Gordo, who was watching the tumbles our pursuers were taking in the rear-view mirror and took advantage to accelerate through a network of empty streets and get us out of that ghost town or half-built housing development we'd ended up in.

'The frustrated robbery of the gas station in Sils had at least two consequences. The first was that, although nobody made any comments on my behaviour that afternoon (or I didn't hear any), I felt ashamed of my cowardice and swore that it wouldn't happen again; at least not in front of Tere. The second was that Zarco decided to change objectives, and the consequence of that consequence was that from then on we stopped robbing shops and gas stations and started robbing banks, because, according to Zarco – and it was all he said to justify his decision – robbing a bank was less dangerous than robbing a gas station or a shop, aside from being more lucrative. The comment didn't strike me as nonsense, and much later I understood that back then, before the epidemic of bank robberies that later swept the country had started, maybe it wasn't, or not entirely, but the truth is it still astonishes me that it never even occurred to me to somehow try to put the brakes on that hell-bent scheme. It's also significant that no one asked any questions or had any qualms about this change in strategy; significant because it reveals again our absolute trust in Zarco: one day he simply tells us we're going to rob a bank and a few days later, after planning the job and watching a branch of the Banca Catalana beside the port in Palamós for several mornings in a row, we robbed it.

'We met mid-morning on the chosen day, had something to drink in La Font and on the way out of the district we stole a Seat 124 station wagon. On the way to Palamós Zarco went over the plan one last time and divided up the roles: he and Tere would go into the branch – Tere with one sawn-off shotgun and him with the other – I would wait for them on the street with the Star, guarding the entrance, and Gordo would wait for us at the wheel of the car, ready to take off. We listened to the instructions and assignments without complaint, but I spent the trip digesting a decision I'd been chewing over since Zarco had suggested the bank hold-up. So, just after we arrived in Palamós and parked in a little square, with the Banca Catalana branch on our left and the sea on our right, I broke the silence in the car as we watched people coming in and out of the bank. What I said was: I'll go in. To my surprise, the phrase didn't sound like an announcement or an offer but almost like an order, and maybe that's why no one said anything, as if no one entirely believed what they'd just heard. I looked away from the entrance to the bank and looked for Zarco's eyes in the rear-view mirror; finding them I explained, emboldened by my own words: You and I'll go in. Tere stays outside.

Zarco held my gaze. Don't talk rubbish, Gafitas, said Tere. It's not rubbish, said Gordo. Girls are easier to recognize than guys. And I have to drive. Gafitas should go in. Zarco and I were still looking at each other in the rear-view mirror while Tere and Gordo got involved in the beginning of an argument, until Zarco asked me: Are you sure? Tere and Gordo shut up. Yeah, I answered, and I said again, more for myself than for him: You and I'll go in. I turned around and looked at him directly, as if trying to make it clear that I had no doubts, and Zarco nodded his assent so slightly that it almost looked like a nod of capitulation. OK, he said to everyone. Gafitas and I'll go in. Then he added: You stay outside, Tere. Give the shotgun and nylons to Gafitas.

'Tere gave me the stocking and the shotgun, I gave her the Star, we both looked at each other for a second and during that second I saw a mixture of pride and astonishment in Tere's eyes and felt invulnerable. Then Zarco went over the plan again and, when there were only a few minutes left before two o'clock, which was closing time for banks, Gordo switched on the engine of the 124, drove around the little square and parked on the pavement on the other side, right in front of the entrance to the branch. Zarco, Tere and I all got out of the car at once. While Tere stationed herself by the door holding the pistol at her waist, under her T-shirt and handbag, Zarco and I pulled the nylons over our heads, walked into the bank and pointed the guns at the two customers and three employees – three men and two women – who were there at that moment. What happened next was easier than we'd expected. As soon as they heard us shout at them to lie down on the floor, the customers and employees obeyed, frightened to death. After that only Zarco spoke, with an unexpectedly slow and deliberate voice or at least unexpectedly slow and deliberate for me, who was still pointing at the three men and two women with the sawn-off shotgun, sweating and forcing myself not to tremble while he tried to calm everybody down saying in his strange unhurried voice that nobody wanted to hurt them and that nothing was going to happen to them if they did what he told them to. Then Zarco asked who the manager was, and when he identified himself ordered him to hand over the money they kept in the branch; the manager – an almost completely bald man in his sixties with a double chin – obeyed immediately, filled a plastic bag with several bundles of notes and handed it to Zarco without looking at him, as if fearing he'd recognize his face disfigured though it was by the nylon. Zarco didn't even open the bag and, as we backed away towards the door, he simply thanked everyone for their co-operation and advised them not to move for ten minutes after we left.

'Outside we took the stockings off our heads and got in the car. Gordo drove normally down the main street of Palamós, without jumping a single red light, and once we were out of town took a detour towards a tennis club, but a short time later Gordo stopped in a lot where there were several parked cars, we got out of the 124, took a Renault 12 and drove back out to the highway. As we drove away from Palamós, sure now that we weren't being followed, Zarco counted the money; most of it was hundred- and five-hundred-peseta notes: the total was less than forty thousand. Zarco announced the sum, and the silence that followed betrayed his disappointment; Tere and Gordo also seemed disappointed. As for me, I cared much less about the miserable amount of the booty than about having made up for my cowardice during the car chase that followed the hold-up of the gas station in Sils, so I tried to cheer them up with my enthusiasm.

'It was no use. Zarco and the others experienced the success of our first bank robbery as a failure (and that false failure blurred my bravery, although I was so proud of myself, and especially of the pride I saw in Tere's eyes just before the hold-up, that it almost didn't matter to me). Maybe this explains why we blew that money even faster than usual, as if we looked down on it even more than usual. Whatever the case, speed calls for more speed, and from that moment on our accelerated impatient life accelerated even more and we became more impatient than ever. While we were surviving on a base of routine jobs (mostly purse-snatchings, sometimes the odd house), the mirage of the perfect heist obsessed us, as if we all planned to give up that outlaw frenzy after we did it, which was not true. We planned several bank jobs, called at least two of them off at the last minute and in the end only two came off: one at a branch of the Banco Atlántico in Anglès, which yielded loot almost as paltry as the job in Palamós, and another at the Bordils branch of the Banco Popular.

'I remember the heist in Bordils very well and one of the hold-ups we called off. The heist in Bordils I remember because it was the last one and because for a long time barely a day went by when I didn't think of it; I remember the frustrated hold-up because, immediately after we called it off, Zarco and I had our longest conversation of the summer. Maybe I should say our only conversation. Or at least the only conversation we had on our own and the only time back then that he and I talked about Tere. In any case, it's the only one I remember in detail.'

'The other day you told me that your relationship with Tere didn't change after sleeping with her on the beach at Montgó.'

'And it's true. I thought it would change (or I should say: I would have liked it to change), but it didn't change. Of course we didn't sleep together again. Nor did we talk more than before or become more involved with each other than before or closer. In fact, I'd almost say that, instead of improving, our relationship deteriorated: Tere even stopped flirting with me, like she used to do sporadically; and if I got up my courage to get down off the barstool and out onto the dance floor at Rufus and started dancing beside her as I'd done at the Marocco, the night of Montgó beach, her response was always cold, and I soon gave up and swore never to try again. I didn't know what to attribute her disinterest to, and I never dared ask her or remind her of what had happened on Montgó beach (just as I'd never dared to remind her of what happened in the arcade washrooms). Of course, Guille's death and Chino, Tío and Drácula's arrest might have had some bearing; the appearance of the weapons might also have had some bearing and the fact that with them everything became rougher, more serious and more violent, as if that change had isolated us more and made us become more introverted and more aware of ourselves, or more grown-up. In any case, just as I never had the impression that Tere regretted what happened between us in the arcade washrooms, now I did have the impression that she regretted having slept with me on Montgó beach.'

'And in spite of that it never occurred to you to think that Tere had slept with you to get even with Zarco, because that night he went off with another girl.'

'No: I already told you the last time we talked. It didn't occur to me then. But by then I no longer thought that Tere was Zarco's girlfriend. Or I didn't exactly think she was. I thought she was his girlfriend but not his girlfriend, or that she was his girlfriend but in an elastic and occasional way, or that she had been his girlfriend and wasn't any more but might be again or he thought she might be again. I don't know. I told you before that I'd never seen them behaving like a couple, never seen them kissing, for example, although I had seen Zarco, especially very late at night, at Rufus, trying to kiss or caress Tere and her pushing him away sometimes with irritation and sometimes with an amused or even affectionate gesture. Anyway. The truth is I didn't really understand too well what the relationship was between them, and I wasn't interested in understanding it either.'

'Do you know if Zarco found out that summer about what happened in the arcade washrooms between you and Tere?'

'No.'

'He didn't find out or you don't know if he found out?'

'I don't know if he found out.'

'Do you know if he found out that you and Tere slept together on Montgó beach?'

'Yeah. He did find out about that. I know because he told me himself, in the conversation I was just telling you about, a couple of weeks after the night on Montgó beach. That afternoon, like I said, we'd called off a heist. It was in Figueras or in some town on the outskirts of Figueras. We called it off at the last minute, when we were just about to go into the bank and a Civil Guard car drove past and we had to buzz off. The escape lasted for quite a while, because for quite a while we feared we'd been identified and that they were following us. Actually I think we only calmed down when our car was travelling under the mid-afternoon sun on a mountain road that snaked between hillsides divided by low stone walls and covered by pines, olive trees, prickly pears and shrubs. After a while we came to a town of white houses crowded together in front of the sea that turned out to be Cadaqués. We wandered the streets drinking beer in the bars along the board-walk, and when we came out of one of them I saw a brand-new Citroën Mehari and hot-wired it with Zarco and Gordo's permission and then, with Zarco beside me and Gordo and Tere in the back seat, drove out of Cadaqués with no intention other than to enjoy the ride.

'I drove along the edge of the sea northwards and passed a couple of pebble beaches and a fishing village. The road got emptier and narrower and the surface more irregular and full of potholes. The wind coming in off the sea threatened to blow the top off the Mehari, and at some point (by then it had been a while since we'd seen any other cars) the road ran out, and became almost a dirt track or a half-paved track. Where are we going?,

Zarco asked. I don't know, I said. Zarco was sunk down in the passenger seat, with his bare feet resting on the dashboard; I thought he was going to tell me to turn around but he didn't say anything. In the back seat, Tere and Gordo hadn't even heard Zarco's question, and didn't look impatient but rather exhausted or bewitched by the silence and desolation of that suddenly lunar landscape: a plateau of slate, grey crags and dry bushes in which only here and there, between bare gullies and rocks, did we get a glimpse of the sea. I carried on avoiding rough patches until at the end of the track I caught sight of a headland crowned by a lighthouse and beyond it an expanse of water almost as big and as blue as the sky.

'We had ended up at Cap de Creus. None of us knew it, of course, but that was where Zarco and I had that conversation I was telling you about. We passed in front of an abandoned hut, climbed up to the headland and I parked the Mehari by the lighthouse, a rectangular building with a tower rising out of it with a cupola of iron and glass, topped by a weathervane. When we stopped we realized that Tere and Gordo had fallen asleep. We didn't wake them up, and Zarco and I got out of the car and started walking along the esplanade in front of the lighthouse until the esplanade ran out and in front of us was nothing but a precipice that descended to a labyrinth of coves and inlets and, beyond them, a sea that stretched to the horizon, wavy and open and a little bit shadowed already by the beginning of twilight. Both of us stood there, our faces to the wind. Zarco murmured: Fuck, it looks like the end of the world. I didn't say anything. After a while Zarco turned around, walked away from the cliff, went and sat down against the wall of the lighthouse and started rolling a joint out of the wind. I walked away from the cliff too, sat down beside Zarco, lit the joint when he'd finished rolling it.

'That's where the conversation started up. I don't remember

how long it lasted. I remember that when we started talking the sun was starting to set, staining the surface of the sea a pale red, and that on the right a boat appeared on the horizon sailing parallel to the coast, and when we left, the boat was about to disappear on the left of the horizon and the sun had sunk into the now dark water; I also remember how the conversation got started. We'd been sitting there for a while not talking when I asked Zarco what he was thinking of doing when summer was over; I'd asked the question most of all to escape from the uncomfortable silence, and it sounded a little incongruous, a little out of place, so Zarco brushed it off saying he'd do the same as always, and half-heartedly asked what I'd do. As well as half-hearted, my answer was innocuous – I said I'd do the same as always too – but it seemed to arouse Zarco's curiosity. And what do you mean by that?, he asked. That you're going back to school? It means I'll do the same as this summer, I answered. I don't plan to go back to school. Zarco nodded as if he approved of the answer and took a pensive toke. I stopped going to school when I was seven, he said. Well, maybe eight. Doesn't matter: it was a pain. You don't like it either? No, I said. I used to like it, but not any more. What happened?, asked Zarco. At that moment I hesitated. I told you before that I'd never mentioned Batista in front of Zarco and the rest; now, for a second, I thought I might; the next moment I discarded the idea: I felt that Zarco wouldn't be able to understand, that telling him about my previous year's ordeal would be to relive it, relive the humiliation and lose the self-respect I'd gained over the summer and force Zarco to lose respect for me. Then, with a blend of amazement and joy, I thought how, although the ordeal had happened just a couple of months ago, it was now as though it had happened centuries ago. Then I said: Nothing. I just stopped liking it and that was it.

'Zarco kept smoking. The wind whipped around the lighthouse

and blew our hair about and we had to smoke carefully, so a gust wouldn't blow the end off the joint; in front of us the sky and the sea were an identical, immense blue. And your folks?, asked Zarco. What about my folks? I asked. What are your folks going to say if you don't go back to school?, asked Zarco. They can say what they like, I answered. Whatever they say it's over. I'm not going back. Zarco took another toke, handed me the joint and asked me to tell him about my family; without taking my eyes off the sea and sky and the boat that seemed suspended between the two, I told him about my father, my mother, my sister. Then I asked him the same question (and not just because he'd asked me: I told you before that I'd barely heard him talk about his family). Zarco laughed. I looked at him: like me he had his head leaning back against the lighthouse wall and his hair tangled by the wind; a bit of saliva had dried in the corner of his mouth. What family?, he asked. I never knew my father, my stepfather got killed years ago, my brothers are in jail, my mother's too busy just trying to get by. You call that a family? I didn't answer. I turned back towards the sea, finishing off the joint, and, when I stubbed it out on the ground, Zarco started rolling another.

'When he finished rolling it he passed it to me and I lit it. What I don't understand is what the fuck you're going to do if you don't go back to school, said Zarco, picking up the conversation again. The same as you guys. Zarco curled his lip in a way I didn't know how to interpret, passed me the joint and turned back to look at the sea and the sky, still immense, less and less blue, both turning towards a reddish darkness. Fuck, he said. I took a drag on the joint and asked: What's up? Nothing, said Zarco. What's up?, I repeated. Can't I do the same as you guys? Sure, said Zarco. I don't know if I was satisfied by his answer, but I turned back towards the sea and sky as well and had another toke; after a few seconds, Zarco changed his mind: Actually you can't, he said.

Why not?, I asked. Because you're not like us, he answered. We stared at each other: that was the argument I'd used with him, at the beginning of the summer, to refuse to rob the Vilaró arcade (and then again with Tere to refuse to break into a house in La Montgoda). For a moment I thought Zarco remembered and he was turning the tables on me; then I thought he didn't remember. I smiled. Don't tell me you're going to give me a sermon?, I asked. In reply, he just smiled back. We kept quiet. I smoked in silence. And I said: Why aren't I like you guys? And he said: Because you're not. And I said: I do the same things you guys do. And he said: Almost the same, yeah. But you're not like us. And I insisted: Why not? And he explained: Because you go to school and we don't. Because you have a family and we don't. Because you're scared and we're not. And I asked: You guys aren't scared? And he answered: Yeah, but we're not scared the same way you are. You think about the fear, and we don't. You have things to lose, and we don't. That's the difference. I made a sceptical face, but didn't push it. I smoked. I passed him the joint. For a while we kept staring at the sea and the sky and listening to the howling wind. Zarco took two or three more tokes, put out the joint and then went on: Do you know what happened to Chino the day he went into the Modelo prison? He paused; then said: He was raped. Three sons of bitches gave it to him up the ass. He told his mother and his mother told Tere. Funny, eh? He paused again. Oh, by the way, he added, did I ever tell you the story of Quílez? It happened the first day I was in the nick.

'I was waiting for him to tell me the story of Quílez when I heard him say: Look at her. I turned around: it was Tere, who'd just come around the corner of the lighthouse and was walking towards us. I conked out, she said when she came up beside us, crouching down. And Gordo?, I asked. Out for the count, she answered. Zarco rolled and lit a joint and passed it to Tere, who smoked for a while before passing it to me. Then Tere stood up and walked over to the cliff and stayed there, facing the sea, her hair whipping around like crazy in the wind and her silhouette standing out against a cloudless, darkening sky and choppy, darkening sea. That was the moment Zarco started talking to me about Tere. First he asked if I liked Tere; I pretended he was asking what he wasn't asking and quickly said of course. Then Zarco said that's not what he meant and I, knowing what he meant, asked him what he meant and he answered that he meant would I like to shag her. Since I'd guessed the question, I didn't have to improvise the answer. No, I lied. Then why did you shag her?, asked Zarco. I froze. Just at that instant, as if she'd caught a snippet of our conversation (impossible, because she was too far away and the howling wind and the noise of the iron and glass rattling in the lighthouse cupola drowned out the words), Tere turned around and opened her arms wide in a gesture of admiration or incredulity for the sky and sea behind her. I passed the joint to Zarco, who held my gaze for a second with a neutral look in his eyes; the dried saliva had disappeared from the corner of his mouth. What did you think?, he asked. That I didn't know? I didn't answer, and we both looked back at Tere: shielding her eyes with her hand from the sun's last rays of the evening, at that moment Tere was looking towards an abandoned building a hundred metres or so to our right, on the same headland. Who told you?, I asked. She did, he answered. It was only once, I lied again; I specified: The night we went to the Marocco. Are you sure?, he asked. Yes, I answered, thinking about the washrooms at the Vilaró arcade. Yeah, said Zarco. And he passed me the joint. I took it, smoked and watched how Tere pointed to the empty building and shouted something and started walking, jumping from one rock to the next and holding her bag against her body, towards where she'd been pointing. So it was just once, said Zarco. Yeah, I said. What's the matter?, he asked without irony. Didn't you like it? Of course I liked it, I answered, and immediately regretted the reply. So?, he asked. I reflected. I took several drags on the joint. I said: I don't know. Ask her. I passed the joint to Zarco and that was it.'

'You didn't talk any more?'

'No. Zarco didn't push it and I was desperate to change the subject.'

'And you were thinking that Tere wasn't Zarco's girlfriend.'

'I thought she was and wasn't, I told you already. Anyway, I don't know . . . I think that at some point I had a sense that this friendly conversation might be a trap, that it might actually be a scheme of Zarco's, a way of testing me or an attempt to make me talk; ultimately, that it might be his way of telling me that Tere was his and that I should keep my distance. I don't know, it was just a feeling, but a very vivid feeling, and I did not feel comfortable. It's even possible that later I began to think that Zarco had been looking for an opportunity like that for a while to bring up the subject of Tere and the night on Montgó beach, and I might have also thought that, deep down, what Zarco wanted was for me to leave the gang so I'd get away from Tere.'

'Did he tell you to leave the gang?'

'Yes. That same day, just before we left the lighthouse. I, to stop talking about Tere, had started talking about that afternoon's thwarted heist, and then we were silent for a while smoking and listening to the wind rattling the iron and glass of the lighthouse cupola, watching Tere approach the abandoned building and wander around it and disappear behind it, and the sun beginning to sink into the sea and the boat to disappear off to the left of the horizon, and at some point Zarco asked what we were talking about and I said that afternoon's thwarted heist and he said: No, before. I said I didn't remember although I remembered perfectly well and then, to my relief, I heard him say: Oh yeah, the story of Quílez.

'And then he told me about Quílez, a long story that he later left out of his memoir and never told in any of the interviews he gave or any of the ones I've read, something which I at least found rather shocking because, as you know, Zarco told the journalists everything. What he told me is that the story had happened on his first day in prison, in the Modelo in Barcelona, at the time it would have been more or less a year before. He told me that afternoon, when he came out to the main courtyard at exercise time, he met two friends of his brother Juan José who'd been locked up in the prison for months (though not in the same cell block as him) and started talking to them. He told me the yard was full of prisoners calmly talking and walking and playing football. He said the calm shattered when the crowd seemed to stop all of a sudden while a circular wall of men formed in the middle of the yard, and in the middle of that wall was a blond, corpulent man, and in the blink of an eye another man, this one pale and very thin, hurled himself on him and, with a homemade stiletto fashioned from a mattress spring, with a single slash, opened his chest and then ripped out his heart and held it up in his hand, fresh and gushing blood in the afternoon sun. And he told me that as he displayed his trophy the murderer let out a long rejoicing shriek. He also told me that it all happened so fast that, before falling down dead, the victim didn't even have time to shout in horror or for help. And he told me how the prison guards evacuated the yard and left the heartless corpse sprawled on the ground, and that he didn't ask anyone anything but soon knew that the murderer's name was Quílez and the murdered man was a guy reputed to be a snitch who'd arrived at the Modelo that very day, just like he had, except that he'd been transferred from another prison. And finally he told me – and when he told me this, I thought his voice trembled – that night, after the guards locked up Quílez in solitary confinement, his name was chanted in a righteous murmur that travelled through the cell blocks of the Modelo like a prayer or a triumphal lullaby.

'When Zarco finished telling me the story of Quílez we sat in silence. After a few seconds he stood up and stretched and took a few steps away from the lighthouse towards the cliff, stuck his hands in his pockets and stood there for a while in front of the darkened sea and sky. Then, all of a sudden, he turned back towards me and spoke with an irritated look on his face. Look, Gafitas, I'm going to tell you, he began. You do whatever the fuck you feel like, but at least don't say that I didn't tell you. After a pause he went on: If it's up to me, you can stay with us. You turned out to be tougher and more of a son of a bitch than you look like, so there's no problem there. Do what you want. Now, he added, if you want my advice, drop it. He took his right hand out of his pocket and cut the air with a horizontal slash, much more violent than his words. Drop this, he repeated. Don't come back to La Font or the district. Get lost, man. Forget the gang. Go back to your family, go back to school, go back to your life. There's no more to this, don't you see? You've already seen all there is to see. Sooner or later we'll get caught, just like they caught Guille and the others. And then we're fucked: if you're unlucky you end up dead like Guille or in a wheelchair like Tío; and if you're lucky you end up in the slammer, like Chino or Drácula. Although for a guy like you I don't know which would be worse. I spent a few months in the slammer, but the slammer'll crush you, it'll be the end of you. That's another reason you're not like us. Besides, we don't have a choice, this is the only life we have, but you have another one. Don't be a dickhead, Gafitas: drop it.

'That's more or less what he said to me. I didn't answer, in part because I had nothing to answer and in part, as I told you before, the conversation about Tere had made me uneasy, but especially because at that moment Tere showed up at the lighthouse with the news that the abandoned building was a Civil Guard post and the suggestion that we should check it out. It was almost dark by then. Zarco pointed the long, dirty fingernail of his index finger at me and said as if he hadn't heard Tere's suggestion: Think about it, Gafitas. I stood up. Tere looked at me; then she looked at Zarco. What does Gafitas have to think about?, she asked. Zarco patted her on the ass and answered: Nothing. We went back to the Mehari and drove away.'

'And that was the last time you and Zarco talked about Tere that summer.'

'Yes.'

'Did you consider leaving the gang after Zarco advised you to?'

'Yes, I think so. Not because I wanted to leave, but because I had the suspicion that Zarco had advised me to leave the gang and return to my previous life to get me away from Tere, and that there was a threat hidden behind that advice. In any case he didn't mention the matter again, and the truth is there was barely any time for me to consider it seriously: shortly after the conversation at Cap de Creus it was all finished.'

'You mean the gang.'

'Of course.'

'When did it finish?'

'In the middle of September, a couple of weeks after my parents got back from their holiday. That was the worst moment of the summer for me. On the one hand I felt increasingly ill at ease in the gang or in what was left of the gang, because that conversation with Zarco had injected me with the poison of distrust. On the other hand my relationship with my parents didn't improve on their return; quite the contrary: after a few days of truce even the rows and shouting matches multiplied and worsened, especially with my father, who must have seen me as an unrecognizable and furious monster, full of contempt. I don't know: now I think I probably felt trapped, and felt that everything could explode in those days at home or in the gang; finally everything exploded in the robbery of the Banco Popular branch in Bordils.

'It was our last job and it was a disaster. The reason for the disaster is obvious. For a start it has to be said that we planned it all in no time and so clumsily that we didn't even check out the branch and barely had a look around outside it. Add to this that the people who participated in the heist were not the best suited: we couldn't count on Tere, who was in Barcelona because one of her sisters had just had a baby, and, after Zarco sounded out the district, Latas and some other guys, the one who ended up filling in for her was Jou, who'd never robbed a bank and had no experience with guns. And to top it off we were unlucky . . . All this is true, but it doesn't explain the disaster; the explanation is simpler: there was a tip-off. We never found out who it was, or at least I never found out. It really could have been anybody: any of the guys Zarco sounded out to participate in the heist, any of the guys those guys talked to, any of the guys we'd talked to. Keep in mind as well that all the bars of the red-light district were full of police informers, starting with La Font; there were also snitches at Rufus. We knew it and, although Zarco was always demanding discretion, the truth is we talked to too many people and too cheerfully. And the first to do so was me.'

'Do you mean that it might have been you who let it slip?'

'I've often thought so.'

'Why?'

'Because two days before the heist, when we were all set to go and just needed to find someone to take Tere's place, I spent a couple of hours drinking beer with Córdoba while waiting for my friends in La Font. I've told you about Córdoba, right? I don't remember what we talked about that day, but Córdoba and I were friends and I trusted him, although I've often thought since that he wasn't trustworthy. I don't know. It might have been him. Which is to say: it might have been me.'

'Haven't you asked Inspector Cuenca?'

'No. I've never talked to the inspector about those days: I never wanted to talk to him and he never tried to talk to me about it. What for? Besides, I don't think he could tell me anything I don't know. The thing is there was a tip-off and, thanks to that, the police were able to set a trap for us.

'At first we didn't notice that they were waiting for us, and everything seemed to go according to plan. We arrived in Bordils at about one or one-thirty, Gordo parked very close to the door of the bank, in a sidestreet that led to the highway and, a few minutes later, Zarco, Jou and I got out of the car and walked into the branch pulling the nylon stockings over our heads. That was the first unusual thing I noticed: only two of us should have gone into the branch, not three; the role Zarco had assigned to Jou was to stay outside guarding the door: that's why he had the pistol. I soon noticed other unusual things. At the same time as Jou and I aimed our weapons left and right and Zarco pronounced the words he'd prepared in his habitual tone ("Good day, ladies and gentlemen. Don't be nervous. Nothing's going to happen. Please don't be heroes. Keep still and nobody'll hurt you. We just want the bank's money"), I saw that there was an alarming number of customers in the branch, among them two women with children; I also saw that there were two doors instead of just one: the main door we'd just come through and a back door that seemed to go into an alley; and I noticed that the employees were isolated from the rest of the branch in a reinforced booth or a booth that looked reinforced, and that booth was not open. Zarco must have noticed these things too, or at least the first and the last, because while he asked the women and children to lie down on the floor and some of the children began to cry, he ordered the employees to open the door of the booth. There were three employees, but for the moment none of the three moved; there's no way of knowing if one of them was weighing up the insane idea of resisting the robbery or if they were simply paralyzed by panic and, to clear up the doubts, Zarco grabbed a customer by the collar of his shirt, dragged him to the door of the booth, put the barrel of his sawn-off shotgun under his chin and said: Open up right now or I'll shoot this guy.

'They immediately opened the door. The man who did looked like a hunting dog with a face as white as plaster. While the children's crying filled the branch and began drilling into my head, the man stepped away from the door stammering that he couldn't open the safe. Zarco let his hostage go, approached the man and asked: Are you the manager? I can't open the safe, answered the man. Zarco slapped him. I asked if you were the manager, he repeated. Yes, said the man. But I can't open the safe. Open it, said Zarco. Open it and nothing will happen to anybody. I can't, the manager whined. It has a delayed opening mechanism. How long does it take to open? Fifteen minutes, answered the manager. Then Zarco hesitated, or I sensed him hesitate; the hesitation was logical: if he didn't force him to deactivate the delay mechanism, the result of the robbery would be a failure: another one; but, if he forced him to deactivate it, the fifteen-minute wait for the safe to open would be the longest and most anguished fifteen minutes of our lives, and nobody could guarantee that we could keep the situation under control during that time. I mustn't have been the only one guessing at Zarco's doubts, because at that moment a man who was on the floor by the back door took the opportunity to open it and escape (or maybe he hadn't been on the floor by the back door, but had crawled or dragged himself to it without us seeing him). Everything happened in a second, the same second in which Zarco hesitated or in which I sensed Zarco hesitating: the next second Jou shattered the glass of the

125

door the man had escaped through with a shot; the next an insane uproar erupted in the bank and the next Zarco tried to quiet it down by firing his shotgun at the ceiling and shouting that everyone should stay on the floor until we'd left. Then Zarco ordered the manager to forget the safe and give us all the money that wasn't in it. The manager obeyed, we grabbed the money and rushed out of the branch.

'On the street the police were waiting for us. As we ran as fast as we could towards the car we heard a shout to halt; instinctively we kept running, instead of surrendering, and, before we could get into the almost moving car, the shots began. All at once I heard them and felt a burning in my arm. All at once we got in the car and Gordo headed for the highway to Gerona while the shooting behind us intensified and my arm smarted and started to bleed. Although I must have been swearing out loud, nobody noticed that I was wounded, among other reasons because at the Bordils ramp there was an undercover cop car parked across the road. Gordo braked or took his foot off the accelerator, until Zarco screamed at him to step on it; he slammed the pedal to the floor, and with a single charge rammed the cop car almost onto the hard shoulder. The blow opened up a spectacular gash on Gordo's brow, which had hit the steering wheel and began to bleed copiously. In spite of that he floored it again and we kept going, at first pursued by two undercover cars that we started to pull away from as we crossed Celrà and Campdorà running red lights and stop signs, overtaking and dodging everything in our way, so by the time we got to Pont Major we had the impression that we'd left our pursuers behind. At that moment a helicopter began flying overhead. It was obviously after us, and Jou seemed to realize that at the same time as he noticed the blood flowing from my arm and Gordo's brow, and he lost his nerve and started shouting that they were going to catch us, and then Zarco told him to shut up and

Gordo turned right and crossed the bridge over the Ter in the direction of Sarrià while the undercover cars reappeared in the distance behind us, coming down the road from Campdorà. They must have been a kilometre or a kilometre and a half away, and Gordo took advantage of that to try to lose them once and for all in the narrow streets of Sarrià. For a while he seemed to have managed it, but in all that time the helicopter stayed hovering in the sky, without losing sight of us for an instant, and after a few minutes the undercover cars appeared again in the distance. Gordo floored it again and got us out of Sarrià and back onto the main highway, only this time not on the coastal road but the one that goes to France but instead of taking us to the border and away from the city it was taking us back to it. Gordo was following new instructions from Zarco and I suppose he was acting sensibly, because it seems like it would be easier to escape a helicopter in a city than in open country, but the truth is that, as soon as I saw where we were going, I felt we were getting ourselves into a rat trap and were not going to get out of it.

'I was right. At the beginning of La Barca Bridge just at the entrance to the city and already with La Devesa in sight, a big truck loaded with gas cylinders was heading straight for us; Gordo tried to miss it by yanking the steering wheel, lost control of the car and we flipped over and started rolling across the tarmac. What happened after that is difficult to tell. Although I've tried to reconstruct the sequence of events many times, I'm not entirely sure I've been able to; I have been able to reconstruct some links of the sequences: enough, I think, to have an approximate idea of what happened.

'They're six links that are six images or six groups of images. The first link is formed by the image of myself lying facedown on the crushed roof of the car, dazed and feeling around for my glasses and finding them intact, hearing meanwhile a sharp buzzing in my head and hearing Jou groaning and cursing and hearing Zarco shout that Gordo was unconscious and that we had to get the fuck out of the car. The second link is formed by the image of myself trying to crawl out of the twisted metal of the car through one of the back windows as I see how thirty or forty metres away a car brakes and two plain clothes cops get out and run towards us. The third link is not formed of one image but two: the image of Zarco yanking me out through the window and the image of both of us running across La Barca Bridge behind Jou, who's a few metres ahead of us and who, out of instinct or because Zarco shouted it, at the end of the bridge turns off up Pedret and heads for the district. The fourth link is not formed of two images but rather a sort of chain of images: first Zarco and I get to the end of the bridge and run towards La Devesa in the hope of giving the police the slip there, then Zarco trips on the uneven slope that goes down to the park and hits the ground, then I stop short and run back and grab Zarco's arm and he grabs me and for a few seconds we try to keep going like that, stumbling, Zarco running on his hurt leg and me dragging him; finally Zarco falls down again or throws himself on the ground while shoving me away and saying in a low, hoarse, panting voice: Run, Gafitas! And there's the fifth link, the penultimate image of the sequence: lit by the midday sun that shines through the crowns of the plane trees of La Devesa, Zarco is still kneeling on the ground and I am still standing at his side while the two cops are about to reach the slope into the park and catch us. The final image is predictable; it's also a double image: on the one hand it's a diaphanous image, the image of myself running through La Devesa leaving Zarco behind; on the other hand it is a blurry image, half-seen as I turn around to see if they're following me: the image of Zarco tangled up in a jumble of arms and legs, struggling with the two cops.

'That's where the six links end, and that's all I remember.'

'So you abandoned Zarco.'

'What was I going to do? What would you have done? He couldn't save himself; I couldn't save him: sacrificing myself would have been stupid, it would have done no good. So I decided to save myself. It's what Zarco would have done; that's why he told me to run, to go. And maybe that's why he fought with the police (or that's why I've always thought he fought with them): to give me time to get away, so I could save myself.

'That's what I did. I ran through the empty park like a flash, passed the football pitch, the rifle range and the model-plane runway and ended up taking shelter in a grove of poplars stuck in between the Ter and the Güell, between the sports pavilion and the municipal dump. Dazed, I stayed in that hiding place for a while, trying to get over my fear, the pain of my wounded arm and the buzzing in my head. Although the buzzing soon stopped, the wound wouldn't stop bleeding and the fear rushed back when the police helicopter flew low over the grove a couple of times, but I managed to think with sufficient clarity to understand that I should get out of there immediately and that I only had one safe place to go.

'Making sure no one saw me, I left the poplar grove, got to Caterina Albert and went home.

'When I got there everything happened very fast. When I went in, my whole family was eating. My mother and my sister cried out to high heaven when they saw my T-shirt soaked in blood; my father reacted differently; without a word he took me to the bathroom and, while I explained to all of them that I'd fallen off a motorcycle, he examined my wound. Once he'd examined it, my father asked my mother and sister to leave the bathroom. This is not from a fall, he said coldly when they left, pointing at my arm. Go on, tell me what happened. I tried to insist on my lie, but my father interrupted me. Look, Ignacio, he said. I don't know what mess you've got into, but if you want me to help you, you have to tell me the truth. Without affection, he added: If you don't want me to help you, you can leave. I understood he meant it, that he was right and that, no matter how badly he reacted to the truth, it would be a thousand times worse if the police arrested me; besides, by then I was coming down hard off the adrenaline and was so scared it was as if I'd injected myself in one single shot with complete awareness of the danger I'd exposed myself to in my forays of the past months.

'I agreed. As best I could I told my father the truth. His reaction calmed me down a little, almost disconcerted me: he didn't yell at me, didn't get furious, he didn't even seem surprised; he just asked me a few very specific questions. When I thought he'd finished I asked: What are we going to do? He didn't even take a second or two to think. Go to the police station, he answered. A chill made my legs go weak. You're going to give me up?, I asked. Yes, he answered. You said you'd help me, I said. That's the best thing I can do to help you, he said. Dad, please, I begged. My father pointed at my wound and said: Wash that off and let's get going. Then he left the bathroom and, while my mother came back in and washed the wound with the help of my sister, I heard him speaking on the phone. He spoke for quite a while, but I didn't know what about or with whom, because the telephone was in the front hall and my mother and my sister were harassing me with questions; they were also trying to comfort me, because I'd started to cry.

'Back in the bathroom, my father asked my mother to pack a suitcase for him and for me. I looked at him with my eyes full of tears; my father looked at me as if he'd just recognized me or as if he was about to burst into tears as well, and at that moment I knew he'd changed his mind, and that he wasn't going to turn me in. Where are you going?, my mother asked. Pack the suitcase, my father repeated. I'll explain later. In silence and without looking at my face again, my father finished cleaning out the wound, disinfected and bandaged it. When he finished he left the bathroom and for a couple of minutes I heard him speaking to my mother. He came back to the bathroom and said: Let's go.

'I followed him without questions. First we went to Francesc Ciurana Street and parked outside the door of a building where a close family friend lived, a lawyer from my parents' hometown called Higinio Redondo. My father got out of the car and asked me to wait and, while I waited, I deduced that it had been Redondo he'd spoken to on the phone, after I told him what happened. After a while my father returned to the car alone and we crossed the city and left it by the highway to France. On the way he told me we were going to a summer home that Redondo had just bought in Colera, a remote coastal village; he assured me that, if the police went looking for me at home on Caterina Albert (something which was highly probable), my mother would not hide our whereabouts; he explained in detail what I had to tell the police in the event, also highly probable, that they came to Colera to interrogate me (what I had to say was, in short, that we'd spent a week there, just the two of us, stretching out the last days of the summer holidays). An hour later we arrived in Colera. The village streets were deserted; Redondo's house was very close to the sea. As soon as we got in, my father started unpacking our things and arranging them in the wardrobes, or rather disarranging them and messing up the dining room, the kitchen, the bathroom and bedrooms, so it would look like a house where we'd been living for several days. Then he went shopping and I stayed in one of the rooms, lying on the bed and watching a tiny portable television. I hadn't recovered from the fear or the exhaustion. I fell asleep. When my father woke me up I didn't know where I was. Someone had turned off the TV and the light in the room was on. My arm didn't hurt; I vaguely sensed that it was night-time. There's some-one out there who wants to talk to you, my father whispered. He'd crouched down beside me; running his hand down my other arm he added: It's a policeman. He didn't say anything else. He stood up, left the room and Inspector Cuenca came in.'

'Did you know him?'

'Of course. And he knew me. We'd often seen each other in the district and he'd interrogated me at least a couple of times. That night he interrogated me too. Standing beside the bed, without asking me to get up – I had sat up just a bit: I was sitting on the mattress with my legs flexed and my back leaning against the wall – he asked the predictable questions and I gave him the answers my father had told me to say. While I was speaking I read in the inspector's eyes that he wasn't believing me; he didn't believe me: when the interrogation was over he told me to get dressed, to pack some clothes in a bag, that I had to go with him. I'll wait outside, he said, and walked out of the room.

'I realized that all was lost. I don't know exactly what happened during the minutes that followed. I know that fear suffocated me and I didn't obey the inspector and didn't get up off the bed; I know that I battled the imminence of the catastrophe by imploring in silence that all that had happened over the past three months hadn't happened or had been a dream, and that I implored as if I were crying or as if I were praying, begging for a miracle. No miracle occurred, although what did happen is the closest thing to a miracle that has happened in my life. And do you know what it was?'

'What?'

'Nothing. At some point the door to my room opened and Inspector Cuenca appeared. Naturally, I thought it was the end. But it wasn't; in fact, it was the beginning. Because what happened was that Inspector Cuenca just stood there, silent, standing still, looking at me for a couple of endless seconds. And then he left.

'Nothing else happened that night. Inspector Cuenca slammed the door on his way out, and after a moment my father came back into the room and sat down beside me on the bed. His face was as rigid as wax. As for me, at that moment I realized I was sitting on top of sheets that were drenched in sweat. I asked my father what had happened and he said nothing. I asked him what was going to happen. Nothing, he repeated. Although I had just woken up, I had the feeling of not having slept for months; I must have looked it, because my father added: Go to sleep. Obedient, as if I'd just suffered a sudden regression to childhood, I slid down and stretched out, not caring about the dampness of the sheets, and the last thing I noticed before sinking into sleep was my father getting up off the bed.'

8

'Up until the beginning of July I wasn't really pursuing Zarco's gang. Why did it take me so long? Well because, as I said, up till then I hadn't managed to find a clue – the clue I dragged out of Vedette – and I didn't have the slightest suspicion that the gang I was after was Zarco's gang.

'Why should I lie to you: from the start I was too optimistic, thought it was going to be an easy job. After all my idea was that I was confronting a group of kids, and I didn't think it would be complicated to catch them; the reality is that it took me more than two months to break up the gang. This delay can, of course, be put down to the fact that Zarco was razor sharp and knew every trick in the book; but it's especially down to the fact that, at least during the month of July, my bosses' interest in catching Zarco and his gang was more theoretical than actual, and I could never count on the support and men that I needed. The summer, moreover, was a bad time to do a job like that: you can imagine that between people off on holiday and Operation Summer – a surveillance measure that came into effect for the season every year on the Costa Brava – the station was often down to a skeleton staff. The first result of those two things was that, although I tried to make Deputy Superintendent Martínez and Inspector Vives understand that Mejía, Hidalgo and I couldn't cope and that without more help we would take a lot longer to accomplish the mission we'd been assigned, they always had good arguments to refuse my requests for reinforcements; and the second result was that, since neither Hidalgo nor Mejía gave up their vacation time, and since both of them were sometimes detailed to Operation Summer (especially as bodyguards for politicians on holiday), I often found myself working on my own, wandering the alleys and strip clubs of the red-light district looking for a clue that would guarantee that the criminal gang I was after was Zarco's gang and give me the chance to catch them.

'At the beginning of August I thought the chance had arrived. That was when we arrested several members of the gang after they tried to rob a farmhouse in Pontós, near Figueras, and they crashed their car on the Bàscara bridge while trying to outrun a police car; one of them died in the accident and another ended up a quadriplegic, but I was able to interview the other two in the station. During the interrogations I confirmed without any room for doubt that the gang I was looking for was Zarco's gang. That was the good news; the bad news was that I realized that Zarco wasn't a typical *quinqui* like the others and catching him was going to be more difficult than I'd thought. The two gang members I interrogated were called Chino and Drácula. I knew them from the district, just like the rest, and I knew they were Zarco's subordinates and not tough guys, so, when I started interrogating them, what I was after was not to charge them with the frustrated robbery of the farmhouse in Pontós and a few other jobs – I was already taking that for granted – what I wanted, as well, was for them to give up Zarco and the rest of the gang, but especially Zarco, because I was sure that bringing down Zarco would bring down the whole gang. Although to be honest, that's also what I would have been after if Chino and Drácula had been tough guys and hadn't just been mere subordinates.'

'I don't understand.'

'What I mean is that back then everything was possible in the station, not like now, for us that was still a time of – how shall I put it? – impunity; there's no other word: although Franco had been dead for three years, at the station we did whatever we liked, which is what we'd always done. That's the reality; later, as I say, things changed, but that's what it was like then. And, frankly, in those circumstances, it was unlikely that a sixteen-year-old kid, no matter how tough, would endure, without caving in and singing everything singable, the seventy-two hours we could hold him in a station house before bringing him before a judge, seventy-two hours without the right to a lawyer that the kid would spend between a darkened cell and interrogations lasting hours and hours during which the odd fist might slip, and that would be a best-case scenario for him. Frankly difficult, like I say. So imagine my surprise when Chino and Drácula held out. How do you like that? The thing is that's the way it went: they took all they had no choice but to take, but they didn't give up Zarco.'

'Do you have an explanation for that display of bravery?'

'Sure: that it was no display of bravery; in other words: Chino and Drácula were more scared of Zarco than they were of me. That's why I said that was when I realized that Zarco was a real tough guy and catching him was going to be harder than I'd thought.'

'I'm surprised you say Zarco was a real tough guy; for some reason I'd got the idea that you thought he was just unfortunate.'

'And he was. But real tough guys are almost always unfortunate men.'

'It also surprises me to hear you say his friends were scared of him.'

'You mean the kids in his gang? Why does that surprise you? The soft ones fear the tough guys. And, maybe with the odd exception, the kids in Zarco's gang were softies; so they were scared of him. Starting with Chino and Drácula.'

'How can you be so sure?'

'I told you already: because, if they hadn't been very afraid of Zarco, they wouldn't have spent seventy-two hours in the station house without giving him up. Believe me. I was with them during those three days and I know what I'm talking about. And as far as whether or not Zarco was really a tough guy, just look at what he did after Guille's death and the arrest of the others.'

'What do you mean?'

'Getting hold of guns and starting to hold up banks.'

'I've heard that back then it was less dangerous to rob a bank than a gas station or a grocery store.'

'That's what Zarco said.'

'And isn't it true?'

'I don't know. It's true that the person behind the counter of a gas station or a grocery store was sometimes the proprietor and might feel tempted to resist the robbery, while the employees of banks would almost never entertain such crazy thoughts for the simple reason that they wouldn't lose anything in the robbery of the bank, which anyway had the deposits in all their branches insured and gave their employees orders that in the case of a heist not to run needless risks and hand over the money without a second thought; and it's also true that back then we hadn't imposed the security measures on banks that two or three years later were obligatory and finally ended the craze for bank robberies: armed guards, double entrance doors for branches, security cameras, bullet-proof enclosures for the tellers, hidden retractable drawers, correlatively numbered bank notes, push buttons that activated alarms that sounded in the headquarters or even at the police stations . . . Anyway: all that's true. But, man, it's also true that it takes balls to walk into a bank armed with a rifle, threaten the employees and customers and make off with the money that's there; especially if you're sixteen years old, don't you think?'

'Yes.'

'Well, that's what Zarco started to do in the middle of that summer. And by doing that he began to run greater risks every time. And, the greater the risks he ran, the closer we came to the moment of catching him.

'It seemed to be coming, but it didn't arrive. During the month of August, while the pressure from my bosses grew to crush this gang as soon as possible, we were on the brink of catching them a couple of times (one afternoon at the beginning of August, near Sils, after they hit a gas station that we knew they'd been lurking around the previous day because the owner had filed a complaint, Hidalgo and Mejía chased them by car until flipping over on an embankment while they got away; in Figueras, a couple of weeks later, a Civil Guard thought he recognized them outside a bank and followed them for several kilometres, but also ended up losing them). The fact is that by the beginning of September I was desperate: I'd been working on the case for two months and things had only got worse; Deputy Superintendent Martínez and Inspector Vives knew it, so when they came back from their holidays they put me between a rock and a hard place: either I solved the problem or they'd have to assign someone else to solve it. Relieving me of the case would have been a tremendous failure, so I got my act together and in the second week of September found out that Zarco's gang was going to hold up a bank in Bordils.'

'How did you find out?'

'I found out.'

'Who told you?'

'I can't tell you that. There are things a policeman cannot say.'

'Even when thirty years have gone by since they happened?'

'Even if sixty had gone by. Look, I once read a novel where one character said to another: Can you keep a secret? And the other replied: If you can't keep it yourself, why should I keep it for you? We cops are like priests: if we're no good at keeping secrets, we're no good as cops. And I'm good at being a cop. Even if the secret is a trivial one.'

'Is this one?'

'Do you know any that aren't?'

'Cañas thinks he was responsible. Apparently, two days before the Bordils hold-up he was drinking beer with Córdoba, an old district character he'd befriended.'

'I remember that guy.'

'Cañas thinks he might have got carried away and told Córdoba about the planned heist and Córdoba took the tale to you.'

'It's not true. But if it was true I'd still tell you it wasn't true. So don't insist.'

'I won't insist. Go on about the Bordils hold-up.'

'What do you want me to tell you? I suppose, when I add it all up, it's one of the most complicated operations I set up in my whole career. I can't say I didn't have the time and resources to prepare it, but the truth is I was so reckless that Zarco and company were on the brink of getting away. My only justification is that back then I was an ambitious greenhorn and I'd expended so much effort to nab Zarco that I didn't want to put him in jail just to have him released a few months later. That's why the operation I set up was designed to catch Zarco once he'd committed the heist and not before, so the crime he'd be charged with wouldn't be a minor offence or an attempted offence and that the judge could lock him away for a good long time. Of course, letting Zarco act in this way, not arresting him before he went into the branch office and held up the bank, meant running an enormous risk, a risk I shouldn't have run and only a couple of years later wouldn't have run. Keep in mind that we couldn't give the manager or employees of the branch prior warning, so they wouldn't let the cat out of the bag and not to alarm them over nothing, because we couldn't be sure our tip-off was good, or even, supposing it was true, that Zarco wouldn't back out at the last minute. In any case, the truth is that Martínez and Vives came through, they trusted me and gave me command of the operation and half the squad: eight police inspectors in four undercover radio cars. Those were the forces at my disposal. First thing in the morning I put a car on the way into town and, as time went on, the rest of us set about positioning ourselves discreetly (one on the way out of town, another in the parking lot to the left of the branch and mine twenty metres in front of it), in such a way that, when we finally saw Zarco and two of his guys go into the branch after midday, the trap was set to close around them.

'But, in spite of all that preparation, everything seemed to go wrong straight away. Three or four minutes had passed when a shot was fired inside the branch; almost immediately there was another. When we heard them, the first thing I did was alert the other cars and tell those on the way in and out of town to cut off access to the highway; then I called the station and told them I'd changed plans and was going in. I didn't finish talking: at that moment Zarco and the other two kids who'd gone in with him came out of the branch taking the stockings off their heads. I shouted at them to halt, but they didn't stop and, since I was afraid they were going to escape, I fired a shot; beside me, Mejía fired too. It was no use, and before we knew it the three of them had jumped in the car and were fleeing towards Gerona. We went after them, saw them charge into the car blocking the ramp onto the highway and carry on, and then I had a good idea. I knew that, in a car chase, they'd have the upper hand, not because the car they were driving was better than ours, but because they drove as if they knew no fear, so I called the station and talked to Deputy Superintendent Martínez and told him that, if he didn't send us one of the helicopters they were using for Operation Summer, the armed robbers would get away again. Again Martínez came through for me and the helicopter soon appeared and thanks to it we didn't lose their trail (or we lost it but we found it again). Finally their car overturned as they took the curve onto La Barca Bridge, on the way into the city, and that was the end of Zarco.

'It happened more or less like this. We arrived at the bridge just after they'd flipped over, just when they were crawling out of the car, which had stopped upside down on the asphalt. There were four of us, two cars, we stopped twenty or thirty metres from the accident and, when we saw the robbers take off running across the bridge, we ran after them. Although there had been four in the car, there were three running, and we instantly recognized Zarco, but not the other two, or not with certainty. One of my officers stayed to examine the overturned car and, when we got to the other side of the bridge, I shouted to the other to run after one of them, who'd fled on his own in the direction of Pedret. Mejía and I followed Zarco and the other kid. We were lucky: on the way into La Devesa Park Zarco tripped and fell and broke his ankle, and that's how we caught him.'

'And the other one?'

'The one who was with Zarco? If you've been talking about this with Cañas, you already know what happened: he got away.'

'You didn't follow him? You let him get away?'

'Neither. What happened is that Zarco kept us busy long enough that Gafitas was able to get away.'

'Do you think he did it on purpose?'

'I don't know.'

'Were you sure the guy who'd got away was Gafitas?'

'No, but that was my impression, and Mejía's too. What I was sure of (I think I told you this already) is that, as soon as we brought Zarco down, the gang was finished.

'And it was. That very evening I began to interrogate Zarco and the other two members of his gang we'd nabbed that afternoon, who turned out to be two kids called Jou and Gordo (Gordo, who lost consciousness in the accident on La Barca, I interrogated a few hours after he'd been admitted to hospital; Zarco didn't even get there: a doctor put a cast on his leg in the station house). The interrogation lasted the regulation three days but there was no surprise; it wasn't even a surprise that from the start all three detainees piled as much shit as they could at the doors of Guille and Tío, who could take all the shit in the world because one was dead and the other quadraplegic. I don't know if it was a strategy they'd prepared beforehand, in case they got caught, or if it occurred to each one on their own, but it was the most sensible thing they could do. Of course it didn't surprise me that Zarco was astute enough not to cop to any more than strictly necessary either, and much less that he didn't give anyone up for anything; I knew this was what was going to happen: not only because Zarco was the toughest in the gang and the one with most experience, but also because he was their leader, and a leader loses all his authority if he turns into an informer. However, I did get Gordo and Jou to give up Zarco for a couple of things (I tricked them: I told them he'd already copped to it himself, and they swallowed it), but I didn't get them to give up Gafitas, or the girls or any of the others who'd participated at some point in the gang's misdemeanours without actually being part of it. This didn't matter to me too much – why should I lie to you – because, like I said, I thought that once I'd thrown the book at Zarco the gang would be out of action, and sooner rather than later the fringes would end up coming undone and falling of their own accord. So I rushed through the interrogations, took the greatest of care writing up the affidavit and put Zarco and the rest before a judge. And that was it: the judge sent them to the Modelo prison to await trial and I never saw Zarco again. In person, I mean; like everyone else, I later saw him often on TV, in magazines, newspapers and such. But that's another story, and you know it better than I do. Are we done?'

'More or less. Can I ask you one last question?'

'Sure.'

'What happened with Gafitas? Did he end up falling of his own accord?'

'Why don't you ask him?'

'I've got Cañas' version already.'

'I'm sure it's right.'

'I don't doubt it. But I'd like to hear yours as well. Why don't you want to tell me?'

'Because I've never told anybody.'

'That makes it even more interesting.'

'It's got nothing to do with your book.'

'Maybe not, but that doesn't matter.'

'Will you give me your word that you're not going to use what I tell you?'

'Yes.'

'OK. You'll see. At dusk on the day I arrested Zarco I showed up alone at Gafitas' house. I didn't want to waste time: I'd just interrogated Zarco and his two accomplices in the Bordils bank robbery for the first time at the station and, while I left the three of them stewing in their cells before waking them up in the early hours to begin the interrogation again, I decided to go after him, who was the one I suspected of being the fourth. As soon as his mother opened the door I knew I'd guessed right. It wasn't the poor woman's terror that betrayed her but the huge efforts she was making to hide her terror. She was so distraught that she didn't even ask me why I was looking for her son, all she managed to say was that for the last week he had been with his father at a friend's place, in Colera, taking advantage of the last days of the holidays; then, before I had time to ask for it, she gave me the address. An hour later I got to Colera, an isolated little seaside village, near the border at Portbou. I asked where the house was and found it not far from the beach; it was dark and looked uninhabited, but there was a car by the door. I parked beside it. I let a few seconds pass. I went and rang the bell.

'It was his father who opened the door, a man in his forties, thin, dark-haired with no grey, who at first glance looked very little like his son. I introduced myself, told him I wanted to talk to Gafitas; he answered that he was sleeping at that moment and asked me what I wanted to talk to him for. I explained. There must be a mistake, he replied. I was with my son all morning out at sea. Are there any witnesses to that? I asked. Me, he answered. No one else? I asked. No one else, he answered. That's a shame, I said, and added: In any case I still need to talk to your son. With a gesture that combined resignation and surprise, the man invited me in and, as we walked through the dining room, told me that he and his son had been in Colera for a week and had been going out fishing every day, although that morning they'd come back earlier than usual because of an accident. My son got a scratch from a lure when he was casting, he told me. On his arm. It was a bit gory but nothing serious; we didn't even have to go to the doctor: I saw to it myself. When we got to the door of a room he asked me to wait there while he woke him up. I waited, seconds later he showed me into the room and I asked him to leave me alone with his son.

'He agreed. Gafitas and I talked for a while, him sitting up in bed leaning against the wall, with his arm bandaged and his legs wrapped in a tangle of sweat-drenched sheets, me standing at the foot of the bed. Just as with his mother, I only needed to look in his eyes – more bewildered than frightened behind the lenses of his glasses – to know what I already knew: that he was the fourth man in the hold-up of the Bordils bank. I asked him a couple of procedural questions, which he answered with fake composure; then I told him to get dressed and bring a change of clothes, and finally I told him I'd wait for him in the dining room. He didn't even want to know where we were going.

'I walked out of the room and told the father I was arresting his son. The father listened without facing me, sitting in a rocking chair in front of the empty fireplace, and didn't turn around. In a whisper he said: It's a mistake. Maybe so, I accepted. But a judge will have to decide. That's not what I mean, he clarified, turning towards me in the rocking chair, and looking at him I had the impression that he'd just removed a mask with features very simi-lar to his own; when he spoke again I didn't note in his voice supplication or anguish or sorrow: just total seriousness. I don't know if my son has done what you say he's done, he explained. I'm not saying he didn't. But we've talked and he's told me he's sorry. I believe him; I'm only asking that you believe him too. My son is a good kid: you can be sure of that. Besides, everything that's happened is not his fault. Have you got children? He waited for me to shake my head. Of course, you're still very young, he went on. But I'll tell you one thing in case you do have some one day: loving your children is very easy; what's difficult is seeing things from their perspective. I didn't know how to put myself in my son's shoes, and that's why what happened has happened. It won't happen again. I guarantee it. As for you, what will you gain from putting him in prison? Think about it. Nothing. You told me you've arrested the ringleader, that you've broken up the gang; well, now you've got what you wanted. You'll gain nothing from putting my son in jail, I tell you, or you'll only create another criminal, because my son is not a criminal now but he'd come out of prison converted into one. You know it better than I do. What is it you're asking of me?, I cut him off, feeling uncomfortable. Without an instant's hesitation he answered: That you give my son a chance. He's very young, he'll mend his ways and this will end up just being a bad memory. He's made mistakes, but he won't make them again. Forget about all this, Inspector. Go home and forget about my son. Forget we ever met. You and I don't know each other, you haven't been here tonight, you never entered this house, never spoke to me, it's as if this never happened. My son and I will be eternally grateful. And you'll thank yourself too.

'Gafitas' father stopped talking. During the silence that followed, as I held his gaze, I thought of my father, an old Civil Guard about to retire back in Cáceres, and said to myself that he would have done the same thing for me that Gafitas' father was doing for his son, and that he might be right. You might be right, I said. But I can't do what you're asking of me. Your son has made a mistake, and he has to pay for it. The law is the same for everyone; if it weren't, we'd be living in the jungle. You understand, right? There was a silence and then I went on: For my part I understand, and I'll do what I can to soften the affidavit; with a bit of luck and a good lawyer he won't spend more than a year or a year and a half in prison. I'm sorry. That's all I can do. I expected Gafitas' father would answer, maybe had the silly expectation that he'd admit I was right, or partially right; he didn't, of course, but he nodded his head slightly as if he did, took a deep breath and, without a word, turned back to the fireplace and slumped back down in the rocking chair.

'I waited for Gafitas, but, since he didn't come out, without saying anything to his father I went to get him. When I opened the door to his room I found him exactly as I'd left him: sitting on the bed and leaning against the wall, his bare legs sticking out of a tangle of sweaty sheets; exactly as I'd left him or almost: the difference was that there was no longer any trace of the faked composure and his eyes weren't the bewildered and startled eyes of Gafitas, but those of a little boy or those of a rabbit dazzled by the headlights of the car about to run over him. And then, instead of demanding he get dressed and come with me, I stood there in the doorway, quietly staring at him, without thinking anything, without saying anything. I don't know how long I was there; all I know is that, when the time passed, I turned around and left. How do you like that?'

'I don't know.'

'Me neither.'

'Is that the end of the story?'

'Almost. The rest isn't of much interest any more. Although this is a small city and everybody knows each other here and everybody's paths cross, I didn't see Gafitas again for a long time. I did see his father a couple of times, in the street, and both times he recognized me, looked at me and greeted me with an almost invisible nod, without approaching or saying anything to me. Gafitas reappeared many years later, ten or twelve at least, but by then he was no longer Gafitas but Ignacio Cañas, recently graduated from Barcelona and starting to make a professional name for himself in the city. The first few times we met in that period we pretended not to know each other, didn't even say hello, but at the beginning of the nineties I was named the civil governor's security advisor and, since the civil government building is almost right across the street from Cañas' office, we began to see each other with some frequency and more than once we had to talk about work-related things. That was when our interaction changed; I won't say we became friends, but we did maintain a cordial relationship. Needless to say we never talked about the past, about when we'd met and how we'd met and such. In fact, I think a moment arrived when I almost forgot that Ignacio Cañas had been Gafitas, just as he must have forgotten that I'd been the same cop that had pursued them, him and Zarco's gang, through the dives of the district. Later I left my job at the civil government and Cañas and I practically stopped seeing each other. And that is the end of the story.

'And now we are done, right?'

9

'After the robbery of the Bordils branch of the Banco Popular and Inspector Cuenca's visit to Colera, my father and I stayed in the village for several more days. I don't know why, though I imagine that the fact that the morning after our arrival I woke up with a fever must have had something to do with it. It was a Thursday, and for forty-eight hours my temperature remained high and I didn't get out of bed, sweaty and tortured by nightmares of persecution and prison, victim of a simple summer cold according to the doctor who came to see me, victim of a panic attack as I now believe. My father didn't leave my side. He brought me fruit, water and instant soup and spent hours sitting by my bed, reading newspapers and cheap novels that he bought at the kiosk in the plaza, barely speaking or asking any questions, whispering into the phone in the dining room every once in a while to my mother, who he convinced to stay home.

'On the Saturday I felt better and I got up, but I didn't go outside. That was when my father's questions started coming. There were so many, or I had so much to tell him, that we spent the whole morning talking. Right after the bank robbery in Bordils, in the bathroom at home and during the trip to Colera, I had told my father the basics; now I told him everything, point by point: from the day Batista moved to our school to the day of the bank robbery in Bordils. My father listened to me without interrupting, and when I finished made me promise not to set foot in the red-light district again and to go back to school as soon as classes began; he in turn promised that Batista would not bother me again. I asked him how he was going to manage that; he answered that when he got back to work he'd talk to his father, and asked me to forget about the matter.

'For lunch we ate a roast chicken with potatoes that my father bought in the village restaurant and in the afternoon we watched a movie on TV. When it ended, my father went to turn it off, but just at that moment I noticed that an episode of *The Water Margin* was starting and I asked him to leave it on. It wasn't just any episode: it was the final one. I had almost stopped following the series when I'd joined Zarco's gang and, as soon as the episode began, it struck me that it seemed to belong to the same series and at the same time to a different series. The opening, for example. It was the same as ever, but changed at the same time, because the images, which were the same as ever, now meant other things: now the ragtag army of men on foot and horseback carrying weapons and standards was a known army, an army formed by honourable men who in the previous episodes had been cast out beyond the confines of the law by the evil Kao Chiu and who, episode by episode, had been joining up with Lin Chung and the rest of the honourable outlaws of Liang Shan Po. The phrase recited in a voice-over at the beginning of each instalment ("The ancient sages said: Do not despise the snake for having no horns, for who is to say it will not become a dragon. So may one just man become an army") now also had another meaning: it was no longer conjecture but fact, because Lin Chung had now become an army and the snake without horns had become a dragon. At least that's how I have always remembered the opening of the episode and the whole episode: the same and different. And a couple of nights ago, knowing I was going to talk to you about the days in Colera, my curiosity was piqued and I downloaded the episode and confirmed that it was just as I remembered it. Shall I tell you?'

'Go ahead.'

'As the episode begins, Lin Chung and the outlaws of Liang Shan Po are threatening the capital city of China, where Kao Chiu, the emperor's favourite, has his lord practically sequestered and the population subjugated by martial law, misery and fear. Kao Chiu has devised a plan to take power: he means to take advantage of the fear of war provoked by the arrival at the gates of the capital of the army from Liang Shan Po with the aim of accusing the emperor of weakness, assassinating him and founding a dynasty of his own. To thwart this strategy, Lin Chung opts to strike with a *coup de main*; he and his deputies will infiltrate the city, get to the emperor, reveal Kao Chiu's deceit and then do away with him. The *coup de main* is successful and, thanks to Lin Chung's courage and cleverness and that of his deputies, the capital rises up against the tyranny and Kao Chiu is left with no choice but to flee the city in defeat.

'Here begins a sort of epilogue that abandons the realism of the series to delve into a hallucination. Kao Chiu flees across a desert of black sand in the company of several soldiers who collapse one by one, weakened by hunger and thirst, until the emperor's former favourite is left alone and, as he falls from his horse, which runs off, and drags himself pitifully across the sand, reality dissolves around him in a delirium inhabited by his victims from times gone by, with threatening expressions on their faces, with illusory lances, horses, riders, standards and fires that drive him mad and threaten to devour him, until the Liang Shan Po men finally find him and Lin Chung kills him in single combat. This is the finale of the adventure, but not of the episode or the series, which ends with two didactic speeches: the first is delivered by Lin Chung and it is a speech to his deputies in which he announces that, although they have now defeated evil in the form of Kao Chiu, evil can return in other forms and they must remain ever vigilant, ready to fight and defeat it, because Liang Shan Po is not really just the name of a river but rather an eternal symbol, the symbol of the struggle against injustice; the second speech is delivered by an off-camera voice and it is a prophesy: while Lin Chung and his deputies ride off into the sunset, the voice-over announces that the heroes of Liang Shan Po will reappear whenever necessary to prevent the triumph of injustice on earth.

'That last image is no more than flatulent cliché, a postcard sweetened by epic sentimentalism, but when I saw it that afternoon, in Higinio Redondo's summer home, I burst into tears; I'm lying: actually I'd already been crying for a long time. I cried for a long time there, in silence, sitting almost in the dark beside my father in that half-empty dining room of some house in a village in the back of beyond, with a despair I neither recognized nor recalled, with the feeling of having suddenly puzzled out the complete meaning of the word failure and having discovered an unknown flavour, which was the taste of adult life.

'That happened on a Saturday. Sunday morning we drove back to Gerona, and that day and the following ones I was anxious. Classes were just about to start again and, as I told you, I'd promised my father that I would go back to school and not go back to the red-light district. I kept my word, at least as far as the district was concerned (and intended to keep it about school as soon as I could). No, the anxiety didn't come from that side; it didn't come from my family either: suddenly, in just a few days, my relationship with them went from being very bad to being very good and, as if we'd all decided to respect a code of silence, nobody at home mentioned the escape to Colera or the circumstances surrounding it again. I insist: the anxiety was not from there; it came from the uncertainty. I didn't understand why Inspector Cuenca hadn't arrested me in Colera, and feared that at any moment he might come back to my house and arrest me. Also, during the feverish days in Colera I'd begun to nurture the suspicion that it could have been me whose tongue had slipped before the bank robbery in Bordils, unintentionally provoking the police ambush, and I was scared that Zarco, Gordo and Jou would have arrived at the conclusion that I had provoked it intentionally and had decided to inform on me in revenge. So I was plagued by a dilemma during those days. I didn't want to break the promise I'd made to my father not to go to the district and I didn't want to run the risk entailed in going to the district (especially the risk of bumping into Inspector Cuenca), but at the same time I wished I could go there. I wanted to know if Zarco, Gordo and Jou were going to give me up or had already given me up and if any of the others had been arrested and were thinking of giving me up, but most of all I wanted to see Tere: I wanted to make clear to her that I hadn't given anybody up or caused the police ambush outside the bank in Bordils, at least not on purpose; I also wanted to make myself clear about her, because, although part of me was starting to feel that she'd been left behind and had just been a strange and fleeting summer fling, another part was feeling that I was still in love with Tere and I wanted to tell her that, now that Zarco was off the scene, nothing was standing in our way.

'On the Tuesday at midday I resolved my dilemma: I went to the district without going to the district; in other words: I went to the prefabs to look for Tere. I told you some days ago that I'd never been there and didn't know exactly where they were; the only thing I'd known since I was little was that they were just across from La Devesa on the other side of the Ter. So I walked from one side of La Devesa to the other (retracing in reverse the route I'd taken the previous week, as I escaped from the police after the bank robbery in Bordils), left the park and crossed La

Barca Bridge. On the other side I turned left, went down some steps that led to the river bank, went back up and, walking along a dirt track, passed by a wheat field, a farmhouse with three palm trees by the door and a ravine where reeds, poplars, willows, ash and plane trees all grew together. The prefabs stood at the end of the track. As I also told you some days ago, I had always had a vague and legendary idea about the prefabs, adorned by romantic suggestions from adventure novels, and somehow none of the anecdotes and comments about them I'd heard that summer in Zarco's gang had done anything to contradict it; on the contrary: those stories had been the perfect fuel for my imagination to add to the prefabs epic tinges of honourable outlaws from a Japanese television series.

'That's as far as my fantasies went: as I got closer to the prefabs I began to understand that the reality had nothing to do with them.

'At first sight the prefabs struck me as a sort of workers' housing colony composed of six rows of semi-detached barrack huts, with concrete walls, corrugated roofs and floors raised a few centimetres above the ground, but as I walked along one of the streets that separated the barracks – a street that was not a street but a mire that stank of sewage where swarms of flies hovered above naked babies, domestic animals and heaps of junk, from empty rabbit cages to broken bedsprings and old or useless cars – I began to feel that, rather than workers' housing, that garbage dump was the apotheosis of misery. Fascinated and disgusted at once, I kept going, jumping over streams of foul water, leaving behind the barracks whose walls had once been white, bonfires in broad daylight, children with dirty faces and children on bicycles who stared at me with indifference and mistrust. I went on sleep-walking, my courage shrinking by the second, and when I reached the end of a street I snapped out of it and was about to turn around and flee, but at that moment I noticed a woman watching me from the door of the last barrack hut, just a few steps away from me. She was an obese woman, with extremely white flesh, sitting in an office chair; she had a baby in her arms, her hair wrapped in a dark scarf, her big eyes fixed on me. The woman asked me what I was looking for and I asked after Tere. Since I didn't know her surname, I started to describe her, but, before I could finish, the woman told me where she lived: In the third hut on the last street, she said. And she added: The one closest to the river.

'The barracks hut where Tere lived was identical to all the rest, except for the fact that a double row of clothes were hung out to dry across the front and a slightly taller television antenna stuck out of the roof. It had two windows closed with blinds, but the door was ajar; as I pushed it I heard some cartoon laughter, my nostrils were saturated with a sickly-sweet smell and, as I stepped over the threshold, I took in the whole dwelling in a single glance. It was barely forty square metres lit by a couple of naked bulbs and divided into three separate spaces by curtains: in the main space there was a woman cooking on a portable stove, with a dog curled up at her feet, three children were glued to the TV on a sofa made out of a sheet of wood and a mattress, and, beside them, sitting on a folding chair by a brazier table, a very young mother was breastfeeding a baby; in the secondary spaces I just saw some mattresses lying on the floor on top of a bed of straw. Tere was standing on one of them, in front of an open chest of drawers, with a pile of folded clothes in her hands.

'As soon as I stepped inside everybody turned towards me, including the dog, who stood up and growled. Noticing that Tere was blushing, I blushed and, before anyone could say a word, my friend left the clothes on top of the chest of drawers, grabbed me by the arm, said she'd be right back and dragged me outside. A couple of steps away from the door to the hut she asked: What are you doing here? Looking for you, I answered. I just wanted to know if you were all right. Have you got any news of Zarco and the other guys? My words seemed to calm Tere, who soon went from defensive surprise to curiosity: as if she hadn't heard me, she pointed to the bandage on my arm and asked what had happened. I began to tell her about the bank robbery in Bordils. She didn't interrupt me until I explained that the police were waiting for us when we came out. They must have got a tip-off, she said. Yeah, I said. Then she said she wasn't surprised, and I looked at her uncomprehending. She clarified: It's Zarco's fault. As soon as I told him I couldn't go with you guys he started talking to anyone who would listen; and it never fails: when you talk to anyone who will listen you end up talking to someone you shouldn't have talked to. He was the first to make the rule and the first to break it.

'You can't imagine how relieved I was to hear Tere say that. Free of the need to demonstrate that I'd had nothing to do with the tip-off, I continued my tale, though I didn't say anything about what had happened after our car rolled over on La Barca Bridge: nothing about Zarco's arrest, nothing about fleeing to Colera with my father, nothing about Inspector Cuenca's visit to Higinio Redondo's house. When I finished, Tere told me what she knew about Zarco, Gordo and Jou. She told me that the three of them were all right, though Zarco had a cast on one leg, and that, after having been interrogated at the station house over three days and nights, they'd been handed over to a judge, who'd sent them to Barcelona and had them locked up in the Modelo. Now they're awaiting trial, Tere concluded. But who knows how long that'll take; you know how long ago Chino and Drácula got nabbed and they're still waiting. But nobody's going to save them from four or five years, that's for sure: they're going to have to take the rap for the guns, car theft, bank robbery and at least three or four other charges. Not as bad as it could have been, but it won't be nothing. They haven't said anything about us, nothing about you, nothing about me or anybody else, and they won't. If you were worried about that, you can forget it.

'I was a little humiliated that Tere guessed what I was thinking; but only a little: by then the opinion Tere might have of me had begun to stop mattering. While she kept talking I glimpsed over her shoulder, across the river and into the trees, no more than three hundred metres away, the apartment blocks on Caterina Albert, and at that moment I thought – it was the first time I thought this – that my house and the prefabs were at once very close and very far apart, and only then did I feel that it was really true that I wasn't like them. Suddenly all that had happened over the past months seemed unreal, and it felt comforting to know that I belonged on the other side of the river and that the waters of the blue border had now returned to their course; I suddenly understood that I had cleared up my feelings about Tere and that Tere had just been a strange and fleeting summer fling.

Tere kept talking while I had started to look for a way to get out of there. She was talking about Zarco; she was saying that, whatever sentence was passed on him, he wouldn't spend much time in prison. He'll escape as soon as he can, she said. And that'll be soon. I nodded, but made no comment. Two little boys on bikes followed by a dog went by a couple of metres from where we were, splashing mud on my shoes. Just then the hut door opened and the sounds of a fake gunfight and a real baby crying came from inside at the same time as the head of the girl I'd seen breast-feeding the baby peeked out and told Tere she was needed. I'll be right there, answered Tere, and the door closed again. Tere touched the beauty spot beside her nose; instead of going in she asked: Have you been back to La Font? No, I answered. Have you? Me neither, she answered. But if you want we could meet there tomorrow afternoon. I'm seeing Lina. I thought for a moment and said: OK. Tere smiled for the first time that day. Then she said goodbye and went into her house.

'The next day I didn't go to La Font and I didn't see Tere again until the middle of December. Over those three months of autumn I completely changed my life; or rather: in a certain sense I went back to my former life. The life I'd had before Tere, before Zarco, before Batista and before everything. Although, as I say, I only went back to it in a certain sense, because the person going back was no longer the same one. I told you when we started talking about Zarco: at the age of sixteen all borders are porous, or at least they were back then; and it's true that the border formed by the Ter and the Onyar rivers was as porous as that of the Liang Shan Po, or at least it was for me: three months before I had gone from being a middle-class *charnego* to being a *quinqui* from one day to the next, and three months later I stopped being a *quinqui* overnight and went back to being a middle-class *charnego*. Things were as simple as that. And as quick. The disbanding of Zarco's gang made it all easier, of course: most of them were in prison or not around any more, the ones who were still on the outside didn't come looking for me and I didn't go looking for them. That radical change in my relationship with my family also made it easier. I told you already that after those days in Colera my relationship with them became really good again and that, although my father knew everything that had happened that summer, he never asked me any more questions; my mother and my sister didn't either, so in my family it was as if what had happened that summer hadn't really happened.

'But what made my return to this side of the water margin irreversible was going back to school, or the way I went back to school. Term started two days after my visit to the prefabs. The first day of school started with a clear sunny morning, the sky a perfect blue and the football pitch gleaming as if it had just been watered. In the octagonal courtyard outside the entrance to our wing, while waiting for the doors to open and classes to start, I greeted some of my old Caterina Albert Street friends from a distance, but not Batista, who didn't show up first thing. In spite of that, I didn't even have a chance to consider the possibility that he might have changed schools because the teacher read out his name from the list when he took attendance.

'Batista came in halfway through the morning, though we didn't exchange a word until classes finished at lunchtime. I was on my way out by the back door, where the parking lot was, when, as I rounded the corner of the school cafeteria, I saw him a few metres away from me, leaning on the gas tank of his Lobito, which in turn was leaning against the wall; in front of him, talking to him, were all the guys: Matías, the Boix brothers, Intxausti, Ruiz, Canales, and maybe one or two others. As soon as I appeared they fell quiet and I knew it was a chance encounter; also, that I had no alternative: unless I wanted to avoid them ostentatiously or turn around and go back inside and out the front door of the school, I had no choice but to walk past Batista and the rest of them. Plucking up my courage I kept walking but before I walked by Batista he stood up from the Lobito and blocked my way by holding out his arm. I stopped. Long time no see, *catalanufo*, said Batista. Where've you been? I didn't answer. In light of the silence, Batista nodded at my bandaged arm. What's that?, he asked. A mosquito bite? I heard some nervous or stifled laughter; I didn't know who was laughing and didn't bother looking around to find out. Then, without having planned it, I answered in Catalan. No, I said. It was a bullet. Batista laughed loudly. You're so funny, Dumbo! he said. After a silence he added: Hey, don't tell me you're only going to speak in Catalan now? At that moment I turned to him, and got a surprise as I looked him in the eye. With an unexpected sensation of victory – feeling almost like Rocky

Balboa on my pinball machine, muscular and triumphant, wearing shorts with the American flag printed on them and raising my arms to the cheering stadium while a defeated boxer lies on the canvas in the ring – I realized that I didn't care if Batista called me Dumbo or called me a *catalanufo*. I realized that Batista was just a half-assed bully, a harmless loudmouth, a weak, spoilt brat, and I was astonished at myself for ever having been scared of him. Even more astonishing, I realized that I no longer felt any need to get revenge on him, because I didn't even hate him any more, and that's the best revenge.

'Batista held my gaze for a second, during which I was sure that he knew what I'd realized, what I was feeling. His laughter froze in his mouth and, as if in search of an explanation, he looked at Matías and the others; I don't know what he found, but he turned back to me and slowly, without taking his eyes off me – eyes in which there was no longer the slightest trace of sarcasm or contempt, only bafflement – lowered his arm. As I carried on towards the exit I said in Catalan, loud enough so that everyone would hear: Well, I'm not speaking Spanish to you, Batista. That day I had lunch with my father, my mother and my sister. After we'd finished, my father took me aside and asked how the first day of term had gone; he'd already asked during the meal, and I repeated my reply: I told him that everything had gone well; then I asked him if he'd already talked to Batista's father. Not yet, said my father. I was thinking I'd do it tomorrow. No, don't, I said. You don't need to any more. My father stared at me. It's all sorted out, I explained. Are you sure?, my father asked. Completely, I answered.

'I wasn't so sure, of course, but it turned out I wasn't wrong and our encounter in the school parking lot must have convinced Batista of the fact that over the summer I had changed from a serpent into a dragon. So Batista's first defeat was his last, and from the second day of term he seemed like a different person. He didn't bother me again, he avoided me systematically, barely spoke to me and, when he found himself obliged to do so, it was always in Catalan. My friends from Caterina Albert also seemed like different people: Matías immediately, and gradually the rest, began to distance themselves from Batista (or maybe he distanced himself from them) and tried to seek my friendship again, and I learned that power is lost as easily as it's gained and that one on one people are always inoffensive, but in groups we're not.

'The reconciliation with my friends from Caterina Albert Street was a done deal, but towards the middle of that autumn, without any shrillness or bad vibes, also without any explanation – as if it were obvious that our friendship had run its course and given all it had to give – I began to spend less time with them and more with a group of students doing their COU (*Curso de Orientación Universitaria*), in their final year of high school before going on to university. That's how I met the first girl I ever went out with. Her name was Montse Roura and, despite the fact that she wasn't doing her COU at the Marist Brothers' school (she was actually only in her second year, and with the Carmelites), she was part of the gang because her brother Paco was. Montse and Paco were from Barcelona, had moved to Gerona two years earlier, when they were orphaned, and they lived in a building with several of their aunts and uncles in the old part of the city, a building where they had a flat to themselves. This made them the centre of the group, because their door was always open and not many Friday or Saturday nights went by when we didn't get together at their place to listen to music, talk, drink and smoke. Also to take drugs, although that only happened once I'd started hanging out with them, simply because I was the only one who knew anything about them and how to get them, which turned me into the group's dealer. In short: that was a magnificent time in my life, full of changes. During the week I studied hard and on the weekends I cut loose with my friends and Montse. I recovered my self-esteem and then some. I signed a definitive peace accord with my parents. I almost forgot Zarco and Tere.

'It was my role as weekend drug dealer that led to my seeing Tere again. I already told you it happened in the middle of December; however, I haven't told you that on that day I was with two of my trusty escorts on those weekly incursions into the underworld: one was Paco Roura and the other Dani Omedes, another regular in our gang. Paco had passed his driving test that summer and had the use of a Seat 600 belonging to one of his uncles, so every Friday evening he'd drive me over to the Flor, in Salt, where a couple of the dealers Zarco, Tere and the rest of us used to buy drugs from in the summer still hung out: Rodri and Gómez. That evening neither of the two was in the bar, and no one could tell me where I might find them. We waited for more than an hour, and eventually had no choice but to start driving around the city, first looking for them and then looking for any small-time dealer. We asked here and there, a bit by chance, in some bars in Sant Narcís and in the old town – at the Avenida, at the Acapulco, L'Enderroc, La Trumfa, the Groc Pub – and didn't find anything. At some point I felt tempted to go back to La Font, but I resisted. It was almost ten when somebody told us about a bar in Vilarroja. Without much hope we went up to Vilarroja, found the bar, I left Paco and Dani in the car and went in.

'As soon as I was through the door I saw her. She was sitting at the back of the bar, a tiny place, filled with people and smoke, with porcelain plates adorning the walls; beside her, around a table full of beer bottles and overflowing ashtrays, were three guys and a girl. Before I could get over to her table, a smile of recognition lit up her face. She stood up, made her way through the crowd, came up to me and asked me the same question she'd asked three months earlier, when I went to look for her in the prefabs, except in a cheerful and not suspicious tone: What are you doing here, Gafitas? As I already told you, during those three months I'd almost forgotten Tere and, when I did remember her, I only remembered the domestic, miserable, defeated *quinqui* that I'd fled from that day in the shithole of the prefabs; now I saw her again as I'd seen her the first time I laid eyes on her at the Vilaró arcade and as I saw her all summer long: sure of herself, teasing and radiant, the most gorgeous girl I'd ever seen.

'I avoided her question by asking if she wanted a beer. She smiled, accepted, we went to the bar, ordered two beers and she asked again what I was doing there, on my own. I answered that I wasn't on my own, that two friends were waiting for me outside, in the car, and I asked her how she was. Fine, she answered. While they poured our beer it occurred to me that Tere could probably get me some gear, but also that I was obliged to ask another question. I asked the other question: How's Zarco? Tere replied that he was still in jail, that like Gordo and Jou, he was still awaiting trial in the Modelo, and that she'd gone to Barcelona two or three times to see him and he'd seemed fine. Then she went on: she told me that – unlike Zarco, Gordo and Jou – Chino and Drácula had been tried and sentenced to five years, which they were serving in the Modelo; she told me that she hadn't been going to La Font or the district for a few months now because after the arrest of Zarco and the others things had got ugly and there had been raids, arrests and beatings; she told me that the raids, arrests and beatings had not been confined to the district but had reached the prefabs and some bars in Salt and Germans Sàbat, that harassment from the cops had ended up dispersing the remnants of the gang and that, although none of the rest of them had been arrested, many people had ended up in jail. Do you remember the General and his wife?, asked Tere. Of course, I answered. He's in the nick, said Tere.

They accused him of selling weapons to Zarco. But they killed his wife. Well, they had to kill her: when the cops went to pick them up at their house, she started shooting at them; in the end she took one of the pigs down with her. Tere looked at me with an expression of joy or admiration, or maybe of pride. You see, she said. And there we were thinking the old gal was blind.

'She finished bringing me up to date with a piece of good news or what she considered good news: she didn't live in the prefabs any more; actually, the prefabs no longer existed: they'd torn them down and, just over a week earlier, the people who were still in them had been relocated to La Font de la Pòlvora, nearby, where they had gone from living in barrack huts to living in recently constructed flats in recently constructed tower blocks in a recently constructed neighbourhood. While Tere was talking about her new life in La Font de la Pòlvora, it occurred to me that the end of the prefabs meant the end of Liang Shan Po, the definitive end of the blue border, and when she finished talking I feared she would ask about my life since we'd last seen each other. Before she could change the subject I did. I need some hash, I said. I went to the Flor, but neither Rodri nor Gómez were there, and I've spent all evening trying to find some. You need it right now?, she asked. Yeah, I answered. How much?, she asked. Three *talegos* should do me, I answered. Tere nodded. Wait for me outside, she said.

'I paid for the beers, went outside and walked over to the field where my friends were waiting in the Seat 600. Dani rolled down the window and asked: What's up? We're in luck, I said, standing beside the car. Paco looked like he hadn't taken his hands off the steering wheel, as if he was ready to start the engine and get out of there. I hope so, he said. This place gives me the creeps. After a few minutes Tere came out of the bar and I walked over to meet her. She reached into the pocket of her raincoat and pulled out three thin little bars of hash wrapped in tinfoil; she handed them to me: I took them in one hand while passing her three one-thousand-peseta notes with the other. Having made the exchange, we looked at each other in the shadows, standing between the long light extending out the door of the bar and the circle of light shining from a nearby streetlamp. The night was damp and cold. We weren't very close to one another but the double spiral of vapour coming from our mouths seemed to envelop us in a shared mist. I pointed vaguely towards the Seat 600 and said: They're waiting for me. Three men came out of the bar and walked past us; while they walked away up the street talking, Tere turned towards them and, without taking my eyes off her in the dimly lit street, I suddenly thought of the washrooms of the arcade and Montgó beach and for a moment I wanted to kiss her and almost had to remind myself that I was no longer in love with her and that she had just been a strange and fleeting summer fling. Tere turned back to me. I have to meet some friends tonight, I said very quickly, with the feeling I'd been caught red-handed and that I'd already said that; I asked: Are you busy tomorrow? No, answered Tere. If you want we could meet up, I suggested. You're not going to stand me up this time?, asked Tere. I immediately knew she was referring to the last time we saw each other, at the door of her hut in the prefabs when we'd arranged to meet at La Font the next day as we said goodbye and then I didn't go. I didn't want to pretend that I'd forgotten. Not this time, I promised. She smiled. Where should we meet?, she said. Wherever you want, I said, and remembered the moment when Tere taught me, in the Marocco, that to dance you don't have to know how to dance you just have to want to move, and added: Do you still go to Rufus? Not any more, said Tere. But if you want we can meet there. OK, I said. OK, she repeated. She kissed me on the cheek, said see you tomorrow and went back inside the bar.

'I went back to the car. Have you got the hash?, asked Dani as soon as I opened the door. I said yes and, as he put the car into first gear and accelerated, Paco celebrated. Cool, he said. And the chick? What chick?, I asked. The one who sold you the gear, Paco said. What about her?, I asked. Quite the *quinqui*, he said. Where do you know her from? Dani interrupted: Yeah, she's a *quinqui*, sure, but is she a fox or do all chicks look good at night in the distance? She's pretty good-looking, I said. But don't get your hopes up, I only know her to see her. I'm not getting any hopes up. Though get to know her a bit better she might suck you off. Stopped at an intersection, Paco let go of the steering wheel for a moment to simulate a blowjob. Hopes?, he said, grabbing the steering wheel again. Fuck, I wouldn't let that chick suck my cock if I was dead: she might bite it off. Dani burst out laughing. Say what you like, dickhead, I said. But don't you dare say anything to Montse. I don't want her ripping mine off, and for nothing. She's a right one, your sister. Now it was Paco's turn to laugh. We'd left Vilarroja, were driving past the cemetery and I suddenly felt sick, as if I was carsick or coming down with something. In the front seats, Paco and Dani kept talking as we drove back into the city centre.

'I spent that night and the next day thinking about Tere. I was full of doubts. I wanted to see her and didn't want to see her. I wanted to go to Rufus and didn't want to go to Rufus. I wanted to leave Montse and my friends for one night and didn't want to at the same time. In the end I didn't see Tere or go to Rufus or abandon my friends, but Saturday night was a strange night: although I was at Paco and Montse's place until very late, I couldn't get the thought out of my head that I'd stood Tere up again or stop imagining her at Rufus, bombarded by the changing lights that flashed over the dance floor, dancing to the same songs or almost the same songs as the summer before that I'd watched her dance to so many times from the bar while her body adapted to the music as naturally as ever – as naturally as a glove fits a hand and as a fire gives off heat – dancing alone while waiting for me in vain.

'On Sunday morning I woke up feeling anxious, with the guilty certainty of having committed a serious mistake the night before, and to remedy it I decided that very afternoon I'd go and look for Tere at the bar in Vilarroja where I'd run into her. But as the morning wore on reality weakened my determination – I had no one to drive me to Vilarroja, I couldn't ask Paco, couldn't be sure of finding Tere and, on top of everything, I'd arranged to meet Montse and the others after lunch – so, feeling like that really was the end of the water margin, that afternoon I didn't go to Vilarroja. And it turned out really to be the end, because it was all over then.'

'Do you mean that was the last time you saw Tere back then?'

'Yes.'

'You didn't hear anything more about Zarco either?'

'No.'

'How about we leave it there for today.'

'That'd be just fine.'

Part II

Over Here

I

'Do you remember when you next saw Zarco?'

'At the end of 1999, here in Gerona.'

'He was no longer the same then.'

'No, of course not.'

'I mean that he'd had time to create and destroy his own myth.'

'In a manner of speaking. In any case it's true that, for Zarco, everything went very fast. In fact, my impression is that when I knew him, in the late seventies, Zarco was a sort of precursor, and when I saw him again, in the late nineties, he was almost an anachronism, if not a posthumous persona.'

'From precursor to anachronism in just twenty years.'

'That's right. When I knew him he was a forerunner in a way of the masses of juvenile delinquents who filled the jails, the newspapers, radio, television and cinema screens in the eighties.'

'I'd say he not only announced the phenomenon: he played the part better than anybody.'

'Could be.'

'Tell me the name of a delinquent from back then better known than Zarco.'

'OK, you're right. But, be that as it may, by the end of the nineties it was over; that's why I say that by then Zarco was a posthumous persona, a sort of castaway from another era: at that time there was no longer the slightest media interest in juvenile delinquents, there were no longer films about juvenile delinquents, or hardly any juvenile delinquents. All that was passé: the country had completely changed by then, the hard years of juvenile delinquency were considered the last throes of the economic misery, repression and lack of liberties of the Franco years and, after twenty years of democracy, the dictatorship seemed to have been left very far behind and we were all living in an apparently interminable intoxication of optimism and money.

'The city had also completely changed. By that time Gerona was no longer the post-war city it still had been at the end of the seventies but had become a post-modern city, a picture postcard, cheerful, interchangeable, touristy and ridiculously pleased with itself. Actually, little remained of the Gerona of my adolescence. The *charnegos* had disappeared, annihilated by deprivation and heroin or dissolved into the country's economic wellbeing, with secure jobs and children and grandchildren who went to private schools and spoke Catalan, because with democracy Catalan had become an official, or co-official, language. The ring of *charnego* neighbourhoods that used to menace the city centre had also disappeared, of course; or rather had transformed into something else: some neighbourhoods, like Germans Sàbat, Vilarroja or Pont Major, were now prosperous neighbourhoods; others, like Salt, had become independent from the city and were flooded with African immigrants; only Font de la Pòlvora, the last bastion of the final inhabitants of the prefabs, had degenerated into a ghetto of delinquency and drugs. I don't know if I told you that the prefabs themselves were demolished: now the ground where they had stood was a park in the middle of Fontajau, a newly built neighbourhood of small duplexes with garages, gardens and backyard barbecues.

'Over here, on this side of the Ter, La Devesa was still more or less the same, but La Devesa was no longer an outlying suburban neighbourhood; the city had absorbed it: it had grown to both sides of the river and the fields and orchards that surrounded the tower blocks of Caterina Albert in my childhood had been developed. The Marist Brothers were still in their place, though not the Vilaró arcade, which closed not long after I stopped going there and Señor Tomàs retired. As for the red-light district, it had not survived the city's changes; but, unlike La Devesa, which had turned into a middle-class neighbourhood, the district had become an elite neighbourhood: where twenty years earlier the narrow stinking streets swarmed with the city's riffraff, grimy bars, decadent brothels, dark poky little rooms, now there are cute little plazas, terrace bars, chic restaurants and lofts done up by trendy architects for visiting artists, foreign millionaires and successful professionals.'

'Like yourself.'

'More or less.'

'Do you consider yourself a successful professional?'

'It's not that I consider myself: I am. Fourteen people work for my firm, among them six lawyers; we deal with around one hundred significant cases a year. I call that success. How about you?'

'Me too. Although, if you don't mind me saying, you don't talk like a successful professional.'

'And how do successful professionals talk?'

'I don't know. Let's say you don't seem to have a killer instinct.'

'Because I put it away in a drawer, as Calamaro's song says. But I did have it, no doubt about it. Who knows, maybe I'm getting old.'

'Don't be cute. You're not even fifty.'

'What's that got to do with it? At my age, not long ago, people were already old, or almost. My father died at fifty-seven; my mother didn't live much longer. Now everybody wants to be young; I understand, but it's a bit stupid. It seems to me the fun in all this is being young when you're young and being old when you're old; in other words: you're young when you don't have memories and you're old when behind every memory you find a bad memory. I've been finding them for a while now.'

'Yeah. Well. Let's go on then. Tell me about your life after you lost sight of Zarco until you saw him again.'

'There's not much to tell. When I finished high school with the Marist Brothers I went to Barcelona. I spent five years there studying law at the Autónoma and living in student flats. I lived in three different flats; the last was on Jovellanos Street, near the Rambla, and I shared it with two classmates: Albert Cortés and Juanjo Gubau. Cortés was from Gerona, like me, but he'd studied at the Vicens Vives Institute, like my sister; Gubau was from Figueras, and his father was a court solicitor. We studied hard, didn't do drugs and went home on weekends, except during exams. At the beginning of my time in Barcelona I was still going out with Montse Roura, but after a year we split up and that ended up disconnecting me from my group of friends from the Marist school, who by then had otherwise all pretty much gone their separate ways. Then I went out with a few girls, until in third year I met Irene, who was also studying law but at the Central University. Three years later we got married, moved to Gerona and had Helena, my only child. By then I had started working in Higinio Redondo's firm. I told you about Redondo before, I don't know if you remember him.'

'Of course: the man who lent your father the house in Colera to hide you, no?'

'Exactly. And also the one who convinced my father that afternoon not to take me to the police station; or at least that's what I've always believed . . . He was an important person in my life. I mean Redondo; so important that, if it hadn't been for him, I most likely would not have become a lawyer: after all I never had any lawyerly vocation. Redondo was from my parents' hometown and had set up a criminal-law practice, and at some stage of my adolescence I admired him a lot, maybe because he was the opposite of my father, or because he seemed like it to me: my father didn't have money and he did; my father didn't have a degree and he did; my father didn't go out at night and he went out almost every night; my father was a political moderate and voted for the centre parties and he was a radical: in fact for years I believed he was a Communist or an anarchist, until I discovered he was a Falangist. In any case he was a good lawyer and a good person and, although he was also a frivolous, irascible kerb-crawler, drinker and gambler, he loved my family and he loved me. He encouraged me to study law and, as I said, when I graduated he took me on to do articles in his practice, taught me what he knew and after a few years made me his partner. A little while later something happened that changed both our lives completely. What happened was that Redondo fell in love with the wife of a bankrupt client; he fell in love for real, like a teenager, left his wife and four children and went to live with her. The problem was that when the client got out of jail thanks to Redondo's efforts, the woman left him and went back to her husband. Then Redondo went crazy, attempted suicide, finally disappeared and we had no news of him until four years later we learned that he'd been killed while crossing a street in downtown Asunción, Paraguay, run over by a delivery truck.

'That's how I became the senior partner of Redondo's firm. By then Irene and I were getting divorced and she moved back to Barcelona and I began to see my daughter only every second weekend and on holidays. But professionally it was the height of my career. Redondo, as I told you before, had taught me many things — among them that a lawyer can't be a good lawyer if he's not able to set aside his moral scruples every once in a while

– although I learned others on my own – including how to manage the press. I also learned that, if I wanted to grow, I needed to delegate, and I was able to hire good people: I contracted Cortés and Gubau, who were then working for a firm in Barcelona, and later made them partners, though I remained the senior partner. Anyway, I had my killer instinct intact, I was obsessed with being the best and I was, to such an extent that, as Cortés started to say, not a punch was thrown in Gerona without the thrower or receiver passing through our office.

'Then suddenly everything changed. Don't ask me why; I don't know. The thing is that precisely at that moment, when I had achieved the money and position I'd been fighting to achieve for years, I was overcome by a sense of futility, the feeling of having already done all that I needed to do, that what I had left to live wasn't exactly life but rather life's residue, a sort of insipid deferral, or perhaps the feeling was that, more than insipid or bad or deferred, the life I was leading was an error, a life on loan, as if at some moment I'd taken a wrong turn or as if all that was a small but terrible misunderstanding . . . That's how bad or muddled I was seeing things just before Zarco reappeared, or maybe that explains in part – a small part – what happened with him.'

'As well as a successful lawyer you're an unusual lawyer.'

'What do you mean?'

'Before becoming a lawyer you were a delinquent, which means knowing first hand both sides of the law. That's not so common, is it?'

'I don't know. What I do know is that a lawyer and a delinquent are not on two different sides of the law, because a lawyer is not a representative of the law but an intermediary between the law and the delinquent. That converts us into equivocal, morally dubious types: we spend our lives with thieves, murderers and psychopaths and, since human beings function by osmosis, it's normal that the morals of thieves, murderers and psychopaths end up rubbing off on us.'

'How is it that you became a lawyer if you have this opinion of lawyers?'

'Because before I became a lawyer I had absolutely no idea what it meant to be a lawyer. Well, I've told you my life story.'

'Yes. I'd like you to tell me now what your relationship was with Zarco during the years you didn't see him; that is: how did you follow the creation and destruction of the Zarco myth?'

'First you tell me exactly what you understand by the word myth.'

'A popular story that is true in part and false in part and that tells a truth that cannot be told only with the truth.'

'You've obviously given it some thought. But tell me: whose truth?'

'Everyone's truth, one that concerns us all. Look, these kinds of stories have always existed, people invent them, can't live without them. What makes Zarco's a little different (one of the things that makes it a little different) is that the people didn't invent it, or not only people, but most of all the media: the radio, the newspapers, TV; also songs and movies.'

'Well, that's how I followed the creation and destruction of the Zarco myth: through the press, books, songs and films. Like everyone. Well, not like everyone: after all I'd known Zarco as a kid; or rather: not only had I known him but I'd been one of his guys. Of course that was a secret. Apart from my father and Inspector Cuenca, no one who hadn't hung out in the district back then knew that at the age of sixteen I'd belonged to Zarco's gang. But my father had never made the slightest mention of the matter and, as far as I know, neither had Inspector Cuenca, at least until I said you should talk to him. The thing is that during those years I assiduously followed everything that appeared about Zarco, clipped out and saved articles from the newspapers and magazines, watched the films based on his life, recorded the reports and interviews they showed on television, read his various memoirs and the books others wrote about him. That's how I put together the archive I lent you.'

'It's magnificent. It's making my job much easier.'

'It's not magnificent. There are things missing, but nothing important is missing. Besides, a lot of things I didn't get hold of when they appeared, but years later, in newspaper libraries and street markets. I'm sure my wife and friends thought my passion for Zarco and for everything that had anything to do with *quinquis* odd and sometimes irritating, but not much worse than a childish fixation with stamp collecting or model railways.

'I remember, for example, the day I went with Irene to see *Wild Boys*, the first of the four movies about Zarco that Fernando Bermúdez made. I knew more or less what it was about because I'd read about it in the papers, but, as the story advanced and I realized that it was in part a re-creation of some of the things that had happened to us in the summer of '78, I started to get palpitations and to sweat so much that after a quarter of an hour we had to rush out of the cinema. The next day I went back on my own to see the movie. I actually saw it three or four times, obsessively searching for the reality hidden behind the fiction, as if the film contained a coded message that only I could decipher. As you can imagine, I was mostly interested in the Gafitas character: I wondered if that was how Zarco saw me or had seen me in the summer of '78, as a faint-hearted middle-class teenager who toughened up when he joined the gang and seems ready to betray him to contest his leadership and his girlfriend, and at the end of the story he does, he betrays him and on top of that he's the only one to escape from the police in that unexplained finale that disconcerted so many people and I thought was the best thing in the film.

'I also remember how I saw on television the press conference that Zarco gave in Barcelona's Modelo Prison, in the spring or summer of 1983, when he managed to convert a frustrated escape into the most famous prison riot in the history of Spain. The night of the day that happened was the first time I went to Irene's family's house, so I remember very well that she'd introduced me to her parents and we'd been having an aperitif with them for quite a while when suddenly I saw on the other side of the dining room, on a television with the sound turned down, the image of Zarco. It was a confusing image: Zarco's hair was very long and he was wearing a tight, short-sleeved T-shirt that accentuated his pectoral muscles, and he was lit by television lights and flashbulbs, surrounded by journalists and prisoners, he seemed to be requesting silence, with the bicep of one arm squeezed by a rubber band he held in his mouth and a syringe in his hand, about to inject himself with a shot of heroin with which he apparently meant to denounce the massive presence of drugs in the prisons. At that moment I was talking with Irene's father and, as she told me later, without giving the least explanation I stood up, leaving the good man in the middle of a sentence, walked over to the TV, turned up the volume while behind me Irene was trying to save face by making a joke. I never said he was perfect, she said, or says she said, because I didn't hear her. He has a weakness for *quinquis*; but, if the *quinqui* is Zarco he goes off the deep end. Would have been worse if he'd gone in for wine, don't you think? (Later, when we separated, Irene was less generous and less jovial, and often threw my obsession with *quinquis* in my face as a symptom of my incurable immaturity.) I also remember having seen on the television at Xaica, a self-service restaurant on Jovellanos Street where Cortés, Gubau and I used to go for lunch, the final images of the escape from the high-security prison Lérida II, the images of Zarco lying facedown on the asphalt of a suburban street corner in Barcelona, beside two of his accomplices, all three of them with their hands cuffed behind their backs, the three surrounded by plainclothes cops walking among them brandishing their pistols, perhaps waiting to take complete control of a situation they seemed to have completely under control, perhaps waiting for an order to remove the fugitives, perhaps simply savouring the minute of glory they were due for having caught, after a 24-hour search by land, sea and air, the most famous and most wanted criminal in Spain who in spite of being on the ground and facedown did not stop talking or screaming or protesting for an instant between the furious screeching of the sirens, according to him complaining to the police that he had a bullet in his back and needed a doctor, according to the police threatening them and cursing their families and their dead, according to some witnesses alternating between the two. And of course, I remember very well that because of Zarco I lost a possible client for Redondo – who moreover was an acquaintance of his or of his wife's – shortly after starting to work at his firm. What happened was that, while the lady in question was almost in tears telling me something about an inheritance, on the television in the café bar in Banyoles where we were having the meeting the incredible and chaotic images appeared of Zarco's escape from the Ocaña penitentiary during the cocktail party for the press screening of *The Real Life of Zarco*, Bermúdez's last film, when, in the presence of a group of journalists, Zarco and three other inmates in cahoots with him took Bermúdez, the prison superintendent and two guards hostage and walked out of the prison without anyone being able to do anything to prevent their escape. I forgot Redondo's acquaintance's tears and her inheritance and stood up to see the footage and listen to the news standing in front of the television in the midst of a circle of seated people, open-mouthed and in silence, totally oblivious to the drama and incredulity of my client, who had left by the time I returned to our table, which resulted in

Redondo coming down on me like a ton of bricks that same afternoon.

'Anyway, I could tell you lots of similar anecdotes, but they're not worth waiting for. The thing is that part of me was ashamed of having belonged to Zarco's gang, and that's why I kept it secret and was almost frightened at the idea that it might come to be known; but another part of me was proud of it, and almost wanted to publicize it. I don't know: I suppose it was like having a chest buried in my own garden not knowing whether it contained treasure or a bomb. Otherwise, another possible reason that might explain why my interest in Zarco and other *quinquis* lasted so many years was a kind of gratitude or relief, the certainty of the implausible luck of having belonged to Zarco's gang and having survived it: after all, from the end of the seventies until the end of the eighties Spain had swarmed with hundreds of gangs of rootless kids from the outskirts like Zarco's, and the immense majority of those kids, thousands, tens of thousands of them, had died due to heroin, AIDS or violence, or were simply in jail. Not me. The same thing could have happened to me, but it hadn't. Things had gone well for me. I hadn't been locked up in jail. I hadn't tried heroin. I hadn't contracted AIDS. I hadn't been arrested, not even after the bank robbery at the Bordils branch of the Banco Popular. Inspector Cuenca had left me in liberty instead of arresting me. I'd had, in short, a more or less normal life, something that for someone who'd belonged to Zarco's gang was perhaps the most abnormal life possible.

'Until I dug up the chest buried in the garden and realized that it contained both treasure and a bomb. That was at the end of 1999. One day in November Cortés burst into my office announcing at the top of his voice: News flash! Your idol has just landed in the city. My idol, naturally, was Zarco. Cortés was just coming back from the prison at that moment, and told me that, according to what the inmates he'd been to visit had told him, Zarco had been there since the night before; as was to be expected, his arrival had caused a certain stir, because it was a very small prison and he was still a very notorious character. Cortés had also found out that the prison board had assigned Zarco to a cell where he had a personal computer and television at his disposal, and for the moment he had almost no contact with the rest of the inmates. I listened to my partner with a slightly melancholic astonishment: ten, even five years earlier, each of Zarco's movements was as complicated as those of the top football players or rock stars, so that, when he was transferred to a prison in one of the provinces or when he passed through one of them on his way to trial or to another prison, the directors of the centres would find themselves overwhelmed with petitions for interviews, and his court appearances were held under strict security measures to prevent the harassment of photographers, television cameramen, journalists and admirers and busybodies who pressed up against the police cordons and shouted encouragement to him, blew him kisses, said they wanted to bear his child or clapped rumbas that sang the story of his invented life; now, instead, not even the two local newspapers had devoted a miserable line in the Society section to his arrival. It was one of the differences that marked the gulf between a myth at its height and a myth that's outlived its usefulness.

When Cortés finished giving me news about Zarco he asked: Well, what do you plan to do? I didn't have to think before answering. Tomorrow I'll go see him, I said. Cortés made an affectedly polite gesture and asked, lowering his voice: Should I take this to mean that you plan to offer him our services? What do you think?, I answered. Cortés laughed. You're going to get us into one hell of a shitstorm, he said, going back to his normal voice. But if you didn't I'd kill you.

'Although my partner knew nothing about the relationship I'd had with Zarco, what he said was not contradictory: all Zarco's relationships with his lawyers had ended badly (and some of them very badly); in spite of that, Zarco was still Zarco and, if the matter was handled skilfully, defending him could still be very lucrative for a legal firm. Besides, I'd often felt tempted to offer to defend Zarco, but, for one reason or another, I'd always resisted; now, when Zarco had just returned to Gerona almost like an archaeological relic or a forgotten wretch, when for everyone else he was little less than a hopeless or closed case after having spent his life in prison and having wasted several opportunities for rehabilitation, I thought it was the moment to give in to temptation.

'I wasn't the only one to think so. That very afternoon, while I was working on my submissions for a court appearance the following day, my secretary told me two women were waiting to see me. A little annoyed, I asked her if the two women had an appointment and she said no, but added that they'd insisted on seeing me to talk about a certain Antonio Gamallo; even more annoyed, I told her to make an appointment for the two women for another day, and then asked her not to disturb me again. But I still hadn't gone back to concentrating on my papers when I looked up from my desk and heard myself repeat out loud the name my secretary had just uttered; I stood up and rushed out to the waiting room. There were the two women, still seated. They turned towards me and I recognized them immediately: one I'd seen in photos recently, alone or with Zarco; the other was Tere.'

'Our Tere?'

'Who else? Over those last twenty years I had thought of her sometimes, but it had never occurred to me to look for her or ask about her whereabouts; nor would I have known where to look or who to ask. And now, suddenly, there she was. An intense silence settled on the waiting room while Tere and I stared at each other without moving; or almost without moving: I quickly noticed that her left leg was going up and down like a piston, just as it did when she was sixteen. After a couple of very long seconds, Tere stood up from her chair and said: Hiya, Gafitas. At first I thought she'd hardly changed, perhaps because her lean body and jeans and worn leather jacket and handbag strap across her chest gave her a youthful air; but I soon spied the ravages of age: the tired skin, crow's feet, circles under her eyes, the corners of her mouth turned down, a sprinkling of grey hairs; only her eyes were just as green and intense as they were twenty years ago, as if the Tere I'd known had taken refuge there, indifferent to the passage of time. I held out my hand mumbling exclamations of surprise and mean- ingless questions; Tere answered cheerfully, ignored my hand and kissed me on the cheek. Then she introduced me to the woman with her. She said she was called María Vela and that she was Zarco's girlfriend, although she didn't say girlfriend she said part- ner and she didn't say Zarco but Antonio. I did shake María's hand. And only then did I actually notice her, a somewhat younger woman than Tere, skinny and plain, short, chestnut-coloured hair, very pale skin, wearing a heavy, poor-quality, black coat over a pink tracksuit zipped up to the neck.

Once the introductions were done, the two women went into my office. I offered them a seat, coffee and water (they only accepted the seat and the water) and Tere and I began to talk. She told me she was living in Vilarroja, working at a cork factory in Cassà de la Selva and studying nursing by correspondence. Really?, I asked. Does that surprise you?, she answered. I found it very surprising, but I pretended it didn't surprise me. Tere seemed very happy to see me. María listened to us without taking part, but without missing a word of the conversation; I didn't know if Tere had told her about my former friendship with Zarco and with her, and at some point I pretended that Cortés hadn't told me of Zarco's arrival that morning and asked how he was. He's here, answered Tere. That's why we've come to see you.

'Then Tere got to the point. She told me they wanted me to defend Zarco at a trial to be held in Barcelona in a few months' time, a trial in which Zarco would be accused of assaulting two guards at the Brians prison. Of course, Tere took it for granted that I knew, as everyone did, who Zarco had turned into over the years, so she skipped straight to putting me in the picture and backing up her proposal drawing an exultant panorama of Zarco's situation: she told me that three years earlier they'd managed to get him back to a Catalan prison, specifically the Quatre Camins, and that, after three years of good behaviour and the Catalan government's new director-general of prisons, Señor Pere Prada, taking an interest in his case, he had just been transferred to the Gerona prison, a perfect prison because María also lived in the city and because it was a small, secure prison with a high rate of rehabilitation; she also explained that Zarco was innocent of the offence with which he'd been charged, handed me a copy of the indictment and his prison record in a cardboard file folder, assured me that his physical condition and his morale were excellent, that he'd stopped using heroin, that he was very keen to get out of prison and that she and María were doing everything they could to get him out as soon as possible. Up till that moment Tere spoke without looking at me, setting out the case as if she had set it out before, or as if she were reciting it; for my part I listened to her while feigning to read through the documents she'd handed me and looking back and forth from her to María. Right, Tere concluded, and we finally looked at each other. We know you have a lot of work, but if you could give us a hand we'd be grateful.

'She fell silent. I sighed. Tere had beat me to the proposal I was planning to put to Zarco the next day; so, in theory, it was all very easy: both sides wanted the same thing. But instinct told me it wasn't in my interest to let my visitors know, that what suited me would be to offer a little resistance before accepting, to earn their gratitude letting them think I was making a sacrifice accepting Zarco's defence, that I was only accepting reluctantly and in any case they should consider it a privilege that I might want to be their lawyer. I put the folder with the indictment in it down on the coffee table and began by asking: Does Zarco know about this? I was about to explain what I meant when María intervened. We would prefer you not call him Zarco, she reproached me in a timid voice with a pained expression on her face. His name is Antonio. He doesn't like to be called that; and we don't like it either. Zarco was another person: none of us want anything to do with him. Surprised by María's reprimand, I nodded, apologized and looked to Tere, but couldn't catch her eye; she was concentrating on lighting a cigarette. I cleared my throat and carried on, directing my question to María: What I was asking is whether Antonio knows that you two have come to ask me to defend him. Of course he knows, said María, scandalized. I never do anything behind Antonio's back. Besides, the idea that you should be his lawyer was his. Antonio's?, I asked. Yes, said María. And since when does Antonio know that I'm a lawyer?, I asked. María looked at me as though she didn't understand the question; then she looked at Tere, who rubbed the mole beside her nose with the same hand that held her cigarette before answering: I told him. She smiled and said: You're famous, Gafitas. The papers talk about you all the time. On TV too.

'That was all I wanted to know: just as I was aware of who Zarco had become, Tere was aware of who I'd become. I don't know if she read my mind, but she added as if to downplay her words: Besides, there are only three criminal lawyers in Gerona; so we didn't have a lot of choice. The other two are good, I said, now feeling confident enough to joke with her. Yeah, Tere conceded. But you're the best. The flattery meant that this time it was me who smiled. Besides, Tere went on, we don't know them, and we do know you. Not to mention that I'm sure they're more expensive than you. They don't interest us. Us knowing each other is not an advantage, I lied. And don't worry: no lawyer's going to charge you anything, much less in Gerona. I clarified: At the moment defending Zarco is still good for business. Tere insisted: That's precisely why we're not interested in your colleagues. We're interested in you. And please don't call him Zarco again: María told you already. Tere's words were sharp, but not the tone in which she said them; even so, I couldn't help but wonder if, whether or not María knew that I'd belonged to Zarco's gang in my youth, Tere and Zarco were thinking they could black-mail me with the threat of revealing that secret past. Tere stubbed out her cigarette, took a sip of water and, opening her arms a little in an interrogative gesture, looked at me, looked at María and looked back at me. Well, Gafitas, will you or not?

'I don't know if I thought that I'd got what I was looking for (or that I couldn't aspire to more), but the thing is I stopped pretending and accepted.'

'Tell me something: were you scared that Zarco and Tere might reveal that you'd been part of their gang?'

'Of course not. I might not have liked the idea of them telling, because I didn't know what consequences it might have, but nothing more. It was one of the risks of defending Zarco; the rest were advantages. They already were before Tere had shown up, for the free advertising for my practice and because I was enormously curious to see Zarco again after more than twenty years (and perhaps also because, at a moment when almost everything bored me and the feeling of misunderstanding and that I was living someone else's life I was telling you about earlier, I sensed that this unexpected novelty could be an incentive, the change I was waiting for); in any case, Tere showing up, and her being so happy at us seeing each other again, made it all much better. And of course, defending Zarco was risking unearthing a dangerous past, but wasn't it better to dig it up once and for all, now that I had the opportunity to do so? Wasn't it less dangerous to unearth it than to leave it buried? Wasn't I obliged to a certain extent to unearth it?'

'What do you mean?'

'Well, that in some way I felt in debt to Zarco. I always suspected that before the heist of the Bordils branch of the Banco Popular I had run my mouth off to Córdoba, and that was the cause of the disaster, the reason that Zarco, Gordo and Jou got caught. I told you before. I always suspected that and I always suspected that Zarco suspected it too.'

'You wouldn't be thinking of the Gafitas in the first part of *Wild Boys*, would you? Although that character reflects in part how you saw Zarco, it's a fictional character. And he doesn't shoot his mouth off, of course: he informs on Zarco, betrays them all. That Gafitas has almost nothing to do with you.'

'Almost: you said it. In any case, the Gafitas of his memoirs does have something to do with me, he isn't a fictional character and he does shoot his mouth off. You'll remember that too.'

'Perfectly. Only that in the memoirs it's not clear either that Gafitas shoots his mouth off.'

'That's true, it's not clear. But most likely he did, most likely the Gafitas of the book did shoot his mouth off, and was responsible for the bank job going wrong. At least that's what Zarco thinks, or that's what he seems to think. And even if he hadn't thought so. Even if it wasn't true that I'd shot my mouth off to Córdoba. Maybe I didn't. Even so, I felt that Zarco had lent me a hand when I most needed it: the least I could do was lend him a hand now that he was the one in need, right? Especially since by lending him a hand I would also be lending myself one.'

'Zarco lent you a hand? I would say rather that he used you and turned you into a delinquent. Is that what you call lending a hand? You yourself recognize that he was on the verge of forcing you to share the fate of all the members of his gang.'

'If that's what you understood, I explained it badly: Zarco didn't force me into anything; I chose it all. The truth is the truth. And don't forget that he saved me, at the last moment but he saved me, or that having come so close to catastrophe was good for me: before meeting Zarco I was weak, and knowing Zarco made me strong; before meeting Zarco I was a boy, and knowing Zarco turned me into an adult. That's what I meant when I said he lent me a hand.'

'I understand. But let's get back to the story, if it's OK with you. Did you go to see Zarco after Tere and María left?'

'No. I saw him the next day, in the afternoon. During those twenty-four hours I studied his prison record in detail and verified unsurprisingly that his official résumé was in the same league as his legend. Zarco had spent more than twenty-five years in prison or as the subject of manhunts and recapture and had been on trial fourteen times and accused of having committed almost six hundred crimes, among them no fewer than forty bank robberies and no fewer than two hundred robberies of gas stations, garages, jewellery stores, bars, restaurants, tobacconist's and other shops, as well as a multitude of muggings and car thefts and break-ins. He'd been wounded six times in confrontations with the police and Civil Guards and another ten times in street or prison fights. Only twice had he been tried for homicide, and both times he was acquitted: the first time he was accused of having shot dead at the door of his house a Santa María prison guard with whom he'd long been in confrontation and who he'd denounced for persecution and torture; the second time he was accused of stabbing a fellow inmate during a riot at the Carabanchel prison in Madrid. Apart from that, he'd been to seven different reformatories, including all the elite ones, and sixteen different prisons, including all the maximum-security ones; moreover, he had escaped from all the reformatories and many of the prisons where they'd locked him up and, in spite of the number of altercations he'd had with the prison guards and the number of fines, punishments and disciplinary sanctions they'd imposed on him, he'd lived in permanent rebellion against his confinement and the conditions of his confinement, in a sort of permanent denunciation of the Spanish prison system: he'd participated in a multitude of riots, had organized several, had initiated two hunger strikes, had presented an infinity of complaints against his jailers and had inflicted injuries on himself as a sign of protest (several times he'd cut open his veins, several times he'd sewn his lips shut with twine). All this was more or less known, or more or less known by me. What I didn't know and discovered then is that, from the point of view of defending him, Zarco's story wasn't as bad as I'd feared: to begin with, Zarco didn't have to answer for any violent crimes, and the hundred and fifty years he had yet to serve in theory were not the result of a long sentence but a series of shorter consecutive ones, which could facilitate their conversion to concurrent sentences and the granting of special leaves and other penitentiary perks; moreover, it was easy to argue that Zarco had now paid his debt to society and then some, among other reasons because he'd barely lived in liberty since, at the age of sixteen, just after the robbery of the Bordils branch of the Banco Popular, he'd gone to prison to serve a six-year sentence, so most of the crimes he'd been accused of had been committed in prison. During those twenty-four hours I also revised my archive on Zarco, watched bits of Fernando Bermúdez's four films inspired by him, reread passages from his two volumes of memoirs and revisited my memories of adolescence; what I didn't do was speak to Tere again (or, indeed, with María): I didn't want to do so until having spoken with Zarco.

'I remember very well the first conversation I had with him. It was in the prison interview room, a minuscule little room where lawyers met with their clients, something I did frequently ("You visit the clients at least once a week," Higinio Redondo used to repeat when I first started working for him. "Remember we're the only hope these rogues have."). The interview room was to the left of the entrance; two rows of bars with a pane of glass between them divided it down the middle: on this side, up against the wall, was a desk and chair; on the other side there was an identical space, the only difference being the prisoner didn't have a desk and that, instead of sitting facing the wall, he sat facing the lawyer, looking towards the double bars and glass. I didn't have to wait long before Zarco appeared. As had happened the previous afternoon with Tere, I recognized him straight away, but I wasn't recognizing the *quinqui* I'd last seen on the way into La Devesa Park, rolling about with a couple of cops, but the one who since then had illustrated the comings and goings of Zarco in newspaper photos and on cinema and television screens.

'When he saw me, Zarco gave the hint of a tired smile and, as he sat down he urged me to do the same with a gesture. I did. What's up, Gafitas?, he said in greeting. Long time no see. His voice was husky, almost unrecognizable; his breathing was gravelly. I answered: Twenty years. Zarco smiled fully and gave me a glimpse of his blackened teeth. Fuck, he said. Twenty years? Twenty-one, I specified. He shook his head seeming somewhat amused and a bit overwhelmed. Then he asked: How are you? Fine, I answered. Yeah, I can see that, he said, and, like in the old days, his eyes narrowed until they became a couple of inquisitive slits. He'd put on weight. He seemed to have shrunk. The flesh of his cheeks and chin looked soft and old, though his arms and torso gave the impression of conserving, beneath the shirt and sweater that covered them, some of their old vigour; he had much less hair and it was almost grey and badly cropped, but still parted in the middle; his skin looked rough, unhealthy, mouse-coloured; his eyes were still very blue, but they were dull and reddened, as if he had conjunctivitis. I asked: How are you doing? Fucking great, he answered. Especially now that I know you're going to get me out of here. Is the prison so bad?, I asked to keep the dialogue going. Zarco made a face that looked bored or indifferent, pushing his shirt and sweater sleeves up to his biceps inadvertently showing me – my first impression had been false – the soft and old flesh of his arms and forearms, covered in scars; actually, his whole body as far as I could see was covered in scars: his hands, wrists, the edges of his lips. The prison's not bad, he answered. But it's a prison: the sooner you get me out of here, the better. I don't know if it's going to be that easy, I warned him; I continued: For the moment Tere told me about a trial for something that happened in the Brians prison. Yeah, he said. But that's just for the moment; then comes all the rest. Be patient, Gafitas: you're going to end up sick to death of me.

'That's how our re-encounter began. Zarco soon started talking about himself, as if he urgently needed to bring me up to date. He told me that over a year ago he'd fallen out with his last lawyer and with his family or with what was left of his family, and since then he hadn't had a lawyer and hadn't spoken to his family, even though some of them lived in Gerona, including his mother and two of his brothers. He also talked about Tere and María. What he said about Tere mustn't have been relevant, because I don't remember it; however I well remember something he said about María. Don't pay much attention to her, he advised me, in a tone somewhere between ironic and disdainful. María just wants to be in the magazines. That's what he said, and I was surprised – and not just because I was there precisely because I'd paid attention to María – but I didn't say anything. As if to compensate him for his confidences I told him a couple of things about me, in which he didn't even pretend to show interest, and then asked him about our mutual friends. I was surprised that he had news of all of them, but not that they were all dead, with the exception of Lina – who Tere apparently saw every once in a while – and Tío – who was still living with his mother in Germans Sàbat and still in his quadriplegic's wheelchair. Jou and Gordo, he said, had overdosed on heroin, Jou just after he got out of prison, where he had spent a couple of years for the bank robbery of the Bordils branch of the Banco Popular, and Gordo three or four years later, when he seemed to have cleaned up and was about to marry Lina. Chino had also died of an overdose, in the washroom of the Babydoll, an Ampurdán brothel, a relatively short time ago, and Drácula had died of AIDS not too long ago either. Colilla's death, however, had never been entirely cleared up: according to some he'd fallen down the stairs of the building where he lived in Badalona one night; according to others he'd tried to get out of a drug debt and his creditors had beaten him to death and then made it look like he'd fallen down the stairs by accident.

'That, more or less, was that for personal matters; from that point on Zarco changed his tone and the subject. He began by summing up his prison record in his own way: although he still had more than two decades' worth of sentences hanging over his head, Zarco considered that within a year he could be eligible for conditional release, which would allow him to spend his days outside the prison, and within two or three at the outside he could be free. I was optimistic about his future (more optimistic at least than I had been before studying his prison record), but not that optimistic; even so, I didn't raise any objections to his predictions or make the slightest commentary. It's true that Zarco didn't ask for my opinion either: he just went on talking about the first trial pending, the trial for which Tere and María had asked for my help. From the start he flatly denied having assaulted the Brians prison guards who had reported him. I didn't beat them, he said. They beat me. Are there any witnesses to that?, I asked. Witnesses?, he asked. What witnesses? Some other inmate, I answered. Zarco laughed. Are you crazy, Gafitas?, he said. You think they're going to beat me up in front of another inmate? They beat me up in my cell, behind everybody's back; I just tried to defend myself. That's what happened. How many were there?, I asked. Four, he answered, and listed their names by memory; pointing to the papers I had on the desk, he added: They're the same ones who filed the complaint. I nodded. And the others?, I asked. I mean the other guards. Did they see their colleagues beat you up? Would they be prepared to testify in your defence? Now Zarco stared at me, clicked his tongue, looked away and seemed to think it over for a moment, stroking his hollow, badly shaven cheeks; then he looked back at me, this time with an air of superiority. When have you ever seen one jailer testify against another?, he asked. Look, Gafitas, if you're going to be my lawyer you have to know a couple of things. And the first one is that everyone in jail wants to fuck me over, but the ones who most want to fuck me over are the guards. All the fucking guards in every fucking jail. Got that? I kept quiet; he went on: And you know what? Maybe they're right: if I were them I'd want to fuck me over too. I interrupted him, feigning innocence I asked him why they would want to fuck him over. Because I fuck with them, he answered. And because they know I plan to keep fucking with them, so they don't fuck me over. That's why. And that's why they make up stories like the one from Brians, except that this

194

time it's not going to do them any good because we're going to take it apart. Yes or no, Gafitas?

'I kept my mouth shut, but I knew that, in part, what he said was true. Zarco's reputation in the prisons was terrible, and not only due to the resentment his fame and the privileges his fame brought with it caused: for years he had devoted himself to denouncing or insulting prison guards in books, documentaries and declarations to the press, branding them fascists and torturers and, in many of the incidents he'd been involved in, he'd attacked and taken many of them hostage; moreover, wherever he might be, Zarco meant a headache for the guards: they had to keep an eye on him, guarding him at all hours and treating him with the utmost consideration, which didn't prevent him from constantly demanding his rights and constantly filing complaints against them. The result of all this was that, as soon as Zarco was sent to a new prison, all the guards who worked there plotted against him to make his life impossible. Yes or no, Gafitas?, Zarco repeated. I answered with a gesture that meant: I'll do what I can. This seemed to suffice; as if granting his consent he added: OK, now tell me how you plan to do it.

'We devoted the rest of the interview to discussing the matter. I explained the defence strategy I'd sketched out over the past twenty-four hours. Zarco didn't like it; we argued. I won't go into details: they don't matter. But there is one detail that does matter, a detail I intuited in a confusing way when we started arguing and by the time we finished seemed obvious. The detail is that there was something very contradictory in Zarco's attitude. On the one hand, just as Tere had in my office, he had sought my complicity from the beginning and had treated me like a friend: just like Tere, he called me Gafitas, reclaiming in this way our old camaraderie; just like Tere, he corrected me each time I called him Zarco and asked me to call him Antonio, as if declaring that he was a man of flesh and blood and not a legend, a person and not a persona.

'That, as I said, on the one hand. But on the other Zarco seemed to wish to establish distance, to put up a barrier of vanity between us. I mean that, at a certain moment – when we started to talk about his next trial and play the roles of a lawyer and his client – things changed, I noticed that he wasn't prepared to let me forget that he was not just any old inmate, I felt that he wanted subtly to make me aware that I had never had nor would I ever have a client like him, who, although he was a man of flesh and blood, he was still a legend, and who, although he was a person, was still a persona. It's not just that he tried to examine my knowledge of the law and argued with me over judicial particulars, even quoting the penal code a couple of times (both, by the way, incorrectly); this amused me and, to be honest, didn't entirely surprise me: Zarco was famous for doing this kind of thing to his lawyers. What really shocked me was his arrogance, his haughtiness, the condescending impatience with which he listened to me, the tense conceit of some of his comments; I didn't remember Zarco as stuck-up or self-important and, as I've always thought arrogance hid a feeling of inferiority, I soon interpreted this change as the clearest sign of Zarco's helplessness. That's also how I interpreted – as an indication of his private weakness, or his fragility – the way he displayed, in an almost high-handed way, his awareness of being a special inmate, of enjoying a special status in prison and of that being backed up by the prison authorities, because after all someone who knows himself to be strong doesn't need to display his strength, don't you think? Have you spoken with my friend Pere Prada yet?, Zarco asked as soon as we started arguing about his defence. With whom?, I asked. With my friend Pere Prada!, he repeated, as if he couldn't believe I didn't know who he was. I soon remembered: Prada was the Catalan government's director-general of prisons, the same man who, according to what Tere had told me the previous day, had taken an interest in Zarco's case and facilitated his transfer to Gerona. No, I confessed, a little perplexed. Shit, what are you waiting for!, Zarco urged me. Pere doesn't know anything, but he's in charge, I've got him wrapped around my little finger, he's eating out of my hand now. Call him and he'll tell you what you have to do . . . Anyway. This was the essential contradiction that jumped out at me that first afternoon: Zarco both wanted and didn't want to go on being Zarco, he wanted and didn't want to bear the weight of his legend, his myth and his nickname, he wanted to be a person rather than a persona at the same time as wanting to be, as well as a person, a persona. None of what I heard Zarco say or saw him do from that day on refuted that contradiction or made me think he'd resolved it. Sometimes I think that's what killed him.

'When we finished talking that day, Zarco and I stood up to go – he back to his cell, me back to my office, or home – but I hadn't left the visiting room when I heard: Hey, Gafitas. I turned around. Zarco was looking at me from the opposite corner of the room, with one hand on the knob of the half-open door. Have I said thanks yet?, he asked. I smiled. No, I answered. But there's no need. And I added: You scratch my back and I'll scratch yours. Zarco stared at me for a couple of seconds; then he smiled too.'

2

'Let me make one thing clear from the start. I don't like talking to journalists, I don't like talking about Antonio Gamallo, and what I like least of all is talking to journalists about Antonio Gamallo; in fact, this is the first time I've spoken of the matter with a journalist.'

'I'm not a journalist.'

'Aren't you writing a book about Zarco?'

'Yes, but . . .'

'Then it's as if you were a journalist. I'll tell you the truth: I wouldn't have agreed to talk to you if it hadn't been the daughter of a good friend of mine who asked me to, and because she promised my name would not appear in the book. I understand you'll respect that promise.'

'Of course.'

'Don't be offended: I don't have anything against you personally; but I do have quite a bit against journalists. They're a bunch of tricksters. They make things up. They lie. And, since they tell lies disguised as truths, people live in tremendous confusion. You take what they did to Gamallo, to Gamallo's wife, to Ignacio Cañas; journalism is a meat-grinder: everyone gets crushed, and they'll crush everything you put in front of them. They get nothing from me. Well. Now that we've got that clear, I'm at your disposal, although I have to warn you I spoke very little with Gamallo. There are lots of people who knew him much better than I did. By the way, have you already spoken with his wife?'

'María Vela? She charges for interviews. Besides, everyone already knows her version, she's told it a thousand times.'

'True. And the other woman? Have you talked to her?'

'You mean Tere?'

'Yes. She could tell you lots of things; they say she's known Gamallo all her life.'

'I know. But she's dead. She died a couple of weeks ago, near here, in Font de la Pòlvora.'

'Ah.'

'Did you know her?'

'By sight.'

'Look, I understand your reservations. I understand that you don't want to make statements to the press. And that you don't like talking about Zarco. But, as I said, I'm not a journalist, I don't work for a radio or television station or write in a newspaper, and I'm not even sure I'm going to write about Zarco.'

'You're not?'

'No. That was the idea at first, yes: to write a book about Zarco that denounced all the lies that have been told about him and tell the truth or a portion of the truth. But a person doesn't write the books he wants to write, but those he can or those he finds, and the book I've found both is and isn't that one.'

'What do you mean?'

'I don't know yet. I'll know when I finish writing it. At the moment all I know is that the book will be about Zarco, of course, but also about Zarco's relationship with Ignacio Cañas, or about Zarco's relationship with Ignacio Cañas and with Tere, or about Ignacio Cañas' relationship with Tere and with Zarco. Anyhow: as I said I still have to find that out.'

'I didn't have anything to do with the girl, but I had more to do with Cañas than with Gamallo.'

'I know. That's why I wanted to talk to you. Actually it was Cañas who suggested I should. It seemed like a good idea: after all, apart from Tere and María you're the only person who was in contact with both of them at that time. Cañas also says that he has the impression that you understood things that no one else understood, not even him.'

'He says that?'

'Yes.'

'It might be true: I've had the same impression myself sometimes. You see, it always seemed to me that, deep down, Cañas always thought that Gamallo was a victim. You know: the good thief in his youth, the perpetual rebel, the Billy the Kid or Robin Hood of his day, and then – it turns out to be the same thing except in reverse – the villain who comes to understand the evil he's done and turns into the repentant delinquent; anyway, that story the journalists invented to sell papers, and then so many people bought it, starting with Gamallo himself. How could he not buy it, pretty as it was and with him coming out of it so well in the articles, in the songs, in the books and films about him? And I'm not saying that the story didn't have some truth to it, albeit a small part; what I say is that Cañas was a victim of that myth, or that legend, of that great invention. Cañas believed that Gamallo was a victim of society, but Cañas turned out to be the victim himself: a victim of the legend of Zarco. That's the reality. That he'd known Gamallo when he was young, as we discovered later, mustn't have helped him at all, but I don't think it was the main thing either: for me the main thing is that Cañas had grown up with the myth of Zarco, that it was the myth of his generation, and that, like so many people of his generation, he thought he could redeem him. Of course, he also thought that by redeeming him he'd make money and become famous; one thing doesn't rule out the other: Cañas was no charitable nun. But the truth is at that moment he believed he could help Gamallo, or rather that he could save him and score a bit along the way. And believing that hurt him. And perhaps this is what Cañas has the impression that I and no one else understand, not even him, but actually I think it's not that he doesn't understand it but that he doesn't want to understand.

'But, well, if I have to tell you the story it would be best to start at the beginning. Cañas and I didn't meet when Gamallo arrived in Gerona: we knew each other before; not well, but we knew each other. He always had clients in the prison and he visited them regularly, so our paths had crossed in the entrance foyer and we'd chatted for a moment or two. That was the extent of my relationship with him: the normal relationship of the superintendent of a prison and a lawyer with several clients incarcerated there. Anyway, although I barely knew him I didn't have a very good impression of him; I don't know why: we'd never had any friction, and everybody knew he was the most competent criminal lawyer in the province; or maybe I do know: because Cañas had the unmistakable vanity of guys who triumph too young; and because hardly a morning would go by without his face appearing in the papers: it was obvious the journalists adored him and he adored the journalists and, as you've realized, I distrust people who adore journalists. In spite of that, from the moment Gamallo arrived in my prison and I learned that Cañas was going to defend him, I wanted to talk to him.'

'What for?'

'I'll explain. At the end of 1999, when he arrived in Gerona, Gamallo was no longer the most famous prisoner in Spain, but he was still Zarco, a legend of juvenile delinquency; and although physically he was in bad shape, he still had a lot of fight in him. On the other hand I was sure that Cañas had agreed to defend him to profit from his renown, among other reasons because Zarco was an inmate who couldn't pay him and who had a tremendous history of conflicts with his lawyers. So I wanted to speak to him before Gamallo started causing the troubles he'd caused in every prison he'd been incarcerated in: I wanted him to convince Gamallo not to cause them, I wanted to arrive at an agreement with him and turn him into my ally and not my rival and enemy and, since I thought this could only benefit both of us (or rather all three of us), I was sure that it would be easy for me to achieve it.

'I was wrong, and that was the first surprise I had from Cañas.'

3

'When I finished my interview with Zarco in the prison I had made two commitments: to be his lawyer in a trial for the incident at the Brians prison and to set up a strategy to get him released. Along with the happiness produced by the reappearance of Tere and Zarco, this event worked like a catalyst on me. Suddenly everything changed. Suddenly I had, in the misunderstanding of the anodyne life I was leading, the flavour of a goal and the passion of a challenge: defending Zarco and getting him out on the street as soon as possible.

'That's what I immediately started to do. The morning following the interview with Zarco I handed my two partners two copies of his prison record and the Brians indictment, asked them to study those papers and buried myself back in them. As soon as I did I began to think that Zarco's predictions about his future were less unrealistic than I'd initially thought; two days later, meeting with Cortés and Gubau again, I realized that they both shared my opinion: none of us were as optimistic as Zarco, but all three thought that, if we took the correct steps, Zarco could be out of prison in three or four years, and that was in spite of having firm sentences adding up to more than twenty. Of course, none of the three of us wondered whether Zarco was prepared to leave prison so soon and, when I left Cortés and Gubau, we still hadn't decided what the steps were that we had to take to get him out, and how to take them (actually, it wasn't urgent that we decide: we couldn't tackle the subject until the Brians trial was over). Be that as it may, over the following days I suspected that, in our case, taking the adequate steps would probably include trying to resuscitate Zarco's media image, because that was the only way to get political support, through popular support, and prison perks and benefits through political support, until we could get a pardon. The problem, I then said to myself, was how to achieve Zarco's media resurrection; that is: how to focus the media's attention on a figure already so overexposed?; how to convince the media that a person from the past could be of some interest in the present?; and most of all, and in light of the more or less serious but failed attempts to rehabilitate him, how to convince the media again and get the media to convince the public that Zarco deserved one final chance, that he'd learned from his past errors, that he no longer had anything to do with the legend or myth of Zarco but only with the reality of Antonio Gamallo, a man approaching his forties with a turbulent past of poverty, prison and violence seeking to construct an honest future for himself in freedom and thereby needing the support of public opinion and the politicians in power?

'Those were some of the questions I asked myself over the days that followed my re-encounter with Zarco. That week of surprises ended with another surprise. Friday evening, as we often did, Cortés, Gubau and I had a few beers at the Royal, a café in Sant Agustí Plaza. When we left the Royal night had fallen. It was raining. I didn't have an umbrella with me, but Cortés and Gubau both did, so Gubau lent me his as he and Cortés were both heading towards the newer part of the city. In a Middle Eastern restaurant on Ballesteries Street I stopped to buy a plate of falafels with yogurt sauce and pitta bread and a couple of cans of beer;

then I carried on home. The streets of the old quarter were deserted and the paving stones shiny with rain under the streetlights, and as I reached the door to my building I had to do a balancing act: holding the umbrella, my briefcase and my dinner in one hand and trying to open the door with the other. I hadn't yet managed to get it open when I heard: Fuck, Gafitas, you practically live in La Font. It was Tere. She was a few metres away from me, having just emerged from the doorway across the street, with her hair wet and jacket collar turned up and hands in her pockets; what she said about La Font, by the way, was true: I have a loft in the same block where La Font was thirty years ago. What are you doing here?, I asked her. I was waiting for you, she answered. She pointed at my umbrella, briefcase and the bag with my dinner in it and said: Can I lend you a hand? She lent me a hand, I opened the door, she handed me back what I'd given her to hold. Do you want to come up?, I asked.

'We went up. When we got inside my flat I left my things on the counter and then went to the bathroom to find a clean towel so she could dry off; as I handed her the towel I asked her if she'd had dinner. No, she said. But I'm not hungry. I ignored that. While I made a salad and opened a bottle of wine and she set the table in the dining room, we talked about my place, a loft I'd bought a few years earlier from a Brazilian couple, he an architect and she a film director, or, to be precise, a director of documentaries and things like that. It wasn't until I'd served her a bit of salad and a couple of falafels that I mentioned to Tere that I'd been to see Zarco. How did he seem to you?, she asked. Fine, I lied. Older and heavier, but fine. He told me he's fed up with prison. He asked me to get him out of there whatever it takes. Tere smiled. As if it were that easy, right?, she said. He thinks it's easy, I said, then added: Maybe it's not so hard. Do you think so?, she asked. I pulled a dubious face and answered: We'll see.

'Tere didn't go on about the matter, and I thought it was premature to discuss my impressions and conjectures with her. While we were eating, Tere asked me about my life; I told her vaguely about my daughter, my ex-wife, my partners, my firm. Then I asked her; to my surprise, Tere replied with such an ordered account of events that it almost seemed prepared in advance. I learned that she'd lived in Gerona until she was seventeen, when the police arrested her after she participated in a bank robbery in Blanes, the summer after we met. That after her arrest she was tried and sentenced to five years in prison, of which she served two, at the Wad-Ras women's prison. That in prison she got hooked on heroin and when she got out she stayed in Barcelona for almost a decade, living most of the time in La Verneda, earning a living with occasional jobs and occasional robberies that occasionally sent her back to prison. That in the second half of the nineties she spent several days in the Vall d'Hebron hospital on the brink of death due to a heroin over-dose, and when she was discharged from hospital she agreed to be admitted to the Proyecto Hombre detox and rehabilitation centre. That she spent a good long while there. That she came out clean. That when she came out she tried to start a new life or what tends to be called a new life, and to do so she left Barcelona and returned to Gerona. That since then she had not had a drop or a speck of heroin or cocaine or any pills (except in the odd relapse). That she'd had lots of jobs and lots of men but no chil-dren. That she'd been working at the factory in Cassà for two years. That she'd started to study nursing that very year. That she didn't like her job but she did like her course. That she was happy with the life she was leading.'

'Didn't you ask about Zarco?'

'As soon as she stopped talking about herself. At first she seemed disinclined to answer, but I got out a second bottle of wine and she was soon talking about the relationship she'd had with him over those past twenty years.'

'Had she gone on seeing him?'

'Of course.'

'It's odd. As far as I recall, Zarco doesn't even mention her in his memoirs.'

'Your recollection is right, but his not mentioning her is more revealing than if he had mentioned her, because it means he took her for granted. Of course that's what I say now, because now I know things I didn't know then . . . In any case, yes: although sometimes sporadically, they had gone on seeing each other. What Tere told me that night was that, during Zarco's first years in prison, she visited him every once in a while and he turned to her when he was out on parole, when he escaped or when he had no one else to turn to. Later, for a long spell, the two of them stopped seeing each other. The reason is that in the middle of 1987, after Zarco escaped from the Ocaña penitentiary by taking advantage of the cocktail party after the press screening of *The Real Life of Zarco*, Bermúdez's final film based on his life, Tere got mad at him and, although in the end she was the one who found him refuge in a friend's house during his days on the run, she refused to visit him after he'd been recaptured. But what separated them completely, still according to Tere's version, was that, once he was back in prison, Zarco began his great change: he went on being a famous delinquent but he tried to no longer be the implacable juvenile delinquent to become the mature repentant delinquent, a change in which he had no need of Tere or in which Tere was simply superfluous, because she was a hindrance from the past that he wanted to overcome. Still, years later Zarco called her again. It was after holding up a Barcelona jewellery store in the city centre and thus violating his third-stage release, one level before getting out on probation that he'd been granted for the first time in his life and which allowed him to spend the days outside and return to the prison to sleep; the absurd stupidity of the robbery meant this privilege was revoked and Zarco was put back on trial again and had many years added to his sentence of many already accumulated years, not to mention the disappointment it provoked in public opinion in general, which had believed in his rehabilitation, and among the politicians, journalists, writers, film-makers, singers, athletes and the rest of the people who'd supported the cause of his release: they all wrote him off as an incorrigible *quinqui*, as a persona with no future from the blackest days of Spain. Again he was defeated and dismissed and with no support from anybody, and again he turned to Tere, who at first told him to go to hell and finally ended up giving in, agreeing to see him and help him and help María to help him, who by then had appeared on the scene. She'd been working with her on Zarco's behalf lately, until they came to see me.

'That's more or less what Tere told me that night, while we had dinner, or perhaps what she told me that night added to what she told me on other nights. Whatever the case, when we finished dinner and Tere finished telling me about Zarco, or she tired of doing so, we were a bit drunk. At that moment there was a rather long silence, which I was about to fill in by praising Tere's loyalty and patience with Zarco or asking after Lina – who Zarco had told me Tere saw once in a while – but, before I could do so, she stood up from the table, went over to the stereo, crouched down and started looking through my few CDs. You still don't like music, Gafitas, she said then. My daughter says something similar, I answered. But it's not true. It's just that I don't listen to it much. Why's that?, asked Tere. I was going to say I didn't have time to listen to it but kept quiet. Looking at the CD covers, Tere added, half-amused half-disappointed: And I don't even know any of them. I got up from the table, crouched down beside Tere, pulled out a Chet Baker CD and put on a song called "I Fall in Love Too Easily". When the music started to play, Tere stood up and said: Sounds old, but nice. Then she started to dance on her own, with the wine glass in her hand and eyes closed, as if searching for the hidden rhythm of the song; when she seemed to have found it she set her glass down on top of the stereo, came over to me, put her arms around my neck and said: You can't live without music, Gafitas. I put my arms around her waist and tried to follow her. I felt her thighs against my thighs, her chest on my chest and her eyes on my eyes. I've missed you, Gafitas, whispered Tere. Thinking it was incredible that I hadn't missed her, I said: Bullshit! Tere laughed. We kept dancing in silence, looking in each other's eyes, concentrating on Chet Baker's trumpet. Seconds or minutes later she asked: Do you fancy a shag? I took a moment to answer. Do you?, I asked. Tere's first reply was to kiss me; the second seemed redundant – I do, yeah, she said – although she immediately added: But on one condition. What condition?, I asked. Tere also took a moment to reply. No ties, she finally said. She soon noticed that I hadn't entirely understood. No ties, she repeated. No mess. No commitments. No demands. Each to his own. I would have liked to ask Tere why she said that, but it seemed like a way of looking for useless complications and a distraction from the essential, so I didn't. It was Tere who asked: Yes or no, Gafitas?

'Those are the last words I remember from that night, the second in my life that I slept with Tere. The following months were unforgettable. Tere and I started to see each other at least once a week. We saw each other in the evening or at night, at my place. There were no fixed days for these encounters. Tere called me in the morning at my office, we arranged to see each other later, at seven or seven-thirty or eight, that day I'd finish work earlier than usual, buy something for dinner in some shop in the old quarter or in Santa Clara or Mercadal and wait for her at home until she arrived, which I never knew when might happen – she was often late and more than once took two or three hours to get there, and more than once I thought she wasn't coming – although she always did eventually arrive. She'd arrive and, especially the first times, as soon as she was through the door we'd be screwing, sometimes right in the front hallway with most of our clothes still on, with the fury of people not making love but war. Later, once we calmed down, we'd have a glass of wine, listen to music, dance, have something to eat and then drink some more and listen to music and dance until we'd go to bed and have sex until late.

'They were clandestine dates. At first I understood this confidentiality as part of the conditions Tere had imposed – part of the no ties and no commitments or demands and each to our own of the first night – so I accepted it without protest, although I sometimes wondered who might be bothered about she and I going out together. Me, answered Tere, when I finally asked her. And you'd be bothered too. It was a categorical reply, that did not allow a rejoinder, and I didn't have one. Otherwise, as far as I recall that was one of the few times, in those early days, that Tere and I talked about our relationship; we never did, as if we both felt that happiness is for living, not for talking about, or that mentioning it might be enough to make it disappear. This is odd, when you think about it: after all there is no subject of greater interest to new lovers than their own love.

'What did Tere and I talk about then? Once in a while we talked about Zarco, about Zarco's situation in prison and about what I was doing to get him out of there, although after a certain point we only talked about that in the presence of María, who in theory was the main interested party. Sometimes we talked about María, about her relationship with Zarco, about how she'd come to be Zarco's girlfriend. Tere liked to talk about her studies and ask me about things at my office, my partners, my sister – who I didn't see more than once or twice a year, because she'd been working in Madrid for many years where she was married and had kids – about my ex-wife and most of all about my daughter, although, as soon as I suggested to Tere the idea of meeting her, she refused without a second thought. Are you crazy?, she asked. What's she going to think of her father hooked up with a *quinqui? Quinqui*, what *quinqui?*, I answered. There are no *quinquis* left any more! Zarco's the last one, and I'm about to turn him into a normal person. Tere laughed. Getting him out of jail would be enough!, she said.

'We often talked about the summer of '78. I remembered pretty well what had happened back then, but on a few points Tere's memory was more precise than mine. She, for example, remembered better than I the two times I'd stood her up after our last two encounters: the first, when I didn't show up at La Font, and the second three months later, when I didn't show up at Rufus. Tere mentioned those episodes without resentment, making fun of herself and the scant attention I seemed to have paid her twenty years earlier; and when I tried to deny it with the evidence that in reality it was her who paid no attention to me, or who'd paid me intermittent and very partial attention, she asked: Oh yeah? Then why did you stand me up? I couldn't tell her the truth, so I laughed and didn't answer; but, at least on this point, my memory of that summer was crystal clear: I had joined Zarco's gang mainly for Tere and my impression was that, leaving aside the incidents in the washrooms of the Vilaró arcade and on Montgó beach, during those three months Tere had done nothing but avoid me and sleep with Zarco and others. All this shows, now that I think of it, that it's not true that Tere and I didn't talk about our love – at least we talked about our frustrated love from two decades before – but I was telling you for another reason and it's that, after Tere brought up those two episodes a couple of times, more than once I wondered if her insistence was due to some hidden reason, if she wouldn't be provoking me to catch me in a lie, if at some moment the repeated slight of standing her up twice hadn't put her on a wrong track and hadn't led her to the mistaken conclusion that, after the failure of the robbery of the Bordils branch of the Banco Popular, I had disappeared and hadn't returned to the district not because I didn't like her any more or because I didn't want to be with her and considered her just a fleeting summer fling, but because I was the snitch who'd tipped off the police. And I wondered whether Zarco had arrived at the same conclusion on his own or if Tere had told him and convinced him it was true and that explained in part the role of traitor that Gafitas played in *Wild Boys*, or at least why he was portrayed as untrustworthy or possibly untrustworthy in *The Music of Freedom*, the second volume of Zarco's memoirs. And, if the reply to this wondering was affirmative, perhaps there was another reason why Zarco wanted me to be his lawyer: not just because he knew me and because I lived in Gerona and was known to be a competent lawyer nor only because our former friendship might make me more manageable and more tolerant with him and might save him fights like the ones he'd faced with his previous lawyers; but also so I could pay for my betrayal or snitching or untrustworthiness, so that it would be me, who twenty years earlier had put him behind bars, who would now get him out.

'But I don't want to give you a mistaken impression: the truth is that I was not very worried about that old story; and it's also true that what Tere and I talked about at my place was far and away not the most important thing that happened on those nights of surreptitious love. The most important is that, as I said, they were happy nights, although of a strange and fragile happiness, as if separate from real life, as if every time Tere and I got together at my place we segregated ourselves inside a hermetic bubble that isolated us from the outside world. The secret nature of our dates and the fact that at first Tere and I only ever saw each other within the perpetual penumbra and four walls of my home contributed to this sensation. Music also played a part.'

'Music?'

'You can't live without music, Tere had said to me the first time she came up to my place. Remember? Well, I decided that Tere was right and that up till then I'd lived without music or almost without music and now I was going to correct that mistake. And the first thing that occurred to me was to get hold of the music that used to play at Rufus when Tere and I used to go there and she would spend the nights on the dance floor and I would spend them propping up the bar watching her dance.

'The day after Tere's first visit to my place was a Saturday, and that afternoon I went to a record shop on the Plaça del Vi, called Moby Disc, and bought five CDs of late-seventies artists with songs I remembered hearing at Rufus or that I associated with the time we used to go to Rufus – one CD by Peret, one by the Police, one by Bob Marley, one by the Bee Gees, one by Boney M. – and that Tuesday night, when Tere came back to my place, I had "Roxanne" playing at full volume as she arrived. Fuck, Gafitas! said Tere as she walked into the dining room, starting to dance as she pulled her handbag strap over her shoulder. This one's old too, but it's something else! From then on I devoted many hours of my weekends to looking for records from the second half of the seventies and first half of the eighties. At first I always bought them at Moby Disc, until an acquaintance recommended two shops in Barcelona – Revólver and Discos Castelló, both on Tallers Street – and I started going to them almost every Saturday. I took great pains over what music to play for my midweek encounters with Tere and tried to follow her taste, although the truth is she liked everything or almost everything: rock and roll as much as disco or rumba, Rod Stewart or Dire Straits or Status Quo as much as Tom Jones or Cliff Richard or Donna Summer, as much as Los Chichos or Las Grecas or Los Amaya. We both loved to listen to the corny Italian and Spanish hits from back in the day every once in a while, the songs of Franco Battiato and Gianni Bella and José Luis Perales and Pablo Abraira we had heard for the first time in Rufus. I'll never forget the night we screwed up against the dining-room table, listening to Umberto Tozzi singing "Te amo".

'This idyll lasted for several months, more or less until the summer. At first I must have had satisfaction written all over my face, because everyone noticed something strange, starting with my daughter, who arrived home the day after Tere's first visit and spent the weekend joking with lethal marksmanship (I don't recognize you, Dad, she sprung on me several times, laughing. Anyone would think you got laid this week), and ending with Cortés, Gubau and the rest of the people at my office, who benefited from my good mood though they also suffered from my absenteeism, or my inattention. I mean that I began to deal almost exclusively with Zarco's case and to delegate the rest of the work to Cortés and Gubau, provoking consternation in the office and complaints from some clients, accustomed to being looked after by the senior partner in the firm. But I was too absorbed by my happiness and paid no attention to the complaints or the disconcertion. That doesn't mean I didn't work. I was reading, studying, collecting information, arguing details of Zarco's case with Cortés, with Gubau, sometimes with other lawyers. I often went to see Zarco. On those visits we mostly talked about judicial and prison matters, about his situation in prison and how to improve it; but neither Zarco nor I evaded talking about the past, not even the summer of '78, especially if we considered some detail or concrete episode from back then

214

could serve to clarify some detail or concrete episode from his later life, and in this way he was able to give me tools with which to defend him. Anyway, our relationship was strictly professional, or almost. I would say we were weighing each other up. In his case I don't know what the initial balance was in that weighing up; in mine it was that, in spite of his visible physical deterioration and secret moral vulnerability, Zarco was all there: he thought clearly, his behaviour was reasonable, he had a real desire to get out of prison and begin a different kind of life and he seemed capable of doing it.

'During that time I also saw María Vela with some frequency. We always or almost always saw each other at her flat on Marfà Street, in Santa Eugènia, where she lived with her daughter, a precocious and graceless teenager who was the spitting image of her mother. Seeing her – seeing María, I mean – many must have asked how it was possible that such a woman had become Zarco's woman. When she and Tere showed up at my office I already knew the story from the press; what I didn't know was that that story wasn't the whole story.'

'I only know what I've read in your archive.'

'The whole story is more interesting; I pieced it together in those first weeks, thanks to María herself, and also thanks to Zarco and Tere. As far as I now understand, the story goes more or less like this. María had started off being one of the many admirers Zarco corresponded with from prison when his media profile was at its peak; there were all sorts among those women: compulsive liars, opportunists, Samaritans, naive women, thick ones, adventurers, I don't know. In general, at the same time as going along with them, Zarco had known how to manage them and get them to work for him, because he understood very early that a great part of his wellbeing inside depended on help he got from the outside, getting his case moving with barristers, solicitors, officials, judges and politicians. My impression is that María must have combined ingredients of all or almost all the types of admirers, but the fact is the press chose to present her as a Samaritan in love.

'I'm not saying that she wasn't in part, at least at the beginning. She first got in touch with Zarco towards the end of the eighties, when he was locked up in the Huesca prison and announced in public declarations to *El Periódico de Aragón* his intention to start a magazine and asked for volunteers to help him. María was one of the people who offered to collaborate in the production and distribution of the magazine, and, although they didn't manage to publish a single issue, from that moment on she began to write to him regularly. That's how Zarco found out she was four years younger than him, that she'd been married and was separated, that she had a two-year-old daughter and had always lived in Barcelona but had just moved to Gerona, where she worked in a school cafeteria; and that's how he found out later, as María levelled with him and her letters grew inflamed, that she had been reading everything written about him for a long time, that she'd fallen in love with him without ever meeting him, that she was willing to do anything for him, that she was sure that – as she had done years ago for her ex-husband, for whom she'd managed to get a special pardon – she could get him out of prison and begin a new life with him. Zarco didn't pay too much attention to this offer, perhaps because María's photos didn't make her look too seductive, perhaps because at that time he was receiving similar offers from his epistolary harem of women who flirted with him from a distance; remember that, although he was behind bars, Zarco was then one of the guys most in demand in this country, a sort of icon of the recent democracy: they were making films about him, writing books and songs about him, publishing his memoirs, the newspapers and radio stations interviewed him on the slightest pretext, the intellectual journals dedicated special issues to him, his photograph appeared everywhere beside politicians, football players, bullfighters, actors, singers, writers, film-makers and celebrities, and the gossip magazines claimed he had romances with Socialist politicians, Andalusian aristocrats, beauty queens, high-school teachers, female prison guards and television presenters. So, although María kept writing to him, in the midst of that whirlwind Zarco tired very early of answering her letters, and didn't do so again until, in the mid-nineties, he himself destroyed his public image with a couple of failed attempts at rehabilitation, the media's interest in him plummeted and his harem of admirers disappeared. María did not miss her moment. No longer with any competition, she started to claim Zarco's attention again, she won it and began to visit him and to have encounters alone with him in prison (face-to-face encounters they call them: a euphemism to avoid calling them sexual encounters); Zarco for his part went along with it. That was when María became what she was when I met her in my office: Zarco's official girl-friend and the person on the outside who looked after his affairs.'

'And in that capacity she visited you that day.'

'That's right.'

'And Tere? In what capacity did Tere go to your office?'

'As María's helper or bodyguard and as someone Zarco trusted. That was the role she'd been filling for years and that she more or less carried on doing for a while. María was ideal for Zarco for tons of reasons: because she was a normal woman, with no criminal record, because she was a mother and aside from that a respectable separated mother, because she was in love with him, because she was always available, for her air of vulnerability, for everything; but even though she was ideal, Zarco didn't think she was smart and didn't trust her, or he thought Tere was smarter and more trustworthy, and so he started to ask her to accompany

María, or Tere herself offered to do so. And that's how that singular couple came to be.

'But I was telling you about my conversations with María. I saw her at least once a week too, at her home on Marfà Street. That was where I began to realize her character had some duplicity and that, more than vulgar or insignificant – which is what she seemed at first – she was one of those people of such obvious ingenuousness and such total transparency that they ended up being enigmatic. One of the things that surprised me was that María still had the idealized vision of Zarco that the media had propagated for years, a vision according to which Zarco was a noble, brave and generous youth condemned by the fate of his birth to a life of delinquency; I found it even more surprising that María still had an idealized vision of her relationship with Zarco: according to her, her story was a love story of a good, simple and unlucky woman for a good, simple and unlucky man, a love story that overcomes all, a romantic love that, once Zarco had his freedom, was going to give her and her daughter the husband and father they'd lost and Zarco the family he'd never had. In those first interviews María told me the same story several times (or different stories that deep down were variations of the same one), and one afternoon, unexpectedly, as I was walking towards my car after having spent hours listening to her I seemed to understand that the story was the answer I'd been looking for, the key that could unlock the flow of media interest in Zarco and, therefore, the key also to Zarco's freedom: he had told his life story to the press many times as a repentant and reformed delinquent, unjustly kept behind bars; but, after he himself had refuted it so many times by reoffending, it was difficult for anyone to believe it, especially if he was the one telling it; but, if that same story, corrected, improved and expanded, was told by a school cafeteria worker, a relatively young woman, on her own, decent, poor and separated, wrapped in an air of submission and disgrace and with a daughter as well (a daughter who could also allow Zarco to present himself as a future head of a household), then the possibility existed that the media might believe it or at least believe that it was credible, spreading it, reviving interest in Zarco and helping me get him out of prison. In any case I reached the conclusion that, without that help, it would take me much longer to get Zarco released, if I ever could; I also arrived at the conclusion that it was at least worth trying.'

'So it was your idea to turn María into a media darling.'

'Not at all. My idea was just that María should tell her story and Zarco's to the journalists; nobody could have predicted what happened afterwards: I at least have nothing to do with that.'

'Of course you do. You encouraged María by believing that you could use her and keep her under control; but that woman bolted and turned against you. Some people might say it serves you right: you can't start something without knowing how it's going to turn out.'

'Nonsense. No one would ever start anything, if that were the case, because no one knows how anything's ever going to turn out, no matter how it starts. Anyway, if you're interested we can talk about this next time. I have to get going now.'

'I didn't mean to upset you.'

'You haven't upset me.'

'OK; I won't keep you any longer. But before we finish for the day, let me ask you one last question.'

'Go ahead.'

'If I've understood you correctly, in that first moment everyone around you was optimistic about Zarco's future. Is that right?'

'Yes . . . Well, no. One person was not.'

'Who?'

'Eduardo Requena, the superintendent of the prison. A strange guy. He knew Zarco well at that time, because he saw him every day, and he had a peculiar vision of his character. I didn't see much of him, but we ended up forging some sort of friendship. I sometimes have the impression that he understood things that no one else understood, or that I took too long to understand. You should talk to him.'

4

'I remember the first time Cañas and I met in my office, at my request, a few weeks after Gamallo was transferred to the prison. I'd only spoken to Gamallo a couple of times then and only in passing (I never talked much with him, I didn't tend to talk with any of the inmates), but the group of specialists who worked under me at the prison had already examined him and made a diagnosis, so I had quite an accurate idea of his real condition.

'That was the first thing I said to Cañas that afternoon, after shaking his hand and offering him a seat on the settee in my office. The second thing I told him was that I'd asked him to come because I wanted to share the information I had at my disposal, to simplify our work and act by mutual agreement. Cañas listened to me very attentively, his eyes looked intrigued behind the lenses of his glasses, leaning back against the sofa cushions, knees far apart and his fingers laced together in his lap; as usual he was impeccably dressed: white shirt, blue three-piece suit and shiny shoes. When I finished speaking, he raised his eyebrows and unlaced and relaced his fingers, inviting me to go on. I went on. I explained that Gamallo was a heroin addict and HIV-positive, which he must have already known as he didn't seem surprised to hear it; I explained that he had an added problem, which was that he was not aware of how much harm heroin was doing him, as he believed he was in control when actually heroin controlled him, that he was unable to admit his drug addiction as a disease or was only able to pretend to admit it in order to take advantage of it, and without truly admitting it he could not combat it. I added that, in spite of all this, at the Quatre Camins prison they had managed to get him onto a methadone treatment programme. Then I said that Gamallo was perhaps the most institutionalized inmate I'd ever come across.'

'Zarco! Institutionalized?'

'Look. All prisons are different, but they're all similar; Gamallo had spent more than half his life locked up in prison, he knew all or almost all of Spain's prisons, knew better than anybody the tricks of prison life and knew how to manipulate them in his favour better than anybody, so he was the king of subterfuge behind bars, the champion schemer. That's what it means to be institutionalized. Naturally, Gamallo considered that for him it was a strength, and he was right; what he didn't know was that it was also his weakness. In any case, the specialists' diagnosis was very clear; I summed it up for the lawyer: the report spoke of Gamallo's manipulative character, his work-resistant temperament and his persecution complex (I remember that one of the psychologists wrote, more or less: I'm not saying that some prison guards haven't persecuted him at times; but that's the problem: the worst thing that can happen to someone who believes himself persecuted is to actually be persecuted); the report also alluded to his tendency to see himself as being victimized and the parallel tendency to always hold others responsible for his own misfortunes, and most of all it alluded to his inability to come to terms with the legend of his juvenile delinquency, to digest it and live with it.

'This was the basic thrust of the report. The rest consisted of an unsurprising repertoire of news about Gamallo's family, childhood and youth, a résumé of his criminal history and prison record and an inventory of his rehabilitation attempts. I handed Cañas the report and let him take a look through it; while he did so I explained: Look, Counsellor, I've been working with prison inmates for thirty-five years, I know the most complicated prisons in Spain and have been running this one for almost thirty. Forgive me for saying so but mine is quite an unusual case, mainly because the job of prison superintendent is so tough that few last for three decades and because it's also a political appointment and that means I've survived the change of a dictatorship for a democracy, of one party for another and of the central government for that of the autonomous Catalan government. I'm not telling you all this to boast; I'm just trying to tell you I know what I'm talking about. I paused and then said: And what is it that I've learned from all this time spent among prison inmates?, you'll be wondering. The most important is something very simple: there are inmates who can live in liberty and those who cannot, there are inmates who can be rehabilitated and those who cannot; and that those who can be are a tiny minority. Well then, I can assure you of one thing, I concluded. Gamallo is not one of them.

'I waited for Cañas' reaction, but there was no reaction. I took it as a good sign: Cañas was an intelligent and experienced lawyer (although he was still young), so I thought that, if anything might surprise him about that encounter, it wouldn't be what I was saying, but that I'd summoned him to say something as obvious as what I was saying. The thing is that for a second he remained silent, looking at me with the specialists' report in his hands, as if he guessed that I hadn't finished. I sighed and confirmed his intuition. But the authorities want him to be rehabilitated, I said. Then I went on. I said that Gamallo's rehabilitation had become a political matter. I said that the Catalan government had decided that Gamallo gave them a chance to show up the government in Madrid, by doing well what they had done badly or hadn't known how to do. I said that, as well as a political matter, rehabilitating Gamallo was a personal matter, or at least it was for the new Director-General of Correctional Institutions, Señor Pere Prada . . . Señor Pere Prada. I had just met him, and at first he'd seemed like a good person; unfortunately, that's not all he was: he was also a daily Mass Catholic, full of good intentions and a believer in the innate goodness of human nature. In short, a dangerous character. I told Cañas that Prada had taken an interest in Gamallo and that, after talking to him a couple of times in Quatre Camins, he'd decided to take charge, commit himself personally to his rehabilitation and commit the entire Justice Ministry, beginning with the minister himself. I said that because of that, among other reasons, Gamallo had been transferred to Gerona: because the director-general thought that in a small prison like Gerona Gamallo could receive more individualized and better attention. Finally I went on to describe to Cañas the regime that would be guiding Gamallo's life from that moment on, a regime in which all his steps would be regulated and where, at Prada's express suggestion, he would enjoy all comforts.'

'In other words you were working towards Gamallo's rehabilitation without believing that Gamallo could be rehabilitated.'

'Exactly. But I didn't try to deceive anybody. I told Prada from the beginning and the people at Correctional Institutions. And I repeated it to Cañas that afternoon, in my office: I did not believe Gamallo could be rehabilitated. And much less did I believe he could be rehabilitated in that way. To begin with, transferring him to Gerona had been a mistake: at that time Zarco was still a persona in Catalonia, not to mention in a city like Gerona, where he still had family and friends, although almost none of them had anything to do with him any more; whereas, in some distant prison in Castilla or Galicia or Extremedura, in the middle of nowhere, Zarco was no longer known, his myth was practically non-existent or it had faded and that was good for Gamallo, because until Zarco was nobody Gamallo couldn't be anybody, or rather, because Gamallo could only survive if Zarco died. I'm not sure if I've explained myself.'

'Perfectly.'

'On the other hand, in the prison itself we did nothing but nourish that myth by not treating Gamallo like just another inmate and by granting him privileges. Those privileges were counterproductive, because Gerona Prison, like all prisons, was ruled by two laws: one was imposed by the superintendent and the other was imposed by the inmates; and I could tolerate the privileges, though they seemed wrong to me, but the inmates could not. I'll say more: privileges are bad for prison life, because they provoke the ill-will of those who do not enjoy them, but they're even worse for getting out, because they led people to believe that Gamallo was a special inmate and not a regular inmate like all the rest, and thus continued to fuel the legend of Zarco. Anyway: that's more or less what I said to Cañas.'

'And what did Cañas say to you?'

'That's when I was surprised. You know? I think to be a good lawyer you have to be a bit cynical, because a lawyer has the obligation to defend thieves and murderers, and on top of that, naturally, he'll be pleased when thieves and murderers are not convicted. Justice is based on this injustice: even the worst of men has the right to have someone defend him; if not, there is no justice. This might seem disagreeable to you, and it is, but the truth is almost never agreeable. Anyway, I had Cañas down as a good lawyer, as I said, so I was sure that, in public, he would be airing the legend of Gamallo as a victim of society, the tearjerking myth of the good, repentant thief and all that: after all, it was the best way to defend him in court; but I was also sure — that's why I'd summoned him to my office — that deep down

Cañas knew that Gamallo was not a victim of society nor a rebel from a movie but a complete bully, an unredeemable savage, and that, in private, speaking one on one to someone like me (who knew that he knew), he'd admit the truth or at least act as if he recognized it, and we could come to an understanding and spare ourselves some problems.

'I was mistaken. The first thing Cañas said when he stopped listening to my explanations was: I'd like to know why you've told me all this. He'd left the stapled pages beside him, was sitting on the edge of the sofa and had his elbows resting on his knees, but he still had his fingers laced together. I told you, I answered. I think it's my duty. I also think that, if we're going to work together on this, it's best if I lay my cards on the table and we come to an agreement. The lawyer murmured: I understand. But he didn't ask me what I wanted us to come to an agreement on, and what he said after a pause made me think he didn't understand. Tell me, Superintendent, he began. How many times have you and I been in this office, talking about one of my clients? Although I saw where the question was aimed, I didn't dodge it. None, as far as I recall, I said; but then I added: It didn't seem necessary. However, now it does seem necessary to me, just as it has before with some of your colleagues. This last bit was true, but Cañas nodded with a smile of magnanimous scepticism. It's a first for me, he said. And I've been coming to this prison every week for almost fifteen years. Which could mean something, don't you think? He answered his own question: What it means is that, no matter what you say, Gamallo is not a normal inmate. He paused, unlaced his fingers, raised his elbows off his knees and straightened up to look me in the face. Look, he went on, in a different tone, I'm grateful you had me come here, and I'm especially grateful for your frankness; let me be frank with you too. Whether you like it or not, Gamallo is a special inmate, and it's logical that he's treated as a special inmate. But his being a special inmate doesn't mean that he can't be rehabilitated; quite the contrary: he's a special inmate precisely because he belongs to the tiny minority you spoke of, because he already is rehabilitated and for some time now he should no longer have been an inmate in any prison. That's the reality. Of course, it looks as if it will be difficult for you and I to come to an agreement on this. No matter. What matters is that your bosses think as I do and you'll have to do what they tell you to. I'm glad: I repeat that I believe Gamallo has paid his debt to society and is ready to be a free man. For my part I can only say that I'm going to use my best efforts to help him get out of here as soon as possible.

'That was basically what Cañas had to say. And it surprised me. They didn't seem to be the words of the reasonable or reasonably cynical lawyer I thought he was, but those of a deluded dreamer: a completely deluded dreamer, who had been led down the garden path by the Zarco myth and believed what he was saying because he'd lived his whole life under the shadow of that myth, or a dreamer but also an unscrupulous individual, or rather a shameless swindler, who needed me to believe what he was saying (although he himself did not believe it) because he didn't only want to benefit from Zarco's fame by defending him in court, but also wanted to achieve a great media triumph by getting him out of prison even knowing that he should not, or that it was premature or dangerous to do so.'

'I imagine that back then you had no idea of the real relationship between Gamallo and Cañas.'

'Of course not, I told you: nobody had any idea of that. I knew that when he was young Gamallo had lived in Gerona and that he had family here, but I didn't know anything else; that Cañas had been part of his gang I learned much later. In any case, that afternoon I realized that Cañas was right on at least one score: given

227

that my bosses supported him, I was bound hand and foot and I couldn't do anything or I could only carry on doing what I'd already begun to do, which was work towards Gamallo's rehabilitation without believing that Gamallo could be rehabilitated, as you said. And I also realized I'd stuck my foot in it with Cañas and that for the moment I would not come to any agreement with him and it would have been best to leave things as they were. So I wrapped up the conversation as fast as I could that day by saying that perhaps I was the one who was mistaken, and in any case I had no choice but to follow Correctional Institutions' guidelines, as he had said, and that meant that we'd both be pulling in the same direction after all; finally I told him he could count on me for whatever he might need, he thanked me with his victorious air intact (a gentlemanly winner, who didn't need to draw blood or flaunt his victory) and that was that.'

'Tell me just one more thing: were you really so convinced then that Cañas was wrong?'

'Yes.'

5

'The trial over the accusations from the Brians prison guards was in March or April of 2000, when Zarco had been incarcerated in Gerona Prison for several months. The hearing was held in a Barcelona court. There I discovered something important: at least in Catalonia, at least in Barcelona, Zarco's myth had not disintegrated, and Zarco was still Zarco. It's true that his public appearance didn't arouse the kind of expectation it would have done ten years earlier, when he was a celebrity, but it attracted enough journalists and spectators so that, in order to avoid interruptions or disturbances, the judge ordered the courtroom cleared and wouldn't allow anyone in who didn't have something to do with the trial. The fact that Zarco still enjoyed considerable pulling power with the media was, for me, a first success; the second was the outcome of the trial: Zarco was sentenced to three months' imprisonment, much less than we'd anticipated, so we were all satisfied and didn't even have to appeal the judgment. Tere and I toasted the triumph with French champagne, one night at my place, and Zarco and María thanked me and congratulated me though not effusively; none of the three asked how much they owed me, but that victory made me decide to set out for them the plan I'd been secretly thinking through – secretly from everybody, including Tere – since I'd taken over Zarco's defence and in that first interview he had asked me to look after not just this initial trial, but all those he had pending.

'My plan's objective was to get Zarco out of jail in two years. To achieve this I had to begin presenting, in the Barcelona court that had ruled on the Brians matter, an appeal for commutation or accumulation of sentences, so that the many convictions and the hundred and fifty years of prison time he had pending would be reduced to a single thirty-year sentence, the maximum time an inmate can spend in a Spanish prison. This was as far as the judicial phase of the operation went. Success was guaranteed this far; or almost: it was very improbable that the court would not grant what we were requesting, but if it did not, it was always possible to present an appeal for annulment before the Supreme Court. Be that as it may, once the sentence accumulation had been successful Zarco could apply for and obtain leave and, eventually day release, which would authorize him to spend the workday outside the prison and return at night to sleep there.

'At this point the political phase of the operation began, more complex and less certain. It began with the petition for a partial reprieve and ended ideally with the granting of a pardon and conditional release, a round-the-clock freedom subject only to the condition that Zarco not commit another crime. The problem, of course, was that getting a pardon was not easy, and much less so in Zarco's case. The application for the pardon could be submitted to the Ministry of Justice as soon as Zarco returned normally to prison after his first leave; then the Minister of Justice would have to raise it before Cabinet, which would have to approve it. The matter then consisted of how to get the Minister of Justice to approve our request. In accordance with my plan, this was only possible if three conditions were fulfilled. In the first place – and most importantly – we had to revive Zarco's media profile; and to revive it we had to mount a press campaign that would bring back part of his lost prestige and convince public opinion that he deserved a pardon and his freedom. Although Zarco himself, Tere and I would have to participate in the campaign, most of the weight, according to my plan, had to be carried by María: she was the one who had the key to Zarco's liberty because she was the one who could move the journalists and public opinion with her idealized vision of Zarco and her relationship with Zarco. In the second place, once the press campaign was launched we had to get personalities from public life to support the request for the pardon and we had to make sure the Catalan government would endorse the request before the central government. And, in the third place, we had to provide Zarco with a family and work situation that would make his fitting into society credible.'

'And what did that mean?'

'It meant that Zarco had to find a job and he had to marry María. Neither of the two things were difficult, but Zarco's face twisted into a grimace as soon as I mentioned them, one afternoon in the prison interview room. Look, Gafitas, he huffed. I can see myself working, but do me a favour and don't bust my balls about María. Naturally, I had foreseen this reaction: by this stage I was already aware that Zarco just considered María as the last and pathetic admirer from his glory days, and the only thing that linked him to her was a dry practical interest; and, because his reaction didn't take me by surprise, I immediately insisted, reminded him of what he already knew: I argued that, for a judge, matrimony was a guarantee of stability and that, for our purposes, María was the ideal wife and perfect propagandist, I reminded him that if he wanted to get out of prison he had to make sacrifices, I assured him that the marriage didn't have to be anything more than a mere formality or last any longer than strictly necessary. With no comeback to my arguments, a shadow seemed to fall over Zarco; he shrugged, said: Yeah. But then he came back to life to add: And what if María doesn't want to? Why wouldn't she? I asked. Well, he answered. Our thing is a circus: in prison it might be fun for her, but out there it won't be. Don't worry, I said, blocking that way out for him too. She'll want to. Remember that for her it's no circus.

'We were sitting in our usual way in the interview room, Zarco on his chair and facing the bars and the glass, me at my desk and facing the wall, leaning over my notebook. I remember it was a Friday and as usual in those days I was elated: Tere had phoned me that morning at the office and we'd arranged to get together that night at my place; after work, I'd have a couple of beers with Cortés and Gubau at the Royal; my daughter was arriving from Barcelona at noon the next day. That afternoon my only concern was to convince Zarco to approve my plan; once he'd approved it, I'd explain it to Tere and María and put it into action.

'I raised my eyes from my notebook, and Zarco and I looked at each other. I don't know, he said, before I could insist again. Maybe you're right. I leaned over my notebook again and said: I can't see any alternative. I also said: We have to be realistic. Or something equally trite. Then, with the reckless confidence of one who thinks he's the winner before he's won, I added: Unless you were going to marry someone else, of course. Someone else?, asked Zarco. Who else? I turned to him and joked: Anyone but Tere. Why would I want to marry Tere?, replied Zarco, surprised. I regretted my recklessness. It was a joke, I reassured him. Besides, I didn't say you wanted to marry Tere. Sure you did, he insisted. That's what you just said. I didn't say that, I insisted. I only said, and as a joke, that you can marry anyone you want except Tere. And why can't I marry Tere?, he asked. I was about to say: Because I'm going out with her; or worse still: Because I'm going to marry her. I didn't say it, and I wonder if, in spite of Tere's demands of confidentiality, she had told Zarco that we were seeing each other. I gave his question a professional answer: It would be inadvisable. She's your lifelong accomplice, she's been in jail, she's been on drugs, no one would believe you'd reformed. I repeated: It would be inadvisable.

'Zarco said nothing. Suddenly, a smile revealed his blackened teeth. What's up?, I asked. Nothing, he answered; then he contradicted himself: You've always thought Tere and I were hooked up, haven't you? I wasn't expecting the question; I asked: And weren't you? The smile still on his face, he seemed to reflect on it. For a moment I thought of reminding him of the first part of *Wild Boys*, where Zarco is going out with a girl that could be Tere and with whom Gafitas falls in love; but Zarco and I had still never discussed Bermúdez's films, and I felt there was no sense arguing against reality with fiction. Zarco asked: Do you know how long I've known Tere? I said no. Since we were four or five, answered Zarco. Her mother and my mother are cousins. Actually that's why my mother and stepfather moved to Gerona. And why I came later. I waited for him to go on with the story, not knowing where he was going with it. He didn't go on. Got to hand it to you, he said. What?, I asked. He answered: You thought Tere and I were hooked up and meanwhile you hooked up with her. Zarco was referring to the night when Tere and I did it on the beach at Montgó, after coming out of Marocco. I told you about that, don't know if you remember.'

'Of course I remember.'

'Zarco remembered too. I again felt tempted to tell him what was going on between Tere and me; for the second time I resisted. I defended myself, I don't know what from: It was just one night, I said. Yeah, said Zarco. But you did screw her. Weren't you scared I'd get pissed off, if you thought I was going out with her? He immediately forgot the question and qualified: Although, thinking about it, well, it must have been her who screwed you. Could be, I said, remembering how jealous I felt in the summer of '78 because Tere slept with other guys. Anyhow, she did what she wanted and with whoever she wanted. Yeah, yeah, said Zarco sarcastically. But with you it was different, eh? I raised my eyes from the notebook and this time I looked at him without understanding; Zarco was looking at me the same way; after a few seconds he said: Don't fucking tell me you never noticed. I asked him what he was talking about. Zarco laughed: openly. I can't fucking believe it, he said. I already knew you were a fool, Gafitas, but I didn't think it was that bad. I don't know what you're talking about, I repeated. Seriously?, Zarco insisted. Seriously, I insisted. Zarco asked: You really didn't notice that Tere had the hots for you? I was left speechless. I told you before that, during our furtive encounters at my place, Tere had reproached me more than once saying that in the summer of '78 I had shied away from her, but I'd always taken it as an implausible joke, or an almost cruel flirtation. How could I take it any other way when my memory of that time is completely clear and in it, as I've told you, Tere paid no attention to me or only did very sporadically, just as she did with so many? I avoided answering Zarco's question, but he guessed the answer from the look on my face. Fuck, Gafitas, he repeated. What a mess you were! I don't know how I managed to change the subject – perhaps I pretended not to be concerned about it, perhaps simply that it mattered much less than the matter that had brought me to the interview room – but the thing is I managed to get our conversation back to what we were talking about before and finally, not without having to argue for quite a while longer with him, I managed to get Zarco, although reluctantly, to agree to my plan; my complete plan: including his marriage to María.

'The first thing I did when I left the prison was to call María from my office and suggest that we meet the next day at the Royal; by phone I told her that I wanted to talk to her and that Tere would also come to the meeting. María was a bit surprised, but she didn't raise any objections. (She was surprised because I always saw her during the week, and I told you already the next day was a Saturday, one of the days that she went to see Zarco at the prison: unlike lawyers who could see prisoners during the week, relatives and friends could only visit on weekends.) That night, at my house, I laid out the plan for Tere and told her that Zarco had agreed. Perfect, she sounded pleased. Now we just need to get María to agree tomorrow. I asked: She'll agree, won't she? And then, before she could ask me why I was asking, a concern that had struck me in recent days, while I talked with María at her place, occurred to me. I said: I don't know. Sometimes I get the impression she's not as naive as she seems, or that she only pretends to be naive to play hard to get. What do you mean?, asked Tere. I don't know, I answered. Sometimes, especially lately, she gives me the impression that she knows it's all a farce and that we're using her, and that at any moment she might get fed up and tell us all to go to hell. Tere dismissed my suspicions. Don't worry, she said, trying to calm me down. She'll agree to your plan.

'Later, while we were dancing in the half-light of my dining room to "Bella sin alma" by Riccardo Cocciante, I told Tere what Zarco had told me at the prison. Tere laughed without letting go of me; she was dancing with her arms around my neck, her body pressed against mine, her face close to mine. It's a lie, isn't it?, I asked. It's true, she answered. I've told you a million times. Then why were you always slipping away?, I asked. Why did you ignore me? Why did you go off with other guys? I didn't slip away, Tere answered. And the one who ignored me was you. Tere didn't throw back in my face the two times I'd stood her up, but she did remind me of the afternoon in the washrooms of the Vilaró arcade and the night on Montgó beach, and then asked me: Who went after who? You after me, I accepted. But only those two times. Then I was after you, and you slipped away, you went off with

235

other guys. Because you ignored me, Tere repeated. She seemed like she was going to add something but she didn't; then, in a resigned tone, almost apologetic, she added: And because I always do what I want, Gafitas. Inevitably I remembered: No ties, no commitments, no demands, each to his own. Unnecessarily I asked: Now too? Tere winked at me. Now too, she answered. And Zarco?, I carried on asking. What about Zarco?, she carried on answering. I always thought you were Zarco's girlfriend, I exaggerated. Yeah I know, she said. And you weren't?, I asked. Did anyone tell you I was?, she answered. Did he tell you? Did I tell you? Who told you? Nobody, I answered. So then?, she asked. Just like that afternoon in the interview room at the prison while I was talking to Zarco, I remembered the love triangle in *Wild Boys*, but again I didn't dare mention it (or it simply seemed inappropriate) and I didn't answer; besides, I felt that Tere was telling the truth. I smiled. We kissed. We carried on dancing. And, as far as I recall, we didn't mention the matter again all night.

'The next morning Tere and I walked over to the Royal. María showed up when we'd already had our first coffee; we each ordered a second and María ordered her first and I began to explain to her and to Tere the plan to get Zarco freed. I did so pretending that I hadn't already explained it to Tere, of course: we didn't want María to guess what was between us, or, since she was going to be Zarco's wife and to play a fundamental role in my plan, as well, for her to feel relegated or undervalued or for her to get jealous if she knew I'd spoken to Tere before her. Both women listened to me as we drank our coffee, Tere pretending that it was the first time she was hearing the explanation, and, at the moment when I said that Zarco and María should get married and added that Zarco was enthusiastic about the idea, a smile lit up María's face. Really?, she asked. Really, I replied.

'I finished speaking and asked their opinions on the plan. Tere rushed to give me hers. If you and Antonio think it's good, it seems good to me, she said. Me too, said María. Well, she corrected herself immediately, timidly. All except for one thing. What?, I asked. María seemed to reflect for a moment. She had come alone, without her daughter, and, as she'd told us as soon as she sat down, later she was going to see Zarco at the prison. Although it was a sunny day, she was wearing her black overcoat, and underneath it had on a blue skirt and a speckled sweater; her hair was pulled back in a ponytail. She answered: I don't want to talk to journalists. Why not?, I asked. I feel embarrassed, she answered. Embarrassed?, I asked again. Yes, she answered again. It's scary. I don't know how to talk. I won't do it right. Tere should talk. Or you talk. While María was talking I remembered a comment Zarco had made that at the time I thought I'd misunderstood or that I'd taken seriously what must actually have been meant ironically ("María just wants to be in the magazines"). I summoned my patience and explained: I can't talk, María. And Tere can't either. You have to be the one to talk to journalists, because you're Antonio's companion and you're going to be his wife, and that's why you're the only one who can convince them. And don't worry; it won't be scary: Tere and I will go with you to the interviews, won't we, Tere? Tere said yes. María insisted. But what do you want me to convince them of?, she asked with an impatient whisper. What do you want me to tell them? The truth, I answered. What you've told me so many times. Tell them about Antonio, tell them about your love for Antonio, tell them that Antonio isn't Zarco any more, tell them about yourself and your daughter and your future and your daughter's future with Antonio. María listened to me shaking her head, her eyes fixed on her empty coffee cup, her ponytail moving behind her. I won't be able to, she repeated. Sure you will, Tere chimed in. Like Gafitas said: he and I will go with you wherever we need to and, if there's any problem, we'll be there to lend you a hand. Exactly, I said, and then I improvised: Besides, if you want I'll tell you what things would be good for you to say. Or I'll discuss it with Antonio and between the two of us we'll tell you. That's it: if you want, we'll give you a sort of script and you can memorize it and say it in your own way and then, as you feel more sure of yourself, you can add your own things until eventually you'll just be talking on your own account. What do you think? María looked up from her cup and regarded me with a mixture of curiosity and suspicion, as if asking: Are you sure? Before she could add another objection I persisted: Yes, that's what we'll do: Antonio and I will write down what you should say, which will just be what you've always said; and then you learn it and tell it in your own way. You'll see, it'll be really easy. María kept shaking her head weakly. She did so for a few more seconds, in silence, until she sighed and sat still.

'It took still more effort, but finally, with Tere's help, María ended up saying yes, and that very Saturday I got down to work. I had lunch with my daughter, who for weeks hadn't stopped asking me about my new squeeze (which is what she called Tere, not knowing her name), reproaching me for not introducing her and making fun of the traces of her having been in our house (I'm not surprised you don't want to introduce her to me, she said when she noticed the shelves in the dining room were starting to fill up with CDs of seventies and eighties music. What an old square she must be), and in the afternoon went into the office to draft a request for a cumulation of sentences and prepare a sketch of a script to discuss with Zarco and then present to María. On the Monday I asked Cortés and Gubau to read the request for the sentences to be served concurrently, finished polishing it up and had it sent to the court in Barcelona, and at about four, with my sketched-out script in hand, I went to visit Zarco. I spent almost the whole afternoon with him. I told him that María and Tere had agreed to my plan and he said he knew that already: María had told him that weekend. I explained that as I envisioned it, the campaign for his freedom would be like a piece of theatre in which María would play the starring role on the stage and we would be the directors in the wings. And Tere?, asked Zarco. Tere would be the assistant director, I answered. I don't know if Zarco knew what an assistant director did, but he seemed satisfied with my reply. Then he took a couple of folded pieces of paper out of his back pocket and told me to call the duty guard so he could give them to me. The guard appeared immediately, unlocked the little paper-passing drawer and I took the pages and had a look at them: it was a long list of names and phone numbers of journalists and personalities who'd had something to do with Zarco at some point or had been interested in his case and who, according to him, I could ask for help. Thanks, I said, putting the pages away. These are going to be very useful; but not yet. Zarco's brow crinkled. This time things have to be done differently, I explained. We won't start at the top but from the bottom. I reasoned that, for the national media, he practically didn't exist; for the local media, however (as we'd seen from the hearing for the last trial), he was still someone, so first we'd have to fully reactivate his figure in the local media and turn him back into a cause, in order to later be able to claim the attention of the national media.

'Zarco watched me curiously, a little surprised, but he didn't protest, so I deduced that the surprise was a welcome one and that he approved my strategy, and we devoted the rest of my visit to discussing the script that should guide María's public remarks. In the end, what we prepared was more of a sales pitch than a script, an arsenal of laments, good intentions and reasoning saturated with philanthropic and sentimental clichés, accompanied by something like an instruction manual. According to the pitch, Zarco was a generous and noble person, condemned by the chance circumstances of his birth to a life of criminality, who had spent half his life behind bars without ever having spilled any blood and who had more than paid for his missteps, had matured and learned from his mistakes; in short, Zarco was no longer Zarco but Antonio Gamallo, a man with whom María, a good, simple, unlucky woman, had fallen in love, and it was a love that had overcome all obstacles and would give her and her daughter the husband and father they deserved, and Zarco the family he'd never had and a free and decent future. That was the sales pitch; the instructions that went with it said more or less the following: so that María and Zarco could be married as soon as the prison authorities granted him leave, María should request a partial pardon from the government and, in order to achieve that, she needed to gather the maximum number of signatures in support of her request; for that reason, in all her public appearances María would request support for her cause from readers, listeners or spectators, who should send their signatures to the address that María herself would give them during the interview, an address that would be that of my office, thus converted into a sort of general headquarters of the campaign for Zarco's freedom.

'That was in short what Zarco and I agreed that afternoon at the prison. The next day I summoned María to my office, explained it to her and gave her some notes and an outline. I like it, she said, once she'd heard me out and had read the notes and outline. It's the absolute truth. I'm glad, I said, knowing that at least fifty per cent was absolute lies. But what matters is not that it's true, but that it's convincing. And that's where you come in. I'm going to get you a couple of interviews this week. Do you want us to rehearse what you're going to say? No need, said María, brandishing the papers I'd just given her. If you and Tere come with me, I have enough with what it says here. Are you sure?, I asked, surprised by her new self-assurance. I think so, she answered.

'She wasn't short of reasons to be. During that week I met separately with two journalists from two local papers: *El Punt* and *Diari de Girona*. Both owed me favours, I explained to both of them that I'd taken on Zarco's defence and asked them to interview María who would describe Zarco's current situation and give them a new point of view on his character; both their reactions were predictable, identical: a mixture of scepticism, pity and irritation, as if I were trying to sell them some fourth-hand merchandise. I had to do my utmost. I reminded them of the favours they owed me, promised to make it up to them, appealed to the human dimension of the matter, praising María and her efforts to get Zarco out of jail, the populist dimension, exaggerating the turnout of journalists and public at Zarco's last trial and finally the political dimension: the Catalan government had taken over responsibility for prisons within the region years before, and I predicted that what left-wing Madrid centralism hadn't been able to achieve in Zarco's case conservative Catalan nationalism was going to be able to do.

'That was enough. The two interviews took place on the Friday in my office; just as we'd promised María, Tere and I sat in on them, Tere in her capacity as María's friend, I in my capacity as Zarco's lawyer. And that's when we got a surprise. The surprise was María, who not only told her story to the journalists, but she unfurled the arguments Zarco and I had prepared so naturally and with such surprising eloquence, and on top of that played with absolute conviction the role of the righteous woman in love ready to do anything to liberate her man, fulfil her love and protect her family. As I witnessed that spectacle I remembered Zarco's phrase again, and only then did I begin to suspect that it contained, as well as a serious and not an ironic opinion, an opinion that was spot on. You can't imagine how pleased I was.

'Both interviews were published that Sunday and were a

success: both were given a whole page; both used quotes of María's as headlines, in which she protested against the injustice being committed against Zarco; although obviously the journalists had not agreed to describe her this way, both called María – one in a subtitle, the other in the lead-in to the article – "a woman of the people", and neither of them hid the sympathy she inspired. These two simultaneous interviews managed to call attention to María, who the following week spoke to a couple of local radio stations and a regional magazine that put her on the cover that same month. It was just the beginning. Then came the Catalan newspapers, radio and television stations, then the newspapers, radio and television stations from the rest of Spain, so that in just a few months Zarco recovered a notoriety he hadn't enjoyed for many years, as if instead of being forgotten he'd been asleep and the country waiting for him to wake up. It was María who achieved this remarkable feat, not Zarco. This woman is full of surprises, I'd say to Tere every time we saw each other at my place. I told you María just wanted to get into the magazines, Zarco told me every time we saw each other at the prison. For some time people racked their brains trying to figure out what turned María into what she turned into. I don't know; I can only repeat that none of what happened later was planned in advance, and that I was the first one to be surprised by that woman, who initially seemed terrified at the thought of facing a journalist, from one day to the next turning out to be imperious and feeling right at home in front of a microphone. In the press interviews her capacity for seduction was extraordinary, but on the radio and television, where she expressed herself without intermediaries, the effect she produced was devastating: at times María spoke with the sadness of a wounded little girl, at times with the fury of a mother whose children someone was trying to take away, at others with the wisdom of an old woman who had known love, poverty and war. But it wasn't just what she said and how she said it; on the radio and television María spoke also with her voice, her gestures, her glances, her way of dressing, and all this went into composing an irrefutable personality who began to draw the attention of many and with whom many began to identify: an average woman able to transfigure herself to the point of being invested with the greatness of an ancient heroine or a modern Pietà, and consequently able to convince anyone that such greatness was also within their reach. Furthermore, the fact of that kind of woman – a wounded, honest, valiant mother – being in love with and engaged to Antonio Gamallo allowed people to imagine that Zarco no longer existed and that Gamallo was just an ordinary man with an exceptional past who deserved an ordinary future.'

'So that's where it all started. I mean that's where María's story started.'

'Just as I've told it to you. No one meant to create a new media personality. With Zarco's celebrity we had enough: what we wanted was to get it back into circulation, back into existence, for people to remember him. The rest, I repeat, was pure coincidence.'

'I believe you: if anyone had put forward the idea of creating a media personality like María Vela, they would have failed.'

'Exactly. All those theories that paint me as the genius who invented María and then María backfiring on me don't hold water. The reality is that at most, as you say, I encouraged her; but she immediately dispensed with me and went on her way. What I really reproach myself for is not having seen earlier that María was taking control of our story, that she rather than Zarco was beginning to be the centre of the interviews, and that she'd turned into a celebrity as popular as Zarco.'

'When did you realize that?'

'I don't know. Late. I should have noticed almost from the start, for example when the Catalan station aired a programme about Zarco, at peak viewing time, after years of silence. It was called *Zarco: Democracy's Forgotten Inmate*. I don't know if you've seen it, it's one of the things missing in my archive.'

'I haven't seen it.'

'Well, get a copy: you'll be interested. I had quite a bit to do with it, among other reasons because at first the prison superintendent denied the producers of the programme permission to film inside and they appealed to me and I appealed to the Director-General of Correctional Institutions, who resolved the problem. The thing is that in theory Zarco was the protagonist of the documentary; and yes, the documentary did contain recent images of Zarco and statements he'd made, but María dominated, and one finished watching it with the sensation that it was María and not Zarco who society was punishing by keeping Zarco in prison: in the images we saw her talking of her love for Zarco, of the promise of happiness that a future at Zarco's side represented for her; we saw her serving at the school cafeteria and doing housework in her single-mother's flat with her daughter at her side; we saw her look directly at the camera almost defiantly and beg viewers to join the campaign for Zarco's liberty and send their signatures to my office address, the address appeared at that moment along the bottom of the screen; wearing the same black overcoat and the same pink tracksuit as the day I'd met her in my office, and holding her daughter's hand, we saw her go into the prison and come out again in the desolate gloom of a Sunday evening in winter . . . Anyway, the programme was enormously successful, and in the days following its broadcast, messages of solidarity for Zarco and petitions for a pardon rained down on my office.

'That triumph should have put me on my guard, but all it did was contribute to my happiness. Of course in those days there was nothing or almost nothing that didn't contribute to my happiness. My idyll with Tere was in full swing, my work was absorbing, my life had direction and meaning and I'd put in place a strategy to free Zarco that was working even better than I'd expected it to. Of course, I would have liked to see more of Tere, spend the odd weekend with her, introduce her to my daughter and my partners, but every time I suggested it, she claimed I was breaking the rules of the game and there was no reason to change them because they were working fine so far, and I had no choice but to put up with it and admit she was right or partially right: when all was said and done I was happy, and so was she; what did it matter that we only saw each other outside my house for work and that I barely knew anything about the rest of her life or that I'd never been inside her house, in Vilarroja, in spite of having driven her to her door a couple of times. Even María was happy, or seemed to be. Not only did she seem to like playing her new role but she seemed delighted to accept her sudden fame, as if she'd always been used to being interviewed by journalists and recognized and greeted by strangers in the street; her duplicity fascinated me: in front of the microphones or cameras she was a heart rending popular heroine, but when the cameras and microphones left she turned back into an irrelevant and grey, completely anodyne woman. Tere and I still accompanied her to her interviews for a long time, not because she needed us to, but because she asked us to or because, since it was the only way Tere and I could see each other outside of my house, I made sure she asked us to. In short: I was pleased, but Tere and María were too; the only one who wasn't pleased was Zarco.'

'Zarco?'

'It doesn't surprise me that you're surprised; I was surprised too. I didn't understand why, precisely when we started to glimpse a way out of his situation, his good mood of the initial days evaporated and he seemed increasingly pessimistic and complaining.

Much later I understood there were two reasons for this. The first is that by that stage Zarco was mediapathic: he had spent more than half his life appearing in the papers, on radio and television on a daily basis and it was hard for him to live without being the protagonist of the film or appearing in the media; that, I'm sure, is one of the reasons he approved the campaign I proposed to reactivate the popularity of his persona. The problem was that, since he was used to being the centre of attention, he didn't like it at all that María took over that position.'

'But María had become the centre of attention to get him out of prison!'

'And what's that got to do with anything? A mediapath is a mediapath, don't you get it? Zarco's irritation was not rational; the proof is that, if anyone had told him he was irritated, he would have responded that he wasn't. What was happening was simply that it wounded his self-esteem as a media star that the press had put the focus on María instead of putting it on him. Nothing more. Although that explained only one part of his disgruntlement; the other, which was perhaps fundamental, took me still more time to understand.

'Actually, I didn't understand it until one day towards the end of spring. That morning, more or less six months after taking charge of Zarco's defence, much sooner than we'd imagined, the Barcelona court consolidated all of his sentences into a single thirty-year sentence. It was the news we were waiting for, great news, and, as soon as I received it, I phoned Tere and María to tell them, and in the afternoon I ran over to the prison to tell Zarco. His reaction was bad, but I'd be lying if I said I was surprised. It disappointed me, but it didn't surprise me. By then, as I said, I had been noticing for weeks that he was tense and nervous, irritable, hearing him complain about everything and rant and rave about the prison, about the persecution a couple of the guards were subjecting him to and the passivity of the superintendent, who (according to him) allowed the persecution to go on. When I noticed his anxiety I rushed to speak to María and Tere, but María said she hadn't noticed anything and Tere had accused me of exaggerating and, as usual, played down the matter. Don't pay any attention to him, she said, referring to Zarco. Sometimes he gets like that. It's natural, don't you think? I would have gone crazy if I'd been locked up in jail for more than twenty years, almost without setting foot outside. Then she advised me: Patience. He'll get over it.

'I followed Tere's advice, but Zarco's uneasiness did not pass, at least not over the next few weeks. That's why I said I wasn't surprised by his reaction, that afternoon in the visiting room: when he heard the great news I'd gone to tell him, he wasn't pleased for himself, wasn't pleased for me, didn't even cheer up; he just asked in a demanding tone whether the consolidation of his sentences meant he could soon get out of prison. In spite of the fact that he had asked me the same question many times over recent weeks, I answered it once again: I told him that, although we didn't know when we could get him definitely released, in a couple of weeks we could start requesting day passes and in a few months he might be out on conditional release/probation. He reacted as if he didn't know the answer in advance and, with a contemptuous look on his face, he snorted. That's a long time, he said. I don't know if I can stand it. Clicking my tongue, I smiled. What do you mean you can't stand it, man?, I asked, with an unworried air. Just a few weeks, a few months, no time at all. I don't know, he repeated. I'm fed up with this prison. That's natural, I said. What I don't understand is why you haven't escaped yet. But it's not worth it now: in no time at all, like I said, you'll start to get out on leave. Yeah, he answered. To go back inside the next day. I don't want to go back inside. I don't want to come back

247

to this shit. I'm sick and fucking tired of it. I've made up my mind. What have you decided?, I asked, alarmed. I'm out of here, he answered. I'm going to ask to be transferred. I'll talk to my friend Pere Prada, tell him I'm fed up and I want to be moved. I can't take it here any more. And then he started cursing the prison, the superintendent and the two guards who seemed to be harassing him. I tried not to let us get buried in the avalanche of complaints, but the way I did so was mistaken: interrupting him every couple of sentences, I carried on joking, I was trying to play down that list of grievances, I assured him that when he started to go out on leave everything would change; finally when he mentioned his "friend" Pere Prada again and I reminded him in a sarcastic tone, as if accusing him of self-importance, that Prada was not his friend but the Director-General of Correctional Institutions, he cut me off: Shut your fucking mouth! Between the four walls of the inter-view room, Zarco's order exploded like slander. When I heard it, I thought of standing up and walking out; but, when I started to follow that impulse, I looked at Zarco and suddenly saw in his eyes something I don't remember ever having seen and that, to tell you the truth, I never expected to see and much less at that moment, something that seemed to me to be the complete expla-nation of his anxiety. Do you know what it was?'

'No.'

'Fear. Pure and simple fear. I couldn't believe it, and the surprise made me swallow my pride, I shut up and sat back down at my desk. I waited for Zarco's apology, which was not forthcoming; the only thing that reached me, in the silence of the visiting room, filtered by the glass that separated the two rows of bars, was his laboured and hoarse breathing. I stood up, stretched my legs, took a deep breath, sat back down at my desk and, after a pause, tried to get Zarco to see reason. I said that I understood but that this was not the moment to think of transfers, I assured him I'd speak to the superintendent as soon as I could and demand he put a stop to the guards' persecution, I asked him to endure it for a little longer, I reminded him that he had within reach what he'd so long been fighting for, I begged him to calm down, not to ruin everything. Zarco listened to me with his head hanging, still furious, still panting a little, although when I finished speaking he seemed to have cooled off; he let a few seconds go by, hinted at a smile that almost seemed like an apology or that I interpreted as an apology, accepted that I might be right and finally asked me to talk to the superintendent as soon as I could so that the harassment of the guards would stop and accelerate as far as possible the granting of weekend passes and conditional release. I said yes to everything, promised that as soon as I left the interview room I would go to see the superintendent and, without any more explanations, we said goodbye.

'I did what I'd promised. And approximately three weeks later Zarco enjoyed his first weekend pass in a long time.'

'So do you think it was a blend of jealousy and fear that made Zarco lose his initial optimism, that worried and infuriated him?'

'Yes. Although the fear was the fundamental thing.'

'But fear of what?'

'That took me even longer to understand. Do you know what it's like to want something and be afraid of it at the same time?'

'I think so.'

'Well, that's what was happening to Zarco: there was nothing he wanted more than to be free, and at the same time there was nothing he feared more than being free.'

'Are you telling me that Zarco was afraid to get out of jail?'

'Exactly.'

6

'Was Gamallo afraid of leaving the prison? Of course he was! How couldn't he be? Did Cañas tell you this? And when did he figure it out? Because if he'd figured it out in time, he would have been spared a lot of unpleasantness, and would have spared the rest of us too. And the thing is if you think it through it wasn't that difficult, eh? Gamallo had been living in prisons for decades; prison life is bad, but over the years you start to master the rules and get used to it, and it can end up seeming like a comfortable life. That's what happened to Gamallo, who actually didn't know any other kind of life. For him prison was his home, while liberty was the outdoors: he'd forgotten what it was like out there, what was out there, how to behave out there, maybe even who he was out there.'

'Cañas basically said that, in theory, there was nothing Zarco desired as much as getting out of jail, but deep down there was nothing he was so frightened of.'

'He's right: when he was far from freedom, Zarco did what he could to get closer to getting it, whereas, when he got too close to getting freed, he did whatever he could to get away from it. I think this explains in part what happened. When he came to the Gerona prison at the end of the year, Gamallo was quite a balanced inmate without much appetite for trouble, he rather seemed to want to go unnoticed, to join in with the rest of the inmates and to co-operate with us; four or five months later, when he became eligible to start applying for weekend passes, he'd turned into a gruff, rebellious and angry inmate who was confrontational with everyone and saw enemies everywhere. The prospect of freedom unhinged him. I insist that, if Cañas had understood all this in time, perhaps he wouldn't have proceeded in the worst possible way, which is how he proceeded: trying to get Gamallo out of prison as soon as he could and by any means possible, instead of being prudent and letting time take its course and letting him mature and letting us prepare him for freedom (supposing we could have done so, of course); and, especially, running that disastrous press campaign that put Gamallo back on the front pages.'

'Did you tell Cañas all this?'

'Of course. As soon as I could. As soon as it was clear to me.'

'When was that?'

'The second time we saw each other in my office. On that occasion it was he who requested the meeting. Or rather who improvised it. That afternoon I was negotiating with a contractor who was going to carry out some work that we'd been needing to get done at the prison for some time when my secretary interrupted me to tell me that Cañas wanted to see me urgently. I told her it was going to be a while before I finished and to fix an appointment for the lawyer for any day that week, but my secretary answered that Cañas insisted on seeing me immediately and I agreed to let him come in. I cut short my dialogue with the contractor, but as soon as I saw Cañas walk into my office I realized I'd made a mistake and should have made him wait a little longer so he could calm down. I shook his hand and offered him a seat on the sofa, but he didn't sit down, and we both stood there beside the redundant piece of furniture. The first thing Cañas said to me was that he'd just spoken to Gamallo and had come to present a protest, and the first thing I thought when I heard him was that I wasn't surprised he'd come to present a protest in Gamallo's name and that, although he was probably puffed up by the triumph of the media offensive he'd launched in favour of his client and by the political and popular support he'd won with it, Gamallo had managed to infect him with his recent nervousness. I thought of saying to him: For this you kicked up a fuss with my secretary? Although in the end I only said: Tell me.

'Without further ado Cañas threw in my face the mistreatment to which, according to him, two guards were subjecting his client. He rounded off his complaint with the threat of bringing a lawsuit against my two subordinates, of talking to the director-general of prisons and of taking the case to the newspapers. Then he concluded, emphatically: Either you stop this or I do. Cañas pointed his index finger at me, his eyes wide open behind the lenses of his glasses; the gentlemanly and proud winner of his first visit had disappeared, and in his place was an irate, high and mighty *señorito*, panicking that he might lose. I stood staring at him in silence. He lowered his finger. Then I asked him the names of the two guards and Cañas told me: they were two of my most trusted men (one, head of service; the other a guard who'd been working under me for twenty years). I sighed and again offered him a seat, this time in front of my desk; the lawyer again refused, but I pretended he'd accepted and sat back down. Don't worry, I said. I'll open an investigation. I'll speak to both guards. I'll find out what has been going on. In any case, I added straight away, leaning back in my armchair and making it turn, let me be honest with you: I was expecting this. Cañas asked me, impatiently, what it was that I expected. I reflected for a moment, tried to explain: I assured him that for some time all my specialists had been noticing a physical and psychological backslide in Gamallo, that for a couple of weeks at that point Gamallo had been refusing the methadone treatment he was on to combat his heroin addiction (which could only mean he'd found a way to get drugs and was using them again), that his relationship with the guards and with the rest of the inmates was getting worse by the day and that the whole prison-management team felt that an important part of the blame for the mess fell on the uproar of the propaganda campaign in favour of a pardon and especially on the unexpected new life that this uproar had given to Zarco's personality.

'Up to that moment, Cañas had listened to me visibly holding back his desire to interrupt, but here he could restrain himself no longer. I don't know what you're talking about, he said. Zarco is dead. Zarco is alive, I contradicted him gently. He was dead, but you resuscitated him. If that poor woman didn't spend her days telling fairy stories to journalists, with you by her side, perhaps this wouldn't be happening. I was referring to María Vela, of course, who Cañas was using as a battering ram in his campaign for Zarco's freedom; it goes without saying that what I'd told him was what everyone knew, but Cañas did not like to hear it. He took a couple of steps forward, put his hands on my desk, leaned towards me. Tell me something, Superintendent, he spat out. Why don't you stick to your business and leave the rest of us in peace? Cañas was breathing hard, his nostrils trembled and, rather than speaking, he'd babbled out the words, as if his fury had hobbled his tongue; as you know, I had tried to avoid a confrontation with him since the beginning, but now realized I could not back down. I answered: Because this business is also mine. As much mine as yours, Counsellor. Believe me: I wish it wasn't, but it is. And, since it's also mine, I have the obligation to tell you what I think, and I think you're the one who should leave Gamallo in peace. Whatever life he has left, you are helping him fuck it up. I understood that this truth would really irritate Cañas; I understood that he would reply: The ones who have always tried to fuck up Gamallo's life are people like you. And he added, standing back up again: Only this time you're not going to be able to. Having said this, Cañas seemed to consider the interview finished, walked to my office door and opened it, but before going through it he stopped, spun around and again pointed his furious *señorito*'s index finger at me. Make sure those guards don't bother my client again, he demanded. And another thing: we're going to start requesting weekend-release passes; I hope you'll grant them. I asked him if that were a threat. No, he replied. Just a piece of advice. But it's good advice. Take it. Sure, I said, leaning back in my chair and raising my hands in a gesture both sardonic and conciliatory. What choice do I have?

'The lawyer slammed the door on his way out and left me perplexed. I still didn't know whether Cañas was utterly naive and believed everything Gamallo told him or if he was an utter cynic and pretended to believe him and in reality he was just after fame at the expense of Gamallo's fame. Whatever the case, I resigned myself to receiving another phone call from the director-general, to whom Cañas had appealed a few weeks earlier to force me to authorize some television cameras to film Gamallo inside the prison. But the director-general didn't call, no one gave me any indication of how I was to deal with Gamallo, no one filed any complaints against anyone and the issue did not come out in the papers. Not only that: although two days later I received a request for a weekend-release permit in Gamallo's name with Cañas' signature, that afternoon the lawyer returned to my office to apologize for his behaviour during his previous visit. That was when my opinion of Cañas changed and I began to like him, because more courage is needed to admit a mistake than to persist in it, and much more to make peace than to declare war. That afternoon I thanked Cañas, told him he had no reason to apologize, and considered the matter resolved and explained that, as I'd only received his request a few hours earlier, it was too late for Gamallo to get out that weekend, but that he'd be able to the next one.

'Over the following days I spoke to the two guards that Gamallo had accused of harassing him and asked them to stay away from him, I spoke to members of the prison staff and asked them to use extreme caution with our man, and the next weekend Gamallo went out on leave for the first time in a long while.'

7

'The Saturday that Zarco got out on his first weekend release I arranged to meet Tere at noon in front of the post office, and from there we went to Marfà Street to pick up María and her daughter. When we got to the prison there was already a cloud of journalists around the door, who fell on María and her daughter as soon as they got out of the car. María dealt with them and, after answering a few questions, went inside the prison with her daughter. Tere and I remained outside, chatting a few steps away from the journalists, whom I kept at bay with jokes on the grounds that it was Zarco's day and not mine.

'Ten minutes later Zarco came out. His exit seemed staged by a set designer: María and her daughter each held one of his hands; the three of them smiled at the cameras. During the seconds they spent in the prison yard, Zarco answered reporters' questions and then, still pursued by photographers' flashes and television cameras, they walked out to the street and got in the car. Tere and I were waiting for them inside; María and her daughter sat in the back, with Tere; without saying a word of greeting to either Tere or me, Zarco got in the front, beside me. The journalists surrounded the car and for a moment all of us inside remained still and silent, as if time had stopped or we were frozen or trapped inside a glass ball, but then Zarco turned towards me with total joy in his eyes and said with a voice so deep it sounded like it was coming from his stomach: Let's get the fuck out of here, Gafitas.

'To celebrate Zarco's release permit I took them all out for lunch to a restaurant in Cartellà, a nearby village. In my memory it was a very strange meal, maybe because it was the first time for almost everything: the first time Zarco was out of prison in a long time, the first time Zarco and María were together outside the prison, the first time Zarco, Tere and María were together, the first time the five of us were together, as well. The truth is that nobody knew exactly how to act, or what role they should be playing, or those of us who did know, didn't know how to play it, starting with Zarco, who turned in a poor performance as the prisoner on weekend release and María's future husband, and ending with me, who turned in an even worse one as the lawyer and former accomplice of the prisoner on weekend release (as well as Tere's secret lover). But worst of all was that, as soon as I saw Zarco and María beside each other, I felt with no room for doubt that such a couple could not function, could not even do an imitation of a real couple for very long: it wasn't just that the combination of authentic *quinqui* and apparent good Samaritan was entirely improbable, it was that Zarco didn't pay the slightest bit of attention to María — neither to María nor to her daughter — and spent the whole meal stuffing his face and knocking back the wine, joking around and telling Tere and I stories while I tried to make conversation with María and her daughter, who barely touched her food and spent the whole time watching everyone with terrified eyes. The consequence of that general casting error and Zarco's terrible manners, or his inability to pretend, was that, as well as being very strange, the meal was also very uncomfortable: very uncomfortable for everyone except him, who seemed to be having a high time; it also turned out to be much shorter than anticipated, thanks to Tere and me (who quickly took charge of the situation and, without any prior decision, tried to cut short María's distress), and that was in spite of the fact that in the end there was no way to get Zarco out of the restaurant, especially when the owner of the place committed the error of asking him to sign the visitors' book.

'Before four in the afternoon I parked the car in María's street. Are we here?, asked Zarco, peering out through the windscreen. María said yes, took her leave and walked towards the door to her building. Well, sighed Zarco. I guess I'm staying here too. He said it without the slightest enthusiasm, knowing it was what I was expecting him to say. He got out of the car and stood next to it, with one arm leaning on the roof, looking in at Tere and at me through the passenger window. He'd had quite a bit to drink, and he seemed more content than resigned. Take it easy this weekend, you bastards, he joked. Don't get carried away. Then he patted the hood of the car and followed María and her daughter.'

'Were you worried?'

'No. I don't think so. Why?'

'Well, you said Zarco and María didn't seem like a very believable couple. Besides, with the expectation Zarco's weekend release had raised, with all the correctional authorities counting on its success and the superintendent opposed to it, any mistake could ruin your whole half-year's work.'

'That's true. But it's also true that I trusted Zarco and was convinced that he wanted to be free and wasn't going to do anything stupid. Although maybe you're right: maybe I was more worried than I remember, or than I was able or willing to recognize. I don't know. In any case I don't remember that as a special weekend either. What I do remember is that after dropping Zarco off I suggested to Tere that we go for coffee and that she turned down my invitation alleging that she had two exams on Tuesday and she had to study, and then I drove her home; I also remember that I spent the rest of Saturday and Sunday indoors without seeing anyone but my daughter, and that on the Monday morning, after Zarco had returned to prison the previous evening, I personally wrote the request for a partial pardon. At midday I went to see Zarco to get him to sign it, and in the afternoon I sent all the documentation to the Ministry of Justice.

'Zarco began to enjoy regular outings like that, at first every three weeks, then every two weeks, then once a week. Naturally, I hoped that these increasing tastes of freedom would improve his mood and his situation in the prison; what happened was exactly the opposite: instead of diminishing or dying down, Zarco's anxiety did nothing but grow, increasingly uncontrollable and increasingly absurd. One example: I managed to get the superintendent to keep the two guards who according to him were making his life impossible away from him, but he immediately began to complain about two other guards. Another example: each time I visited him I begged him to avoid any kind of conflict, but he answered as if he hadn't heard me or as if I'd said the opposite of what I'd said, talking to me about complaints that his insubordination and protests provoked among the prison personnel, and making him feel increasingly proud of them. I still didn't entirely understand the way Zarco worked, or I didn't want to understand it: since our first encounter at the prison I was aware of the duplicity or internal contradiction that was tearing him up – the contradiction between the legend, or the myth, and the reality, between the persona and the person; but, in spite of this precise intuition, I didn't accept that, as the prison superintendent had told me very early, the press campaign that I'd initiated to achieve Zarco's freedom accentuated instead of attenuating that contradiction, because it resuscitated, unfortunately for the person, the legend and the myth of a persona by then almost redundant.

'I suppose that the petulant exhibitionism with which Zarco kept me informed at the time, just when he began to start getting out, of his outrages and the degradation of his life in prison, has in part to be attributed to this resurrection. But being informed of it didn't mean I was able to stop it. When Zarco was out on release we didn't see each other, and, no matter how much I asked him later, he didn't talk to me about those free weekends (only prison matters seemed to loosen his tongue). During the week I couldn't do much to fix things either: in our conversations in the visiting room I could only listen to him, put up with his unpleasantness, swaggering and rudeness and try to calm him down and keep his spirits up and give him encouraging news, and outside the prison all I could do was keep the campaign in favour of getting him pardoned alive and carry on accompanying María (with or without Tere) on her promotional interviews. By then, I also had to go back to taking serious care of things at the office. I'd spent over half a year not doing so, working almost exclusively on Zarco's case, and in that time a certain amount of chaos had been generated that neither Cortés nor Gubau had managed to sort out and that had led to us losing some clients ("I knew this thing with Zarco was going to get us in shit," Cortés used to say as we had our Friday evening beers at the Royal. "But I didn't think it would be this bad"). So I went back to handling the important cases, back to travelling frequently, back to staying late working at the office. These changes affected my relationship with Tere. Not that we stopped seeing each other, but we saw less of each other, and so I started insisting that we move our midweek dates to the weekends, which was when I could have more free time available; but Tere always flatly refused: she said that weekends were the only time she had to study and besides, if we moved our dates to the weekends, they wouldn't be secret any more. That's silly, I replied. And your daughter?, Tere argued. She doesn't come every weekend, I answered. Besides, she wasn't born yesterday, don't you think she already knows I'm seeing someone . . . Not to mention that we could go to your house or anywhere else. Tere wouldn't give in: she would not let me go to her house, or see me on the weekends, or meet my daughter or my friends. Anyone would say you're ashamed of me, I said to her once, exasperated by her intransigence. Tere looked surprised and then smiled an enigmatic smile (or that's what it seemed like to me), but didn't say anything.

'All this – Zarco's personal degradation, my return to proper work at the office and a slight cooling off of my relationship with Tere – explains what happened one night at the end of May or beginning of June, when Zarco had had several consecutive weekend releases. It was an important night for Zarco and for me. I'd gone to bed early and had been asleep for a while when the phone rang. I answered. Cañas? I heard. Speaking, I answered. It's Eduardo Requena, said the prison superintendent. Sorry for calling so late. Still lying in bed and in the dark, I suddenly came back to reality: it was Sunday night and very late; I immediately thought something had happened with Zarco. Not to worry, I said. What's happened? I'm calling about Gamallo, the superintendent answered. It's midnight and he's not back. He's supposed to be in his cell by nine. If he doesn't show up before breakfast we'll be in trouble.

'Requena and I barely exchanged another phrase or two; there was nothing else to say: Zarco hadn't returned from his weekend release and, unless I found out where he'd gone and managed to get him back to the prison, the campaign for his liberty would go down the drain. I hung up the phone, turned on the light, sat up in bed, thought for a moment, picked up the phone and called María, who said when she answered that she wasn't sleeping but watching TV. I told her what Requena had told me and, with a voice that revealed neither surprise nor alarm, she explained that she didn't understand and that it wasn't yet nine o'clock when she dropped Zarco off two hundred metres from the prison door. He said he wanted to go for a walk before going in, María told me. I asked her if anything abnormal had happened that weekend and María said that it would depend what I considered abnormal and for her the question wasn't if anything abnormal had happened but if anything normal had happened. I asked her what she meant by that and María answered, sounding irritated, that she'd meant exactly what she'd said. Not understanding her irritation, I asked her if she had any idea where Zarco could be and María answered, sounding even more irritated, that I should ask Tere. He spent the weekend with Tere?, I asked incredulously. You can ask her that too, she answered.

'I didn't want to argue any more or ask her any more questions, nor was there time, so I asked María to stay home, in case Zarco called her or showed up there. Then I hung up, picked the phone back up and started dialling Tere's number, but I hadn't finished when I changed my mind and hung up again. I got up, tidied myself up a little, got in the car and drove towards Vilarroja. To get to Tere's house you had to go past the neighbourhood church and down three deserted, steep and badly-lit streets, which that night seemed straight out of an Andalusian village in the 1960s. When I got to the place I was looking for – a two-storey building that looked like a garage or a warehouse – I stopped the car, got out and rang the intercom for the second floor. No one answered. I rang the first floor. Tere answered. I told her who it was and without buzzing me in she asked what I wanted and I told her what the prison superintendent had told me. She asked if I'd talked to María and I told her what María had told me and asked her the question María told me to ask her. Tere didn't answer; she asked me to wait. After a few minutes she appeared and, without a word of greeting, pointed to my car. Let's go, she said. Where?, I asked, following her: she was wearing jeans, a white shirt, sneakers and her handbag strap across her chest, like twenty years ago when we'd meet up in La Font to go out and steal cars, snatch old ladies' handbags and rob banks on the coast. To look for Antonio, she answered. Do you know where he is? I asked. No, she answered. But we'll find out.

'Following Tere's instructions I drove out of Vilarroja and towards Font de la Polvora. On the way there I asked her again if she'd been with Zarco that weekend and this time she answered: she said no. Then I asked her if she knew who Zarco had been with that weekend and she said she had an idea. Then I remembered the last time I'd spoken to the prison superintendent, in his office, and I asked her if she knew that Zarco was using heroin again. Of course, she said. And why didn't you tell me?, I asked. Because it wouldn't have done any good, she answered. Besides, when did you want me to tell you? We haven't seen each other for weeks. Not through any fault of mine, I reproached her. She returned the reproach: Don't start with me on what's whose fault, Gafitas. I thought Tere was blaming me for Zarco's bolting, but it seemed so unfair an accusation that I didn't even try to defend myself. After a silence I insisted: Do you know where Zarco scores his heroin? No, said Tere and, I don't know why, but I felt she was lying; then I wondered whether she was lying when she said she hadn't spent the weekend with Zarco; then I wondered whether she didn't spend the weekends with me so she could spend them with Zarco. Tere went on: Anyway, it's easy to get it in prison. And outside prison as well. At least it is for him.

'We'd arrived in Font de la Pòlvora. While we drove into the neighbourhood I asked again: Does María know? About the smack?, she asked, and she answered herself: She pretends not to know, but she knows. What she can't pretend not to know is that she barely sees Zarco on the weekends and when he does go to her place, he robs her. Stop here. I noticed that she'd said Zarco and not Antonio and I stopped on a dirt road without

263

streetlights, between two identical tower blocks or between two blocks of flats that the night made almost identical. Tere got out and told me to wait for her. I watched her go in one of the blocks that looked like a massive shadow dotted with windows of light, I saw her come out a little while later and point to the other building, saw her go in, saw her come out almost immediately. They don't know anything here, she said, as she got back in the car. Let's try in Sant Gregori.

'We tried a bungalow in a housing development in Sant Gregori and a house in the old quarter of Salt. Finally, in a farmhouse near Aiguaviva they assured Tere they'd seen Zarco that evening and directed her to a place in La Creueta, a district in the outskirts, south-east of Gerona. We crossed the city again and, somewhere around four or five in the morning, I stopped in an empty field, beside the roundabout of a bypass, opposite a block of flats that in the darkness of that desolate place looked like a spaceship stranded in the small hours. Tere got out of the car, went into the building, came out a while later, opened my door, and leaning on it announced: He's upstairs. I asked: Did you speak to him? Yes, she answered. I told him that he has to be at the prison before dawn. I don't think he even heard me. I asked: How is he? Tere shrugged and half-closed her eyes in a gesture that meant: You can imagine. Who's he with? Two guys; I don't know them. Have you told him I'm here? No. We looked at each other in silence for a second. Go on up, please, said Tere. He'll listen to you.

'I was surprised by Tere's confidence (also by that "please": she didn't normally ask for favours or say please), but I understood that I at least had to try. So I got out of the car and, walking behind her, entered the block of flats and walked up a narrow and dark stairway, although its darkness dissolved bit by bit as we approached a door left ajar on the landing of the top floor, out of which sprang a strip of light. We opened the door the rest of the way, walked into the flat, down a short hallway and there was Zarco, sitting on a burst sofa, twisting up the end of a joint under the sickly light of a fluorescent tube. Beside him was a redheaded guy sleeping, in a tracksuit, and to his left, legs splayed in an armchair, a barefoot black man in his underwear was watching TV with the remote control lying on one of his thighs; behind him, a big picture window looked out into the night. The room was a shithole: the floor was strewn with ash and bits of food, empty beer cans, empty cigarette packets, unidentifiable substances; also on the floor, in front of the sofa, there was a table made from two upside-down beer cases: at a glimpse I saw, on top of it, a bottle of whisky with barely any whisky in it, three dirty glasses, a crumpled Fortuna packet, a couple of hypodermic syringes, the remains of a bit of cocaine in a piece of tinfoil and a lump of hash.

'Zarco seemed exaggeratedly glad to see me: he said the word fuck several times as he finished rolling the joint with an expert twist of his fingers and then stood up and opened his arms wide in a welcoming gesture and asked Tere why she hadn't told him I was with her. Tere didn't answer the question; I didn't answer the welcome: summoning all my patience I recognized the arrogant thug he could be turned into by the combination of alcohol and drugs, but especially by the combination of alcohol and drugs with the resurrection of his own myth, with the triumph of the persona over the person. Zarco approached me smiling, halfway between smug and somnambulant, threw an arm over my shoulders and turned towards his party pals like an actor addressing the stalls. Hey, guys!, he said, demanding their attention; he got part of it: although the redhead went on sleeping, the black guy looked over, pointing at us with the remote control. Zarco acted as if they were both listening. Believe it or not, he announced, this is my lawyer. A son of a bitch with three sets of balls, badder than a toothache. He laughed loudly revealing two rows of rotted teeth and patted me on the back. The black guy didn't laugh; he turned back to the TV indifferently setting the remote control back down on his thigh. Zarco looked like a vagrant: he stank of sweat, tobacco and alcohol, his eyes were extremely red, his hair was dirty and his clothes dirty and wrinkled; on his feet he only had a pair of socks with holes in them out of which poked enormous and dirty toenails. He urged me to light the joint, but I refused his offer and he lit it himself; then he gestured to the whole room like a drunken host. Well, he said to us recent arrivals. Are you going to have a seat? If you feel like a beer, there should be one left somewhere. Tere and I stood still, in silence, and Zarco sat down and almost at the same moment the redhead woke up and looked at us with fear on his face; Zarco calmed him down: he patted his knee and said something that made him half-smile. Then the redhead sat up and stretched and started to prepare a couple of lines of coke while Zarco watched him, smoking.

'I turned to Tere and interrogated her wordlessly. I don't know if Tere understood the question (she was standing, looking very serious, her left leg moving faster than ever), but I understood that she was asking me wordlessly to try. I tried. I have to talk to you, I said to Zarco, who seemed suddenly to remember I was there and took a last hit off the joint and offered it to me. Great, he said. Tell me. He looked at his companions. Don't worry about these two, Zarco reassured me, pointing at the black guy and the redhead. They don't understand shit. Zarco shook the joint in the air, insisting that I take it; I kept not taking it and finally it was Tere who took it, with an impatient gesture. Zarco stared at me. There's not much to say, I said. Just that you have to go back. He smiled. Feigning terrible disappointment he clicked his tongue, moved his head to the left and right, asked: To the nick? I didn't answer. Zarco added still smiling: I'm not going back. Why not?,

266

I asked. Because I don't feel like it, he answered. I'm fine here. Aren't you? Turning to Tere, he patted the sofa next to him a couple of times and said: Come on, Tere, sit down and tell this guy to take a toke and get over it all. For once we're all partying together . . . Tere didn't say anything, but she didn't sit down beside Zarco or pass me the joint either. You have to go back, I repeated. The superintendent called me and told me he's expecting you: if you go back he'll pretend nothing's happened. Mentioning the superintendent didn't help. Suddenly tense, Zarco replied: Well, you can tell him from me that he can keep waiting. He sat forward on the sofa, poured what was left of the whisky in a glass, knocked it back in one and, after a silence, began to complain, getting more and more upset: he grumbled about the conditions of prison life, he assured us that since he'd begun to get weekend-release passes things had continued to get worse for him inside and several guards and several inmates had decided to make his life impossible with the consent or at the urging of the superintendent, he finished up by announcing that the next day he'd call his friend Pere Prada and then he'd hold a press conference to denounce his situation in the prison.

'I listened to Zarco's complaints with the weary feeling of having heard them all many times already, but I didn't feel like interrupting him. When he finished talking he seemed exhausted and saddened and a little confused. I felt that I should take advantage of that slump to return to the attack and try to convince him, but just then the redheaded guy snorted the first line of coke and, pointing at the last one with a rolled-up thousand-peseta note, invited Zarco to have it; I understood that if Zarco snorted the line it would not be humanly possible to get him back to the prison that night, so, without a second thought, I grabbed the note out of the redhead's hand, stuck one end in my nose and inhaled the line through the other. The redhead and Zarco were astonished. Then, as my brain coped with the hit of coke, Zarco looked at the redhead, still perplexed he looked back at me, his eyes narrow like slits, and finally laughed joylessly. You're something else, Gafitas, he said.

'I snorted the rest of the coke and handed the thousand pesetas back to the redhead. Zarco stopped laughing abruptly, but seemed to relax again straight away, seemed to be back in a good mood; he lit a cigarette and leaned back on the sofa; he said: So you've come to rescue me, eh? This time I didn't answer either. He scrutinized me for a couple of seconds and continued in a relaxed tone: I'm curious about something, Gafitas. I've been meaning to ask you for a while and I always forget. What's that?, I asked. Why did you agree to defend me?, he asked. Why have you set up this whole scene with the journalists and the brainless María? And why are you so compelled to get me out of jail? You know why, I said. No, said Zarco. I know what you told me, but I don't know the truth. What's the truth, Gafitas? Why are you doing this? Are you trying to be sanctimonious, because you want to go to heaven? Or is it that you want me to go to heaven so you take my coke right out from under my nose? It wouldn't be just that you want to screw Tere, would it? Because if it's that . . . He looked at Tere and shut up. I hadn't heard her move, but she had moved, silently as a cat: now she was sitting on top of a beer case, with her back against the wall, with her legs crossed and the almost extinguished roach between her fingers, witnessing the scene at a distance, without showing much interest. Zarco stopped looking at Tere and looked at me, intrigued. During those months I had wondered more than once whether he knew that Tere and I were sleeping together; now I thought I sensed that he didn't even suspect it. I answered: I told you: You scratch my back, I'll scratch yours. In Zarco's eyes curiosity turned to sarcasm, so, before he could say anything, I jumped the gun. And don't forget it's my job, I said as well. This is how I make a living. Fuck off, Zarco replied. People get paid to do their jobs. And you haven't charged me a fucking cent. You haven't asked how much you owe me either, I answered. Besides, I don't charge you money, but that doesn't mean I'm not earning; maybe I should pay you: you're making me famous. Zarco looked like he was about to burst out laughing again, but limited himself to simply tightening his lips sardonically, and making a gesture with his hands as if pushing me away and repeating as his gaze wandered to the TV: Fuck off, Gafitas!

'The TV was showing a car chase across a desert and, for a moment, Zarco became completely absorbed by it, just as the redhead and the black guy were; in the picture window, behind him, the night was turning into dawn. I noticed the coke was starting to speed up my brain. Then, nodding without taking his eyes off the screen, Zarco mumbled something unintelligible several times. Until he suddenly turned to me and asked: You're doing it because of the day of the bank job in Bordils, aren't you?'

'He said that?'

'More or less: I don't remember his exact words, but that's more or less what he said, yeah.'

'What was your answer?'

'None. I didn't know what to answer. It was the worst possible timing to talk about that, or the most unexpected, and the only thing that occurred to me was to wait and see what he did.'

'And what did he do?'

'The same as me but in reverse: waited for my reaction. Then, since I wasn't saying anything, he looked at Tere, looked back at me and, pointing at me, looked back at Tere: Has he ever told you what happened the day they caught us? Well, he corrected himself. The day they caught the rest of us and he escaped. Has he told you? I bet he hasn't, has he? That was when I interrupted. I didn't give you away, I said unthinkingly. If you think I informed on you, it's not true. How was I going to give you away? I was with you, they just about caught me . . . I know it wasn't you, Zarco interrupted me. If it had been you I would have got even by now. I didn't run my mouth off either, I insisted. That I'm not so sure about, said Zarco. And I don't know how you can be so sure. Because I am, I lied. Absolutely. Careful, Gafitas, he warned me. The more you say it wasn't you, the more it seems like it was you and you're trying to hide that.

'He shut up. I shut up. Tere also remained silent. Then Zarco added, in a different tone of voice, Anyway that's not what I meant, or not only that. I was about to ask him what he meant when suddenly I knew; I also knew that he knew that I knew. Then he turned to Tere and kept talking as if I weren't there, as if he were alone with her. Didn't I tell you?, he asked. He's ashamed. He feels guilty. This dickhead has been feeling guilty for more than twenty years. Un-fucking-believable, no? He thinks he left me lying there and I stopped the cops so he could get away. That's what Zarco said. He was talking about what happened in La Devesa after the bank robbery of the Bordils branch, of course.'

'And was he right? Did you feel guilty?'

'No. And that's why I was surprised that Zarco thought I did. Sure, I felt that what had happened that morning in La Devesa had been important, that I'd gambled everything and that I'd come out all right by a miracle. And of course I knew, whether he meant to or not, Zarco had saved me, and I was grateful to him for that. But nothing else. I didn't feel guilty: if Zarco had helped me then it was because he'd been able to help me, and if I hadn't helped him it was because I couldn't help him. That was it, as I already told you. As far as I was concerned no one was to blame.'

'But Zarco didn't believe you; I mean: he didn't believe that you didn't think it was your fault.'

'Evidently not. He kept on about it. He kept talking and

gesticulating, puffed-up and scornful, increasingly heated, only now apparently sober. He said: Come on, tell the truth, Gafitas. You think I saved you, don't you? And I said: The only thing I think is that tonight you're fucking everything up, and you're going to regret it. Zarco laughed again. Sure you do, he said. You take me for an idiot, or what? You think I didn't know? That's what you think and you feel you owe me and that's why you're a wanker and you'll always be a wanker. There's no hope for you: mister big-shit shyster and you've never understood nothing about nothing. Look at yourself, dickhead, look at you coming here to save your little friend. Aren't you embarrassed to be such a wanker? But, don't you realize me and you aren't friends? Shut up now, Tere interrupted him. I don't feel like it, replied Zarco, without taking his eyes off me. You and me aren't friends, he went on. We're not friends now and we never have been. Stop being so holier than thou, for fuck's sake; stop making a fool of yourself. Don't you realize that we've been using you because I knew that you had to wash away your guilt and nobody was going to do more for me than you? I told you to shut up, Tere interrupted again. And I told you I don't feel like shutting up, replied Zarco. Let's see if this guy can figure out that he thinks he's real smart but he's a wanker and he's making a fool of himself. See if you can figure out the truth for fucking once, man . . . And you know what the truth is? He stared at me, breathing hard; then he looked at Tere, looked back at me and seemed to start to cool down. The truth is that we don't know who ran their mouth off that day, he said, more calmly. Maybe it was you, maybe it was someone else; we don't know, and that's what saves you. But what we do know is that I didn't stop anybody or defend anybody; the only thing I did was defend myself: if I'd had to fuck you over to defend myself, I would have fucked you over. Of that you can be sure. Is that clear? I didn't say anything, and the question hung in the room's foul air for a few seconds. During the silence that followed, Zarco tilted a beer can to his lips and, finding it was empty, threw it furiously on the floor. God, he muttered, leaning back in the sofa. That happened a fuck of a long time ago. Can't you leave me alone, at least for tonight. Forget me, man. You don't owe me nothing. And, if you did owe me, you've paid me back already. It's over. End of story. Debt cleared. You can go now.

'But I didn't go. How strange, I thought. The more I say I wasn't the snitch, the more Zarco thinks it was me and, the more Zarco says he did nothing to stop the police, the easier it is for me to accept that he did. How strange, I also thought. Zarco thinks I've done what I've done to repay him a favour; he doesn't know I've done it to have Tere. While I was thinking these things, Zarco had found a twisted cigarette in the Fortuna packet, had straightened it out, lit it and was smoking it while staring with ferocity at the TV, where at that moment two bikers and a woman were sitting on stools in a roadside bar talking. The coke had accelerated my heart as well as my brain; I was fed up with Zarco and the situation I'd got myself into. I looked at Tere and, although I felt no confidence or strength to convince anyone of anything, I decided to make one last attempt. You're going to ruin everything, I told Zarco's profile: his eyes remained on what was happening on the TV. This is your last chance, and you're going to fuck it up. It's up to you; there won't be another one: if you don't go back, forget about any releases, forget about parole, forget about a pardon, forget it all. And get ready for everyone to forget about you and to spend the rest of your life behind bars. I stopped, struck by the certainty that, in a bolt of lucidity, I'd just come to completely understand Zarco. Of course, now that I think of it, I went on, with ill-considered audacity, maybe that's what you want. I left the phrase suspended and waited for Zarco to look at me, or ask. He did neither. Then, as if taking revenge for his bragging and insults, I said: I might be a dickhead, but you're a coward: you're not afraid of spending the rest of your life behind bars; what scares you is spending it on the outside. I hadn't finished the sentence when Zarco jumped up from the sofa, kicked the improvised table out of the way, grabbed me by my shirt collar and nearly picked me up off the floor. The next time you say that I'll break your neck, he threatened as I inhaled his homicidal breath, with his face a centimetre from mine. Is that clear, Gafitas? I was so frightened that I didn't even nod; after a few seconds Zarco let me go and stood staring at me with a grimace of disgust, panting. It seemed as though he was going to say something else or go back to the sofa, but he turned to Tere, who was watching us unmoved, sitting on her beer case, leaning against the wall. And what are you looking at?, he said to her. Nothing, answered Tere, stroking the mole next to her nose. I was thinking about what Gafitas said. Then she stood up, started walking towards the door and added: We'll wait for you in the car.

'While we went down the stairs in the semi-darkness, I murmured: I've had it with that fucking bastard. Did you see that? He was about to strangle me. Don't be silly, Gafitas, said Tere, walking ahead of me. You were great. Yeah, fucking great, I said sarcastically. So were you. By the way, thanks for lending me a hand: if it wasn't for you, I wouldn't be here to tell the tale. Dawn was breaking. We got in the car and I started the engine. Putting her hand on top of mine on the gearshift, Tere said: Wait. He's going to come down. I looked at her hand and then I looked at her. Are you crazy or what?, I said, still very pissed off. He's not coming down, don't you realize? Then I lost it and started shouting and cursing Zarco. I don't remember what I said, or I'd rather not remember. But what I remember very well is that Tere stopped my stream of insults with a slap. And only then did I shut up, stunned. A few seconds later, Tere said: Sorry. I didn't answer.

I turned off the engine and we sat there beside each other in silence, watching the first cars of the day on the roundabout that gave onto the ring road, watching the ash-coloured light of dawn growing on the windscreen. After five or ten minutes I heard Tere say: There he is. I looked in the rear-view mirror and saw Zarco walking away from the tower block on the outskirts that half an hour earlier had looked like a spaceship and now just looked like a tower block on the outskirts of town, I saw him walk unsteadily to my car, I saw him get in and sit in the back seat, I saw him look me in the eye in the rear-view mirror, I heard him say: Let's go, dickhead.'

8

'He showed up about seven, shortly before breakfast. By then I was starting to come to terms with the idea that Gamallo was not coming back and I was waiting for the moment to call the director-general to give him the news and then go home to get a little sleep. I'd spent the whole night in my office. I'd gone out into the yard to kill time, stretch my legs and get a bit of air when a car pulled up at the front gates. It wasn't completely light yet, but before the car stopped I recognized Cañas in the front seat and that girl. What did you say her name was?'

'Tere.'

'Tere, yes: I always forget her name.'

'You already knew her?'

'Of course. I'd only seen her a couple of times in the prison, but I knew she went to see Gamallo every weekend. And I knew she was working with Cañas and María Vela to get Gamallo out of there.'

'Did you know what her relationship was with Gamallo and with Cañas?'

'Someone told me she was a friend or relative of Gamallo's or of Gamallo's family. As far as I recall that was all I knew then; I found out the rest later.'

'Go on.'

'There's not much to tell. Gamallo got out of the car, rang the

275

bell, they opened the gate and, before he went into the prison, he walked past me with his head hanging and his hands in his pockets, without looking at me or saying a word. I didn't say anything to him either. What I did do was walk across the yard to the entry gate and stand there for a moment, in front of Cañas' car, waiting. I don't know what I was waiting for. Maybe that Cañas would get out of his car and give me some explanation; maybe not. The fact is he neither got out of the car nor gave me any explanation. I mean Cañas. He just sat there looking at me through the windscreen for a few seconds, in the dirty dawn light; then he started his car, turned around and drove away.'

'And you looked the other way with Gamallo.'

'Yes.'

'Why? By not showing up at the prison on Sunday night, Gamallo had violated the conditions of his release permit. Why didn't you report the violation? Why didn't you inform the director-general? Why instead of reporting it or informing him did you call Cañas so he could try to solve the problem by finding Gamallo and bringing him back to the prison?'

'Because it was the most sensible thing to do. Rules are not there just to be observed. Besides, it wasn't the first time I did it; I mean it wasn't the first time I phoned the lawyer of an inmate who had violated a weekend release, so they could try to right the wrong before it was too late and beyond repair. OK, Cañas was right, Gamallo was not just any prisoner, but at least in this respect I behaved towards him the way I would have towards any other prisoner. Or almost. Look, I think there's something that you haven't entirely understood. I didn't have anything against Gamallo, and much less against Cañas; leaving aside questions of principle, we disagreed on the means, but not on the ends: Gamallo's failure to reintegrate into society would not have just been a personal failure for Gamallo, for Cañas and for the director-general; it would also have been a failure for me, because Gamallo was in my charge. Don't forget that: Gamallo's failure was my failure, but his success was my success. I was also interested in everything turning out well.'

'Even though you didn't believe it could turn out well.'

'Even not believing it. That's what I meant by a question of principles. Of course I would almost say that, more than a question of principles, it was a question of character. We might say that I am a pre-emptive pessimist: I always expect the worst. That's why I enjoy the best more. Or that's what I believe.'

9

'After dropping off Zarco at the prison, Tere asked me to take her home. I agreed without a word and we crossed the city one last time that Monday from one edge to the other, in silence, while the sun came up and people started going to work. It was daytime when I stopped the car in front of the building where Tere lived, and an almost summery light blazed against the white façades of the houses of Vilarroja. It must have been seven-thirty or eight o'clock. I had barely spoken a word since the slap Tere had given me in La Creueta to make me shut up and convince me to wait for Zarco, and his insults and threats were still stinging; besides, I didn't like the idea that Tere might ask me about what Zarco had said about my participation in the robbery of the Bordils branch of the Banco Popular. So I don't know if what I said to Tere next was a way of alleviating the sting or of avoiding uncomfortable questions (or both at once). Turning to face her I asked: How did you know where to look for Zarco? Tere didn't answer; she was pale and ravaged by the sleepless night. I asked: Is it true you hadn't seen him this weekend? Tere continued not answering and, increasingly furious and fired-up (perhaps still under the effects of the line of coke I'd snorted in La Creueta), I took the opportunity to let off steam. And another thing, I said, do you think I'm a dickhead and a wanker, too? You think I'm a sanctimonious git and that I've been making a fool of myself? Are you using me too?

Tere listened to this string of questions without batting an eyelid and, when I finished posing them, she sighed and opened the car door. You're not going to answer?, I asked. With one foot already on the pavement, Tere turned to look at me. I don't know why you're talking to me like this, she said. Because I've had it up to here, I said sincerely; and I added: Look, Tere, I don't know if you've been with Zarco this weekend or not, and I don't know what kind of things you've got going on: that's between you and him. Now, if you want what's between you and me to carry on, that's going to have to be the way everybody does it; if not, I'd rather we didn't see each other. Tere thought for a moment, nodded and murmured something, which I didn't catch. What did you say?, I said. Nothing, she answered as she got out of the car. Just that I knew this was going to happen.

'During that week we didn't see each other or speak on the phone, but I was reconsidering; on the Saturday I went to Barcelona and spent the afternoon in Revólver and Discos Castelló buying CDs – it had been a while since I'd bought any – and the following week I called her and suggested she come over to my place. I have some new music, I said, and then tried to tempt her by listing what I'd bought. When I finished, Tere said she couldn't accept the invitation. Are you still angry?, I asked. I didn't get angry, she answered. You were the one who was angry. Well I'm not angry any more, I said; then I added: Have you given any thought to what we talked about? She didn't ask me what I meant. There's nothing to give any thought to, she said. Look, Gafitas, this is a mess, and I don't want any mess. No ties, no commitment. I told you. You were right: we can't go out like everybody else does, so it's best that we stop seeing each other. Why can't we go out like everybody else?, I asked. Because we can't, she answered. Because you're what you are and I'm what I am. Well then we'll see each other as we've been seeing each other up till now, I conceded. Come over to my place. We'll have dinner and dance. Like we did before. We had a good time, didn't we? Yeah, said Tere. But that's over; I didn't want it to end, but it's over. And what's done is done. Although we carried on arguing for quite a while, Tere had made a decision and I could not get her to change her mind; the decision didn't mean a break-up, or at least I didn't take it to mean a break-up: Tere just asked me for time to think, to clarify her ideas, to find out, she said, what she wanted to do with her life. All this sounded a bit hollow to me, or rhetorical, like something you hear in movies, but I had no choice but to accept it.

'Tere and I stopped seeing each other that summer, just like that. I phoned her at least once a week, but our conversations were brief, distant and functional (mostly we talked about Zarco and María), and, when I tried to guide them onto a more personal terrain, Tere cut me off or listened in silence and then found a reason to hang up straight away. Towards the beginning of August she stopped answering the phone and I imagined she'd gone away on holiday, but I didn't go up to Vilarroja to find out. Actually I didn't see her again until Zarco's wedding day.'

'Zarco's wedding?'

'Zarco and María's wedding. It was in September, three months after the frustrated escape in La Creueta, and it was the good result of that episode, or the culmination of its good results; so good that for months I could allow myself to think that, for Zarco, that night had been like an alcoholic's last tumble off the wagon or like the last performance of a dying persona. The fact is that the episode had an immediate therapeutic effect, and in a way revolutionized Zarco's life. I myself noticed an improvement in his attitude straight away, his mood and even his appearance, but I wasn't the only one to notice it; the prison reports changed from one week to the next: the guards stopped complaining about him, he went back on the methadone to combat his heroin addiction, started

280

exercising again. This personal readjustment contributed perhaps to the fact that, in spite of the shock of the night of La Creueta, the prison superintendent did not rescind his weekend-release privileges. It's true that I spent Sunday nights on edge, always hanging by the phone, although it's also true that Zarco did not return late back to prison again and I did not receive another distressing phone call from the superintendent.

'But the unmistakable sign that Zarco was another person – a more reasonable and less stuck-up and deranged person, more independent of his own myth, more person and less persona, more suitable for living in liberty – was his wedding to María. At least that's how I interpreted it. That wedding meant as well that the campaign for his freedom that had been running for nine months was still moving forward. Of course by then, when he was on the verge of getting married, Zarco no longer even bothered to hide the fact that the marriage was a farce; strange as it might seem, this was not for me a proof of Zarco's cynicism, but rather of his honesty (and, by extension, of mine): according to my clever interpretation, Zarco was using María to get free, but not at the price of deceiving her, or not at the price of entirely deceiving her. As for María, it's almost as sure that she was still in love with Zarco as it is that deep down she knew her marriage to him was a fraud; although knowing this could sometimes make her uncomfortable, it never managed to calm her impatience to get married: perhaps she thought that in the long run she could make Zarco love her; without a doubt she had become hooked on the drug of celebrity and knew that she couldn't dispense with Zarco because dispensing with Zarco would be dispensing with fame. In spite of all this, at least a couple of times that summer María told me the doubts she was having about her imminent marriage; my reaction was always the same: cutting her off by playing them down or clearing away her uncertainties at a stroke. A logical reaction, after all, because I knew that marriage to María was not only an indispensable prerequisite for Zarco getting his third-level parole, but also for us to successfully conclude the campaign in favour of his getting a definitive pardon, and I trusted that Zarco's freedom would represent the end of Zarco's problems.'

'The end of Zarco's problems and the end of your problems with Zarco.'

'Sure: at least I would have carried out the job of getting him his freedom back. In any case, as well as a farce Zarco and María's marriage turned out to be quite the media event. It was held at the Gerona courthouse. Tere was the maid of honour and I was the best man. During the ceremony we could barely exchange any words other than formalities and practicalities, and afterwards not even that: a crowd of photographers was waiting outside who bombarded Zarco with flashes as he walked down the building's steps carrying María in his arms. There was no wedding reception or celebration of any kind and, before I knew it, Tere had left. Over the following days the image of the bride coming out of the courthouse in the bridegroom's arms monopolized the front pages of the newspapers and magazines, and the television stations were lavish in their attention on the news, magazine and gossip programmes that followed the newlyweds on their honeymoon in a hotel on the Costa del Sol, paid for by an Andalusian builder who had often proclaimed his juvenile admiration for Zarco to the press and in his main office had a portrait of Zarco hanging next to one of Marlon Brando as the Godfather.

'After the commotion of the wedding and honeymoon, every-thing went back to normal for Zarco. A few weeks later, towards the middle of October, Correctional Institutions issued him his third-stage parole. This entailed two important changes for Zarco: on the one hand he no longer had to sleep in a cell and moved to a building adjacent to the yard, where he and other inmates at the same stage of incarceration had their own individual apartments with a kitchen and bathroom; on the other hand, from that moment on Zarco lived his own life outside of prison, which he left every morning at eight and where he had to return each evening at nine. By then I had got him a contract to work at a carton factory in Vidreres, not far from the city, thanks to a businessman who years earlier I'd exculpated from a fraud conviction, so theoretically, Zarco spent most of his day in the carton factory, which he went to and from by bus for eight-hour work days: from nine in the morning until six in the evening, with an hour lunch break; from six until he had to go back inside at night, Zarco was free.

'That was his life from then on. When he embarked on it we had to give up our conversations in the interview room, we stopped seeing each other and I tried to wash my hands of what he was doing or not doing. For a time I thought the story was over, or was coming to an end, and that I'd only find out what Zarco was up to again from the press and when the various stages of his parole expired and I had to intervene to settle the final routines. Or maybe through Tere. Because, although she and I were still not seeing each other and, to spare myself futile brush-offs, I'd even stopped phoning her, now Tere called me. She called me at the office, once or twice a week, to chat for a while. These conversations weren't as cold and utilitarian as those that followed our peaceable split, when it was still me who called her at home, but they were very brief, fairly trivial, as far as I recall we never mentioned the night in La Creueta or the uncomfortable things Zarco said there, or even the limbo that Tere had left our relationship frozen in; but, perhaps for that reason, I always hung up the phone convinced that the wait was about to end happily. Why did Tere keep phoning me? Whatever her reasons, it was in those conversations that she sometimes mentioned Zarco, always in a superficial way and sort of in passing, always to make some comment or give me some bit of news that I never knew where she got, nor did I want to find out.

'All this lasted a short time. I soon understood that the story was not over, nor was it on the verge of being over, and soon it was me who was giving Tere news of Zarco, and not vice versa. One evening, two or three months after he'd started his part-time free-man's life, Zarco showed up unannounced at my office. It was seven or seven-thirty and he was coming from Vidreres; he looked good, he'd lost a bit of weight, was dressed like a person and not like a perpetual convict: corduroy trousers, red sweater and a leather jacket. His presence agitated the whole firm: it was the first time he'd been there and everybody dropped whatever they were working on to see him, say hello, congratulate and welcome him. He smiled and looked happy and joked non-stop with my partners and the secretaries and the rest of the staff until, after a few minutes, he suggested we go out for a drink. I agreed with pleasure. I took him to the Royal and, although the clientele recognized him and were watching us and whispering to each other, they left us alone to talk and drink at the bar for a while. He told me about his new life; we talked about his job, the people he worked with, and especially about his boss, whom he praised to the skies and about whom I told a couple of anecdotes. My impression was that he was at ease with the new state of things, much more at least than with the old one. Before nine I gave him a lift back to the prison.

'Zarco's appearance at my office turned into a habit over the following months. At least a couple of times a week he'd show up there at seven or seven-thirty and we'd go and finish off the work day with a drink. At first those visits cheered me up, I enjoyed Zarco's company and conversation, I felt proud that people saw me with him at the bar at the Royal or walking along Jaume I or under the arcades of Sant Agustí: he was Zarco – hence the pride

– but also – and hence even greater pride – he was a free and reformed man, and his reform and freedom were a triumph that was in part down to me. That was when, perhaps thanks to the optimism Zarco seemed to be radiating, the two of us began to share something resembling closeness; and that was when an event occurred that I'm going to tell you about on the condition that it not appear in the book.'

'I repeat that you can read the manuscript before I submit it to the publisher and I'll cut anything you don't like.'

'Yeah, I know: I just wanted to hear you say it again. Now listen to my story. It's about Batista. Do you remember him?'

'Sure: your high-school bully.'

'Exactly. I'd lost track of most of my friends from Caterina Albert a long time ago, although once in a while I crossed paths with one of them in the street and I knew that they all still lived in the city or at the very least in the province, except for Canales, who was a forestry specialist and lived in a village in Ávila, and Matías, who'd been working in Brussels for many years, as a bureaucrat in the European Parliament. Batista was a case apart. His track had been easier to follow as he'd turned into a relatively popular guy, at least in Gerona, and his story was one of those stories of individual success that newspapers love and that seem to proliferate in times of limitless prosperity like that one. I think I already told you that Batista was from a rich family with deep roots in the city; I must have also told you that his father was for years my father's boss, he'd been chairman of the county council: in fact, he was the last council chair of the Franco era. But, with the arrival of democracy, things began to go less well for the family, and a few years later Batista's father died leaving his family ruined or what a family like that considered ruined. The thing is that Batista, who by then would have been in his twenties, took charge of a small pig farm that had belonged to one of his grandfathers, in Monells, transformed the small pig farm into a larger pig farm, the larger farm into a small sausage factory, the small factory into a large factory and finally ended up transforming himself into one of the main sausage manufacturers in Catalonia, as well as a model young entrepreneur for the Catalan nationalists in power, which transformed the ferocious Españolista of my adolescence into a ferocious Catalanista (and the Narciso of back then into Narcís). That's what had become of Batista over those twenty or twenty-odd years. And one evening, while I was waiting for Zarco at the bar of the Royal – sometimes we met there – I saw a photo of him in a newspaper and, when Zarco arrived at my side, the first thing that occurred to me was to tell him, point blank: I bet you don't know why I joined your gang, why I went to La Font each afternoon, do you?

'Zarco laughed heartily and ordered a beer. What for?, he answered. To sniff Tere's tail, what else? I laughed too. Apart from that, I said. To give us a hand, he added. Because I tricked you. You tricked me?, I asked with curiosity. Sure, he answered happily. You thought we were going to do a job on the old man from Vilaró. And you thought if we didn't it was to do you a favour and that I had to stop Guille and all that. They served his beer, he drank it down in one and burped. You were a dupe, Gafitas, he said. I ordered two more glasses of beer and replied: And you were a son of a bitch. You only just noticed?, Zarco laughed again. Anyway it was Tere's idea. She said it would be better if you came with us of your own free will rather than against it. By the way, he added, have you seen her? Not lately, I said. How about you? Me neither, he said, and it sounded like the truth. And María?, I asked. Sure, he said, and it sounded like a lie.

'Our beer arrived. Zarco took a sip and reminded me of the double question I'd asked him at the start: what I'd joined his gang for, why I'd gone to La Font every afternoon. So I picked up the newspaper and handed it to him, folded open to the page with Batista's photo on it. To get away from this guy, I said, pointing at the photo. While Zarco looked at Batista's face and took sips of his beer, I tried to summarize the story. Fuck, man, he interrupted me halfway through. This guy really is a son of a bitch. I went on with the story. Finally I told him that I sometimes thought that deep down I'd never forgiven Batista, that sometimes, at weak moments, when I saw Batista so smug in the newspapers or on television, the memory of what had happened humiliated me and I sometimes regretted never having taken revenge on him, and at moments like that I felt that, if I could have got rid of him by pressing a button, I would have done it without a doubt.

'That evening we didn't talk about anything else and I ended up pretty drunk, but I didn't mention it again over the following days; for his part, Zarco seemed to forget Batista. Then, two weeks later, it happened. That day a very agitated Gubau came into my office, saying he'd heard on the radio that Batista had just been stabbed at the door of his house in Montjuïc, a neighbourhood on the outskirts of the city. Over the course of the morning more news of the incident came in — Batista had been admitted to the Trueta hospital, where he was fighting for his life, he'd been stabbed seven times, nobody had seen his attacker — and around noon we heard that my old classmate had died.

'Hours later Zarco showed up at my office, ready to go for a couple of beers at the Royal. Remember the guy I told you about the other day?, I said as soon as I saw him. The bully of my school, I specified. Sure, he said. Somebody killed him this morning, I told him. Zarco looked at me and, seeing I wasn't going to add anything, shrugged his shoulders and said: So what? What do you mean so what?, I said. They stabbed him seven times. Not exciting enough for you? I was going to go on but I didn't, because I had the feeling that an almost imperceptible smile was prowling about Zarco's lips. At that moment I remembered that he left the prison every morning just before the time Batista had been murdered, and, dismayed by a sudden suspicion, I went over to my office door, pulled it shut and turned to him. Hey, I asked, lowering my voice. You wouldn't have had anything to do with this, would you? He didn't seem surprised by the question, but his smile widened and he turned his head from left to right. You're too much, Gafitas, he reproached me. Did you or did you not have anything to do with it?, I repeated. Zarco held my gaze, seemed to be thinking over his reply. And what if I did have something to do with it?, he asked defiantly. Are you going to start crying over this son of a bitch now? A son of a bitch is a son of a bitch, Gafitas. Didn't you tell me you regretted not having got revenge on him? It was just an expression, I answered. It's one thing to say something and quite another . . . I didn't finish my sentence, I said: Batista was nobody, he hadn't done anything. Ah, no?, he answered. He fucked you right up, and when you were just a kid who didn't know how to defend himself. That's not doing anything? They locked me up inside for much less. He, on the other hand, never got touched. Well then, now justice has been done. After a pause he continued: And if I took care of it, all the better. Who's going to suspect me, who never even met him? And who's going to suspect you? A clean job, man, he concluded, opening his arms. Just like pressing a button. True or false? I was stunned, trying to process what I'd heard. Zarco pointed at me with his index finger and, as if urging me to say something, added: I scratch your back and you scratch mine, eh, Gafitas? The phrase snapped me out of my paralysis, and in two strides I stood a handspan from him; in the quiet of my office I heard the soles of my shoes squeak against the wooden floor. Tell me the truth, Antonio, I said. Did you have anything to do with it or not? Zarco was again slow to answer; his blue eyes bored into mine. Until he suddenly blinked, smiled broadly and patted me on the cheek. Of course not, dickhead, he finally said.

'That was the last time Zarco and I talked of Batista, or of his murder. A murder that, as happens with so many, was never solved: the police arrived very soon at the conclusion that it had been the work of a professional, perhaps a hitman from some Latin-American country, but they didn't find any trace of the murderer; the police investigated Batista's relatives, friends and business competitors in search of a motive with the same degree of success. Until the case was filed away in the archives.'

'Now I understand why you don't want this story told in the book. Readers might think Zarco killed Batista.'

'Maybe he did kill him. Or had him killed. Sometimes I think he did it, and by killing him thought he was doing me a favour, that it was his way of repaying me for what I was doing for him. But other times I think he couldn't have killed him: that he had no money to hire a hitman (although the truth is that someone like him might not need money for that) and that he couldn't have committed the murder so cleanly and he wouldn't have had enough time, that morning, to get from the prison to Montjuïc and surprise Batista on his way out of his house (although the truth is that perhaps he would have had enough time and that Zarco probably knew how to kill as professionally as any hitman). I don't know. And, now that I think of it, maybe you should recount this story in your book, just as I've told you: after all what it's about is readers getting to know the truth about Zarco. And this, including my doubts, also forms part of the truth.'

'Aren't you afraid some readers might think you're lying, or diluting or massaging the truth, and that it was you who induced Zarco to kill Batista, to get revenge without getting your hands dirty?'

'Do you think I would have told you if I had? Besides, I didn't want to get revenge on Batista, for me it was a forgotten story or almost forgotten, I'm not saying what I said to Zarco was entirely false, I'm only saying it was one of those things that get said sometimes when you have a few too many and nobody takes seriously, or a momentary and unimportant letting off steam, which I immediately regretted . . . Anyway, do what you think best, or what's best for your book: if you think it advisable, tell it; if not, don't. Later we'll see.

'But getting back to our story, because the evenings of cheerful friendship and beers with Zarco at the bar of the Royal soon came to an end. Practically from one day to the next the friendship and good cheer evaporated and Zarco's head betrayed him again; or that's the impression I had: that the persona had once again got the better of the person. Before, during my visits in the interview room at the prison, it was common for Zarco to complain about his lack of freedom, of the stupidity of the regulations or mistreatment from the guards; now, when he'd only been spending his days outside the prison for a few months, Zarco fell back into his unstoppable habit of complaining, and his fatal old blend of arrogance and seeing himself as a victim began to poison our conversations again: Zarco said that his work folding and unfolding cartons at the factory in Vidreres was slave labour, that his hours were slavery hours, that his salary was slaves' wages and that he'd come out of prison to live the life of a slave as bad or worse than the one he'd been leading inside. Hearing this I began to think I'd been too optimistic in judging his state of mind, I went back to fearing his fear of liberty (a liberty that would soon be complete and no longer partial), I began to fight his despondency as best I could. It's not true that you're leading the same life you led in prison, I reasoned. You're leading a much better life. And, of course it's not a slave's life: it's the life most people lead. Look at the other inmates, look at the guys who work with you. And what do they matter to me, Gafitas?, answered Zarco. I don't give a shit what people do: if they want to get fucked, let them fuck themselves; it's up to them. What I give a shit about is not fucking myself up. You get that, right? And right now I'm just as fucked outside jail as in. Several times I told him I knew that the work he was doing wasn't very satisfying, and I could get him another job. Oh yeah?, asked Zarco. Doing what? Whatever you want, I answered. Everybody wants to hire you. Don't talk bullshit, Gafitas, he replied. What everybody wants is to be able to say they've hired Zarco and be able to show me off like a fairground monkey as propaganda for their business, just like my boss does. It's not the same, is it? Besides, he concluded, I don't know how to do anything at all, and by now I'm not going to learn, so all I can do is slave labour.

'With slight variations, conversations like this were repeated for weeks at the Royal between one beer and the next, and I participated in them with increasing anxiety as Zarco's nervousness grew and his physical state degenerated before my very eyes (as I later discovered, in part because he'd gone back to using heroin); also as I watched unfold before my eyes, in the things that he said, the oft-repeated spectacle of the irreconcilable contradiction between his person and his persona: again he wanted the world to forget Zarco once and for all, that it let him be Antonio Gamallo, a normal man with a normal life like the majority of people; but, at the same time, once again he didn't want to be a normal man, he didn't want anybody to forget he was Zarco nor did he want to dispense with his pride and the privileges of being Zarco, among them that of not living the life of slavery that the majority of people lived. He didn't want to and, in part, maybe he couldn't: as much as he aspired to be a normal person, a new person, he panicked at the thought of not being Zarco any more, because that meant no longer being who he'd always or almost always been;

likewise, as much as he aspired to live outside prison, he panicked at the thought of doing so, because it meant no longer living where he'd always or almost always lived.

'But all this is mere speculation, or not much more. What's certain is that at some point, perhaps tired of me arguing with him and telling him what he had to do, or simply tired of complaining, Zarco stopped coming to my office after work and I practically stopped hearing anything about him. Two or three months later – eight months after getting his third-stage parole, to be precise – the government granted him a limited pardon and conditional release. This was the premature culmination of the project we'd set in motion almost two years earlier, and, in spite of my melancholy premonition that Zarco was heading for disaster, I received the news as a triumph: not only because I'd done my work conscientiously and got Zarco out of prison in record time, or because I would be able to get the highest propaganda value out of his case this way; most of all because in those months I'd reached the conclusion that I could only get Tere back when Zarco got his freedom back and we were free of him: our relationship had always been hindered by Zarco, by our need for him as teenagers and by his need for us as adults, by the suspicions and mistakes and doubts those needs had provoked, and I imagined that, once Zarco was no longer depending on us nor us on him, Tere and I could start over again, picking up our relationship where Tere had left it in suspension a few months back, after the night we'd rescued Zarco from La Creueta. So I waited impatiently for news of the pardon and, as soon as I got it, I rushed to phone Zarco to tell him.

'It was a late morning in early June or mid-June. I phoned his workplace in Vidreres and asked for him, but they told me he'd been off sick for a couple of days and hadn't left the prison. I phoned the prison and again asked for him, but they told me he was in Vidreres. The misunderstanding didn't surprise me. For some time the businessman who'd hired him had kept me informed of Zarco's absences from work; this, combined with his constant lack of punctuality and refusal to submit to drugs tests, had led to the prison superintendent drafting a report advising against Zarco's pardon and recommending rescinding his third-stage parole status with the argument that he was not ready for release. Luckily, no one had paid the report any attention, and that morning I wondered whether or not I should call the superintendent. Then I wondered whether or not to call María. I hadn't talked to her for months, but I knew from Tere that she was fed up with her sham marriage and barely saw Zarco, which was not preventing her from turning into an increasingly popular public persona, although in her appearances on the radio, in the press and on television she talked less and less about Zarco and more and more about herself.

'In the end I just phoned Tere. After phoning the factory in Cassà and being told she was no longer employed there, I found her at home. As I told you before, Tere and I talked on the phone every once in a while, but it was usually she who called me rather than me calling her, so, without giving her time to be surprised by my call, I told her what they'd told me at the factory in Cassà. Why didn't you tell me?, I asked. Because you didn't ask, she answered. Have you found a new job?, I asked. No, she answered. I asked her what she was planning to do; nothing, she answered. I've got a few months of dole coming to me, she explained. Maybe I'll go on holiday; or maybe I'll stay home and study: I've got exams next month. Tere fell silent; now it was she who asked: Has something happened? I told her what had happened. Congratulations, Gafitas, she said. Mission accomplished. I didn't notice any enthusiasm in her voice, and I wondered if she was really glad that all this was over. Thanks, I said, without daring to ask her; instead of that I asked: Do you know where he is? Zarco?, she asked: for a while now she'd gone back to calling him that, not Antonio. Isn't he at work? No, I answered. Not at the prison either. Then I have no idea where he is, said Tere.

'I believed her. That night I went to look for Zarco at the prison. Shortly before nine I asked through the intercom by the entrance if he'd arrived; they told me he hadn't and I went back to wait for him in the car. I was there for a while, and I'd already decided that Zarco wasn't coming back and I might as well leave when I saw him get out of a clapped-out Renault parked in front of the yard. Hey, Antonio! I called him, climbing out of my car. He turned towards me and waited on the sidewalk, right beside the prison gate. At first my presence seemed to annoy him – What are you doing here, Counsellor?, he asked when he recognized me – but as soon as I gave him the news his expression relaxed, he took a deep breath, opened his arms wide and said: Come here, Gafitas. He hugged me. He smelled intensely of alcohol and tobacco. Well, he said as we finished hugging; I looked in his eyes: they were red. When do I get out? I don't know, I replied. Tomorrow they announce the news, so pretty soon, I suppose. Then I hastened to warn him: But the problem is not when you're going to get out but what you're going to do when you're out. During my wait I'd loaded up with arguments, and now I reproached him for not having gone to work for the last two days and asked him what he was going to live on if he lost that job and told him I knew it had been a long time since he saw María and asked him where he was going to live if not with María. Zarco didn't let me continue. Take it easy, man, he said, putting a hand on my shoulder. I just found out I'm a free man. Save the lectures for another day; let me enjoy it for now, eh? And don't worry about me, for fuck's sake, I'm a big boy. For a moment that drunken laid-back attitude irritated me. I'm not worried, I replied. I just want you to understand that this hasn't ended and it'll all go to hell if you don't live a normal life from now on. With all the work we've put in . . . I understand, Zarco interrupted me again. Fuck, how am I not going to understand? The way you go on about it. He took his hand off my shoulder and gave me a pat on the cheek; then he pointed at the building where he slept, on the other side of the prison fence, on the far side of the inadequately lit yard, and added: Well, Gafitas, it's damn late: if I don't get in there right now I'll be left without a pardon. Zarco had already called through on the intercom and they'd opened the gate to the yard when I suggested: Tomorrow we could celebrate the news with a drink at the Royal. I clarified: When you get off work. I added: I bet Tere would join us too if you invited her. She's lost her job. The news didn't seem to make much of an impression on Zarco, and I thought maybe he already knew; or that he was so absorbed in his own stuff that he'd barely heard. Tomorrow?, he asked, almost without turning back to me. Tomorrow we'll have to hold a press conference and all that, no? Well, maybe I'll call you and we'll talk about it.

'He didn't call, we didn't talk about it, we didn't celebrate the pardon. The press conference, however, was held. It was two days later, in the prison itself, and it was the Director-General of Correctional Institutions who called it. I didn't attend the event because no one asked me to; neither María nor Tere attended either, not even the superintendent, at least according to the reports of it I read the next day in the papers. They all included a photo of Zarco and the director-general, both smiling and both with their index and middle fingers raised in a victory sign; they all reproduced the director-general's statement, according to which Zarco's liberty represented "a triumph for Antonio Gamallo, a triumph for our prison system and a triumph for our democracy", and a few words from Zarco thanking all those people "who'd done their bit, however small, to make this moment possible"; they all highlighted María's absence, and all related this fact to the rumours of the couple's separation that had been circulating lately.

'That very day Zarco disappeared from the media and didn't show up again until four or five months had passed. Just as I'd suspected (or desired), during that time I no longer saw him. But I still received news of him. Thanks to my former client from Vidreres I found out that, once he'd regained his freedom, Zarco had not set foot in the carton factory again. A little while later María made some casual or apparently casual statements to a reporter on a television programme in which she confirmed that she and Zarco were living apart and hadn't seen each other since months before the pardon was granted, and in which she also insinuated that, almost from the start, their relationship had just been staged. These words unleashed a storm of gossip, conjecture and demands for explanations among the tabloid and romance journalists that María fed with silences and rudeness, which filled many minutes of television and whole pages of magazines for several weeks and which I interpreted as the swansong of the media soap opera starring María and Zarco.

'The exact opposite of what my incurable optimism had predicted ended up happening with Tere. For the first few weeks things stayed more or less the same as they'd been up till then: she phoned me every once in a while and I waited for the opportunity to take a step forward, as if I were afraid to rush things or feared that if I didn't get it right the first time, I wouldn't get a second chance. But after a month and a half Tere stopped calling me, and then I made up my mind; I started calling her, started pressuring her: I suggested we see each other, that we go out for lunch or dinner, that she come over for lunch or dinner, that we give it another try; I assured her I was ready to accept her conditions and that this time there would be no ties, no mess, no commitments, no demands. Tere responded to my suggestions with excuses and to my complaints by saying I was right, especially when I repeated that I'd been waiting for months and was tired. You should try something else, Gafitas, she suggested more than once. I don't have anything else to try, I answered, almost infuriated. I already know what I want. The one who doesn't seem to know what she wants is you. The last conversation we had was not awkward but sad, or that's how I remember it. Resigned to reality, I didn't beg and we didn't argue, but, maybe because I sensed that this was farewell, I asked her about Zarco, something I hadn't done for a while. Tere answered vaguely, told me she hadn't seen him and all she knew was that he was living in Barcelona and earning a living working in the car-repair garage of a former cellmate. That's what she said, and for some reason I thought she was lying and that she was giving me the brush-off again; I also thought that she was telling me without saying so that it was no longer any of my business because my work with Zarco had finished. When I hung up the telephone I remembered Zarco's words in La Creueta: end of story, debt settled, you can go now.

'I stopped calling Tere and tried to forget her. I didn't manage to. The only thing I managed to do was wake up each morning with a crushing sensation of failure. That sensation increased a few weeks later, when Zarco was arrested on the Rambla de Catalunya in Barcelona after having robbed a pharmacy and having tried to steal a car from an underground parking lot. It was less than five months since he'd received the pardon and the conditional release. It was front-page news in the newspapers and magazines and on the radio and television, it unleashed a journalistic debate about the softness of Spanish penal legislation, the insufficiencies of the prison system and the limits of rehabilitation, and provoked a small political earthquake that included a row in the Congress, an exchange of accusations between the Madrid government and the Catalan one and the sacking of the Director-General of Correctional Institutions, Señor Pere Prada. For Zarco the episode also represented an ending. The violation of the conditions of his release meant that from the correctional point of view he went back to square one: he went back to having three decades of imprisonment to serve, to which he'd now have to add, besides, the years he'd get for his last two crimes. All this meant, given his age and given that nobody was going to risk granting him any kind of release, let alone parole, in practice Zarco was condemned to a life sentence. His hopes for liberty ended there. And there ended the myth of Zarco.'

'You mean the myth of Zarco in his lifetime ended there, the one you reactivated with the campaign in favour of his pardon; but the Zarco myth didn't end: the proof is that here we are you and I, talking about him.'

'You're right. Actually, when you think about it, rather than ending at that moment Zarco's myth seemed to transform, or degrade, or took its final shape. I mean that almost from one day to the next Zarco went from being the legendary good delinquent who had finally found the right road and began to be seen as an irredeemable junkie, sordid and dirty, like a perpetual delinquent, ungrateful and glib, like a hopeless *quinqui* without a trace of glamour. In short, he began to be seen as a tyrant and not as a victim. María contributed very much to this transformation from the beginning, from the first time she appeared on television ranting and raving about Zarco; well, ranting and raving about Zarco, and about Tere and about me. Which was the first time I saw her converted into a furious vengeful woman. I don't suppose you've seen that interview, because I didn't record it; anyway these things must be on the Internet, on YouTube or sites like that, no?'

'Probably. I'll find out.'

'Find it if you can: it's worth seeing. The interview went out one Saturday night, quite late, on a magazine show with a huge audience. María was interrogated for more than an hour by the presenter and by several reporters with the idea that she might confide in them about her relationship with Zarco and clear up her insinuations about the wedding having just been a stunt. By then her appearance barely bore any relation to the shy, sad, anodyne woman Tere had introduced me to years earlier in my office: she'd let her hair grow, dyed it blonde and had it curled, her face was caked with make-up, she was wearing a sparkling, violet-coloured, tight satin dress with a plunging neckline. That night María more than fulfilled her mission: she clarified, confided, ranted and raved; her performance was worthy of a diva: she accompanied her words with dramatic silences, with outbursts of rage, affected gestures, challenging looks straight at the camera. She began by saying that she hadn't seen Zarco for months and had no news of him apart from what she'd read in the press, and then she went on to say that Zarco had hit her many times, that he'd stolen money from her, that he'd abused her sexually and had tried to sexually abuse her daughter, that he'd cheated on her with Tere, that Zarco, Tere and I had tricked her into marrying him in order to get him released, that she had paid me significant sums of money to defend him, that I knew about all the humiliations he and Tere had submitted her to and not only did I not do anything to prevent them but I had encouraged them because I'd belonged to Zarco's gang in my youth and Zarco and Tere were blackmailing me with the threat of exposing my delinquent past. I listened to all this live, alone in my loft on La Barca Street, more fascinated than furious or scandalized, as if they weren't talking about me but about my double and, as soon as María started to spill the beans, I began telling myself that a good lie is not a pure, free-standing lie, that a pure lie is an implausible lie, that, to make it plausible, a lie needs to be constructed in part out of truths, and I spent the programme wondering how much truth María's lies contained: I knew, for example, that it was true that Zarco had stolen money from her (though not that María had paid me a single euro to defend Zarco), and I wondered if it was also true that Zarco hit her and had tried to sexually abuse her daughter; I knew that it was true, of course, that when I was young I'd been in Zarco's gang and that in a certain sense Zarco, Tere and I had tricked María so she would marry Zarco so we could get him freed, and I wondered if it was also true that Zarco cheated on María with Tere and if from the moment he started to get out on weekend-release passes, more than a year before, the two of them had been seeing each other behind my back and that explained why since then Tere hadn't wanted to go back to seeing me and had kept me at a distance, keeping my hopes up through telephone conversations. I asked myself many questions similar to these, but I didn't give myself any answers. I didn't want to.

'Or I couldn't. As soon as the programme began Gubau called me, and almost immediately after him my daughter called and then Cortés; before I got into bed I spoke by telephone with no fewer than ten people. All of them were watching the programme or had seen it and all of them wanted to comment on it and find out how I was, but from there on in the reactions differed: most of them tried to calm me down, took it for granted that the woman was crazy, that she just wanted to be on television and that what she said was false. But there were also different reactions. In my sister's tone of voice, for example, I thought I detected, well covered by the obligatory indignation, a tiny shade of resentment, as if she were pained by the public prominence her little brother had just acquired, but also a shade of respect, as if she'd just discovered, proudly, that I had finally become somebody. Is it true that you were in his gang?, my ex-wife asked for her part, with a mixture of admiration and astonishment. Crikey, you could have

300

told me: now I understand why you were so obsessed with Zarco . . . The truth is that, sometimes with one ear on the television and the other on the receiver while my mobile was ringing, I tried to deal with them all, answer their questions and play down the importance of the programme and María's accusations, but when I finally disconnected the phones I'd realized that this was just the beginning and that, supposing it didn't end up affecting me personally, it was obviously going to affect the opinion others had of me, which was a way of affecting me personally.

'In the days that followed the gossip magazines and radio and television chat shows repeated María's accusations, and that Monday morning I read in everybody's eyes, in the office and at court, that yes, that was just the beginning. That afternoon my secretary put through an unexpected call. It was the producer of the programme María had appeared on two days before. He introduced himself, said his name – López de Sol, I remember he was called – and, without any further explanation, he offered me the possibility of defending myself the following Saturday against María's accusations: it would simply entail allowing myself to be interviewed at the same time and on the same set by the same group of journalists that had interviewed her. I thanked him for the offer and turned it down. The producer told me not to be hasty, to think it over, that he'd phone back that evening. I answered that I'd already thought about it and he could save himself the trouble of calling back. Here the producer changed his tone, with an inflection at once friendly and paternalistic he mentioned a sum of money, not particularly high, and then explained María's appearance on his programme the previous Saturday had been a hit, that they planned to continue with the story next Saturday and that, if I didn't agree to be interviewed, they would most likely interview María again. Then I flew off the handle: shouting, furious, I told him he should do what he thought best, but that, if María continued talking about me on television the way she had the time before, I'd be bringing two lawsuits to court, one for slander and another for defamation of character, one against María and the other against the programme. My threat did not upset the producer; I heard him click his tongue, heard him sigh; before hanging up on him I heard him say: You haven't understood anything, Counsellor.

'That Saturday night María was on the show again. I decided not to watch it, and I didn't see it, but on Sunday I learned that her second appearance had been even more brutal than the first, so for several days I considered the possibility of carrying out the threat I'd made over the phone and filing suits against María and the programme. Cortés and Gubau talked me out of it; their arguments were irrefutable: I knew it wasn't easy to win such a lawsuit, but my partners made me see that, even supposing we did win and María was sentenced to withdrawing her insults and accusations and the programme obliged to broadcast a retraction, the person most harmed would still be me, because the trial would destroy my reputation, and the main beneficiaries would be them, because the trial would only increase María's fame and the programme's audience. So I chose to keep quiet, to try to stay out of it, to go on as if nothing were going on. Maybe I was mistaken. Maybe I should have filed a suit. Who knows. The thing is that over the following weeks the sensation of failure and shame multiplied and began to devour me like a cancer.'

'Didn't you try to talk to Tere? Didn't you try to get in contact with her?'

'I tried, but I couldn't. I phoned her, but she didn't answer. I went to her house, but she wasn't in. Someone told me she wasn't living in Vilarroja any more. I don't think finding her would have done any good, anyway. Of course, it didn't even occur to me to try to find out which prison Zarco had been sent to, although I thought of him far too often. And do you know what I remembered most of all? The night in La Creueta, of the binge he went on of telling me I was making a fool of myself and calling me dickhead and wanker. Because that was the honest truth, that's how I felt then: like a dickhead and a wanker who'd made the most ridiculous fool of himself.

'During the following months I again tried to force myself to forget about Tere. Also to forget about Zarco. María, however, was much harder to even try to forget, because as a result of her two appearances on the Saturday-night TV programme she blasted off for stardom and began to show up in magazines, on the radio and television much more often than she had up till then, taking Zarco's place to a certain extent. Not that Zarco was suddenly obliterated from people's memories, but that, thanks to María, he seemed at times to turn into a different character, hazy and secondary, into the minor bad guy of a tragedy or a melodrama no longer his own: up till then María had just been Zarco's wife, while he was the real protagonist of the story; from then on María became the protagonist and Zarco became merely the beast who had made her a victim par excellence. As far as everything else went, that was a bad time for me. I'd just turned forty, but I felt washed up, and that feeling sunk me into a foul pit of self-pity: I saw myself wallowing about in absolute failure, in absolute drought and desiccation, in absolute futility; my old feeling of living a borrowed anodyne life returned, stronger than ever, my impression of having taken a wrong turn and of being trapped in a misunderstanding. I lost interest in my work, lost my capacity for joy, I wore out physically in no time. Some mornings I woke up crying; some nights I cried myself to sleep; some days I stayed in bed, unable to get up and go to my office. Just then I made what I thought was a great discovery; I thought I discovered a truth that I'd always had in view and hadn't wanted to see, a truth that changed everything except the sensation of having been a dick-head and a wanker and made the most ridiculous fool of myself, which became even sharper.

'The discovery happened in a trivial way, one morning when I was talking to a bunch of colleagues in the courthouse corridor and someone mentioned Higinio Redondo, my father's friend, I don't know if you remember . . .'

'The friend who lent you his house in Colera after the bank robbery in Bordils.'

'That's right: my mentor, the lawyer I began my career with. At a certain moment someone brought up his name while we were talking. I don't know who it was or what they said, perhaps they were remembering one of Redondo's anecdotes or jokes, something like that, which wasn't unusual either, as I told you before Redondo was a real character, people at the courthouse still remember him. The thing is that Redondo's name acted as a trigger: I suddenly stopped listening and mentally left the small group and the courthouse; suddenly, like I say, I believed I saw the truth, as if it had always been right in front of my nose, barely hidden by a semi-transparent veil, and the unexpected mention of Redondo had revealed it. I don't remember what happened afterwards, or how the conversation ended. The only thing I remember is that for several days I walked around stunned by the humiliating certainty that my story was actually a mediocre copy of Redondo's story, a version of a story as old and ridiculous as the world: I already told you that Redondo had fallen in love like a schoolboy with the wife of a penniless client who used him to get her husband out of prison and that, as soon as she got what she wanted, she left him.'

'And you believed your story with Tere was similar?'

'It's not that I believed it: it's that it struck me as obvious. And not that it was similar: it was even worse. More ridiculous. More humiliating. I suddenly felt that everything fell into place: Tere was Zarco's girlfriend when I met her, in the Vilaró arcade, she still was while Zarco's myth grew up in the prisons and she probably still was now, when he himself had destroyed or degraded his own myth and now knew for sure that he would never live in freedom again. That didn't mean Tere hadn't loved me, or that she hadn't been in love with me when we used to see each other at my place to make love and listen to old CDs, or even that she hadn't been during the summer of '78, like Zarco and she herself claimed. Why wouldn't she have been? Who can say that in her own way Redondo's lover wasn't in love with him? Women are like that: they turn their interests into feelings; they always have and they always will, at least as long as they're weaker than us. So no, that didn't mean that Tere hadn't loved me: it just meant that she'd loved me in an occasional and conditional way, while she loved Zarco in a permanent and unconditional way. It meant that probably everything or almost everything Tere had done with me she'd done for Zarco: in the washrooms of the Vilaró arcade she'd seduced me because Zarco needed to recruit me, and that same summer, as you suspected, she'd seduced me again on Montgó beach to get even with Zarco, who was sleeping with another girl that night; and at my place on La Barca she'd seduced me again, twenty years later, because she wanted to make sure I'd work conscientiously to get Zarco out of prison and, when Zarco started to get out on release, brushed me off so I wouldn't bother them, but she used her wiles to keep hold of me, although at a distance, so I wouldn't abandon them before Zarco was freed and she could run away with him . . . It all fell into place. And worst of all I felt that I'd always known the truth and at the same time had never wanted to know it, that it was such an obvious truth that neither Tere nor Zarco had bothered much about hiding it from me, and that, precisely for that reason, I'd been able to ignore it or pretend

I didn't know. I understood Tere's attitude that night in La Creueta, trying to get Zarco to shut up when, drunk and drugged up, he let off steam and almost let out the brutal truth and called me a dickhead and a wanker and said that the two of them were using me and that I didn't understand anything. I understood the irony of two professional sharks like Redondo and I falling for such an old and well-known trick. I understood Redondo's horror when he discovered the snare he'd fallen into and immediately started planning to imitate him by leaving the practice in the hands of Cortés and Gubau and abandoning the city for a good long while. And I understood that the great misunderstanding of my life was that there hadn't been any misunderstanding.'

'So you did as Redondo had done? You dropped everything and left?'

'No, I didn't leave. I stayed, not because I wanted to but because I didn't even have the energy to leave. What happened was I went to a doctor who diagnosed depression, and for more than a year I underwent psychiatric treatment and a massive diet of antidepressants and anti-anxiety medication. As time passed, I began to recover gradually: I continued in treatment and, although I didn't give up the psychotropics, I reduced the doses and managed to return to work and more or less resume my old life. It's true that during that period I felt like some sort of survivor, but it's also true that I began to think with increasing frequency that the worst was over and that, since I'd already made all or almost all the mistakes a person can make, what I did from there on in I could almost only get right. It was naive: I'd simply forgotten that, no matter how bad things got, they could always get much worse.'

'Does that mean you heard from Zarco?'

'Bingo. One day in May or June of 2004, almost three years after seeing him for the last time at the gates of the Gerona prison, I received a letter from him. It was the first sign of life I'd had from him since the press reported his final arrest. The letter came from the Quatre Camins prison and was written by hand, with careful rounded handwriting and in the formal tone of a request; I read it twice: the first time I thought Zarco was using that handwriting and that tone to impose a professional distance between us (or perhaps to tell me without saying so that he was annoyed with me for all the time I'd wanted nothing to do with him); the second time I guessed that he used them because they were the only ones he knew. Zarco began with an overly formal salutation, and then immediately asked me to be his lawyer again; then he gave the reasons for his request: he stated that days earlier, in the prison yard, a skinhead had given him a beating that had left him almost unconscious and that, while they were transporting him to the emergency room of Terrassa General Hospital, two members of the Catalan police force had stopped the vehicle, made him get out and brutalized him. Now he was back at the prison, isolated from the rest of the inmates in a hospital unit, and he wanted me to denounce the two beatings; as well as taking charge of this case, he also wanted me to defend him against a charge of insubordination, and most of all he wanted me to start proceedings to get him readmitted to Gerona Prison and do whatever necessary to get them to accept him. At the end of his letter, Zarco managed to wrench a pitiful note out of his orthopaedic handwriting and inform me that he was ill, begging me to help him through this rough patch and asking me to get in touch with Tere so she could bring me up to date and fill me in on the details.

'I don't know if I finished rereading Zarco's letter more furious than incredulous or more incredulous than furious. It was like a message from an alien. I thought it was incredible and infuriating that, after having cost me two years of work and having betrayed my trust and that of all those who had supported the campaign for his liberty, he didn't offer the slightest excuse or show the slightest sign of remorse. I thought it was incredible and infuriating that he showed no sign of feeling guilty, or even of remembering his own outrages, and instead was still trying to present himself as a victim. Most of all I thought it was incredible and infuriating that, after having deceived me and making Tere deceive me, having treated me like a dickhead and a wanker and having forced me to make a fool of myself, he would still come to me using the same old bait and believing I would bite for a third time (although I couldn't help but notice that the letter didn't contain Tere's address or phone number, so I could get in touch with her). All this meant that I didn't feel the slightest pity for him or the slightest cordial impulse towards him or his situation; just the reverse: I knew that ninety-five per cent of my feelings of absolute futility and drought and desiccation and failure that had dragged me into depression should be attributed to Tere's deceit and her having left me, but at that moment I realized that the remaining five per cent should be attributed to my absurd attempt to take responsibility for the actions of someone who didn't take responsibility for his own actions and to save someone who deep down didn't want to save himself; and I also realized that the best thing I could do would be to stay away from him. From him and from Tere. The result of this reflection was that I didn't even answer Zarco's letter. And the result of this result was that I suddenly felt buoyant and independent, as if someone had just taken a lead collar I didn't know I was wearing off my neck.

'That happened on a Monday. The following days were euphoric. I started showing up for work with the same joy as in the early years, I flirted with a young attorney at the courthouse and a couple of times went to the Royal for a few beers with Cortés and Gubau after work. This state of light-heartedness vanished suddenly on the Thursday morning, when Tere showed up unannounced at the office. She'd barely changed in those three years:

she was dressed in her eternal teenage style – jeans, white shirt and handbag strap slung across her chest – and her hair was still damp and uncombed; she seemed very happy to see me. I, however, could not and did not want to hide my annoyance; without even saying hello I asked: What are you here for? Instead of replying, Tere gave me a fleeting kiss on the cheek and, before I could invite her in (or not), stole into my office. She sat down on the sofa. I followed her, closed the door and stood across from her. Zarco's written to you, hasn't he?, she said straight off the bat. I answered her question with another question: Did he tell you that? No, she answered. He gave me the letter and I left it in your mailbox. At that moment I understood why Zarco's letter didn't have Tere's address or phone number: it had been written for her to hand to me in person. And why didn't you come up and give it to me?, I asked. I didn't want to overwhelm you, she answered. I thought you should have a few days to think it over. I nodded and said: No need. There's nothing to think about. I'm pleased to hear it, she said. Don't be pleased, I said. I don't plan on falling into the trap again. What trap?, she asked. You know what trap, I answered; then I added a half truth: Being his lawyer. It's not a trap, she said. And I don't understand why you don't want to help him. The question isn't why I don't want to help him, I argued. The question is why should I help him. Because if you and I don't nobody will, she answered. He's completely alone. Well, he's earned it, I replied. When we tried to help him it did no good at all; or rather: all it did was fuck us all up and make us waste our time and money. As far as I know, the only one who got fucked over was him, replied Tere. Oh, yeah?, I said. I was about to reproach her for leaving me, I was about to tell her about my depression; I spoke of María. What's wrong?, I asked. Don't you watch TV, don't you see any magazines, don't you go outside? Have you not heard about the mountains of shit María has piled on top of us? That's

309

water under the bridge, replied Tere. It wasn't true, but almost; although over the last year María hadn't disappeared from the media, her star was fading: she still showed up on the odd chat show and sometimes appeared in the gossip magazines, but she was no longer a relevant figure in the media circus, her story and her celebrity were wearing out and, in spite of her efforts, she seemed incapable of reviving them. Tere continued: Besides, it was all lies. Not all of it, I corrected her. Almost all, she conceded. And nobody pays her any attention any more. They didn't before either. Don't you realize it's all a comedy and everybody knows it's a comedy?

'She fell silent. I did the same. I was upset and didn't want to argue with Tere: I just wanted to get the matter out of the way swiftly, without giving her time to use any wiles to make me vulnerable again and make me accept her suggestion. I sat in one of the armchairs, beside her, still on the sofa, watching me expectantly and almost still, except for her left leg moving with its unstoppable piston rhythm. Look, Tere, I began. I'm going to tell you the truth. I'm fed up with this story. I'm fed up with Zarco and with you. With both of you. You tricked me when I was a kid and you're deceiving me now. You think I don't know? You think I'm an idiot? Zarco was right: I have made a ridiculous fool of myself and been a dickhead and a wanker and let myself be used. And I've suffered a lot. I loved you, you know? And I suffered like an animal when you left me. I don't want to suffer any more. It's over. Understand? It's over. I don't want to have anything more to do with you. Not with you and not with him. Don't ask me to defend him again because I'm not going to. No way. I don't want to know anything more about Zarco. And, if you had any sense, you'd do the same. He's made you make a fool of yourself too. He uses you too whenever he feels like it. But have you really not figured out what a fucking son of a bitch he is, as well as a pathological media whore? Tere had been stroking the mole beside her nose, her head had slumped between her shoulders and her eyes fixed on the parquet and her gaze turned inwards. Meanwhile I went on cursing her, more and more upset, her and Zarco; I swore at them until I realized Tere was saying or murmuring something. Then I shut up. Tere repeated: He's my brother. An absolute silence filled the room. I'd heard perfectly, but I asked: What did you say? Tere looked up at me: her green eyes were empty, inexpressive; three very fine lines had just appeared on her forehead. That he's my brother, she repeated. His father was my father. We don't have the same mother, but his father is my father. She looked at me, touched the mole beside her nose and shrugged in a gesture that seemed like an apology, but she didn't say anything else.

'I didn't know what to say either, so I stood up from the armchair and took a few steps towards my desk; when I got to it I turned back towards Tere. Is that true?, I asked. Tere nodded. It can't be, I said. Tere kept nodding. Nobody knows, she explained. My mother and his mother. And me. No one else. What about Zarco?, I asked again. Zarco neither, she answered. My mother told me we were sister and brother when he showed up in Gerona, not long before we met you. She told me because Zarco and I were always together, she knew we loved each other a lot and she didn't want anything to happen between us. She fell silent, pensive, or perhaps as if not knowing what else to tell me, or not wanting to tell me. I asked another question: Why didn't you tell Zarco? What for?, she answered. It was enough for one of us to know. And I could live with it, but he might not have been able to: he's weaker than you think. And had you . . . ?, I asked. I realized Tere was crying: big fat tears started rolling down her cheeks, falling onto her shirt and leaving little wet spots. I had never seen her cry. I sat in the armchair, beside her, I held one of her hands: it was damp and warm. We were just kids, she said. We didn't know what we were doing, nobody ever told us anything, you know? She kept crying, without mopping up her tears, as if she hadn't noticed she was crying, and I understood she wouldn't say anything else.

'For a while we sat in silence; I ran my fingers over her knuckles with my mind blank: I didn't even think that here was a real misunderstanding, only a resolved misunderstanding, and that now, probably, everything did fall into place. When Tere stopped crying and started wiping her face with her hands I stood up, left the office, came back with a packet of Kleenex and gave her a few. Sorry, she said as she dried her eyes. I don't know why I told you that. She finished tidying herself up, looked at me. Then she looked away and we were quiet for a while longer. She blew her nose and dried her tears; I had been left speechless. At a certain point she said: Well, I do know why I told you. What I told you is the truth: Zarco has nobody; you and I are all he has left. And he's ill. She turned back towards me, her eyes still shining: You'll help him, won't you?'

IO

'When Gamallo got his pardon and the conditional release and left the Gerona prison with everyone's felicitations, I hoped it would be the last I'd see of him. A short time later he committed another crime and was sent to Quatre Camins Prison, but still I hoped. I was mistaken. His lawyer was to blame for everything.

'After Gamallo was released, Cañas and I still saw each other, almost every time he visited one of his clients at the prison. As I told you before, we'd had a clash over Gamallo, but thanks to that my opinion of him had improved and now our relationship was excellent, so, if we bumped into each other on his way in or out of the prison (sometimes even in town), we'd say hello and chat for a while, though we always avoided talking about Gamallo. However, things must have got pretty complicated for Cañas when, shortly after Gamallo got sent back to Quatre Camins, that nutcase started accusing him on television of being complicit in the barbarities Gamallo had done to her . . . I mean his wife. But, anyway, I imagine Cañas will already have told you all this; I only know what everybody knows. The thing is that for a while I didn't see him. I asked about him and was told he was having health problems, though nobody specified what kinds of problems he was dealing with; then there was also a lot of talk about his involvement with the girl who visited Gamallo, it seemed to become the talk of the courthouse for a while, and ended up reaching me.

Later, after some months (many months, maybe more than a year), Cañas reappeared: he started visiting his clients again, our paths started crossing again once in a while here and there and we went back to talking about anything except Gamallo again, until a moment arrived when I almost forgot Gamallo or when I stopped associating Cañas' name with that of Gamallo.

'It was around that time that Cañas showed up in my office again one afternoon. Years had gone by since he'd last done that and I thought he was coming to talk to me about one of the inmates. We chatted for a while and, when I thought he was going to leave and that it had just been a courtesy call or something like that, the lawyer put me right: he told me he'd come to see me because he'd agreed to defend Gamallo again and because he was going to put in an application for his transfer from Quatre Camins to Gerona Prison. I couldn't believe my ears. You're incorrigible, was all I could manage to say. Cañas smiled. You're mistaken, he answered. I'm just a lawyer. And Gamallo is my client. I'm just doing my job. Sure, I said. Though I think you're the one who's making a mistake. In any case, I added, I appreciate your inform-ing me of what you plan to do. Well, Cañas said then, and his smile turned a bit mischievous, a bit childish. Actually I haven't come just to inform you. He took a sheaf of photocopies out of his briefcase and put it on my desk as he said: I'd like you to support the application. I looked at the pile of pages, without touching it. The decision to transfer an inmate rests with Correctional Institutions, but Cañas knew that the opinions of the prison super-intendents (that of the receiving prison and that of the current one) were important; he also knew it wasn't going to be easy to convince me to support his move, so he had come to the meeting prepared. He explained what the sheaf contained: the main thing was a report from the superintendent of the Quatre Camins prison supporting Zarco's transfer, and a series of reports from various specialists; according to Cañas, only one thing could be deduced from these reports, and it was that the Zarco of today bore very little relation to the one who had first come to the Gerona prison, because the illness, the years and his own errors had taken away the strength and the halo of youth and converted him into an inoffensive inmate. Cañas ended up playing a sentimental tune. He said, more or less: When he arrived here last time, Gamallo was coming to recover his freedom; now he just wants to be allowed to live his final years in peace. I don't think anyone has the right to deny him that.

'As soon as Cañas finished speaking I sat up a bit in my chair, took the sheaf of pages, leafed through it for a moment without reading it and then I sighed and put it back down where it had been. Look, Counsellor, I said. Maybe you're right: maybe Gamallo is no longer what he used to be. I'm not saying you're not. What I do say is that, even half dead, that man is a headache. I paused and then continued: You know something? In a little over two years I'm going to retire. Don't you think I too have the right to live this time out in peace? You know better than anybody that when Gamallo was in this prison my life was unbearable, and on top of that it did no good; I don't want to go through that again. Besides, what good would it do to transfer him? Naturally the superintendent of Quatre Camins wants to be rid of Gamallo, but the truth is that his prison is much more modern and much better equipped than mine, especially to deal with Gamallo. So, don't take it personally, but, if I can spare myself the presence of that man here, I'm going to. I hope you'll understand. Cañas did not understand, or did not want to understand. We argued for a few minutes more. In the end we went our separate ways amicably, and, though the lawyer managed to get me to keep the reports on Gamallo, he did not manage to get me even to promise that, since I wasn't going to support the move, I would at least not oppose it.'

'But in the end you supported it.'

'How do you know?'

'I didn't know, I guessed. Why did you?'

'Support him? To be frank, I don't know. One day Correctional Institutions called me to ask if I thought it would be good for Gamallo to return to Gerona and I simply couldn't think how to say no. I suppose Cañas and the Quatre Camins reports must have convinced me between them that Gamallo was no longer a problem, that he was on his last legs.'

'And were they right?'

'Yes, this time they were. When they brought Gamallo to the prison I was surprised that a man could deteriorate so much in such a short time. He was skin and bones, had difficulty walking, he'd lost most of his hair and his face looked like a preview of his skull, with his black teeth, sunken eyes and fleshless cheeks. My first impression was that the man was no more than a walking skeleton; the medical reports confirmed it: he had once again exchanged heroin for methadone, but AIDS was devouring him from within and he was very weak, which meant that, at any moment, any minor illness could overcome his defences and wipe him out.

'His myth had also collapsed. Not only did the press not mention a word of it, when he arrived in the city, but even in the prison his arrival didn't provoke the slightest agitation. In spite of everything I decided to hedge my bets and assigned him his own individual cell with the idea of keeping him separate from the rest of the inmates. For Gamallo, this was a humiliating measure, which equated him with the lowest of the low – informers or rapists – but he didn't protest, I think he already knew that because of the combination of his former celebrity and his physical weakness he was an irresistible target for the kids looking to make themselves respected, kids he no longer had the strength to confront; he didn't protest when I tried to impose an activity programme that would keep him busy from morning till night either. How ingenuous! The activity programme, I mean: in his physical state, Gamallo couldn't carry out any programme and, when I realized that, I understood that Cañas was right and the only thing we could do for him was to let him end his days in tranquillity. And that's what I tried to do.'

II

'At the end of the spring or beginning of the summer of 2005 Zarco returned to Gerona Prison and I started seeing him once a week again, often more than once. It wasn't until then, almost thirty years after I met him, that I started to feel that what linked us was starting to resemble a friendship. Of course, I was still his lawyer, but the problem (or the advantage) was that, once we got him transferred to Gerona, he practically didn't need a lawyer, or he needed one much less than he had before: after all, any fantasy of rehabilitation was ruled out, as was any hope of getting any release permits, and the legal matters we could deal with had been reduced to a minimum. By then, Zarco was physically a wreck; morally too: as Tere had told me, he was alone, nobody wanted anything to do with him, he was totally discredited outside and inside the prison and he no longer even seemed capable of playing the part of Zarco. This is important: as soon as I saw him again, still in Quatre Camins, before we managed to get him transferred to Gerona, I had the impression that the struggle within him between the person and persona was over, that the tendency to see himself as a victim and the arrogance were coming to an end and the magnificent façade of the myth was about to come tumbling down, revealing the prematurely aged, defeated and ill man in his forties behind it. At first, as I said, it was just an impression, but it made me see him in a different way, just as knowing that he was actually Tere's brother changed my way of seeing him; it changed, although I don't know how it changed: I didn't know exactly what his relationship with Tere had been like – and I don't think I wanted to know – but the truth is that he no longer interfered in my relationship with her, and nor did she in my relationship with him.

'All this explains why I started to go to see Zarco at the prison almost immediately, more to chat for a while than for work, and that our conversations became much more intimate than they had ever been before. Obviously it never occurred to me to tell him what Tere had revealed in my office; actually, as far as I recall, we barely talked about Tere except in passing. We talked a lot, however, about his mother (who was living in Gerona, like some of his family, and with whom he hadn't been on speaking terms for years), and especially about his three older brothers, three *quinquis* who he'd got to know when he was eleven or twelve, with whom he'd lived for a very short time and who'd been the idols of his youth; all three had died more than a decade before in violent circumstances: Joaquín, the youngest, crashed into a moving van at an intersection in El Clot, in Barcelona, while fleeing the police in a stolen car; Juan José, the eldest, while trying to slip down a rope from the window of the Madrid prison hospital, where he had been moved from a prison where he was serving thirty years for homicide; Andrés, the middle brother and for many Zarco's model, at a police roadblock on the way into Gerona, after robbing a bank in Llagostera, when the police shot him when they saw him reaching for his pistol. But you know all these things: they're in the cuttings in my archive and besides, if I'm not mistaken, Zarco recounts them in his memoirs.'

'You're not mistaken.'

'Of course: actually, most of the things he told me then he'd already told in his memoirs, sometimes even in the same way and almost in the same words, so I sometimes had the impression that Zarco wasn't telling me what he remembered but what he remembered having told in his memoirs. Anyway, I enjoyed listening to him a lot, hearing him talk about the riots and escapes he'd played a starring role in, the books he'd signed or that had been written about him and the movies he'd been in, the journalists and film directors and actresses and musicians and football players he'd met. In this way I discovered something that surprised me, and it's that, in his memoirs and interviews, Zarco had lied or adorned the truth much less than I'd thought (and less in the second volume of the memoirs than in the first, according to him, through the fault of Jorge Ugal, the ghostwriter who later, in part thanks to that book, went on to have a short political career); or to put it another way: what I discovered was that it hadn't been Zarco who'd constructed his own myth, but most of all the newspapers and the films Bermúdez made, and all he did was to approve it, make it his own and spread it.'

'So you think his memoirs are reliable.'

'I think so. Except on particular points, of course.'

'For example?'

'For example on the death of Bermúdez. From the first moment everybody thought Zarco was the one who killed him, who shot him up with that overdose of heroin and set up that scene to look like a ritual sacrifice or a sexual crime . . .'

'But in the memoirs he denies it.'

'What else was he going to do? I'm sure it's true.'

'Did he confess?'

'No: he denied it. But at that time I could tell when he was lying and when he was telling the truth, and on that matter he lied to me. I'm sure. Or almost sure. You should have heard him bitch about Bermúdez; he really badmouthed him, but not because Bermúdez was homosexual, as some have said: he didn't care about that, in fact I think he always knew Bermúdez was in love with him and he played with that, or tried to. No, I think he hated Bermúdez for other reasons: he thought that, with Zarco's saga and his other films about young *quinquis* starring real *quinquis* that followed, Bermúdez had made a fortune and won prestige in the film world at his expense, and on top of that he'd done so by presenting himself as a sort of philanthropist who wanted only to save him and other kids like him; he claimed that Bermúdez's Catholic altruism was hypocritical, a stomach-turning way to sell his films; he said he'd swindled him from the start, that he'd stolen his life to make into films, that he'd promised he'd get to star in them and that it's not true that he didn't star in them because the supervising judge wouldn't let him leave the prison (as was generally thought), but because in the end Bermúdez wanted someone else to star; he also said that he paid him much less money than they'd agreed he would pay, that it was a lie that he'd legally adopted him while they were filming his last movie and even more of a lie that he'd disinherited him as a punishment for having taken advantage of the press-screening cocktail party, at the Ocaña penitentiary, to escape . . . Anyway, I think by the end his relationship with Bermúdez had gone sour, and as Bermúdez said, that Zarco staged that escape in part to fuck him over and to fuck up his film and that later, when the police were looking for him, he appealed to Bermúdez again and things got out of hand or he bumped him off on purpose, or had him bumped off. Zarco was like that: if he came to the conclusion that someone was a real bastard, or had acted like one, he would make that person pay if at all possible.'

'As might have happened with Batista.'

'For example.'

'It's strange then that he didn't make María Vela pay for what she did.'

'No, not strange: the thing is he didn't consider María to be a real bastard. And he was probably right. María was just a mediapath, like him, or rather, like the Zarco character; at most she was an opportunist. But not a bastard. And maybe that's why Zarco, in the conversations we had then, never spoke badly of her, always downplayed the importance of what she said about him in the press (or what she was still saying, which was less and less as there were fewer and fewer people paying any attention) and he didn't seem at all irritated by all the visibility in the media she'd achieved at a certain moment by messing with us; more than that: my impression was that Zarco spoke more cordially of María now than he had done when they were together and she spent all her time trying to get him out of jail.

'But what Zarco and I discussed most – where I believe the complicity I told you about sprang from – was none of that, but the summer of '78. In fact, we could spend all of my afternoon visits in the interview room remembering the guys in the gang, reliving purse snatches, robberies and binges, recalling the General haggling with his wife – who Zarco insisted was actually blind not pretending to be blind – telling each other details of a visit to La Vedette or trying to rescue from oblivion the names and faces of the regulars at La Font or Rufus. Those conversations at times turned into fierce tournaments in which Zarco and I competed in eagerness for precision about the past; thanks to them – and to those I'd had with Tere years earlier, in our nights of romance in my penthouse on La Barca – I was able to reconstruct the summer of '78, and that's why I remember it so well. Of course, Zarco often talked about the prefabs, and one day I told him about the only time I'd been there, shortly after the robbery of the Bordils branch of the Banco Popular, although I didn't tell him that I'd actually gone there that day to see Tere and especially to find out if the gang thought I'd been the one who had given the game away (and, if so, to refute it). This doesn't mean that we didn't talk about that matter then, actually we discussed it several times, but always in the way we discussed all the details of the summer of '78, a slightly strange way, very cerebral, almost with the coldness with which you might discuss a chess problem; what-ever the case, I always arrived at the conclusion that Zarco thought that the snitch or informer could have been anybody that day, but that anybody didn't exclude me.'

'You mean you didn't convince Zarco that it hadn't been you?'

'That's it: I tried, but I didn't manage it. Or I don't think so. He always had a shadow of a doubt. Although he didn't say so, I knew he did.'

'Perhaps he had some doubt because you did too, because you weren't entirely sure that, before the Bordils robbery, you hadn't run your mouth off.'

'Could be.'

'Another thing. You say that, when he returned to Gerona Prison, Zarco was a physical wreck. Didn't he improve later?'

'No. Although the prison treated him well, he was ill and exhausted, and he had nothing left. While I talked with him in the interview room I often had the sensation I was talking to a zombie, or at least a very old man. And in spite of that (or perhaps thanks to it) during that time I discovered three important things about him and about my relationship with him: the first two demonstrate that deep down I had a vision of Zarco for years that was guileless and mythologized, ridiculously romantic; the third demonstrates that Zarco himself shared that vision. Perhaps by this point you've guessed the three things I've come to tell you, but I didn't discover them till then.'

'What do you mean?'

'Look, I've always heard it said that, in personal relations, the first impression is what counts. I don't think it's true: I think the first impression is the only one that counts; all the rest are just additions that do not alter anything essentially. At least that's what I think happened to me with Zarco. I mean that there in the Gerona prison, Zarco might have looked like human scum, and he surely was, but that didn't mean I could stop seeing him as I'd seen him with my teenage eyes the first time I'd seen him, walking into the Vilaró arcade with Tere, and as I'd seen him during that summer. That's the first thing I understood: that for three months of my adolescence I had admired Zarco — I'd admired his serenity, his courage, his audacity — and since then I haven't been able to stop admiring him. The second thing I understood is that, as well as admiring him, I envied him: now, in the Gerona prison, seen with the perspective of time, Zarco's life could seem like a wasted life, the life of a loser, but the truth of the matter is that, if I compared it with mine — which had so often seemed to me a false and borrowed life, a misunderstanding or, even worse, an insipid yet convincing simulation of a misunderstanding — his seemed to me like a full life, that had been worth living and that I would have traded for mine without hesitation. The third thing I understood is that Zarco had always been aware of playing the role of Zarco, or at the very least he was aware now of having played this role for years.'

'Is that what you meant when you said that at this moment the persona disappeared and only the person remained?'

'Exactly. Let me tell you about one of the last conversations Zarco and I had, in the prison's interview room. That afternoon we'd been talking for a while as usual about the summer of '78 when, after I mentioned the prefabs in passing, Zarco interrupted me and asked me what I'd said. At that moment I understood that, without realizing it, I'd just called the prefabs by the nickname I'd always had for them, so I said I hadn't said anything and tried to change the subject; Zarco wouldn't let me, and repeated the question. Liang Shan Po, I finally confessed, feeling as ridiculous as a guy who accidentally says his lover's pet name out loud in public. That's what you called the prefabs? Zarco asked. I nodded. I tried to keep talking so I wouldn't have to give him an explanation, but I couldn't; Zarco frowned, his eyes narrowed until they looked like two slits and he asked: Like the river in *The Water Margin*? Zarco greeted my surprise with a black and toothless smile. You remember the series?, I asked. Fuck, Gafitas, Zarco protested. You think you're the only one who ever watched TV? He immediately started talking about *The Water Margin*, about the dragon and the snake, about Lin Chung and Kao Chiu and Hu San-Niang, until he stopped short in mid-sentence, frowned again and looked at me as if he'd just deciphered a hieroglyphic on my face. Hey, he said. You didn't fall for that old song and dance too, did you? What song and dance?, I asked. He took a couple of seconds to answer. The Liang Shan Po thing, he specified. The honourable bandits. All that shit. I wasn't sure what he meant. I told him so. He explained: You didn't believe that whole *Water Margin* spiel, did you? That whole story about you lot on that side being worse sons of bitches than we are on this side, and vice versa; that thing about the only difference between me and you is that I was born in a wrong neighbourhood of the city and on the wrong side of the river, that society's to blame for everything and I'm innocent of everything and this that and the other. You didn't believe that, right?

'At that moment I knew it. It wasn't only in his words, it was in the sarcasm that drenched his voice, in the disappointment and irony and sadness of his old man's eyes. What I knew was that Zarco was definitely finished, that the persona had disappeared and only the person barely remained, that lonely, ill and washed-up *quinqui* I had in front of me, on the other side of the interview room. And I also knew or imagined that, deep down, Zarco had never believed in his own persona, had never seriously thought that he was the true Robin Hood of his time, or the great reformed delinquent; it had just been a pretend, strategic identity, which he'd used when it suited him but never really believed or he'd only believed it fleetingly and almost without meaning to, an identity that he hadn't believed in for a long time in any case and that, in those days of terminal lucidity when he no longer had the energy to laugh or cry, was only pitiful.

'That's what I knew then (or what I imagined), thanks to that conversation.'

'I would have imagined something else as well.'

'What's that?'

'The opposite: that perhaps Zarco no longer believed in his own persona, but he believed that you did believe in it. That he believed, in some way, that you still believed he was an innocent victim, that you were the last one who thought of him as the Robin Hood of his day, or as the great reformed delinquent. That you weren't really either his lawyer or his friend, but the last admirer he had left. Or the last deputy: the last honourable man Lin Chung had left on the far side of the Water Margin. After all, the questions Zarco had asked you were rhetorical, weren't they?'

'You might be right.'

'And didn't you say anything? Didn't you try to disabuse him of that notion?'

'More or less. I told him I hadn't believed his song and dance, as he'd called it, that of course I'd never thought that society was to blame for everything and he was just a victim of society. Zarco replied by asking then why did I call them the outlaws of Liang Shan Po, and I answered because at first I did believe it, that after all in the summer of '78 I was sixteen years old and at sixteen you believe things like that, but later I stopped believing it, only by then it was too late to change the nickname so it stuck. That's what I told him, more or less, though I realized he didn't believe me and I didn't want to insist.'

'So you let Zarco hold onto a false idea of what you thought of him.'

'Yes. I suppose so.'

'I thought the truth was very important to you.'

'It is, but a virtue taken to extremes is a vice. If one does not understand there are things more important than the truth one doesn't understand how important the truth is.'

'You didn't talk about the matter again?'

'No.'

'And neither of you mentioned the Liang Shan Po again?'

'Not that I recall.'

'And Tere? You haven't even mentioned her today.'

'She hasn't come up. What do you want me to tell you? That summer we saw each other quite often. Tere had lived in Barcelona for a while but the last two or three years she'd moved back to Gerona, or rather to Salt, where she had a job cleaning various council properties. She'd given up her nursing studies and was going out with the local librarian, a guy with a ponytail and a goatee who went everywhere on his bicycle, spoke Catalan-inflected Spanish and rented an allotment on the banks of the River Ter where he grew tomatoes and lettuces. His name was Jordi and he was ten years younger than Tere. We got along well immediately (as far as he was concerned I was just Zarco's lawyer, and Zarco was just Tere's famous, unruly relative), so some Saturdays I'd show up at the allotment and spend the afternoon watching him and Tere working the land, talking politics (he was a separatist) or about Salt (he'd been born there and hoped to die there, though he'd travelled all over the world) and having the odd toke of his marijuana; when it got dark we'd go back into the city, them on their bikes and me in my car, and have something to eat at Jordi's place or in some bar in the old quarter.

'Sometimes, not many times, Tere and I would meet on our own. For this I would have to invent some important matter to do with Zarco, which was not at all easy. I remember one Saturday I'd met her at midday in a bar in the Sant Agustí Plaza and, after we finished our coffee and dealt with my bullshit, I accompanied her to the farmers' market they have every weekend on the boardwalk between La Devesa and the banks of the Ter; and I remember while Tere was doing her shopping I thought I might lay a trap for her and suggest crossing the river over to the ground where years before the prefabs had stood. Have you ever been back?, I asked. No, she said. It doesn't look anything like it used to, I told her, and then went on to describe the immaculate park of freshly mown lawns, with brand-new wooden benches and swings and slides that had replaced the lines of miserable barrack huts crisscrossed by streams of pestilential water swarming with flies where she had lived, until I noticed she was looking at me strangely. And if it doesn't look anything like it used to what do I want to see it for?, she asked curtly. That's how Tere was then: invulnerable to the lures of nostalgia, reluctant to talk more than necessary about the past we shared. Even so, one of those Saturdays we met to talk about Zarco she suggested a café in Santa Eugènia, and when I got there I found her with a large woman who greeted me with a big kiss. Don't you know who I am?, she asked. I had trouble recognizing her: it was Lina. She was still just as blonde as she had been in La Font days, but she'd put on twenty-five or thirty kilos, looked very much worse for wear and shouted when she talked. She didn't say a word about Gordo, but told me she'd married a Gambian, that she lived in Salt too, that she worked in a hair salon and had three kids. It was an odd encounter. Tere and Lina had never completely lost touch

328

although it had been a while since they'd seen each other, and at some point Lina started talking about Tío, who apart from us was the only member of Zarco's gang still alive: it seems she'd bumped into him by chance not long before, at the Trueta hospital, and she told us he was getting around in his wheelchair and she'd been really happy to see him (and him to see her); finally she suggested the three of us go visit him in Germans Sàbat, where he still lived with his mother. Tere and I agreed to her suggestion, and we arranged to meet the following week at the same time and in the same place to go together to Tío's house. But the following Saturday I didn't show up to meet them; days later I found out that Tere hadn't shown up either.

'More or less around the middle of October I stopped seeing Tere and Jordi, not for any reason; Tere simply stopped calling me and I was starting to get the impression that, after the novelty of the first few months, my company was starting to be annoying and they'd rather be alone. The fact is I didn't see Tere again for almost three months. This time it was by chance. That afternoon I'd gone to La Bisbal to visit a client, at dusk I was returning to Gerona and as I drove into the city by Pont Major I recognized Tere in a group of women and children waiting for a bus at the stop closest to the prison, sheltering from the cold under a little roof. It was Sunday, the last Sunday of the year. I stopped the car, waved to Tere, offered to give her a lift home. Tere accepted, got in beside me and, as soon as we pulled away from the bus stop, told me that Zarco was in very bad shape, that both Friday and Saturday he'd had a fever and that morning they'd diagnosed him with pneumonia. A bit surprised, I said I'd seen Zarco on Wednesday and he hadn't said anything and I hadn't noticed anything either; I asked: Did you see him? Tere said no, but she'd been able to speak to the senior supervisor. They were thinking of taking him to hospital, she said. Which hospital?, I asked. I don't know, she answered. I took my eyes off Pedret Avenue for a moment and looked at her. Don't worry, I said. Tomorrow I'll talk to the superintendent. And I added: I'm sure it's nothing. The conjecture filled the car like an unavoidable lie as we approached the city, which at that hour, covered in Christmas lights, sparkled in the distance. To dispel the silence I asked after Jordi. Tere told me distractedly that she hadn't been seeing him for a while; I waited for an explanation, some comment, but neither was forthcoming, and I didn't want to keep asking.

'Tere's house was on the outskirts of Salt, near the overpass and the highway to Bescanó, in a tower block planted in the middle of a dirty site covered with rubble and weeds. I stopped in front of the building and again promised Tere that I'd talk to the prison superintendent the next day; Tere nodded, asked me to please do that and said goodbye, but as she stepped out of the car she seemed to hesitate. Outside the darkness was almost total; the silence too, except for the growl of the traffic coming from the highway. Without turning back towards me, Tere asked: Do you want to come up?

'It was the first time she'd ever invited me into her home. We went up a stairway with scaly walls lit by fluorescent tubes, and on the way up we crossed paths with two Middle Eastern women with their hair covered by scarves. When we went inside her apartment Tere ushered me into a tiny dining room, turned on the gas heater and offered me tea or camomile tea. I said I'd have camomile. While Tere made the tea I noted the underprivileged order that reigned in the room: there was nothing but a table with two chairs, an imitation-leather armchair, a sideboard, a small CD player, a portable television and the heater; there were also three open doors leading off the dining room: behind one of them was the kitchen where Tere was bustling, behind the other two I glimpsed or imagined a bathroom and bedroom even smaller and icier than the room I was in. Distracted by that inventory of misery, without realizing it I lost the joy I'd felt at the news that Tere had split up with Jordi, and felt overwhelmed with sorrow at Tere's life in that lonely outlying flat, sorrow at the news about Zarco's health, sorrow of the season and Sunday night sorrow.

'That night Tere and I slept together again. First thing the next morning, instead of going to the office, I went to the prison. At the entrance I was told I couldn't see Zarco because he'd been admitted to the infirmary. Then I tried to see the superintendent and, after being kept waiting for several minutes, went into his office. I asked him straight out how Zarco was doing. By way of reply the superintendent dug a sheet of paper out of the mess of papers on his desk and handed it to me. And what does this mean? I asked, waving the paper around after I read it. It means that, according to the doctor, Gamallo probably won't come out of this one, the superintendent answered. Can't they do anything else? I asked. Aren't they going to take him to hospital? The superintendent made a gesture of indifference or discouragement. If you want we'll take him, he answered. But the doctor advises against it. Gamallo isn't well enough to be moved, and we're taking good care of him here. Can I go in and see him?, I asked, handing him back the paper. I'm sorry, said the superintendent. No visitors are allowed in the infirmary. But I repeat you shouldn't worry. Gamallo is well attended. Besides, you know doctors: they always say things are worse than they are. Who knows if this one might not be wrong.

'When I left the prison I called Tere and told her what the superintendent had told me, but she made no comment.

'The three days that followed were very strange; in fact, I remember them as the happiest days of my life, and at the same time the most melancholy. Tere and I were barely apart. She had a week of holidays, and I took the time off. First I suggested we go away somewhere, but she wouldn't; then I suggested she come and stay at my place, but she wouldn't agree to that either; finally it was me who ended up going to stay at her place, arriving with a bag full of clothes and another full of part of my collection of CDs of '70s and '80s music. It was like a honeymoon. We didn't leave home except to eat at L'Espelma, a restaurant in Salt, and we spent morning, noon and night in bed, listening to my CDs, watching movies on TV and making love without the enthusiasm of the first times, but with a care and tenderness that I'd never known. Like a honeymoon, as I said, except a honeymoon troubled by bad omens: in those happy days I had an intuition more than once of how it was all going to end, and that's why they were also melancholy days.

'The fact of the matter is that first thing in the morning on New Year's Day the prison service supervisor woke me up to tell me that Zarco had died in the early hours. From that moment on confusion takes over from the strangeness in my memory, to such an extent that the following hours and days have the texture of a dream for me, or rather a nightmare. I don't remember, for example, how I told Tere the news. I don't remember how she took it, either; I don't remember the two of us at the prison, taking charge of the body or of Zarco's things, although I know we went to the prison and took charge of the body and of Zarco's things, of all the paperwork of the death. The funeral was held on the second day of the year. Inevitably, the newspapers repeated that it was a media event and a manifestation of popular mourning, but my impression is that, for once, the cliché did not entirely betray the reality. Over the last years the country seemed to have forgotten Zarco, or only seemed to remember him every once in a while as a guilty husband and increasingly distant secondary and declining character in the gossip magazines; now, the massive crowd at his funeral demonstrated that it wasn't the case, that the people had not forgotten him.

'Zarco's relatives, friends and acquaintances immediately showed up at the wake. Tons of them showed up. I had never seen a single one of them, I didn't know if any of them had ever visited him at the prison or had anything to do with him over the last few years; Tere, however, seemed to know them all, at least she treated them as if she knew them. The wake was in Salt, in the Salt chapel of rest. As I said before Tere and I had at first shared responsibility for the formalities and paperwork, but she soon turned into a sort of mistress of ceremonies, I think unintentionally. Shortly after we arrived at the chapel building she introduced me to a relatively young woman, still good-looking, with big blue eyes and big blonde hair, and told me it was her aunt, Zarco's mother; then she introduced me to other relatives of Zarco's, including one of his younger brothers (an albino who bore not the slightest physical resemblance to Zarco). I didn't manage to exchange anything more than the typical expressions of condolence with any of them, I don't know whether because Tere always introduced me simply as Zarco's lawyer. Some of them were Gypsies or looked like Gypsies, but none expressed outwardly any signs of pain over Zarco's death, except for his mother, who sighed every once in a while or cried out for her dead son.

'By mid-afternoon the chapel was full of busybodies and journalists on the hunt for quotes. I avoided them as best I could. By then I'd already lost my place, I did nothing but wander aimlessly between one big crowd of strangers and another and I had the impression that, rather than helping Tere, I was annoying her. I talked to her and we agreed that it would be best if I left and she stayed with the family. That night I called her, I suggested we have dinner just the two of us. She said she couldn't, that she was still with people, that she'd be finished late and that I should call her the next day. I called her the next morning, very early; she had her mobile disconnected and, although I tried again and again, it was futile. When I finally managed to get through to her it was almost one. She seemed nervous, she told me she'd argued with someone, maybe with Zarco's mother, she told me about preparations for the funeral; I asked her where she was, but all she answered was that I shouldn't worry and we'd see each other that afternoon. Then she hung up. I was worried, and a minute later I called her back. I got an engaged signal.

'The funeral was held in Vilarroja. There, at four in the afternoon, a huge crowd packed the church and its grounds. I had to make my way through those present, escorted by Cortés and Gubau, who had wanted to come with me. After looking around the church for a while I found Tere in the middle of a circle of mourners. I hugged her. We talked. She seemed to have recovered her serenity, but she also seemed tired, perhaps uncomfortable with the role that had fallen to her or been assigned to her, impatient to get all that over with as soon as possible. When the priest appeared in the vestibule, we separated: Tere sat in the front row, beside Zarco's mother; I stood at the back near the door. The ceremony was brief. While the priest was speaking I looked around the church and saw Jordi, Tere's former boyfriend, behind me; I also saw Lina on the end of an aisle, holding onto a wheelchair where, unmistakable, very pale and crying, Tío sprawled, fatter than thirty years earlier but with the same vaguely childlike air he had back then. Once the ceremony was over, the crowd didn't want to disperse and accompanied the family and the hearse to the cemetery, a few kilometres from the church. It was the most motley funeral cortège: there were mink coats beside rags, bicycles beside Mercedes, elderly people and children, relatives mixed in with journalists, criminals mixed in with cops, Gypsies mixed in with non-Gypsies, people from the neighbourhood, people from the city, people from other cities. I was with my two partners and with Jordi – who was walking his bike and told me he hadn't been able to say hello to Tere – all of us quite distant from the hearse, back where the cortège was starting to thin out; a cortège that, as people had joined along the way, soon filled the cemetery, which made Cortés, Gubau, Jordi and I decide not to go in but stay by the gate, waiting. That was why we didn't manage to witness either the burial or an incident that some newspapers picked up the next day and has to do with María Vela, who it seems had attended the burial (although I didn't see her at the funeral or at the cemetery). Various versions of the incident circulated. The most often repeated claims that, after the ceremony, María had approached Tere, who had returned her greeting; everything would have ended there and there wouldn't have been any incident had not a photographer caught the scene and had Tere not seen him do so; but the fact is she saw him and asked for the memory card from the camera and, when the photographer refused, she grabbed the camera and smashed it on the ground and stamped on it.

'That anecdote is the last thing I know of Tere; after Zarco's funeral she vanished: literally. When the burial ended I was waiting for her with Jordi, Cortés and Gubau at the cemetery gate until we realized that she must have left through another gate with Zarco's family. I called her on her mobile, but she had it switched off. Only then did I understand what was going on. And what was going on was that Tere had been avoiding me almost since I gave her the news of Zarco's death. Cortés and Gubau, who possibly guessed what I had guessed, invited me to go for a drink; I accepted and Jordi said he'd come along, although in the end it wasn't one drink but several and although, while we drank them, I kept dialling Tere's number, always without success.

'I finished up that evening quite drunk, and the next morning began several weeks of bitterness. No matter how hard I tried I didn't understand Tere's disappearance; as well as not

335

understanding it I didn't accept it: I phoned her at all hours of the day and at all hours was waiting for her to call; I went to look for her at her place, and spent many hours sitting on the stairs, waiting for her; I even thought of getting in touch with her through Zarco's relatives who she'd introduced me to during the wake, but I didn't know how to and, after a few attempts to locate them, I gave up. One afternoon, it must have been at least a week after her disappearance, I decided to knock on every door in her building and ask if any of her neighbours knew where she was; I didn't speak to all of them – some weren't in, most were Arabs and quite a few didn't understand Spanish – but from that inquiry I concluded that Tere had clearly not returned home after the burial, although also that she hadn't moved out and might return at any moment. On another day I went to see Jordi at his library and confirmed that conclusion: he told me that he didn't know where Tere was and the only thing he did know was that she'd left her job at the council without explanation. That afternoon I had a few beers with Jordi at a bar next door to the library; we were there till they closed, talking about Tere: since I immediately realized Jordi was still in love with her, I wasn't bold enough to tell him the truth, to tell him about our honeymoon tucked up in Tere's flat, and I spent the whole time trying to console him. When we were saying goodbye, Jordi couldn't hold himself together any more and burst into tears.

'During the weeks that followed I immersed myself in work matters. I was afraid of falling back into depression, into a blacker and deeper depression than the previous one or even a depression with no way out, and I fought it by working. My partners helped me a lot. Cortés and Gubau had the brains to treat me as an unwell or convalescent person and the tact to keep me from noticing that they were treating me as an unwell or convalescent person. They accepted without protest my pathological hyperactivity, my inexplicable absences, my glaring errors and apparent whims, among them eliminating prison visits, from which I invariably returned filled with deadly discouragement. On the weekends Cortés and Gubau took turns trying to distract me: they took me on day trips or out drinking, invited me to the cinema, the theatre or a football match, had me over for dinner or introduced me to single or divorced women friends. Keeping my daughter apart from my misfortunes helped even more, oblivious to what I was going through, which I hadn't been able to do or known how to do during the collapse that followed Tere's penultimate disappearance which had only contributed to making my misfortune worse. It also helped to accept the help of a psychoanalyst, to whom Gubau practically dragged me. Psychoanalysis did me good for three reasons. The first is that it helped me formulate in detail, chewing over and digesting it, what had happened to me at age sixteen with Batista (only then did I realize, for example, that he'd represented absolute evil to me, for several months). The second is that, although perhaps it didn't allow me to entirely digest what had happened with Tere, or with Tere and Zarco, it allowed me to accept it, live with its memory, keeping at bay legions of hostile ghosts in the shape of poisonous conjectures, guilty fictions, regrets without compassion and real or invented memories that fed the torture I mortified myself with on a daily basis.'

'And what's the third reason? What else did psychoanalysis do for you?'

'It got me writing. As soon as I lay down on the psychoanalyst's couch I began to think that, if it was really going to be useful to tell my story out loud to be able to understand it, it would be more useful to tell it in writing, because I thought that writing was more difficult than talking, it requires a greater effort and allows you to go into more depth. So I got into the habit of writing down sketches of episodes, dialogues, descriptions and reflections on Zarco and on Tere, on the summer of '78, on my re-encounter with Zarco and with Tere twenty years later; in short: many of the things I've been telling you about recently. These notes were fragmentary and random, they didn't have a single narrative thread or the slightest systematic, not to mention literary, volition; and, although the stimulus for writing them had been psychoanalysis, they didn't have a healing intention, but the truth is that they worked on me like therapy, or at least they did me good. The truth is, a year after losing sight of Tere and after Zarco dying, I was sure that I had dodged the threat of another collapse and had the impression that I'd recovered myself, and recovered my work and my former habits, including visiting my clients in prison at least once a week. A symptom of my recovery (or perhaps a consequence) was that at Christmas I took a week-and-a-half-long holiday. I spent it in Cartagena de Indias, Colombia, staying in the Hotel de las Américas, swimming in the mornings at the hotel beach or at the beaches on the Rosario Islands, spending the afternoons reading and drinking coffee with white rum and the nights dancing at the Havana Club, a place in the Getsemaní neighbourhood where I met in the small hours of one of those nights a Dutch divorcée I slept with several times and with whom I exchanged an unhealthy number of emails once I was back in Gerona for a couple of weeks, at the end of which the story ended as easily as it had started. A little while later I started sleeping with a linguistics professor recently arrived at the university and a friend of Pilar's, Cortés' wife, a good-looking, cheerful and kind Andalusian woman from whom I fled as soon as I noticed her phoning me too often.

'During this time I knew nothing about Tere; on the other hand, I had lots of news about Zarco (or about what remained of Zarco). His death provoked his last public resurrection and the definitive crystallization of his myth. It was predictable: as soon as Zarco died, everybody must have felt with good reason that the myths of the living are fragile, because the living can still belie them, while, since the dead cannot, the myths of the dead are more resilient; so everybody hastened to construct an invulnerable myth out of the dead Zarco, a myth that he could no longer contradict or disfigure.'

'An invulnerable but modest myth.'

'A modest but real myth. The proof is that here you are, preparing a book about him. The best proof is that, right now, even kids know who Zarco was. If you think about it, that's extraordinary: after all we're talking about a guy who was just a minor delinquent, known most of all because of three or four mediocre films and a riot and a couple of jail breaks. It's true that the image people have of Zarco is false, but one doesn't attain posterity, even a modest one, without simplifications or idealizations, so it's natural that Zarco has turned into the heroic outlaw that, for the journalists and even for some historians, embodies the yearning for liberty and the frustrated hopes of the heroic years of the change from dictatorship to democracy in Spain.'

'The Robin Hood of his day.'

'Yes: the Lin Chung of the Transition. That's the image Zarco's been reduced to.'

'It's not a bad image.'

'Of course it's bad. It's false, and if it's false it's bad. And you should do away with it. You should tell the true story of Liang Shan Po. That's why I've spent all these days talking to you.'

'Don't worry: I won't forget. Although in the book, I might not just talk about Zarco: I'll talk about you and Tere and . . .'

'Talk about whatever you want, as long as you tell the truth. Well, what else do you want to know? I have the impression that I've told you everything.'

'Not yet. Have you seen Tere again?'

'No.'

'You haven't heard anything about her?'

'No.'

'And María?'

'No more than everybody else knows. That she's still out there, gripping her fame with teeth and claws, or what remains of her fame, which I think by now is very little. Zarco's death and reappearance in the media allowed her to return to her origins as the wife of a famous man and exploit the rose-tinted version of her life with Zarco again. Like that, on the basis of lies, María recovered the place she'd lost, though for a very short time. Then she lost it again, and since then I don't know what's become of her, or even if she's moved back to Gerona . . . Anyway, for my part I can only say that at least I didn't knowingly contribute to that bullshit, because, no matter how much they insisted (and I assure you they insisted a lot), I never let any of the reality shows she appeared on interview me. Don't take it the wrong way. It wasn't an ethical matter, I don't consider myself superior to María, I don't even have anything against her any more, and much less against reality shows. Everyone makes a living how they want, or how they can. I deal in legal judgments, not moral ones. But I didn't fancy going on TV talking about my life. That's all. You understand, don't you?'

'Of course. What I don't entirely understand is that, from Zarco's death until now, you've refused to speak of him with serious journalists, people preparing articles, features, documentaries, biographies, things like that.'

'There are two reasons. One is that at first I didn't feel like talking about Zarco: same with Tere, all I wanted was to forget him. And the other is that I don't trust journalists, especially serious or supposedly serious journalists. They're the worst. They're the tricky ones, not the frivolous ones. Frivolous journalists lie but everyone knows they lie and nobody pays them any attention, or hardly anyone; serious journalists, however, lie while shielding themselves with the truth, and that's why everyone believes them. And that's why their lies do so much damage.'

'So you convinced yourself that only you could tell the truth.'

'Don't take me for an idiot. What I convinced myself of is that only I could tell a certain part of the truth.'

'And why haven't you told it? Why have you agreed to tell it to me, who isn't a journalist but might as well be, after all I'm going to write a book about Zarco?'

'Don't you know? Haven't your editors told you? If you want I'll explain, but it's a bit of a long story. How about we leave it for next time?'

'OK. Next time is our last, isn't it?'

'Yeah. Next time I'll tell you the end of the story.'

12

'Gamallo died on New Year's Eve 2005. Or was it 2006? It must have been 2006, because it wasn't long before I retired. The fact is that his death brought the press swooping back down on him, this time in search of carrion. Some journalists tried to get in touch with me then, but I didn't want to talk to them. It was a repugnant spectacle: as if they hadn't made up enough lies about Gamallo when he was alive; now that he was dead and couldn't even defend himself any more they wanted to go on lying. Truly repugnant.

'I lost track of his lawyer again for about a year, maybe a year and a half. In that time he didn't show up at the prison. I asked, and was told that he hadn't stopped working: he'd simply stopped visiting his clients; later I found out that it wasn't just that, Cañas wasn't well: he no longer attended trials, he seemed to have delegated almost everything to his partners, he began to get a reputation for being standoffish and eccentric. I had grown fond of him, and felt bad that what had happened to him had happened to him, that things hadn't gone well for him and had affected him so badly; I especially felt that it had happened because he had not listened to me, because he had got his hopes up and tried to defend Gamallo.'

'Do you think that was the cause of the problems Cañas had?'

'In part yes. I'm not saying his sorry tale with the girl had no bearing, although it had happened a long time before and it would be logical if, by the time Gamallo died, it had been forgotten; but, anyway, I can't give an opinion on that. What I do know is that failure is a bad business, and that Cañas felt he had completely failed with Gamallo, after having invested so much in him. For me the problem was that Cañas had believed the legend of Zarco, as I already told you, and he had decided to redeem him, redeem the great delinquent, the symbol of his generation. That was his proposal, and not achieving it hurt him: fellows used to success don't easily accept failure. So he felt like a failure, and perhaps guilty. Don't you think so?'

'No, but I'd like to know why you think that.'

'Let me finish telling you the story and you'll understand. Cañas took quite a long time before getting back into his habit of visiting his clients, but one afternoon, shortly after hearing that he'd started doing so again, I ran into him at the prison. We happened to meet in the foyer, as I was on my way out of my office having just finished for the day. Long time no see, Counsellor, I said in greeting. We were starting to miss you. Cañas looked at me with a speck of mistrust, as if he suspected I was making fun of him, but he soon smiled; physically he wasn't the same man: he still wore an impeccable suit, but he'd lost a lot of weight and his hair was going very grey. I took a bit of a vacation, he said. So you jumped the gun on me, I replied. That's what I plan to do in a couple of months, except my vacation's going to be longer. You're retiring?, he asked. I'm retiring, I answered. It was true; but it wasn't true that retiring made me as happy as I insisted on pretending: on the one hand it made me happy; on the other it made me uneasy: apart from resting and sitting in the front row for the spectacle of my physical and mental collapse, I didn't know what I'd devote my life to when I retired, or what I'd do with it. I thought that, like Cañas, I was a bit pitiful too; and I immediately thought there's nothing filthier than feeling oneself worthy of pity. Cañas and I kept talking. At a certain moment he asked: Can I buy you a coffee? I'm sorry, I answered. I dropped my car in at the garage on my way to work this morning and I have to go pick it up before they close. If you want I can give you a lift, Cañas offered. Don't trouble yourself, I said. I was just going to call a taxi. Cañas said it was no trouble and settled the argument.

'The garage was on the other side of the city, near the exit for the airport on the Barcelona highway. I don't remember what we talked about on the drive, but I do remember that, as we rounded the bend at Fornells Park, already in the outskirts, Cañas brought up a client of his who'd recently arrived at the prison, a gas-station employee we'd been keeping under protection since he'd been admitted. Then Cañas started talking about Gamallo, who was the last of his clients subject to this exceptional treatment, and I thought that he'd brought up the gas-station attendant in order to bring up Gamallo. The lawyer confessed his disappointment, regretted that Gamallo hadn't been able to live out his last years in liberty. Then he said: Anyway, at least you and I have clear consciences. After all, we did what we could for him, didn't we? I didn't answer. We were driving between a double row of car workshops and dealerships, and we turned right into an alley that led to the entrance to the Renault garage, in the back of the dealership. Cañas stopped his car in front of the open door of the garage, but he didn't turn off the engine. Without losing his thread he continued: At least I think so. What's more, I think almost everyone can have a clear conscience when it comes down to it. No one had as many opportunities as he did. Between the lot of us we gave him every chance, but he didn't take advantage of them. Turning towards me he said: What could we do: it wasn't our fault but his. I felt an awkward contrast between his reassuring words and his anxious gaze, and looked away: I wondered if our encounter in the foyer of the prison had been a coincidence or planned; I wondered if a man who says twice that he has a clear conscience has a clear conscience; I wondered if a man who makes excuses when no one has accused him of anything wasn't accusing himself. I vaguely sensed that Cañas was suffering, I thought that he was still lost in his labyrinth, said to myself that this unburdening was no accident and he was seeking my approval, or rather he needed it.

'I felt pity again, for him and for me, and again felt enraged at feeling pity. Only then did I intercede. Remember what I told you about Gamallo the first time we spoke about him?, I asked; without waiting for an answer I went on: Believe me: I'm sorry that I was right. Anyhow, you're right too when you say that the failure was not our fault; on that count you can rest easy. That said, don't deceive yourself: Gamallo had no chance. None. We offered him all of them, but he didn't have any. You were his friend and can understand that better than anybody. You understand, right? I read in his eyes that he didn't understand; also that he needed to understand.

'I looked inside the garage; they were just a couple of minutes away from closing time and I could only see one mechanic shuffling papers inside a glass-walled office. I sighed and undid my seatbelt. Let me tell you something, Counsellor, I said, and I waited for him to turn the engine off, before I went on. Have I ever told you that I'm from Toledo? My father and mother were both from there too. My mother died when I'd just turned five. My father didn't have any relatives and didn't remarry, so he had to raise me on his own. He was no longer a young man, he'd fought in the war and he'd lost; after the war he spent several years in prison. He had a job at a hardware store, very close to Zocodover Plaza, and, until I was fifteen years old, when I got out of school I'd always go to the store. I'd get there, sit on a stool to do my homework, at a little table near the counter, and wait for him to finish so we could go home. I did that every day of my life for ten years. Every day. Then, just as I turned sixteen, I was awarded a scholarship and went to Madrid to finish school. At first I missed my father and my friends a lot, but later, especially when I started studying at the university, I felt less and less like returning to Toledo. Of course, I loved my father, but I think I was a little ashamed of him; I also think a moment came when I preferred to see him as little as possible. I liked life in Madrid and he lived in Toledo. I felt like a winner and he was a loser. I was grateful to him for having raised me, sure, and, if he hadn't died so early, I would have made sure he lacked for nothing in his old age; but, apart from that, I didn't feel in debt to him, I didn't think he mattered at all as a person, or had influenced me in any way . . . Anyway, nothing out of the ordinary, as you see, normal things that happen between fathers and sons. Why am I telling you this? I paused and looked back inside the garage: the gate was still open and the mechanic hadn't left the glass office yet. I'm telling you because my father never told me where good was and where evil was, I continued. He didn't have to: before I had the use of reason I knew that it was good to go to the hardware store every afternoon, do my homework sitting on my stool beside him, wait for him until the shop closed. Evil could be many things, but that was surely good. I paused again; this time I didn't look at the garage but kept looking at Cañas. I concluded: Nobody ever taught Gamallo any of that, Counsellor. They taught him the opposite. And who can say they weren't right? Who can be certain that, in Gamallo's case, what we call good wasn't evil and what we call evil wasn't good? Are you sure that good and evil are the same for everyone? And, in any case, why wouldn't Gamallo be how he was? What opportunities to change did a kid born in a barracks hut ever have, who was in a reform school at seven and in jail at fifteen? I'll tell you: none. Absolutely none. Barring, of course, a miracle. And with Gamallo there was no miracle. You tried, but there wasn't. So you were completely right: at the very least it wasn't your fault.

'That's more or less what I told him. The lawyer didn't answer; he just moved his head vaguely up and down, as if he approved of my words or as if he didn't want to discuss them, and soon we said our goodbyes: I went into the garage and he started up his car and drove off. And that's how we left it.'

'You mean that was the last time you saw Cañas?'

'No. Since then we've run into each other two or three times – most recently, at the supermarket: he was on his own and I was with my wife – but we haven't spoken of Gamallo since then. Well, we're finished here, aren't we?'

'Yes, but would you allow me to ask one last question?'

'Sure.'

'Were you being sincere with Cañas that day? Did you say what you said to him because that's what you think or out of compassion? So he wouldn't feel unsuccessful and guilty, I mean, to help him get out of the labyrinth.'

'You mean about Gamallo not having any opportunity?'

'Yes. Do you believe that?'

'I don't know.'

Epilogue

The True Story of Liang Shan Po

'The last time we saw each other you told me that today you'd finish telling me the story. You promised you'd tell me why, instead of telling it yourself, you agreed that I should do it.'

'I'll tell you quickly.'

'Don't rush on my account: it's our last day.'

'I know, but a lot of time has passed since we last saw each other and in the meantime I've discovered that what I thought was the end of the story is not. Let's cut to the chase. Have I already told you about the dinner parties Cortés and his wife would sometimes have for me at their house? In theory the idea was to find me a girlfriend; in practice as well, I guess, though most of the time it was just an excuse to get together on Saturday nights. This particular Saturday the guests were, as Cortés had told me earlier in the week, two women in their thirties who had just founded a small publishing house for which his wife was translating a popular philosophy book.'

'My publishers.'

'Silvia and Nerea, yes. I got along well with them, and over

349

dessert, as usual at those dinners, Cortés and his wife steered the conversation round to office matters, so I would feel at ease, on home ground. This minor paternalism almost always irritated me, but that night I took advantage of it to show off, and by the time we were having coffee and liqueurs I started talking about Zarco and my relationship with him. I'd never spoken to Cortés or his wife about the subject, although they knew, as everyone did, that as a teenager I'd been a member of Zarco's gang – María had proclaimed it to the four winds, after all – and of course they knew all or almost all of the ins and outs of my adventures as Zarco's lawyer. In any case, that was practically the only topic of conversation for the rest of the evening, which went on until two or three in the morning.

'The next day, Sunday, I slept all morning and spent the afternoon regretting having told that story to two strangers. At least a couple of times I phoned Cortés, who tried to calm me down by assuring me I'd been brilliant the night before, that I hadn't said anything I shouldn't have and he was sure I'd impressed the two publishers. First thing Monday morning I got a phone call from Silvia, and I immediately thought Cortés or his wife had put her up to it in order to reassure me. That's not why she was calling. Silvia asked if we could have lunch together one day that week; she added that she had a proposal she wanted to make. What proposal?, I wanted to know. I'll tell you when we see each other, she answered. Give me a hint, I begged. Don't leave me on tenterhooks. We want you to write a book about Zarco, she admitted. As soon as I heard the proposal I knew I was going to accept it; I also knew why I'd poured out the story of my relationship with Zarco to Silvia and Nerea: precisely because secretly I was hoping to convince them to make the proposal they'd just made. Almost embarrassed by my cunning, to keep Silvia and Nerea from suspecting that they'd fallen into my trap

I turned down the proposal from the start. I told Silvia that I didn't know how such an idea could have occurred to them and I was grateful to them but it was impossible. Without conviction, I argued: To begin with, I know how to talk, but not how to write. And besides, everything's already been said about Zarco. That's the best reason for you to write this book, Silvia replied easily. Everything's been said about Zarco but it's all lies; or almost all of it. You said so on Saturday. At least you have something true to tell. And, as far as you not knowing how to write, don't worry about that: writing is easier than talking, because you can't edit yourself as you talk, but when writing you can. Besides, Cortés told us you've begun a memoir or something like that. That's what Silvia said, and only then did I realize, with relief, that for her and for Nerea what I'd thought a possibly romantic dinner had actually been a business dinner, if not a trap, and in that matter my novice-writer's hunger had been joined to the neophyte publishers' appetite for success. It's not a memoir, I corrected her, on the verge of dropping the pretence that I didn't want what I actually did want. They're notes, remnants, scraps of memories, things like that; besides, they're not just about Zarco. That doesn't matter, Silvia enthused. That's your book: the one you started to write before we asked you. Now you just need to finish off the remnants and sew them together.

'Frankly, I got enthusiastic too. So much so that, after having lunch with Silvia the next day, I got down to work on it immediately, and for a month devoted my evenings and some entire nights to writing the book. Until I realized I wasn't capable of it, especially because, even though everything I was writing was true, none of it sounded true. So I gave up. That was when Silvia suggested that I should tell another person the story, so they could take charge of writing it; it struck me as a good idea: it occurred to me that, as long as the story's true, it didn't matter who wrote it, and with time I've come to think that it's preferable that someone other than me tell it, someone detached from the story, someone who is not affected by the story and can tell it with some distance.'

'Someone like me.'

'For example.'

'So it was you who suggested my name?'

'No. It was Silvia. Or maybe Nerea. I don't remember. But it was me who approved you; and also who established the conditions. A few days after I accepted her suggestion, Silvia called and said she had the perfect person for the job. The next morning I received your book on the Aiguablava crimes. I hadn't heard of you, but I'd followed the case in the papers, and I liked the book because, contrary to what I had tried to write, everything you told in it sounded true; even better I liked that not only did it sound true, it was, or at least your version of events coincided with that of the judge.'

'It wasn't that difficult.'

'No, but many fantasies were told about that story, and I was glad that you didn't let yourself be fooled by them and you didn't give in to the temptation of reproducing them. I thought that, as well as knowing how to write, you were trustworthy.'

'Thanks. Anyhow I should warn you that, in my case, it's not such an achievement, because I'm one of those who think fiction always surpasses reality but reality is always richer than fiction.'

'The fact is you were chosen, and I soon started telling you the story that we're now almost at the end of.'

'Almost?'

'As I said it turns out that wasn't exactly the end. The end – or what I now think is the end – happened a couple of weeks ago, after you and I saw each other last time. One afternoon, while I was with Gubau at the home of a client we were going to defend against a charge of embezzlement, I received a text message.

"Hiya, Gafitas," it said. "It's Tere. Come and see me as soon as you can." It was followed by an address on Mimosa Street, in Font de la Pòlvora, and ended: "It's above José and Juan's Snack-Bar. I'll be expecting you." I put my mobile away, tried to concentrate again on my client's statement; after a while I realized that I wasn't even taking in what she was saying and I interrupted her. Excuse me, I said, standing up. Something unexpected has come up and I have to leave. What's up? Gubau asked anxiously. Nothing, I answered. You finish here and get a taxi back. We'll talk tomorrow in the office.

'It was about seven in the evening and I was in Amer, so I must have got to Font de la Pòlvora about half past seven. The neighbourhood gave me the same feeling as ever, a feeling of festering poverty and dirt; but the people, who packed the streets, seemed happy: I saw a group of children jumping on a dusty mattress, several women trying on dresses that were spilling out of a van, a group of men smoking and clapping along to a rumba. I soon found José and Juan's Snack-Bar, on the ground floor of a building with a yellowish façade. I parked the car, walked past the snack-bar door and into the building.

'In the hall I tried to turn on the light in the stairwell, but it didn't work and I had to go up in the dark, feeling my way along the flaking walls. It smelled bad. When I got to the door of the flat Tere had indicated I pressed the bell, but it didn't work either, and when I was about to knock on the door I noticed it wasn't closed. I pushed it open, went down a tiny hallway and came out in a little living room; there was Tere, sitting in an old wingback chair, looking out the window with a blanket over her legs. I must have made a noise, because Tere turned towards me; recognizing me she smiled with a smile that had equal amounts of joy, surprise and weariness. Hiya, Gafitas, she said. That was fast. She brushed a hand over her dishevelled hair, trying to fix it up a bit, and added:

353

Why didn't you let me know you were going to come? I immediately realized something fundamental had changed in her, although I didn't know what. She didn't look well: she was very drawn, with big dark circles under her eyes and her bones very visible in her face; her lips, which had been red and full, were dry and pale, and she was breathing through her mouth. Instead of explaining that I showed up so quickly because she'd said to come as soon as possible, I asked: What are you doing here? What do you want me to do?, she answered, almost amused. This is where I live. But that place, in truth, did not look like a home; it looked more like an abandoned garage: the walls of the room were grey and covered in damp stains; there was no furniture apart from a formica table, a couple of chairs and, on the floor, in front of Tere, an old television set, which wasn't on; also on the floor I saw newspaper pages, cigarette butts, an empty litre-bottle of Coca-Cola. Oblivious to the mess, Tere was in her bathrobe, with her hands folded in her lap; under the robe she was wearing a pink nightgown. Can you walk?, I asked. Tere looked at me questioningly; her eyes were a matte, lifeless green. You can't stay here, I said. Tell me where your coat is and I'll take you home. My words erased the joy from Tere's face. I'm not going anywhere, Gafitas, she replied. I already told you I live here. I stared at her; she was very serious now. Come on, she said, gesturing vaguely. Grab that chair and sit down.

'I sat down in front of her. I took her hands: they were just skin and bones, and they were cold; without saying anything, Tere stared out the window. Through the dirty panes I could see the backs of a couple of tower blocks where tons of garbage and useless stuff was piled up, some kids playing football in a vacant lot, and beyond that, tied to a post, an old work horse grazing in a field; dark, rocky-looking clouds covered the sky. I asked Tere if she was ill; she said no, she'd just had a bit of flu, she was on the

354

mend now, that she was eating well and was well looked after. That's what she said, but, since many explanations are less convincing than a single one, and since her appearance was not exactly healthy, I didn't believe her. Julián would be there soon, she added. I didn't ask who Julián was. There was a silence that lasted too long, and I unexpectedly broke it by asking her why she'd abandoned me after Zarco's death, why she'd left without saying anything; I immediately regretted the question, but Tere seemed to think her answer through conscientiously. Before telling me she let go of my hands and leaned back in the armchair again. I don't know, she answered; but she immediately contradicted herself: Besides, you wouldn't understand either. As if in a hurry to change the subject she began talking about Font de la Pòlvra; Tere knew I went there once in a while – once in a very long while – for work, and at some point asked me how I saw the neighbourhood. As usual, I answered. The city changes but this place always stays the same. Tere nodded pensively; after a while she ran her tongue over her lips and smiled slightly. More or less like me, she said. I asked her what she meant. She shrugged, looked out the window for a moment and then looked back at me. Well, she said. I tried to change too, didn't I? And immediately, undoubtedly because she noticed a trace of confusion or bewilderment on my face, she explained: To change, to be someone other than who I was, to be different. I tried. You know I did. I moved away, I tried to study, I went out with you, with Jordi, I don't know . . . All for what. I was an idiot, I thought it would work. And here I am again. She paused, added: at Liang Shan Po. She smiled again, now with a broader almost cheerful smile, and, before I could get over my surprise, she asked: That's what you used to call the prefabs, right? I didn't answer, I didn't ask her if she'd heard that from Zarco: after all nobody else could have told her. Tere unfolded her hands for a moment and with one of them gestured towards everything outside the window, the unre-deemed misery of that ghetto where the last residents of the prefabs had been confined, just after the summer of '78. She said: Well, here you have what's left of Liang Shan Po. I hoped she'd go on, but she didn't; all I could think of to say was: That Liang Shan Po thing is stupid. Tere replied: I told you you wouldn't understand.

'I was going to ask her again what she meant when she took the blanket off her legs and stood up. I have to go to the bathroom, she said. I stood up and, as I helped her to walk, I realized she was even thinner than she looked at first glance: I felt her shoulder blades and hipbones in my hands. There was no light in the bath-room and the toilet tank was broken. Fearing that she might fall, I asked her if she wanted me to stay in there with her, but she said no, handed me a plastic bowl and asked me to fill it with water from the kitchen. I did what she said and, while listening to her urinate behind the door, with the bowl in my hands, waiting for her to finish, I felt that I had to get her out of that place, not for her sake, but for mine. Since she seemed to be taking too long I asked if she was all right; her answer consisted of opening the door, taking the bowl from me and shutting herself in there again.

'When she came out she'd washed her face and combed her hair. She held the bowl out to me and asked me to put it back in the kitchen. I was about to say: Let's just go, Tere. You're sick, you have to see a doctor. Put some clothes on and I'll go get the car. But I waited, I didn't say anything. I took the bowl, Tere started to walk on her own back to her armchair and wrapped herself back up in the blanket. She seemed very tired from the effort and stared out the window; the sky was even darker than before, but night hadn't yet fallen. I left the basin in the kitchen and went back into the room. When she saw me, Tere said: Aren't you going to ask me why I asked you to come over? I sat back down in front of her and reached for her hands again, but she pulled them away and folded her arms, as if she'd just got a sudden chill. What did you ask me here for? I asked. Tere let a few seconds pass; then she said, straight out: I gave you guys away. I heard the words, but didn't understand their meaning; Tere repeated them. Knowing what she was talking about, I asked her what she was talking about.'

'She was talking about the last robbery, no? The robbery of the Bordils branch of the Banco Popular.'

'Right.'

'She meant she was the one who gave them the tip-off.'

'Right. I went quiet, silent, as if she'd told me she'd just seen a UFO or that she'd just been sentenced to the electric chair. Tere unfolded her arms and, as soon as she started to speak (slowly, with many pauses), I looked away from her and fixed my gaze beyond the window and the kids who were still playing football, on the horse that was ambling around his post. Tere assured me that what she'd said was the truth, repeated that it had been her who had informed the police and that's why she'd made an excuse not to participate in that morning's robbery. They scared me, she explained. They threatened me. Although if they'd only threatened me I wouldn't have said anything. They threatened my mother and my sisters, threatened to take the kids away. They were fed up with us, especially fed up with Zarco. They wanted to catch him any way they could; for his own sake and because they knew that, if they caught him, the gang would be finished. They put me between a rock and a hard place. I knew that sooner or later they'd catch us; and I also knew that Zarco would never suspect me and that, if by some miracle he found out that I'd snitched on you, he wouldn't do anything to me. Not to me. So I ended up giving in. What choice did I have? The question hung in the air for a few seconds. I was stunned: I didn't know what to think, except that what Tere said was true. How could it not be? What interest could Tere have in lying about it, and so many years later at that? What could she possibly gain from accusing herself of such a thing? Only I insisted on one condition, she continued. And they agreed. This time she waited for me to ask the question, but I didn't. The condition was that they'd let you escape, she said. I looked away from the window and stared at her. Me?, I asked. Tere touched the beauty spot beside her nose. I had to choose someone and I couldn't choose Zarco, she explained. I told you already: they weren't going to let Zarco escape; you they would. She paused. You understand, right?, she said. That morning the cops weren't after you. Even if Zarco hadn't stopped at La Devesa they wouldn't have caught you; and if they had caught you they would have let you go pretty soon. That was the deal I made with them. And those kinds of deals are kept. You know better than I do.

'That was it: I did know; but I still didn't know what to think, or what to say. I said: Why are you telling me this now? Why didn't you tell me before? Tere answered: Because before Zarco was alive and I didn't want you telling him. She added: And because I don't want you to keep thinking something that isn't true. I want you to know the truth; and the truth is that you never owed Zarco a thing. Tere sat there looking at me expectantly for a few seconds. Since I didn't say anything she asked: Are you mad at me? Why would I be?, I answered. Didn't you say you saved me? Yeah, she said. But before that I snitched on you. You and everybody. And on top of that I let everybody believe that the one who snitched was you. What were you going to do?, I replied, shrugging. First you had no choice but to give us up; then you had no choice but to keep quiet about having given us up. Besides, I continued, after a pause: Do you know how many years ago that happened? Thirty. It doesn't matter to anyone any more. The ones it could have mattered to are dead now. Zarco's dead. Everybody's dead. Everybody except you and me. Tere listened to me attentively, I don't know whether relieved or sceptical, and when I finished talking turned back towards the window. I looked at her sharp profile, at her very pale cheeks and temples, blue networks of veins showing through. Before I could go on, Tere said: Look. It's raining.

'I looked: a heavy, slow shower was falling from the sky, chasing the boys off the vacant lot; the horse, however, stood motionless under the rain. I pulled my chair up closer to Tere's until our knees were touching, and just when I was about to speak I noticed that her left leg was still, quietened, without its perpetual piston movement. All of a sudden I was sure that was the change I'd noticed when I saw her, and that change changed everything. Tere, I said, taking her hands again. She seemed absorbed by the rain, exhausted by the confession she'd just made. I repeated her name; she turned and looked at me. Do you remember the Vilaró arcade?, I asked her. Do you remember the first time we saw each other? Tere waited for me to continue. Do you know the first thing I thought when I saw you? There was silence. I thought you were the most gorgeous girl in the world. And do you know what I think now? Another silence. That you're the most gorgeous girl in the world. Tere smiled with her eyes, but not with her lips. Let me take you to a hospital, I said. Then we'll go home. Nothing will happen to you. I'll take care of you. And we won't be apart again. I promise you. Tere listened to me without batting an eyelid, without losing the smile. When I finished speaking she let a few seconds pass, took a deep breath, sat up a little, took my cheeks in her hands and kissed me; her lips didn't taste of anything. Then she said: You have to get going, Gafitas. Julián will be here any minute.

'She didn't say anything else. I didn't insist. I knew it was futile.

359

We sat there opposite each other, looking out the window in silence while the room gradually grew dark; outside, abandoned beneath the rain, the dray horse seemed to look back at us with an almost human gaze. After a while Tere said again that I should leave. I stood up and asked if I could do anything for her. Tere moved her head almost imperceptibly from one side to the other, before she said no. We're leaving the day after tomorrow, she added. I looked at the chaotic disarray of the flat and noticed the plural. Where to? I asked. Tere shrugged. Somewhere, she said. Then I thought I wasn't going to see her again and took a step towards her. Please, Gafitas, said Tere, holding up one hand. I stopped, stood still there for a couple of seconds, staring at her, as if the suspicion had suddenly hit me that this image of Tere, ill, sitting in that wingback chair, in that desolate flat in that miserable neighbourhood, wearing a blue bathrobe and frayed nightgown, pale, drawn and exhausted, was going to supplant all the others I had of her for the rest of my life, and my memory had already started to struggle against that flagrant injustice. Until, without another word, I turned and left.

'A violent downpour was falling over Font de la Pòlvora when I walked out of Tere's building.

'That night and the next two days were agonizing. I didn't want to phone Tere or return to Font de la Pòlvora, but I sent her several texts. At first she answered. I asked her how she was and if she needed anything and she answered that she didn't need anything and that she was fine. The last text she sent me said: "I'm better, Gafitas. The doctor's given me the all-clear. I'm off. Bye." I replied congratulating her, asking her where she was and where she was going, but she didn't answer me any more. Once the first moment of frustration was over, I calmed down, and then the anguish turned into a bittersweet feeling: on the one hand I thought I wouldn't see Tere again, that this was the end of the story and everything that had to happen to me had now happened to me; but on the other hand I thought I finally knew the truth and that, now, everything did fall into place. The calmness – or at least the calming sensation that everything fell into place – didn't last long. One of those nights, while I was having a drink at home before going to bed, I was struck by a doubt. I spent most of the night battling it, and the first thing I did the next morning when I got to the office was ask my secretary to find me Inspector Cuenca's phone number. I suppose I've told you that after the summer of '78 the inspector and I still saw each other.'

'You mentioned it; the inspector also told me that after that summer you lost touch with each other for some years, after which you began to see each other again as if you'd never met.'

'It's true. We pretended we didn't know each other, and we pretended very well. We mostly saw each other at the time when he worked for the civil government, almost directly across the street from my office, as a security advisor for the governor. We became rather friendly during those years, but even then neither of us ever mentioned anything, much less whether he had been on the verge of sending me to prison for belonging to Zarco's gang. Later we stopped seeing each other again and then, not long ago, I heard that he'd been chief of the airport police station for some time. And there, at the airport, my secretary found him that morning. When I told the inspector I needed to talk to him, he just asked: Is it urgent? It is for me, I answered. He said his morning was pretty busy but we could see each other mid-afternoon, and suggested I come see him in his office at the airport. It's a private matter, I said. I'd rather talk somewhere else. I heard silence at the other end of the line; then I heard: Well, as you wish. He asked when and where we should meet; I said the first thing that came into my head: at six, on a bench in Sant Agustí Plaza.

'At quarter to six I was already sitting in the sun on a bench in

Sant Agustí Plaza, in front of the statue of General Álvarez de Castro and the city's defenders. Shortly after six Inspector Cuenca showed up, out of breath and with his jacket folded under his arm. I stood up, shook his hand, thanked him for coming, suggested we could have a coffee at the Royal. The inspector dropped onto the bench, loosened the knot of his tie and said: First tell me what you want to talk about. I sat down beside him and, without giving him time to catch his breath, asked: You haven't guessed? Still panting, he gave me a look that was halfway between ironic and suspicious; he asked: You want to talk about Zarco? I said yes.

'The inspector nodded. He seemed to be ageing well, but for some reason his face made me think of a tortoise; a sad tortoise. He was facing straight ahead, his gaze fixed on the statue of General Álvarez de Castro or on the maple trees that surrounded the centre of the plaza or on the big white parasols that shaded the terraces of the bars or on the arches or the cream-coloured façades covered with strings of wrought-iron balconies; a drop of sweat trickled down his cheek. Well, he said with resignation, once he'd caught his breath. I suppose it had to happen sooner or later, didn't it? Arranging his jacket on his lap he asked: What do you want to know? Just one thing, I answered. Who was the informer? Inspector Cuenca turned to me as he wiped away the drop of sweat from his cheek; I asked: You know what I mean, don't you? Before he could answer I reasoned: You were waiting for us outside with your people. You knew we were going to rob that bank. Somebody must have told you. Who was it? Inspector Cuenca didn't look away; he seemed more annoyed than intrigued. What do you want to know that for?, he asked. I need to know, I answered. What for?, Inspector Cuenca repeated. This time I didn't answer. Inspector Cuenca blinked several times. I'm not going to tell you, he finally said, shaking his head. Professional secret. For fuck's sake, Inspector, I said. It was thirty years ago.

That's true, said the inspector. And that's precisely why you should have forgotten this story by now. I, however, still have my obligations, especially to people who confided in me. Would you reveal a client's secret, even thirty years after they confided in you? Don't play games, Inspector, I protested. This is not a normal case. Don't play games, Counsellor, he protested. There's no such thing as a normal case.

'We fell silent. I let a few seconds go by. OK, I conceded. I'm not going to ask you to tell me who it was. I'll just ask you to tell me yes or no. I paused and then asked: Was Tere the informer? Now Inspector Cuenca looked at me with genuine unmitigated curiosity. Tere?, he asked. Which Tere? Zarco's girlfriend? I was about to tell him that she wasn't actually his girlfriend but Zarco's sister, but I just said yes. Inspector Cuenca's face gradually lit up, until the laughter illuminated it entirely; I think it was the first time in my life I'd ever seen him laugh: it seemed like a strange laugh, the cheerful laughter of a young man from the disillusioned face of an old one. What's the matter?, I asked. Nothing, he answered. The inspector barely smiled but he wasn't sweating any more, although it was still hot; his thick veiny hands were still holding his jacket on his lap. It's just that I can't believe you're serious, he said; immediately he asked: You liked that girl, didn't you? I blushed. And what's that got to do with it?, I asked. Nothing, said the inspector and, meaning you, he added: The journalist who's going to write about Zarco told me. What he told me is that you joined Zarco's gang for the girl. Is that true? I couldn't see any need to lie, so I told him it was true. I asked the inspector why he asked; he said no reason; he went on: And might I know where you got the idea that the girl was my confidante? I didn't say she was your confidante, I corrected him, I just asked if that time she was your informer. Same thing, he said. Who knows what you've told that journalist . . . But have you forgotten how things worked with Zarco? Do you really think one of his own would have dared talk? Would you have dared talk? Don't you remember how scared everyone was of Zarco? I wasn't scared of him, I hastened to reply. I did what he said but I wasn't scared of him. Of course you were scared of him, said Inspector Cuenca. And if you weren't you were more oblivious than I thought, more oblivious than any of your friends. Zarco was a nasty piece of work, Counsellor. Very nasty. As far as I know he always was. How would any of his own dare to inform on him? And, least of all, that *quinqui* girl; you must have known it: she was as loyal as a dog, I couldn't have got her to give up Zarco even if I pulled her fingernails off.

'I thought Inspector Cuenca was right. I thought that, actually, before talking to Inspector Cuenca I already knew that Tere could not have been the informer, and that I'd only wanted to talk to Inspector Cuenca to confirm it. I have another question, I said to Inspector Cuenca. He was staring straight ahead, with his eyes half-closed against the sun; the jacket placed on his lap concealed his belly. I said: I've always wondered why you let me go that night, why you didn't arrest me. Inspector Cuenca immediately understood I meant the night he came looking for me in Colera, and the proof is that only a couple of seconds went by before he murmured: Now that is a good question. He said it without looking at me, curving his wide mouth and thick eyebrows; since he didn't go on I asked: And what's the answer? He let another couple of seconds go by and said the answer is that there is no answer. That he didn't know what the answer was. That he had no idea. That he had never let any other guilty suspect go on purpose and at first he even regretted having done so, until he reached the conclusion that he might have done it for the wrong reasons. Here he seemed to reflect for a moment and added: Like all the best things I've done in my life.

'I thought he was joking; I looked him in the eye: he wasn't joking. I asked him what he meant. Then he started to tell me about his life: he told me he hadn't been born in Gerona but he'd been living in Gerona for almost forty years and that he often thought that, had he not ended up in this city, his life would probably have been a disaster, in any case it would have been much worse than it had been. And do you know why I ended up here?, he asked. Without waiting for an answer he raised one of his hands and pointed towards the centre of the plaza. For that, he said. I looked in the direction he was pointing and asked: For the statue? For General Álvarez de Castro, he answered. For the siege of Gerona. Do you know there's a novel by Galdós about it? Sure, I said. He asked me if I'd read it and I said no. I have, he said. Twice. The first time was many years ago, when I was eighteen and doing my practical training in Madrid. The book made a big impression on me, I thought it was a great war novel, and that Álvarez de Castro was a fabulous hero. So, when it came time to choose a posting, I decided to come here: I wanted to see the city, wanted to get to know the city where Álvarez de Castro had fought, or Álvarez de Castro's men, I don't know. Inspector Cuenca then told me that a few weeks earlier, exactly when he was talking to you about his relationship with Zarco, he'd mentioned the Galdós novel and what it had meant to him, and having done so piqued his curiosity and he reread it. And do you know what?, said Inspector Cuenca, turning once again towards me. I thought it was shit; rather than a novel about war it seemed like a parody of a war novel, an affected, gruesome and pretentious thing set in a cardboard-cut-out city where only cardboard-cut-out people live. And as for Álvarez de Castro, Inspector Cuenca also said, Frankly: he's a disgusting character, a psychopath capable of sacrificing the lives of thousands of people in order to satisfy his patriotic vanity and not surrender an already defeated city to the French. Anyway,

Inspector Cuenca concluded, after I finished reading the book I remembered that I once heard a professor on TV say that a book is like a mirror and that it's not the person who reads the book but the book that reads the person, and I thought it was true. I also said to myself: Damn, the best thing that happened in my life happened to me due to a misunderstanding, because I liked a horrible book and because I thought a villain was a hero. Inspector Cuenca fell silent; then, without taking his eyes off me, looking at me with infinitely ironic mischief, with absolutely serious irony, he asked: How do you like that?

I thought over my reply, or rather pretended to be thinking it over. I was actually thinking that it wasn't Tere who had lied to me but Inspector Cuenca, and that the inspector was telling me all that to distract me from the fundamental issue, to continue protecting his confidante more than thirty years after she'd confided in him. For a moment I wanted to persist, carry on the interrogation, but I remembered my last conversation with Tere and told myself it made no sense: La Font and Rufus and the district had disappeared decades ago, and Inspector Cuenca and I were nothing but two relics, two *charnegos* from back when *charnegos* still existed, an old cop and an old gang member turned shyster sitting on a bench in the late afternoon like two pensioners talking of a vanished ruined world, of things nobody in the city remembered any more, and that didn't matter to anybody. So I chose to let it go, to keep quiet, not to keep asking: I didn't know if it was Tere who had told me the truth and Inspector Cuenca who lied, or if it was Tere who had lied and Inspector Cuenca who was telling the truth. And, since I didn't know, I couldn't know if Tere had loved me or not, or if she had only loved me in an occasional and conditional way, while she had loved Zarco permanently and unconditionally. Actually, I said to myself then – and I was surprised I'd never thought it before – I didn't even know how

Tere had loved Zarco, because I had no proof that Tere and Zarco were sister and brother and that Tere hadn't lied to me years before, in my office, telling me they were, to convince me to keep helping Zarco up until the end; actually, I said to myself then, I didn't even know either if, supposing it was true that Tere and Zarco were sister and brother, after finding out the real kinship between them that Tere had loved Zarco in a different way than she'd loved him before knowing it. I didn't know anything. Nothing except that it wasn't true that everything slotted into place in that story, and that there was an infinitely serious irony in it or an absolutely ironic mischief or an enormous misunderstanding, like the one Inspector Cuenca had just told me about. And I also thought that after all perhaps it wasn't the end of the story, that perhaps not everything that had to happen to me had happened and that, if Tere came back again, I'd be waiting for her.

'I looked out of the corner of my eye at Inspector Cuenca, and said to myself that in spite of his air of a sad tortoise and disillusioned old man he was a fortunate man. I thought it but I didn't tell him. The question I'd asked him remained unanswered and we sat there in silence for a while, enduring the sun on our faces, watching through half-closed eyes the urban hustle and bustle of Sant Agustí in front of General Álvarez de Castro. Until at some point I stood up and said: Well, now can I buy you a coffee? Inspector Cuenca opened his eyes wide, as if my question had woken him up; then he sighed again, stood up as well and, as we started across the plaza towards the Royal, said: If it's all the same to you, let's have a beer.'

Author's Note

This novel would not have been possible without the collaboration of Francisco Pamplona and, especially, Carles Monguilod, whose book *Vint-i-cinc anys i un dia* was one of the initial spurs to this story. Aside from them, Carmen Balcells and David Trueba read a draft and provided extremely useful observations. I've borrowed from Antony Beevor an expression I heard him use over dinner in London, one evening in the winter of 2011. What the books I've written over the last twenty-five years and I owe to Jordi Gracia would never fit in an acknowledgments note. I am also in debt to the following books: *Hasta la libertad*, by Juan José Moreno Cuenca; *Historia del Julián*, by Juan F. Gamella; *Els castellans*, by Jordi Puntí; *Quinquis dels 80: Cinema, prensa i carrer*, by various authors; and *Memòries del barri xino*, an unpublished manuscript by Gerard Bagué. I'd also like to thank Joan Boada, Josep Anton Bofill, Antoni Candela, Emili Caula, Jordi Caula and Narcís Caula, Jordi Corominas, Mery Cuesta, Daniel de Antonio, Tomás Frauca (not Franca), Pepe Guerrero, Ramón Llorente, Llorenç Martí, Puri Mena, Mariana Montoya, Isabel Salamanya, Carlos Sobrino, Robert Soteras, Guillem Terribas and Fernando Velasco.

Translator's Note

I would like to thank Nika Blazer, Jim Smith and Ben Ward for their helpful suggestions and discussions.

A NOTE ON THE AUTHOR

Javier Cercas was born in 1962. He is a novelist, short-story writer and columnist, whose books include *Soldiers of Salamis* (which sold more than a million copies worldwide, won six literary awards in Spain and was filmed by David Trueba), *The Tenant* and *The Motive*, *The Speed of Light* and *The Anatomy of a Moment*, which won Spain's National Narrative Prize. He taught at the University of Illinois in the late 1980s and for many years was a lecturer in Spanish literature at the University of Gerona. His books have been translated into more than thirty languages. In 2011 he was awarded the International Prize of the Turin Book Fair for his oeuvre. He lives in Barcelona.

A NOTE ON THE TRANSLATOR

Anne McLean has translated Latin-American and Spanish novels, short stories, memoirs and other writings by authors including Héctor Abad, Carmen Martín Gaite, Julio Cortázar, Ignacio Martínez de Pisón, Enrique Vila-Matas, Tomás Eloy Martínez and Juan Gabriel Vásquez. She has twice won the Independent Foreign Fiction Prize: for *Soldiers of Salamis* by Javier Cercas in 2004 (which also won her the Valle Inclán Award), and for *The Armies* by Evelio Rosero in 2009. She was awarded the Spanish Cross of the Order of Civil Merit as recognition of her contribution to making Spanish literature known to a wider public. She lives in Toronto.

A NOTE ON THE TYPE

The text of this book is set in Fournier. Fournier is derived from the *romain du roi*, which was created towards the end of the seventeenth century for the exclusive use of the Imprimerie Royale from designs made by a committee of the Académie of Sciences. The original Fournier types were cut by the famous Paris founder Pierre Simon Fournier in about 1742. These types were some of the most influential designs of the eight and are counted among the earliest examples of the 'transitional' style of typeface. This Monotype version dates from 1924. Fournier is a light, clear face whose distinctive features are capital letters that are quite tall and bold in relation to the lower-case letters, and *decorative italics, which show the influence of the calligraphy of Fournier's time.*